Absolute Garbage, Total Nonsense, and Utter Ridiculousness

By

Gerald Dean Rice

Copyright October 26, 2021

Red Hand Books, LLC

This may come off as convoluted, but I'd like to dedicate this book to the future. To prospects yet to be fulfilled, dreams waiting to come to fruition, and answers to hopeful questions.

Table of Contents

Foreword

I'd been working on a different book of short stories when I got the idea for this one. Originally titled, *Men in Chairs*, it was going to be a collection of just that, stories about men in chairs. It was an aggressive idea—aggressive in thinking I could actually write such a thing. I mean, I had plenty enough story ideas in mind, but in hindsight, maybe not such a good idea for someone with an attention span problem to be writing.

The notion of an author with ADHD sounds incongruous, I'm sure, but I assure you, at least anecdotally, it's more common than you'd think. I edited an anthology a few years back and the process was very eye-opening so far as traits writers have in common. I'm not the *only* weird one.

Like any other writer, though, I created a slush pile. The longer I've written, the more stories I've accumulated that I just never did anything with. Stories I wrote for anthologies that were rejected for various reasons, ideas I came up with on my own and wrote, ideas I started and abandoned—not necessarily bad ones, there certainly were more than a few of those while I was cobbling this thing together that I rejected (I guess my slush pile has a slush pile?). I even had stories I thought were good, but just weren't the proper fit with the theme developing in my mind. Those stories I do intend to get back to. I have an idea for them and the whole thing stands at about 40,000 words right now.

This collection *does* have one particularly bad story in it, but it was included with intention. Written in 1990, it is a straight up-and-down slasher with absolutely zero nuance, elegance, or familiarity with metaphor. I wrote it for a class project in 8th grade and it's the kind of story that would get a kid sent to the school counselor if it were written today.

There's also some godawful poetry I wrote to my girlfriend in high school. Sappy, syrupy, shirt-rending, woe-it's-me type stuff that hopefully juxtaposed with later poetry shows several rungs of growth to where I am today.

I'm immensely proud and nervous to alternating degrees. This is probably the boldest and most revealing work I've had to date and to be honest, I'm unsure how it'll be received. But if I could call myself an artist for at least the briefest of moments, then this is the work I want to put before the public that sparks conversation and thought, both good and bad.

At some point, you have to get out of the bathroom. So, put this back on top of the tank (or just close the app if you are reading on Kindle) and get back to what you were supposed to be doing.

It's only obvious that the very last story I wrote would be first in this collection. Some of the stories are much too serious for such a title. So to bring things back to earth and out of the effluvium of high-minded speech and bottom-of-the-soul scraping poetry, I present to you…

Branch Manager

"That guy can suck my *dick*," Taylor said, balling up a sheet of paper and shooting for the trash basket. It bounced off the lip of the can and she grimaced like it hurt.

"Who?" Michelle said, looking at her cubicle neighbor and best friend. She had her paper basketball ready and took her shot. It landed in the plastic bag. "Two-one."

"Cheater." Taylor scooped up her ball as Michelle prepped another one. "The manager. The new one."

"What's wrong with him? I thought he was a nice guy."

1

Taylor shook her head. "You know I was up for that promotion. He's going to screw me. I know it."

Michelle held her tongue. Since she'd applied for the position and neglected to tell her friend, she felt odd about defending the tree. Especially since Michelle began to believe there was a strong chance she might actually get it. Arv Edmore had dropped out for some reason and he'd been the only shoe-in for the job. That left Taylor, Michelle, and Pat.

Taylor had the smarts but not the focus. Michelle was around the corner from her degree, and Pat was just Pat. There was nothing positive or negative to say.

Michelle had plans. She and Alice were starting to get serious and might be moving in together soon. She was getting tired of the bar scene with Taylor and though she loved her friend, felt they were drifting apart.

"He's a creep anyway. I mean, look at him—he never leaves his office. All day…right there." Taylor gestured toward the office the tree occupied with her palms upturned.

"Tay, he's a tree. I don't think he *can* go anywhere."

"Of course he can, Chelle. They got him in here, didn't they? I bet he walks around after everyone leaves. Probably roots through people's desks."

Michelle could hear her best friend getting worked up. Like the guy whose car she'd keyed after giving him her phone number and shortly after convincing herself he'd ghost her after a couple dates, or the waitress she 'knew' was going to spit in her food.

She had to cut this off at the pass.

Michelle took another shot, easily sinking it in the trash basket even though it wasn't her turn. "Three-one!"

"*Bitch!*"

"Why do you think he has it out for you?"

"I dunno." Taylor tossed the paper ball across her desk. "I mean, I mighta been pulling branches off a tree by the parking lot, but he couldn't have seen that. I dunno—he just has it in for me."

"Why were you pulling branches off a tree?" Michelle asked.

"Is that even the point? You're supposed to be on *my* side." Taylor ran a hand over her curls.

"I'm on your side." Michelle nodded vigorously. "All the way."

Taylor snorted, holding her head in her hands. "Oh my God, you're so cheesy."

"Am not." Michelle smiled, remembering why she'd developed a crush on her best friend and why a relationship between them would never work. Taylor's words always had a bite that Michelle couldn't withstand. It was easy to fall in love with her—she was fun, caring, and beautiful—but loving her up close came with painful consequences.

"Anyways, I'm out." Taylor drummed her fingers on her desk and pushed back in her chair.

"It's not even three o'clock."

Taylor shrugged. "It's Friday. You know I can't concentrate after ten o'clock. That's why I process extra Monday through Thursday. It's not my fault the bartender at The Hideaway is cute. I think I'm going to get his number tonight. He says he has a fiancée but nah."

"How are you going to punch out?"

Taylor tossed her badge to Michelle and gave her a finger wave. "By*eee*!"

Michelle had just wrapped her hair when her cell rang. She just wanted to go to sleep and almost ignored the call, but her Spidey sense was tingling.

"Hey, I'm here."

"Excuse me?" Michelle said. She recognized it was Taylor on the phone, but being 'here' didn't make sense when they were roommates and Taylor obviously *wasn't* home.

"At the office. Remember? Like we talked about."

Michelle knew the conversation and also recalled nothing being said about going back to the office after work.

"What are you doing there?" Whatever Taylor's reason, Michelle knew it was nothing good.

"He's up to something. The manager. I'm gonna get proof of whatever it is so they *have* to give me that promotion."

It was past the point of talking her down from what she'd already started. The most Michelle could do would be to minimize the damage.

"Stay right there. Promise me you won't do anything until I get there."

Taylor was quiet a long moment.

"Promise me!"

"*Okayyyy.*"

Michelle's normal drive to the office was about twenty-five minutes. She made it there in less than twenty. She'd always supposed their badges didn't work after hours, but when she swiped hers, the door buzzed and she pulled it open.

Her first thought was to go to her desk, thinking Taylor would be there, but then she thought again. Her friend probably would be hovering around somewhere, maybe the branch manager's office. She had it fixed in her mind that he had it in for her, so Taylor's reflex was to strike first.

Michelle turned toward his office. A moment later, she saw he wasn't in there. She blinked as if she didn't understand. He had every right to go home just the same as any other employee. But he was a tree.

She tucked her concern in the back of her mind. Michelle was more concerned with finding her friend and getting her the hell out of here. She scanned the cubicles nearby and got into a crouch as she ran to the breakroom. The lights were out in here too, and she went around the corner to the restrooms. Taylor wasn't in either of the stalls, and just to be sure, Michelle checked the men's room too.

And then it hit her. Michelle found her best friend sitting in her cubicle, tossing trash balls in the can. From a brief glance, she was missing a lot more than she was hitting.

"What are you doing here?" Michelle whispered.

"What, you told me to wait for you," Taylor said.

"I mean…I mean *here.* Tay, this is crazy!"

"I'll concede I may have gone a little overboard." Taylor put her hands up in mock-surrender. "But we're already here, so let's go."

"Go?" Michelle asked, but Taylor was already out of her chair and headed in the direction of the manager's office.

"Tay! Tay! Tay!" Michelle said, hurriedly catching up to her friend in a crouch-run.

"What, Chelle?"

"He's not in there."

"I know. That's why I'm going in."

Michelle wanted to make the point that the tree not being in his office meant he was somewhere *outside* of his office, but the point was as left behind as Michelle would have been had she not followed her best friend.

The office door was open and Taylor walked in. Michelle followed a moment later on her hands and knees, turned around, and quietly shut the door.

"Why'd you shut the door?" Taylor asked. "We might need to run out of here."

"Oh. Right." Michelle reached for the door handle.

"No. Leave it shut."

Taylor began rooting through drawers and checking behind picture frames. Michelle didn't help, instead staring at the pictures of trees. One in particular caught her eye of what she guessed was an older tree with two saplings to either side of it.

"Oh, he's got a family," Michelle said.

"Don't buy that bullshit, Chelle," Taylor said. "Those are stock photos or something. Probably came with the frame."

"C'mon, you don't know that."

"That tree isn't dioecious. It isn't male. I just said 'he' because I knew it would be easier for you to understand."

"How do you know it's not di...di-eesh..."

Taylor turned to her. "Know. Thy. Enemy."

She turned back to the desk and began combing over the items inside the overhead compartments.

"I didn't know you knew about trees," Michelle said. "How did you know what kind of tree it was?"

"It's not a tree at all. At least I don't think." There was a locked drawer underneath the desk beneath the keyboard. Taylor tugged at it a few times, then fished into her pants pockets. She tried her own

5

keys, which didn't work, and Michelle sidled up to her with a paperclip.

"Let me try."

She wormed the paperclip around until it was hooked at the end with a couple bumps in it. Michelle slid it in and jiggled it gently inside until she thought she'd felt something click. The drawer came open, and there was Taylor, smiling next to her.

"That's my best friend!" Taylor put her hands out in front of her and began pumping the air in a little dance. She took the few documents out of the drawer and paged through them.

"I *knew* it!"

"Knew what?" Michelle said, her interest piqued. Never had any of Taylor's trips off the beaten path actually led anywhere.

"He's not a tree. Not a tree at all."

"Then what?"

A withered leaf floated down onto the desk, perfectly in the middle of the calendar.

They both looked up.

Vines dropped from the ceiling and wrapped around Taylor's head and shoulders. She lifted off the ground without struggling or making a sound, and a moment later, she'd disappeared in a nest of vegetation.

Michelle stared at the branch manager, her body unable to process the commands coming from the lizard part of her brain. Something that *could* have been munching was coming from inside there, but she didn't want to believe what she was thinking.

Taylor's boot plopped onto the desk, tipping briefly before standing upright. Another line lassoed around it and reeled it back up. Another vine wriggled from the ceiling, and instead of wrapping around Michelle's neck or her leg to drag her into the mouth, or whatever he'd used to eat up Taylor, it laid an apple gently on the desk.

She stared a long moment before picking it up and taking a bite.

Michelle was going to make an excellent branch manager.

I realized I didn't have any new horror poetry in this collection. I haven't written any in a long time, but here goes.

Angels with No Faces

Angels with no faces
Came for me today,
They have no place to go,
They need nowhere to stay,
They asked me for a face
they could borrow,
They took mine today,
And already have
yours tomorrow.

Gerald Dean Rice

This idea popped in my head a few days ago. I don't know if it's trying to say something larger about the universe, culture, or society in general. I just thought it was a freaky story.

Eat

J. Wellington Wimpy. He'd reminded Martina of him—the hamburger guy from the old Popeye cartoons. He was a little rotund and wore a suit but was a little more handsome than his cartoon counterpart. Martina didn't know why she had initially noticed him. Other than the suit, there wasn't anything that stood out about him.

She didn't know his actual name. Half the guys on stage used nicknames anyway. Guy 'The Flame', Meat Vader, and the Bun-Man—had to include the dash—were just a few of the names of the people onstage. Martina particularly liked Cynthia the Crusher, a petite fortyish woman who looked like she'd have difficulty finishing a salad.

Martina had simply mentally noted the man as wimpy once she had laid eyes on him. Gwen had handed her a clipboard of names for her to keep track of how many hotdogs each contestant had eaten. He was number six and an X had been written on the line where his name should have been. Not having a name wasn't expressly against the rules, but no one had done that before. The letter looked like it had been written hastily, last moment, but it didn't rise to the level of making Martina feel she had to care.

Not until much later anyway.

The hot dog eating contest had gone off as could be expected. Two men had thrown up within minutes and a third had all but turned green before getting up and quickly exiting the stage. A very small woman had been a surprise by how she seemed determined to down dog after dog, regardless of her body's capacity to contain them.

Wimpy had been eating each hot dog slowly, as if he were leisurely enjoying himself at a picnic. He was at least four hot dogs behind the next slowest person, by her guess, and showed no sign of stopping or picking up the pace.

The first round was called, and surprisingly, he was still in the running. Two had been eliminated because they'd vomited, leaving Wimpy in the top five by default. He seemed blissfully unaware of the air horn that called an end to the round and picked up his next hot dog and began slowly munching on it.

"Let him," Martina whispered. "Just let him keep eating so he can fill himself up or get sick, and then he's out." She didn't know why the man made her so uncomfortable; it was like the rest of the world didn't exist. His eyes were half-lidded, like he was falling asleep or had nothing but disdain for everyone around him. The pan of hot dogs near each contestant was refilled, and she should have paid more attention when the boy—Kevin, his name was—yanked his hand back from Wimpy's pan and shook his finger.

Kevin looked at her, but other than being generally aware of the teen looking at her, Martina hadn't really noticed him.

He and the other boys filed offstage, and a moment later, the air horn sounded again. Wimpy's hand shook just before he took another hot dog. Martina's heart leapt at the possibility of him being out, but whatever it was passed. He continued his slow pace and she could tell he wasn't going to make it past this round barring someone else vomiting again.

Wimpy slowly and steadily fed hot dogs into his mouth, bite after bite, as if he were savoring a meal. Most of the other contestants had adopted the method of splitting the hot dog in half and dunking it in water before eating, a technique employed by Takeru Kobayashi, but Wimpy didn't even touch his cup of water.

Finally, the round was called, with three contestants moving on to the next round. Wimpy wasn't going to be one of them. Martina breathed a sigh of relief. The other person eliminated stood away from the table, took a dramatic bow, and exited.

Wimpy was still eating.

Everyone to the side of the stage turned to look at Martina. This was her event. She was supposed to be in control of everything happening. But in her three years of managing this particular event, she'd never seen someone eliminated who wouldn't stop eating.

"I guess I need to go up there," she said. Martina handed her clipboard to someone and emerged onto the stage.

She waved to the crowd, wanting to make as little of a scene as possible. It was definitely awkward for her. Martina wasn't the type of person who liked to be the center of attention, but everyone definitely had their eyes on the man who was still eating hot dogs between rounds. Even the other remaining contestants had turned to look at him.

"Excuse me, sir," Martina said, laying a hand on his shoulder.

He took another bite of the hot dog in his hand, chewing lazily.

She gripped his shoulder and gave him a moment to finish what was in his mouth, hoping he would look at her and realize something was amiss. He took another bite.

"Sir!" Martina said as forcefully and quietly as she could. She was still hoping to avoid a scene and laid a hand over the hand holding the half a hot dog.

He continued munching as if he hadn't noticed her.

She willed him to look at her and realize it was over.

Gerald Dean Rice

The man swallowed and opened his mouth to take a breath. Martina felt his arm pull against her palm covering his hand. He didn't push her hand away.

Instead, he reached with his other hand and plucked off her ring finger and popped it into his mouth.

Either it didn't hurt or Martina was too shocked to feel pain. He slurped her finger into his mouth, chewed it a few times, and swallowed.

Martina's mouth worked open and closed as if she *should* have said something, but her mind was blank. What do you say to the person who was eating you? Blood squeezed continually from the fresh wound of the small stump on her hand, soaking into the hot dog bun, the man's shirt sleeve, and the paper tablecloth.

It never crossed Martina's mind to remove her hand from his.

He opened his mouth the same as when he'd finished his last bite of hot dog and reached over with his free hand and picked off another finger from Martina's hand.

This time, shock didn't shield her from the agony, but a part of her was able to marvel at how deftly he'd plucked off her finger, like it'd been detachable to begin with. It went into his mouth, the passive expression on his face never changing.

Martina lifted her hand, but she'd been resting her weight across his hand and, overleveraged, fell across the table in front of him. His hand pulled from underneath her and for a terrible moment of panic, she was certain he was going to take some other part of her, something that would be vital this time.

"Hey!" someone shouted. It could have been one of the other contestants, Martina had no way of telling. There was a degree of shoving and grunting as she tried to rise from the table, but her palm slipped in the puddle of blood, and she smacked back down on her chin, clicking her teeth together and biting her tongue.

Martina rolled away from him, not caring if she fell off the table and the good eight feet or so to the ground. But she bumped against a solid barrier of flesh.

"We gotcha," Kelly, her assistant, said. "We gotcha."

Martina turned her head and saw the two of them, Kelly and Kevin, and realized they were girlfriend and boyfriend. She'd been

12

working with and around these two for the last three weeks and couldn't believe she hadn't noticed before now.

Martina looked to where Wimpy had been sitting and saw an empty space where his chair had been. Two contestants were still seated, staring in shock between her and where several men must have been pinning the man to the floor.

She looked at her three-fingered hand and chuckled once. It didn't look real to her. Then Martina was gone.

She woke up in the hospital. They hadn't put her in a bed or maybe they had and she'd just been in and out of it so long they'd eventually transferred her to a wheelchair.

"How long have I been here?" Martina said, groggy. She held up her wounded hand and saw it had been bandaged to the wrist. Somewhere around the end of her hand, it itched, but the sensation was so distant it was nearly nonexistent. She had to have been on something to keep her calm because the sight of her hand minus an index and pinky didn't seem extremely out of the ordinary.

Whoever was pushing her didn't answer and Martina supposed that might have been because she hadn't spoken loudly enough.

"Where we going?" she asked.

"Tina, I'm sorry, but I need you to come somewhere with me." It was Sheriff Andy. The two of them had dated off and on over the last two years or so. Nothing acrimonious between the two of them, when he gave her that look and she was in the mood, they did something. Sometimes something might last up to two weeks before they went their separate ways again.

She did her best to crane her neck to look up at him behind her, but her neck was stiff. Andy must have taken her gesture for an inquiry.

"It's the jail. He…the man…we still don't have a name—was there since he attacked you."

Martina's rational yet disconnected first thought was, *Why would you take me to see the man who* ate *two of my fingers?* She was cognitive enough to realize she was high as hell, but she didn't pick up on Andy referring to the man in the past tense.

By the time they got to the police station, even Martina could tell Andy was visibly disturbed. He'd always been a self-assured man, to the point of being arrogant. The version of the man that climbed out of his police cruiser and opened the rear door to let her out looked afraid.

"Is everything okay?" Martina asked.

Instead of answering, he shut the door behind her and led her inside. This late, there was normally a skeleton crew of about four people, but as far as she could tell, everyone was here. And they all had the same expression as Andy.

Martina absentmindedly scratched at her bandages, wanting to ask what was going on, but nobody would make eye contact with her. Martina wanted to ask why she was here. The police were the experts in this situation and they were all here. She ran a resale shop and managed a few events at the yearly fair. Why did they need her?

Dirk Malloy opened a door for them, leading to a maze of corridors she knew went to the jail cells. Martina had only been down this way once on one of those evenings when the skeleton crew had been particularly thin. But they went past all four cells to an old door she'd assumed was to a janitor's closet.

Andy took the set of keys off his belt, fished out the one he needed, and unlocked the door. He took a deep breath, his wide back rising and falling.

"What's wrong, Andy?" Martina asked.

He shook his head. "Nothing. I think. I hope. I just need you to see it too." He opened the creaky door, stepping aside to let her go first.

"I'll wait here. Just call if you need me."

Martina's alarms finally began sounding through her drug-infused haze. "You aren't coming?"

Andy shook his head and cast his eyes to the floor. Martina didn't move for a long time, looking from the sheriff to the long flight of the stairs, lit by a lone, naked light bulb.

She couldn't believe she was doing it—despite trusting him, this had been a strange day—

Was it still the same day? As she descended the stairs, Martina realized she had no idea how much time had passed since the contest.

She paused midway down and turned to look back at Andy. There were a lot of questions floating at the edges of her mind, but they were just out of reach.

"I know it's scary," Andy said. "But I promise it's okay. It's safe now."

A question floated in from the periphery.

Safe now? *What did that mean?*

But she was still in the haze of the pills she'd been given, although their effect was waning. She did trust Andy, though, and realizing it in that moment put a different frame around whatever was happening.

He was disturbed by something he'd seen. And he wanted her to see it too. Martina walked into a room she could only have guessed was the original jail cell when the building was constructed.

The floor was stone and had a unique grit underfoot as she walked. There were three cells down here, each with iron bars from floor to ceiling. The first two were empty. Martina realized with sobering intensity that the painkiller she'd been given was rapidly wearing off. She could feel the sweat pricking her brow and wanted to turn around and go back upstairs.

"What do you see?" Andy called from upstairs. His voice was tinny and sounded slightly farther away than it was.

Martina passed the divide between the second and third cells and saw no difference between it and the prior two. Wait, half beneath the bed was a hat. It had to have been the same bowler hat Wimpy had had on.

But there was no Wimpy.

There was no way they would have just let him out. Martina spun around, certain he was right behind her and would start with the remaining fingers on her hand. Her heart hammered as she was confronted by nothing more than a blank gray wall.

"Tina?"

She turned three hundred sixty degrees, fully taking in the entire room. Cobwebs high up on the walls, a crack running along the corner of the ceiling, water stains here and there. The only things that looked out of place were the three cameras mounted on the walls, trained on the cells.

"Tina." Andy came around the corner and a split second before she saw him, she expected Wimpy, using Andy's voice and, even when she saw him, thought he might be wearing Andy like a suit.

But he'd used the nickname she had allowed only him to use. She blinked twice and the stress eased from her shoulders.

"You're okay, right? Did you see?" Andy squeezed her shoulders and she was coming back to herself.

"There wasn't anything in his cell but a hat. Where is he?" Martina resisted the urge to scratch her bandaged hand.

He squeezed her shoulders harder. "I need you to see one more thing." He locked eyes with her and waited until she nodded.

Andy took out his phone. "This is the last copy." He shook it as if Martina should understand. She remained blank-faced until he continued. Andy opened his phone and pulled up a thumbnail. He put a hand around her shoulder and pulled her into him as he started a video with his other hand.

The grainy video began from a high-up angle, the camera pointed into the cell where the bowler hat had been. Wimpy sat on the bed, feet flat on the floor, hands in his lap, blotch on his shirt that had to have been her blood. She could see his wide, flat mouth, lips apparently moving, but there was no sound. Martina wanted to ask Andy what he'd been saying, but she didn't want to interrupt the moment.

Her hand began to throb in time with her pulse and she did her best to ignore the budding pain. Wimpy lifted one blurry hand from his lap and covered the other. Then the first hand rose to his mouth. He repeated the motion, and after a few repetitions, she realized the hand in his lap was getting smaller.

Was he eating his own hand?

Wimpy continued at his leisurely pace, rolling up his sleeve and plucking off pieces of his arm until there was just a nub below the shoulder. Then he leaned forward, grabbed his shoe, and appeared to pull it off. He turned the shoe upside down and shook out his foot before lifting it to his mouth and shoving it down with two visible swallows.

Unless the video was speeding up, Wimpy was picking up the pace. He detached his calf just below the knee, the half empty pant leg drooping over the edge of the cot. The other foot and calf followed, then the rest of his reduced arm and his thighs.

He looked like a sort of scarecrow, real and not real, peculiarly balanced despite not having legs. Martina had moved past the man cannibalizing himself and was currently amazed at how much of himself he was ingesting. She hadn't yet thought about when he would stop.

He unbuttoned his shirt and let it fall from his diminished torso. Wimpy dug inside his pants and pulled out what she could only guess was a fistful of genitalia. He stuffed that in his mouth and pulled out a long columnar thing that, when he started to sag like a blow up doll with an air leak, Martina realized was his spine.

What she was seeing already didn't make sense, but rather than the remains of his body just caving in and falling over, he used that spare arm and tore off the rest of his torso and stuffed it in his mouth while the rest of him rested seemingly on nothing. Now he had absolutely no stomach, yet he was still consuming himself. He ripped off the top of his head, opening wide to eat and, after he sucked his fingers, stuffed his whole hand in his mouth and slurped it down like a giant noodle. His collarbone and the rest of his neck was next, then his jaw, and lastly, his tongue slicked over his lips, wiping them away like an eraser.

And then nothing. He was gone.

"What…what happened?" Martina asked when she rediscovered her voice.

"You saw it." Andy breathed heavily as if he'd been running and she realized she was too. "That's what was on the video. Didn't doctor it. Didn't do anything to it but watch." He turned the phone in his hand so only he could see the screen and poked at it with his index.

"And now it's gone. The last copy."

"What are you talking about? A man died in that cell." Martina found herself having sympathy for this man for some reason. "It has to be reported. He might have a family—"

"Reported to who?" Andy held her gently by the elbows. "Nobody knows who he was. And what would we say to anyone who may have known him? Do we tell them he *ate* himself until he was *gone*? What do we say here, Tina?"

She realized he was searching her eyes for an actual answer and not just asking rhetorically.

"Why?" she asked. "Why me?" Martina had the impression none of them could believe what they had seen and were looking to get to understand for some reason.

Andy let go of her elbows, his mouth a grim line. He reached into his inside jacket pocket and pulled out a glasses case.

"These were in the cell. Under the bed." The itching in her hand ramped up to burning. Martina looked back and forth between his haunted eyes and the case. He held it out to her, a mild tremor in his hand. She took it and he took a step back.

"They're yours," he whispered.

Whatever was inside was heavier than a pair of glasses. Andy didn't help as she struggled to open the case. She dropped it twice before she was finally able to pry it open. Inside were her index and pinky fingers.

They were moving.

I've been feeling something lately. I'll probably be talking more about this feeling on social media, solidifying where this feeling is coming from, even though I hesitate to do that here. By the time you read this, I suspect I'll know one way or another. But this is where I am right now.

Holding Patterns

I have a Walk now,
I run like a snail—
I wanna be there now
But I take my time
With one-handed touches
And wink-eyed stares,
A single handful of heart
With the other waiting behind my back

Gerald Dean Rice

I hop-scotch along your path
And wait for you to unveil the next entry.

There is a truth
That rings,
Regardless of those who don't
Want to bear witness,
Evidence of love, desire, want, completion,
A toll must be paid
to pass this stage of life,
Resist the rising sun
If you must,
But it still crests
the sky and rests
On the tail of the
Moon, waiting for you
To read facts written
on the heart,
I practice,
Etching each word in mid-air
Until you reach out
And strike the lies
You want not a part of record,
To make the blind space
For what's next to blossom,
Love. Is. Here.
And it knows your name,
It will whisper
Until you speak,
And then it will shout in your key,
A testimony and an oath,
To swear by your desire
And live by the words you swear together.

The flame of youth
has turned down for us
As we've walked through

licks of fire

Brittled but hardened,
Ashen-faced and still matched
Smoldering for years yet,
Our coals slowly cooling,

As sparking feelings float light as air
Waiting to catch.

Gerald Dean Rice

The title of this story makes no sense. That's fine. I had another title that didn't make sense but it more closely relates to why what happens happens. The title came from autocorrect going bonkers as I wrote.

Wheedle Pick

Baron didn't know why he was at this party. Brenda was the only reason he was there, but he hadn't seen her yet. And what was the point? It wasn't like she even knew he existed. She'd said hello to him once with all the casualness of swatting a fly.

He probably would be better off going back home now. Baron had a couple sketches he'd half-heartedly begun and maybe he could half-heartedly finish them.

Baron glanced at the cup in his hand. It was allegedly punch, but the smell of alcohol in it was like a thump in the nose. He sat the cup down and rose from the arm of the couch.

Kids he knew from school and a bunch he'd never seen sat, stood, and a few were doing headstands as they chugged beer through a tube. Music pounded every surface, including him, and as he weaved through the thicket of bodies, someone knocked rhythmically on the door. *Ta-tah tah tah tah tah tah tah.*

He thought that was odd, considering he'd used the perfectly good doorbell when he'd arrived and also thought he recognized the song from the cadence of the knock. *You are the Sunshine of My Life* by Stevie Wonder, a household favorite of his parents.

Baron stopped behind a pimply-faced boy with hair pulled into a curly pompom and braces who opened the door right as something punched through it and pierced his chest.

The boy's eyes went wide and whatever it was withdrew. He turned, cup still in hand. He and Baron met eyes for just a moment before the door smashed in and swatted him into the wall.

Baron leapt in surprise, watching the boy crumple to the floor. He gradually looked up to the figure filling the doorway. She was the most muscular human he'd ever seen as she turned slightly sideways to step through, covered with every melee weapon imaginable.

Including the axe she held high up on the handle as she looked around. So far, it seemed like only Baron had noticed her, everyone else deaf to what had happened just a moment before from the ear-pounding music. She gripped the axe near the bottom before tossing it past a dozen people and burying in the back of a petite blonde-haired girl who looked like she was dressed for church.

The spray of blood caught almost everyone's attention as she fell into the lap of a shirtless boy. He screamed and then everyone joined him as an Olivia Rodrigo song came on. People ran into each other, ran into walls, tripped over each other and were trampled on the floor. Amidst the chaos, the killer strode calmly past several teenagers, stabbing and slashing with a long-bladed knife. Baron tripped over his own feet to get out of the way, feeling something spongy beneath him when he fell and turned to see it was a buxom junior whose name he *almost* knew.

He got to his hands and knees, realizing much later the front door had been open and he could have crawled out and avoided the bulk of the massacre to come.

The killer had a pair of brass knuckles and bashed several teens in the face who were still on their feet and within arm's reach. Every punch was a killing blow, the ferocity and power of each one crushing skulls or caving in chests as she savaged anyone in reach.

Someone tried to open the patio door, but before they could unlock it, she had a bow in her hand and pinned the boy's hand to the door with an arrow. He danced in place a moment and quickly lost steam, collapsing to his knees with his hand suspended above him.

She changed direction, strafing between teens, chopping through them with a broadsword, when Baron realized she was headed back in his direction. A brave girl ran at her with a kitchen knife and was roughly cut in half from the waist up. The chorus of screams grew louder than the music, everyone running more in each other's way than actually attempting escape, the killer almost leisurely cutting through teenagers like a thresher through wheat.

Someone bumped into Baron and he yelped.

"Come with me," a girl said, lacing her fingers between his. He looked at her as she dragged him away and realized he was looking at—

—Brenda—

She looked as frightened as anyone, but she led him out of the killer's path and into a closet. The music cut off abruptly, and the screams continued, a chorus of terror-filled voices accompanied by splats of blood and the sounds of melee weapons breaking bones and slicing through flesh.

"We can't stay here," Brenda said. "She's gonna go for the kids upstairs and that's when we run for it."

"She's killing everyone," Baron said much too loudly. "Someone should call the police!"

"Everyone will be dead by the time police get here." Brenda looked him in the eye. "We have to get out."

She listened at the door for a long moment, then squeezed his hand. Baron briefly allowed himself the reminder that he was in love with this woman. His heart raced for more than what was happening on the other side of the closet door.

Brenda took a deep breath, then threw the door open, and she dragged Baron along as they made a beeline for the front door. They were a half dozen feet away when she screamed and went down, taking Baron with her.

A moment later, he was on his feet, seeing what had taken her down. It was a bear trap, painted pink and red. Brenda howled in agony, rolling back and forth on her back. He wanted to help her but honestly didn't know if he'd be making it worse if he tried removing it.

Then an arrow caught him high in the shoulder blade and spun him around. He hit the floor less than a foot away from Brenda. The pain was enormous, seeming to extend past his body into the air around. Baron lay paralyzed on the floor, clutching at his wound, his lame hand somehow connected to one of Brenda's.

The house was nauseatingly quiet. The lizard part of him knew what that meant. The killer had dispatched with everyone in the house. Perhaps some had escaped and were seeking help, but Brenda had been right. Calling the police was no sort of salvation for them in the moment. The killer had been much too efficient.

Bodies were littered about, blood splashed across everything, and deep dark stains in the carpet. Baron could only sit in stomach-queezing silence as he heard her approach.

The killer wore a mask with a beatific face. Her strawberry blonde hair was pulled back in a ponytail and she seemed to regard Baron as she approached.

She knelt in front of him and cocked her head like a dog trying to understand something new. Then she laid a massive paw over Baron and Brenda's hands—she'd fainted from the pain—and said, "Good."

The killer stood, walked to the front door, opened it, stepped out, and gently closed it after herself.

Baron sat in shock, looking over the carnage all around him. An arm draped over the back of the couch, gently swinging back and forth. He grabbed a finger, hoping to tell whoever it was they weren't alone. That there was at least one other survivor.

Then the arm fell in his lap. The wound at the shoulder was ragged, like it had been ripped off. Baron squealed and shoved it away, pressing even harder into the back of the couch.

He just wanted to go home.

Brenda moaned next to him. She blinked several times before she sat up.

"Are you okay?" she asked him.

The question confused him. So, he asked in return. "Are *you* okay?"

"Yeah." She rubbed her eyes and stretched. "I guess." She looked at him and something in her eyes was different. She was looking *at* him. She was looking at *him*. *She* was looking at him.

Baron's heart skipped a beat. His injury suddenly didn't hurt anymore. She laced her fingers between his and they smiled at each other.

Brenda finally knew he was alive.

Gerald Dean Rice

This idea came to me after a podcast I listened to. Bonus points if you can guess what it is.

The O'Brien Show

It was all Danny could do to keep his eyes open during the drive home. Another 2:00 a.m. day and he was going to have to be back at 7:00. He still hadn't gotten the motor on the garage door fixed and didn't feel like messing with the thing to get it open.

Danny parked in his driveway, barely able to haul himself out of his Fiat, almost dropping his keys before he'd made it to his porch. As soon as he tossed his keys on the little dining table someone said, "Woo!" Several whistles and cheers followed along with prolonged general applause.

"Did I leave the TV on?" he said as he tossed his jacket on the couch. He wasn't surprised he'd left the television on, but it was the *Andy Griffith Show*. And when he picked up the remote, a quick thumbing of the mute button informed him the sound had already been off.

"What the hell?" he said and dropped the remote on the couch as he lumbered toward the kitchen.

His cell rang before he opened the fridge. He thumbed on his Bluetooth glasses and answered.

"Danny?"

"Sheila, hey. What are you doing up at this ungodly hour?" His stomach clenched. There'd been a lingering conversation waiting to happen between them for a little while now.

"We need to talk."

"Ooooooooo," a chorus of voices said. Danny peaked up from behind the refrigerator door, looking around.

"Hello?"

"Danny, I'm here—"

"Just a sec, babe. I heard a voice."

Several voices, he thought.

"What do you mean, a voice?"

"Hang on."

He was wide awake now and swiftly rounded his small ranch, including poking in the bathroom last. Danny opened his front door and looked outside. The only thing he could hear was the hum of the streetlights and a dog yarking in the distance.

"Is everything okay?"

"I…I guess so." Danny shut the door and locked it. He backed away slowly, as if expecting it to leap off its hinges and swat him. "Sorry. Sorry." He touched his glasses as if he were touching Sheila's hand. "Uh, hello? I'm back. I'm here."

"Danny, are you all right?"

"Yeah. Yeah." He shook his head as if the voices he'd just heard were only in his head. Then silently prayed they weren't, realizing what that implication meant. "I just heard something weird. Never mind. How are you doing?"

"I'm okay…No, I'm not."

"What's wrong?"

"You know, Danny."

He did. Despite his many put-offs and avoidances, Danny knew why Sheila would be calling him now.

"Sheila…"

"No. Just listen. You know I love you. I do. We've been together five years."

"I know—"

"Shhhhh!"

Danny thought he heard a chuckle but he ignored it.

"I *know* you love me too. Why are we waiting?"

"You know, I love you, babe. It's just—"

"No. I'm not done yet!" Another laugh. "I'm not even talking about us getting married. You know I don't care about that. I just want you. And you want me too. Why aren't we together right now?"

It was the question he'd been dreading because he couldn't come up with a sensible answer. He could relocate to California tomorrow and probably have a job on par with the one he had now. But that would be in large part due to Sheila. He didn't mind in the least that she had a much higher position than he did, but he'd gotten this job with his own sweat and tears. Well, mostly. Taking a job out there would be a red carpet being rolled out for him for work he hadn't done.

"You could move out here. You could move in with me. I wouldn't even care about the job. You could find something on your own. All on your own."

That was true and it wasn't. Danny knew if he moved out there with Sheila, everything would be great in the beginning. But if he really did find a job on his own, it would take time, if ever, and would either end with him breaking down and accepting the offer that came because of her or her resenting him because he wasn't contributing to the life they were supposed to be building together.

He was silent a long time after she'd stopped talking. Danny realized it was finally his turn to speak. There were so many things he could have spoken right then that he didn't know how to say.

"I'm…really tired. I have to be up really early in the morning. Could I call you around lunch?"

There was a long sigh on the other end of the line. "Sure."

The line went dead.

"Ohhhhhhhhhhhhh!" several voices said in chorus.

"What the hell?" Danny shouted as he took the phone from his ear, already forgetting the conversation that might have been signifying the end of his relationship.

He looked around his home again, this time making a more detailed effort, peeking into cupboards and cabinets and examining the corners of rooms to find hidden microphones or speakers.

Once his hackles were down again, he thought he should call Sheila back. He loved her more than he had vocabulary to express and had every confidence she felt the same about him. For a moment, he thought to dash his pride and tell her he'd be on the next flight to her. That he'd get in his car right now and just wait until his flight boarded, no matter how many hours away that would be.

In that moment, he wanted to be with her more than anything. But then he came back to earth.

A tear had trickled down his cheek and he removed his glasses to swab at his eye with the inside of his hand. Danny looked at his glasses, realizing he'd had them on.

"Wait..." he said, thinking about the possibility his eyewear had been hacked. It definitely made more sense than...than whatever else had been going through his mind. Danny narrowed his eyes at his frames mistrustfully before putting them back on.

He grabbed a beer from the fridge and sat on the couch with his phone, swiping through his apps, looking for one out of place. Danny had had a previous girlfriend install a GPS tracking app on his phone to find out where he was. There were a few apps he didn't recognize, but it turned out that was only because he hadn't used them. He deleted the ones he could and examined the ones he couldn't to insure they were actually needed.

So that wasn't it. Danny took another drink as he looked around his home.

At some point, he wound up turning on his television. Back when he was a kid, the only choice would have been to flip through the few stations available, but with at least a half dozen streaming apps with a cavalcade of programming each to choose from, there was as close to an infinite amount of options to choose from as possible.

He finally settled on a show with a bearded foocie he thought he'd seen on Youtube. At some point, another beer had wound up in his hand.

Danny came awake, thinking he was hearing a susurrus of voices like conversation in a restaurant. By the time he'd finished blinking, the voices had stopped.

"Hello?" he said.

The silence seemed extra…silent. Almost like he was being watched. It may have been his imagination, the buzz from the two beers he'd had on an empty stomach, or…

It might have been real.

The tumblers in his brain had rolled into place while he'd been sleeping and he realized his glasses hadn't been on when he'd come home. He hadn't turned them on until Sheila had called.

Sheila…

So the voices weren't in his head.

Danny began examining his house again. Whatever it was, wherever it was coming from, was definitely in here. Someone breaking into his home and installing equipment that monitored and allowed people to react to his actions made little sense, but a live studio audience just for him made way less sense.

He was wide awake, and there was no way he was going to get any sleep before he had it figured out. Danny rechecked everywhere he'd checked before but made a point to pay even more attention. When he walked into a room, he started by examining the threshold first. He had no carpet, so he wouldn't have been able to see footprints. His bed was made and so was the one in the spare bedroom. There were no indentations from knees or hands. Everything in his drawers looked in order so far as he could tell. The blinds were still drawn as he'd left them—no point in opening them if he weren't going to be home at all during the day. The toilet seat was down, no streaks on the mirrors, no bits of trash on the floor. As far as Danny could tell, everything was as he'd left it. Danny even went so far as to press on walls as if that would release doors revealing hidden compartments.

Either whomever had come into his home had been just that meticulous or…or…

He'd had a really long day and was just tired.

That thought gave Danny a great deal of peace. He'd been feeling a knot twisting up in the center of his back and didn't know what he would have done even if he found *whatever* it was. But resting everything on his overactive and exhausted brain seemed appropriate. Even if there were something he had been plainly overlooking, a few hours of rest would give him a fresh perspective, and he could start over again. Danny even thought he'd have a good idea of what to say once he'd had a few hours rest and he could think more clearly.

People in the walls? That *definitely* made no sense and was more than likely a sign of just how tired he was.

"I just need some sleep," Danny said as he sauntered toward the bathroom. He took a leak and washed his hands, taking his time so he could examine his face in the mirror.

"You know you're fucking this up, right?" he said to his reflection. He stared a moment longer before swiping his hands across a drying towel and taking off his shirt as he left the bathroom.

"Ow!" a single voice shouted. Danny covered his nipples with one forearm and put a hand over his crotch even though he still had his pants on.

"Hello?" he asked timidly.

There was an uproar of laughter that made him feel even more self-conscious. His cell phone dinged. Danny reached for it without thinking and thumbed it open to read the message from Sheila.

Maybe we should take a break, she'd texted.

Terror filled him even more than whatever was going on in his home. Danny had to text back. He didn't *want* a break. He didn't want to lose her.

Danny paced back and forth, starting and stopping several messages, erasing each one.

One of Sheila's biggest complaints about him was that he'd always gotten stuck in his own mind. Lucky for him, she also thought he was particularly cute with that slack expression on his face. It was true, though—he did tend to go for long walks in his head.

He had to consider if stress was playing a part in whatever this 'episode' was. And if it were stress, what exactly he was stressing about.

Danny clenched his phone, resisting the urge to throw it. He wanted to be with Sheila and she wanted to be with him. Why wasn't that enough?

As he continued to his bedroom, he worked his belt open with his free hand and whipped it out and onto the floor.

"Ow!"

"You're repeating yourselves, guys," he said as he walked into his bedroom. He ignored a nervous chuckle as he dropped his phone on the nightstand. Danny unbuttoned his pants, let them fall, and stepped out of them.

He'd been standing there a short moment when he realized they were waiting. It was a pregnant pause.

They were waiting for him to take it all off. To get naked. Sheila had been waiting for him to take it all off too, metaphorically. To be naked, vulnerable. He knew what he needed to do.

Danny looked at his phone. Then he looked somewhere into the middle distance, a smirk on his face. Now would have been the perfect time for him to climb in his head again. He figured he may as well give them what they wanted.

Danny stripped out of his boxers, twirled them around on a finger, and then let them spin somewhere away.

The audience howled with delight, the applause increasing in volume until it was a roar in his ears.

He crossed his feet and was about to give a fancy bow when he looked down and screamed.

Danny's genitals were pixelated.

Gerald Dean Rice

I wrote this on a plane after one little bottle of Jack Daniels.

Naked

I am bared to you,
I want you to be mine
And I want to be yours,
I want all your messy,
Dirty things,
And to give you everything
All over again, but clean
Breaks are for the heartbroken
Who need to suckle their wounds, it
Tears me to not be a part of you
One whole, separated by blank space
Where we stand nude and true,
Where you go home to me

Gerald Dean Rice

And I come to the edge of the universe
with you.

I want your fire,
Every second without you
is a cold, wasted moment,
Your lips are the spark
that ignites me,
Your hands on me
like coals
Cooking me medium rare,
Perfect is the standard of young fools,
But I await your chef's kiss,
I will take the configuration
Of whatever presentation
You desire, garnish me
with the reds, yellows, and greens
Of your attention,
Serve me,
And I'll always be back
for seconds.

These feelings didn't die,
They didn't go on layaway
or recede,
I never satisfied
Or absented the need,
I feed on your presence
But lessons have been learned,
I burned,
But passion never left my flame,
I'm the same
Yet I aim
Different,
I hope you see in me
A difference,
A change to remain

For the rest of my life,
An exchange to explain,
The best of this strife,
And other words the rhyme,
If you have the time and a beer,
I'll gladly explain the rest of my years,
No fears,
I'd love to explain what I mean
When I say the word 'mine'.

Gerald Dean Rice

I have no idea what to call this one. This was one of those stories I thought of at night just before going to sleep and I didn't want to get up to jot the idea down. I almost didn't remember it.

X

Mr. Phipps looked across his little desk in his little office at the little couple. They were middle-aged, handsome to a degree, but oddly disturbing.

For starters, the husband was dead.

He wasn't all the way dead? Mr. Phipps couldn't help but note how the man's eyes seemed to lock onto his and occasionally flicker around the room. The couple had walked in his office and sat down, but that had been before Mr. Phipps realized the man was no longer entirely with us.

But he was determined to be professional. Mr. Phipps cleared his throat.

"I'm Matthew Phipps. How might I make your life better?" He mentally kicked himself, realizing he should have skipped asking the agency credo. The Michigan Organization of Redressable Grievances was a quasi-governmental agency that filtered out incidents and accidents that required police action from those that…didn't. Any action MORG could divert away from police and resolve was how they kept the lights on, although there was still a fee involved when something did require police involvement. The last part was so the organization didn't try to hog and underreport actual crimes.

"Mr. and Mrs. Clark," the woman said. She had a cherubic face despite her middle age and short, curly blonde hair. Mr. Clark looked like he'd been handsome in life, lean faced and bald on top with a van dyke and large brown eyes. He looked uncomfortable beyond just being dead, and when Mr. Phipps realized why his face looked so mask-like, it made him uncomfortable all over again.

The sutures emerging from the man's scalp and across his forehead meant his face had been peeled down so a ME could use a Stryker saw to remove the cap of his skull to examine his brain. Mr. Clark had been autopsied.

"Helen, let me address the elephant in the room."

"Mrs. Clark," she said.

"Sorry. Mrs. Clark. I'm sure you're here because of your husband." She nodded, that odd smile still on her face. "I'm presuming this has something to do with his present…condition?"

"Oh, absolutely. I tried to tell them he wasn't dead, but they didn't listen. Nothing can disturb my Harry when he's sleeping. He once slept all the way through a house fire."

Mr. Phipps had only skimmed the file, so he hadn't read anything about this if it were in there. "Excuse me? Slept? How do you mean?"

"He *slept* through it," Mrs. Clark said again. "One morning, I woke up when I smelled smoke. A minute later, the detector went off. I tried to shake him, but I already knew better. He never wakes up until he's done sleeping. He was too heavy for me to drag out of the house, so I got out as quickly as I could and went to a neighbor to call 911. By the time any kind of help arrived, the whole house was in flames. The firefighters couldn't get to him, but he was fine when the fire was out."

"How could he have been fine after the fire was put out?" Mr. Phipps was incredulous. Even if the man hadn't been burnt to death, he would have died from smoke inhalation.

Mrs. Clark shrugged. "They found him in the bedroom under the covers. The alarm went off and he got up."

Mr. Phipps was having difficulty reconciling her story with what he was seeing. Without seeing the dead man in front of him, he wouldn't have believed, even though one technically may not have had anything to do with the other. He thought it might have been best to stay on task.

"Regardless, Mrs. Clark, your husband's condition is…final. There really isn't anything I can do." He skimmed the paperwork until he found the page he wanted. "EMTs arrived on scene, attempted to resuscitate Mr. Clark. They were still administering life-saving measures at the hospital which were continued by hospital staff. He was pronounced at 5:37 a.m. I apologize for my bluntness, but everyone down the line did their jobs. Is there anything you would have me do to improve this situation?"

Mrs. Clark shook her head, forming her mouth into an O before she spoke. "Oh, we're not concerned about that Roger has been declared dead a bunch of times. It never quite got this far, but we're dealing with it." She looked from her husband to Mr. Phipps again, a twinkle in her eye. "In fact, it may have improved things."

"Improved, madam?"

"Yes-yes. Oh, yes. You know that old expression, when you remove one organ, the rest compensate."

Mr. Phipps recalled that expression being about senses and not organs, but he nodded, comfortable he had the gist of her meaning.

"Well, they removed *all* of Ed's internal organs, stuffed them all back in him in a plastic bag. I had to snip him back open to take them out, but our sex life has never been better."

Mr. Phipps blinked several times, understanding but not wanting to understand what she meant. There was a box of tissue on the opposite side of his desk for the many people who had sat in the same chairs as the Clarks and he leaned forward in his little chair—his considerably long upper body giving him a high view of the top of their lower bodies.

It looked like a python had been lying in his lap when Mr. Clark had put his pants on.

"Whu-whu-what do you want me to do?" Mr. Phipps was struggling to maintain his concentration as the constant smile on Mrs. Clark's face took on a new connotation. "If you don't mind that your husband is…y'know…with us in body but not in spirit."

"It's the ME's office," Mrs. Clark said and she reached up to touch the top of her husband's bald head. He hollow-grunted, pulling away slightly. "I can't get anybody on the phone to get his toupee back."

Heart sickness is the genesis of this poem. I won't gc into detail because at the very moment writing this, the entire situation I'm experiencing is evolving, but at 1:18am in a bar in Clawson, Michigan, this is what I was feeling.

Sip of My Health and the Merry of Ye be Whole

You aren't my O2,
Despite my free-floating heart,
There isn't a safe space to land,
I,
Hover,
In your air,
Waiting for you to inhale,
Breathing out
And in,
My rhythm
To the side
While you purify

the capillaries, veins, arteries,
tributaries, and rivers,
My insides
Balloon
As I wait for something
Inside you to swell for me,
I let the air out of the things
I want to swear to you, oaths
held in check,
Promises banked,
Expanding,
Until I can't hold
on, and I…
Pop.

I found this incomplete story on a flash drive. I'd started it years ago and didn't know how to finish it. Sometimes, perspective changes with time. A lot of time.

Kill Her

Brandon sighed. Karen imagined he was finally tired of her ranting about *her*.

He still hadn't told her what was in the big box in the middle of the floor by the dining table.

"Why don't you kill her?" he said, giving her that deadpan stare of his.

She laughed. Sometimes it was so hard to tell if he was joking, although this had to be a joke. His face broke into a smile, and she laughed again, less nervous this time.

"Seriously." He smiled, turning more fully toward her, and put a hand on her thigh. "What if you had her right here, right now, and you could just do whatever you wanted to her?"

"I'd probably wring her neck!" Karen laughed and Brandon smiled.

He gave her a toothless smile. "Would you really?"

"I don't know." She looked off in the distance and shook her head slowly.

"Really. Think about it. What would you like to do to her?"

"Maybe I'd punch her. Or give her a really good slap."

The glint disappeared from his eyes.

"C'mon. After what she did?" Brandon said. "You would have lost your job if it were up to her!"

I almost did. Brandon would never understand the politics of her job, and had she told him that, then he might really have gone down there and done something stupid.

"You know what?" She had an idea. "I would sit down with her, have a glass of wine, and tell her *exactly* how I feel."

"Exactly how you *feel*?" He looked disgusted. "What the hell kind of cop out is that? A woman who wanted to cost you your livelihood? Someone who prides herself on being a shit to every human being she encounters, someone you personally saw having an inappropriate intimate relationship with a manager who lost his job because of it—you just want to *tell* her how you *feel*?"

"Jesus, Brandon, you sound like you're advocating for me to kill her."

"Is that so terrible an idea?"

"Brandon, she's a human being!"

"She's a terrible human being. Did you know she's been divorced three times?"

"So? My uncle has been divorced four times."

"Your Uncle Frank isn't the best representative of all that's good." Brandon gave her a look.

That was true, but she did love him.

"I'm sure she has people who love her," Karen said.

"Sure, she does. But does one negate the other? Because *someone* loves a human being, does that mean their life can t be forfeit?"

"Well…yeah."

"So, the guy who killed Jeffrey Dahmer shouldn't have done it? Dahmer did have a mother at the time and I'm certain she loved him."

"Well…no. He should be punished."

"Right, he should be. But let's be honest. The ones responsible for punishing him probably did it with half a heart. If you found out he just got a month in the hole, would you be disappointed? Be honest."

Karen thought a long moment. "I guess I wouldr't be. But he was punished somehow."

"So sometimes the punishment for murder can be nominally performative?"

"Yes. To declare to society that killing even the worst of us is unacceptable."

Brandon nodded. Then he lifted her arm by the wrist and gently slapped the back of her hand."

Karen giggled. "And what was that for?"

"To let you off the hook," her husband said. "That was your punishment. A pre-punishment."

"A *pre*-punishment?" Karen's eyes flicked to the large box on the floor by the patio door. "Why would I need to be punished? We both are joking, right?"

"You ever heard of Schrodinger?"

"The guy with the cat? Something like it was in a parallel state of existence and non-existence?"

"Something like that. I saw you looking at the box. What if…I had her in there?"

"Had her in there? Brandon, that's not funny."

"It's not meant to be. If emotions can dictate our actions, then can't they also dictate reality to some extent? Take the guy who killed Jeffrey Dahmer. I'm sure he didn't wake up thinking 'tcday is the day I kill JD.' Maybe the thought had crossed his mind a few times, but it wasn't a *conscious* decision."

"What are we talking about exactly?" Karen stood, wanting to put a little distance between her husband and her and hoping being lupine would help clear her thoughts.

"Never mind the Dahmer example." Brandon waved his hand. "There are people who die by the hands of other people all the time. Good people on both sides. People who didn't deserve it and people who didn't mean to do it and are racked with guilt after. And many times, the punishment those people receive is nominal. A few years in prison in comparison to the many years the other person should have had left."

"Brandon—"

"And why should a person who premeditates the death of someone who deserves to die be punished more? To intentionally remove a weed is not worse than accidentally burning down a forest."

"Stop it!" Karen said. "Just stop! We are not talking about weeds or trees. We are talking about people. Maybe I'm being a hypocrite, but I believe we all are to some degree, and I accept my portion of it. But I'm not going to kill *anyone,* no matter how much I hate them or how much they might deserve it."

"So, you think she does deser—"

Karen held up her hand to stop him from finishing.

"Nobody deserves it. Not even hardcore murderers on death row. I accept that there are people who are executed and I even take relief that they are no longer able to hurt anyone.

"But it's like *you* said, one emotion doesn't cancel out the other. Nobody has the right to take someone's love away. Even if there is no one who loves that person. As long as we are alive, no matter how hopeless, we all have the potential to love and find love. My hate doesn't give me the right to take that away. So can we just drop this?" Karen gave her husband an exhausted smile. "C'mon, I'm hungry. I wanna go to dinner." She slapped his shoulder.

His face had fallen. Karen had won.

"I'm hungry too."

"Great, I'll get my jacket." For her, that was code for 'and go to the bathroom' and when she returned, he was still sitting.

"What's wrong?" she asked. "Let's go."

50

"Oh, nothing," Brandon said. "Just one last thing. I forget how the expression goes. Something like all things true are said in jest."

Karen looked at him.

"You were joking about killing her, but be honest with yourself. If you had her by the throat, how *good* would that feel? Just imagine it."

Karen had never seen that look on his face. It was like…an expression of passive hatred, like he could have killed someone and with the press of a button.

"Brandon, are you feeling okay?"

"I feel great! Delicious even."

She narrowed her eyes, processing a sudden truth despite who she was seeing.

"You're not my husband," she said. "Where is my Brandon?"

The thing dressed in her husband's clothes stood. It smiled at her in that same way he did at times and turned its head upward and opened its mouth. A *sound*—less human, but more something else than animal—*escaped* its mouth. Karen pictured a bottle being opened—pressure being relieved.

The thing's body elongated, its ankles and wrists stretching past the cuff of his pants and shirt.

"I'll leave it up to you what you do with that," it said, pointing to Alice's finger, still on the kitchen counter. "I'd put it on a necklace, personally." It made for the front door after shrugging into Brandon's rain jacket. Karen opened her mouth to protest but didn't say anything. It wasn't that she was afraid of it, for some strange reason, she felt she was in no danger. Everything it had touched of her husband's, she didn't want back. She'd take him for a new coat herself after showering him with a thousand kisses. Speaking of which…

"Wait." She stalked over to the thing as it was zipping up and put a hand on its shoulder, turning it toward her. "Where is my husband?"

Its eyes rolled toward the window.

"Stuck on Rochester Road. There was a traffic accident, two fatalities." It held up a hand. "Not me."

"So, he's all right? You didn't…harm him?"

It smiled. "Why would I want to harm Brandon? I love that guy." It turned to go, the door opening of its own accord. Karen followed.

It perched on the rail of the porch and rather than the sun bursting the thing into flames, it seemed to swell even more in daylight. It took a deep breath, let it out, then took in another.

Then it sprang off the rail, its arms spread, and lifted into the sky. For a long moment, Karen kept expecting it to fall and for the earth to open and swallow it up, but it kept going up into the clean blue sky until it was invisible to the naked eye.

She came back inside, shook from what she had just witnessed, forgetting to close the door behind her.

Karen's cell phone rang on the dining table and she knew it was Brandon. The real Brandon. She wanted to go to the table and answer. To hear his voice and know he was fine.

But she would have to go past the box. And despite her spirited argument against the demon-angel-whatever it was, she didn't know what was in the box.

Or what wasn't.

I'm not sure where this story came from. I wrote it while putting this collection together, but the influence? Maybe a little Hellraiser?

Horrorphone

The twins sat across from one another at their small dining table with the box between them. Sefra had found it beneath Father's bed and had sought out Sue for her opinion.

"It's a box," Sue had said. But Sefra had seen the look on her sister's face and had led her to the kitchen so they could talk about it.

Father had died in the house. Despite his advanced age, he'd been in great health. The cause listed on his death certificate had been cardiac arrest, but Sue had said that's what they put when they couldn't figure out an actual cause of death. Technically, everyone died of cardiac arrest. So long as the heart was beating, a body was considered to be alive.

But Sefra was concerned the box might have had something to do with Father's death. It was so strange-looking. It was about five inches square and four inches tall. It was made of what felt like a delicate material—maybe bone—stained a deep shade of violet, but weighty when she hefted it in her hands. She had no idea what could be inside, but she thought she'd felt something move.

"It's a clock," Sue said, tapping an index on the lid.

At least, Sefra assumed it was the lid. The box could just as easily have been upside down—it didn't even have seams.

Sefra shook her head.

No, it wasn't a clock.

"Maybe it's one of those puzzle boxes. Y'know, the ones you have to figure out how to open."

Sefra looked at her. Puzzle boxes looked like puzzle boxes. This was barely more than a rock shaped like an oblong box. Plus, it felt wrong to the touch. The longer Sefra had held it, the more uncomfortable it was in her hands until she felt something akin to nausea by the time she'd put it on the table.

"Okay, so that doesn't make any sense. Do you have a better idea?"

Sefra raised her eyebrows and shook her head again.

"Then let's just throw it away!" Sue shouted.

Sefra clasped her hands together. It had been Father's. It might be important. There might be something inside it.

Sue had to have seen the look on her face. She'd always been the leader, but when Sefra begged, she'd always given in.

"Okay," her sister said. "We'll figure it out." She reached across the table and took Sefra's hand. "Together."

Sefra felt her face relax a little and she forced a smile. Sue squeezed her fingers and they locked eyes.

Okay.

Sefra reached across to grab Sue's other hand and she brushed the box. A small section popped out of the side of it. Twice the thickness of a wooden match and just as long. Whatever material the box was made of, this piece appeared to be the same. She reached…

"Don't touch it!" Sue shouted and slapped her hand. They both stared at it for a long minute as nothing else changed.

"Okay, maybe we should touch it."

Sefra stared at her.

"I don't know. I thought you wanted to figure out what this thing is."

Sefra gradually relaxed then nodded. Sue slowly reached with an index extended and poked it.

Nothing happened.

Sefra squared her shoulders and raised her hand.

"Wait," Sue said. "Just wait another minute." Sefra held her breath until her sister gave a nod for her to proceed.

Just as she was about to touch it, she got a tiny electric shock to her index and immediately snapped her hand back and suckled the tip of her finger.

Then it started moving. It looked like a tiny nest of iridescent black spikes bloomed its way out of the top, but it didn't fold or swing open—the lid cracked, accompanied by a tiny whine that quickly rose in volume and pitch until it was like a blade scraping her eardrums from the inside.

"Ouch!" Sue said, covering her ears.

Sefra covered her mouth in shock as blood streamed from her sister's nose and then began trickling from her eyes.

She pointed, but Sue had to have noticed after blood crested her lip and went in her mouth. The bleeding stopped and Sue gasped for breath, blood soaking into the puffy white sleeves of her blouse.

"Sefra, shut it off," she said, but Sefra had no idea how she'd turned it on.

Had she even turned it on?

And why hadn't she started bleeding too?

She was about to stand to go to her sister when Sue sat upright and vomited all over the table. It was orange with white pearlescent curlicued chunks swimming—wriggling—through it. It smelled like nothing they'd eaten that day and it made a familiar snapping sound like Rice Krispies as it spread across the table and hung off the sides like it was solidifying.

Sue continued gagging and coughing, slamming her hands on the table, audibly breaking her fingers.

The box on the table continued making that eerie whining, but a voice accompanied it now. It was…it was their father's.

And it was screaming.

It went on for a long moment, paused for a deep inhale, then continued.

Sefra had never heard her father like that in life. It was terrible, agonizing, pain wasn't word enough for what assaulted her ears.

This had been what killed him. This box. And these recorded screams were his eulogy.

Sue sat up straight, her face upturned to the ceiling. Bones crackled like rifle shots—Sefra hoped it wasn't her sister's spine. What looked like thin milk ran freely from Sue's eyes.

Something tugged inside of Sefra. So hard she rose out of her seat and plopped back down, jarring her spine.

Sue curled her three unbroken fingers into the table, carving unvarnished rivulets into the wood. Grey foam poured from her mouth and Sefra could see only the whites of her sister's eyes.

That box pulled her out of her seat again as her father's screams turned to agonized moans. This time, she didn't resist, allowing it to carry her up to a half-stand. She leaned over the table until her face hovered over the box. Sefra felt as though her body were on some sort of autopilot as she opened her mouth, dipped her head, and breathed in.

She felt the whines and her father's agonized voice pouring up into her, driving down into the pit of her and spreading like the root of some rotten tree too stubborn to die.

Sue's convulsions stopped. She wiped the foam from her mouth as if she were half aware of it and blinked heavily several times. Sefra noticed her jaw hung crookedly, lower on one side.

"Sefra," her sister said once she was finally able to drag her chin off her chest. "Sef…ra…"

It sounded painful for her to speak. It was definitely painful to hear. Sefra raised her hands to her own throat, achingly sore despite having made no sound since she was three years old.

The sound came to her ears as Sue spoke again, her voice like shattered glass, concern just as present as awe. She leaned forward, reaching across the table and covering Sefra's hand with her broken one. Sefra was full-throated screaming with her father's voice.

Sue rubbed her hand in the same small, circular motions as she had for years, ever since the younger sister had become the protector of the older. "It's okay," Sue said, the broken bones in her hand clicking together. "It's okay."

Gerald Dean Rice

All the stories for this book were in and were just essentially in need of some fine-tuning to one degree or another. I was lying in bed one night, thinking about my kids and monsters. New monsters, specifically, the creation of them and what a collaboration with my kids might be like.

The Goodnighter/Schrödinger's Toe

It had been something to do with the kids. Wayne had taken off work to spend the day with them. Neither he or Trese had realized beforehand the day was a school holiday. He'd rolled back into bed after Trese had left, but the kids were already rumbling around in their rooms before he could close his eyes.

So, breakfast had come next with two children who had way more energy than he was prepared for. Even after a cup of coffee, Wayne had difficulty tracking them, following behind his kids with his eyes—were they always this fast?. Television was out of the question for all three of them; his daughter had internalized their mother's strict regimen of no TV until after six and no more than ninety minutes in a day. And there would surely be a report made if he plopped down in front of the boob tube—was it still called that even though televisions no longer had tubes—while they ran around free range.

Wayne had an idea, though. He figured lunch at McDonald's, an hour or two at the park, and then back home. If he started dinner at four, it would be ready by the time Trese got home around 5:30. So from 2:30 to 4:00, he had a small gap to fill.

They were going to make a monster.

He started with a belch, the physical memory of his Quarter Pounder with Cheese reaching up to remind him of lunch, the three of them sitting down at the dining table, each with a pen and paper, although his son barely knew the alphabet.

"So, what's our guy going to look like?" Wayne asked.

"Super tall and super skinny," RJ said.

It wasn't lost on Wayne that he was tall and thin and his boy might have been using his father as a template. Lana made a face, she'd probably realized it too, but thankfully, she let it pass.

"Okay, tall and thin." Wayne began a bullet list and RJ began doodling a green stick figure with his tri-color pen. "What else?"

"He's got big feet. Real big."

"Like a clown?" Wayne asked.

His son made a face. "No. Regular feet."

Lana had a two-mile stare on her face. "How about you, El? What do you think he has?"

She slowly rolled her eyes over to him. Lana was thirteen and on the edge of finding everything her parents did as corny, cheesy, or wholly designed with the complete desolation of her burgeoning social life in mind.

She took a deep breath and blew it out. "Well, first of all, why does he even have to be a he?"

"It can't be a girl. It's gotta be a boy," RJ said. "Boys make the best monsters! Freddy…Jason…"

"Blooooooooody Mary. Blooooooooody Mary…" Lana lifted her hands toward her little brother like she had a marionette strung to her fingers.

RJ clapped his fingers over his ears as if not hearing the name a third time would protect him once she popped out of the mirror, his complexion blanching considerably for his deep shade of brown.

"All right, all right," Wayne said, a smile creeping to the corner of his mouth. His children knew all the classic horror monsters of his youth, despite his wife protesting they were 'too young for that stuff'. "So, we have a girl monster."

Lana shook her head. "Why a boy *or* a girl? This *thing* isn't real. Why do we have to shackle it with a gender construct at all?"

Wayne felt his brow lift in surprise, but he was proud at the progressive thinking his daughter was displaying.

RJ squinted with one eye, confused. "So, you're saying it's smooth like a Ken doll down there?"

The question caught Wayne by surprise—not because of his son's comparison, but that he'd had to have heard his father make a statement that was a variation of what he was asking.

He'd have to be more careful about what he said out loud around them.

"Who knows what's down there?" Lana said, leaning forward. "Maybe you find out before you die."

"So, is it gonna teabag me to death or something?"

"Guh-*ross*," Lana said. Wayne tried his best and failed miserably to not laugh, the sound coming out of him like a fork caught in a garbage disposal.

Yeah. He was definitely going to have to watch what he said.

"Let's, uh…let's get back on track. We don't have to get into what genitalia, if any, our boogie-*person* has."

"What's jenny…jenna…"

Lana formed her arms into an open V and chopped toward her groin. RJ nodded.

"You mean penis-vagina. Why didn't you say that?" From the look on his son's face, Wayne could tell his son was warming to the idea of a gender-less or mystery-gendered monster.

"Anyway, I think they should wear a cloak and a bowler hat. All the big monsters wear something iconically identifiable—Jason has a hockey mask, Freddy has his Christmas sweater, Michael Meyers has that Shatner mask, Candyman has that big winter coat, and Dracula has that black cape that's red on the inside."

"Oh, I see you got ideas," Wayne said. "Boy, are you drawing all this?"

"On it." RJ doodled in deep concentration, the tip of his tongue poking out of the corner of his mouth. "How about this?" He held up his notepad and showed them the stick figure he'd drawn of a monster with dagger teeth and what looked like a large, hairy snake around its neck.

"Is that a cater—"

"I love it!" Lana said. "They're wearing a black boa!"

"A black boa," Wayne said, as if that had been obvious. He was glad his daughter had cut him off before he could say caterpillar.

"And glass teeth," RJ said. "No. *Diamond* teeth."

"So, they have teeth made out of jewelry?" Lana asked.

Wayne was about to tell his daughter to take it easy on her little brother when RJ responded. "Diamonds are the hardest material known to man!" He seemed to ponder a moment then asked, "What's a Shatner?"

"Diamond sharp teeth." Wayne wrote it down and then looked up at his children. "Now what does our mystery monster do? Let's make it unique. Wayne had a couple ideas, but he was really enjoying what they were coming up with.

Lana and RJ sat quietly in thought. No doubt they were thinking of and passing on monsters that killed horny teenagers, creepy children, bloodsuckers—

"It gets you when you go to bed," RJ said.

"You mean like the Sandman?" Lana asked and rolled her eyes. Despite her tone, Wayne could tell she was invested in the process.

"No," RJ said. "It doesn't get you when you go to sleep or put you to sleep." He smiled slyly and looked between his father and sister. "It gets you if you *don't* go to sleep."

That sent a chill up Wayne's spine and he cleared his throat and shifted in his chair. He didn't think they knew he had problems with insomnia, but then again, he had a history of saying things sometimes without being aware his children were in the room.

"Ooo, that's really good," Lana said, grinning.

Now he definitely couldn't squash the sleep thing.

"Okay, so he watches you while you sleep," Wayne said.

"Dad." Lana looked at him. "First of all—*they*—and second, they watch you to make *sure* you go to sleep."

"Right. Got it." It had been worth trying, but Lana wasn't as distractible as her brother. He wrote the suggestion down and was eager to wrap up. When he finished, Lana and RJ were staring at him.

"What?"

"*Daddy*," RJ said.

"What?"

"You can't forget the most important part!"

For a moment, he felt ice pouring down the column of his spine when the thought of them saying in unison, 'They're right behind you,' popped in his head. His children were separated by seven years, but there was something very twinnish in the set of their faces at that moment.

"What's…the most important part?"

Lana had wrapped her arms in front of her and gestured to her brother for him to say it. "The name. We gotta give them a name."

"Oh. Yeah, we do. What, uhh, what do you guys think?"

"Um, Mr. Goodnight. No, wait. That won't work, will it, Lana?" He furrowed his brow in concentration as Wayne finished recovering.

"How about, The Goodnighter?" Wayne said finally. He could tell Lana was folding back into her own angsty world and he'd be losing her shortly. "Maybe they could pluck off a toe if you don't go to sleep as a warning. Or better yet—"

"Lame." Lana snorted. "Whatever."

"I like it." RJ gave his father a thumb's up.

He could tell the moment had passed and Wayne collected the notepads and tore out the sheets that he and RJ had used. Lana had participated, but she hadn't written or drawn anything in her notepad. That had been about as much as he could have expected.

Wayne noticed the time and quickly put everything away before starting dinner. He was going to make his famous honey and hot sauce chicken that, despite her general indifference, even Lana loved.

By the time Trese got home, dinner was ready. He made au gratin potatoes from the box and steamed some green beans. They kissed hello, and Trese lassoed her children into a hug and asked them about their day. RJ rattled off a million details of which The Goodnighter was only a small part and they followed her upstairs. By the time the three of them came back down, four plates were waiting with two glasses of Pinot Grigio and two cups of Faygo Rock 'n Rye.

"Is this for me?" Lana said with too big of a smile on her face, pretending to belly up in front of a plate with a glass of wine by it. "Kidding," she said when Trese and Wayne responded with blank looks at her.

All four of them sat and ate together and it was so pleasant that The Goodnighter was mostly forgotten. But it remained a tiny knot somewhere in his brain, and no matter how many jokes he told that everyone laughed at, it remained, drawing from him like a tumor. Except it supped his mind, irrigating through synapses, growing not in size but in scope, developing in character like a growing fetus in the womb.

The Goodnighter watched from the darkest corner in the bedroom, waiting until a random appointed hour when everyone should be asleep. Then it floated out of its sliver of corner, expanding like a balloon, compressing the air in the room into an uncomfortable thickness, the black boa crawling around its neck and cinching into a chokehold around the creature's neck. It watched—

"Honey, where'd you go?"

Wayne looked up from the dishes in the sink to his wife. She'd interrupted whatever had just been going through his mind just then and he'd instantly forgotten what it was.

"Sorry. Just lost in thought." Trese continued staring at him and he realized he was supposed to have responded to something she'd said. He tried to scramble back over the shaving of words he'd caught and wasn't able to put them together into something coherent. "I'm sorry, babe. I totally zoned. What did you say?"

"Are you sure you want to go to Margate? You seem hot and cold on it. We could always go to another amusement park. I just figured, it's in the UK…"

"No-no. Yeah. I wanna go." He turned to his wife. "I really do. You know me. I need a Xanax to get on a plane and I hate how that makes me feel."

"You know I'm going to be right next to you. You don't have anything to worry about."

"If only anxiety worked that easily." Wayne smiled.

Trese looped two fingers around two of his. "You know, if you're feeling anxious now…" She gave him a coy smile. "Unless it doesn't work like that."

"Oh no. It works *exactly* like that."

Wayne hustled his wife upstairs. The kids were already showered for the night, his son waiting in bed for a story. Trese gave him a big hug and kiss before saying goodnight to Lana and going into their bedroom for a shower.

"Goodnight, Bro," his son said after Wayne had finished two chapters from the book.

"Don't call me bro." Wayne narrowed his eyes. "Or I will *kill* you where you stand." RJ giggled as Wayne leaned in and kissed his forehead before his son flopped over on his other side.

Finally, his daughter came out of the bathroom, her twists up in a bonnet.

"G'night, Daddy."

"Sweet dreams, El." He kissed her forehead as they passed each other.

"Goodnight, RJ," she said at her brother's threshold.

"Goodnight, Bro!"

"I'm not your bro." Wayne watched as she passed him again, en route to her room, rolling her eyes before she disappeared inside, the door swinging shut behind her.

Before he could step fully into his bedroom, Wayne caught sight of his naked wife in silhouette standing just outside of their bathroom. Both their bodies had changed over seventeen years of marriage and two kids—he'd done more than his fair share of sympathy eating when she'd been pregnant—but right then, he would have preferred this woman than any prior version of her.

"I should take a shower—"

"Close the door."

They lay in bed together after, their hands lingering on one another for several minutes. It had been a while—work, kids, life in general. He'd missed her more than he would have thought, had he actually thought about it, and she had made love to him with an urgency as if their time were limited by a parent who would open the door at any moment.

Trese's hand slid off his pudgy belly as she turned over on her side, drifting off into a near uninterruptible slumber. Wayne would have envied her except his lids had steadily been getting heavier by the moment. His breathing deepened as he rolled with her, spooning his body behind hers, one of her perfectly proportioned breasts filling the cup of his hand. His body relaxed as he tumbled into sleep, conscious of one last breath before he was gone.

Breathing in impending terror, anticipated agony, eventual dread.

The Goodnighter floated just above the floor, the tail of their boa dragging behind their many-toed, filthy feet. He could feel them just beyond the footboard of the bed, the knot that had been in his mind now outside but still attached to him like a bundle of nerves strung out of him.

He kept his eyes shut, hoping to slip back to sleep before they could reach him. The Goodnighter rotated in the air until they were parallel with the bed. He could feel the air between the two of them being squeezed as they lowered over him.

He squeezed his eyelids together, counterintuitive to sleep, but he couldn't help it. The only sound he could hear aside from the susurrus of Trese's gentle breathing was the fingernail scratches against the window of the branch he had clipped from the tree at the beginning of spring.

He felt exposed where his body wasn't covered by the comforter, his head and neck feeling particularly vulnerable. The arm he considered sacrificeable and his foot should have been fine because he always wore socks to bed.

But then something pinched his toe through his sock. He'd had a cat when he'd been a teenager that would play with his feet, but it had run away when he'd left for college twenty years ago.

The lore that had written itself in his head told him the Goodnighter was plucking off his toe, but that had to be ridiculous. His mind was aggressively playing tricks. Too many consecutive nights of poor sleep were impressing a layer of paranoia upon him. He almost believed he could feel its long, slender fingers flexing his toe back and forth through the clingy film of his imagination just before…

Nothing?

Wayne was tempted to sit up in bed, but the impression still draping over him was so palpable, his irrational fear anchored him to the bed. He slowly pulled the rest of his body beneath the comforter, knowing and not caring he was going to sweat the bed.

He didn't want to wake Trese, even though the only thing he wanted was his wife's comfort. Wayne settled for curling up next to her as Trese's breathing deepened.

"Good morning, sleepyhead!" his family shoutec in unison as Wayne shambled into the kitchen. He rubbed his eye as he absorbed the sunlight coming in through the deck window, devouring the crumbs of leftover dreams. Trese had the electric griddle on the table with two pancakes on it and was in the process of pour ng a third. The kids had scrambled eggs and bacon along with two pancakes each, taken from the growing stack on the plate next to the griddle.

He gave them his best smile as he beelined for the Keurig. Trese already had it loaded with his *Walking Dead* mug and he grabbed the sugar and a spoon from the drawer.

"It already has—" Wayne gave his wife a dead-eye stare as he spooned sugar into his mug. He slapped the Keurig closed and started it. He felt himself coming officially awake as coffee scented the air.

"G'morning, guys," he said and sat at the table. "What made you do all this?"

Trese wasn't much for cooking.

"Well, after what you did for me last night, I figured I'd return the favor." She winked at him.

"What's wrong with your eye?" RJ asked.

"Oh *god*," Lana said.

"Well, you're very welcome, madam," Wayne said.

"Oh *god*."

There was bacon at one edge of the griddle and Wayne pinched a couple rashers.

"There's eggs in the fridge if you want some."

"Nah, I think I'm good," he said, reaching for the pancakes. "On second thought, you guys' look good." Wayne scooted back from the table, taking his coffee with him as he went to the refrigerator and rooted around for the eggs. He kept meaning to arrange everything in there and putting it off. The shelves could also use a cleaning and he was relatively sure there was an opened bottle of mini pickles in the back that had been there since RJ was a baby.

He backed out of the fridge with two eggs and something about the pan with the remnants of the scrambled eggs still in it made him think of last night. That crazy dream with the monster he and the kids had made up.

But wait, why did he remember drifting off to sleep *after* then? He'd briefly fallen asleep after he and Trese had made love, but that was always more of a nap. Wayne recalled tossing around until he'd gotten comfortable with half his upper body from underneath the covers. Then *it* came.

No. Then *they* came.

Detail filled his mind like one of those old computers that flashed nonsensical data as they booted up. The scratching at the window by a branch that was no longer there, the air thickening, and something touching his toe.

Them touching his toe.

And then taking payment for putting him to sleep by taking his toe. But that had been just his imagination leisurely galloping, unbridled by his command. It hadn't been real.

It hadn't been real.

Wayne looked down at his foot, still with the sock on he'd worn to bed. He wiggled his toes. He wasn't sure if they were all there.

Gerald Dean Rice

I wrote this story in the early 2000s. For some reason, this was inspired by the song Blue *as sung by Leann Rimes. I can't really recall the connection between song and story but it was going through my head as I wrote it.*

I Only Have Eyes for You

I must be dead. I can't feel a thing, but there's this music echoing far off in the distance. I feel completely at rest until I feel a soft fingertip begin to stroke my forehead between my eyebrows.

Slowly, I open my eyes and look into the most angelic face ever. A beautiful, brown-skinned woman faces me, completely naked at least from the waist up, her golden hair like sunshine. Her eyes are closed, but the way she's smiling, I wanna get up and kiss her or something, but I'm just completely numb with comfort, resting my head in her lap.

Gerald Dean Rice

I think I remember what happened. Me and a couple buddies rented a boat and went fishing on the lake. We didn't catch any fish, but we sure got hammered. So hammered, we got lost. We tried finding our way back to the shore when a storm came out of nowhere, swallowing the daylight in angry, dark clouds. Ted and whatever wasn't tied down got washed away in the first huge wave that hit us. Chris got pitched right off the deck, caught staring at the suddenly blanketed sky, when a huge wave rose abruptly beneath us. Al was still holding onto the steering wheel when we hit a wave so big it almost stood the boat on its stern, the bow pointing into the sky. He dangled by the wheel, and I was hanging onto a sail, arms and legs wrapped tightly around the pole. We hung there in slow motion and I thought we were going to tip all the way over and land upside down. But we rode the wave out and slammed hard right side up. I woke up flat on my back, seeing stars and coughing up water and trying to get my breath back. My vision cleared and I sat up looking over to where Al used to be. As I got my footing, I turned and looked around. The rain was coming down in sheets so thick I never saw the boat heading toward the rocks.

Then I woke up here with her. The longer I lay here in her arms, the more distant all that seems, my memories of everything fading away with each stroke of her hand. The expression on her face is saying, 'You're here with me now. Be safe.'

She blows something off her fingertip and begins to stroke my left leg. A single hair catches in my right eyelash, and without opening her eyes, she deftly plucks it out with her free hand. Something doesn't feel right as she strokes my leg. I try to sit up to see if it's broken, but she gently eases me back down, not saying a word, but telling me to relax.

I rest my head in her lap again and look at that beautiful smiling face, and I don't care about my leg anymore. The discomfort goes away, and she eventually moves to my arm, running her fingers up and down. I reach up to touch her face and see my arm has become translucent. I can see the powder blue sky through it, and the ghost of bones and veins underneath.

Panicked, I open my mouth to scream, to speak, to *something*, but as soon as I think it, her hand is holding mine, taking hold of my fear. I look at her face, and it simply tells me, 'No,' as it radiates love and affection, and I relax again. The music in my head returns, and she begins stroking my arm again. I'm falling in love with her, drowsing and desperately wanting to look into her eyes.

I don't recall waking up. I'm briefly aware she has been rubbing my chest, the after-sensation of her hands touching me, still lingering. She cuddles me like a baby, rubbing my neck and running her fingers through my hair. I feel like I'm still wrapped in a wonderful dream as her hands rapidly go over my face and head. She lovingly traces every crevice, the corners of my eyes, my laugh lines, the little divot under my nose, over and over again.

I want so badly to touch her face as I realize I can't. I don't need touch anymore. She holds all that is left of me in her hands and somehow...somehow I still see. I course through her veins, as much a part of her as she is.

She waits for my answer and I say, 'Yes,' with the little of me that is left. She opens her eyes and there are only empty sockets. She closes her hands over me and when she opens her eyes again, she sees through me. Instantly, the remaining barriers between us disappear, and we meld into one. We look down to where I was lying and there are only the tattered rags left of what was my clothing. We look for a moment, not in mourning but simple curiosity, and then use our tail to push back toward the rising tide and back into the ocean. Our gills open and we breathe, swimming away.

Gerald Dean Rice

I wrote this poem sometime in the early 2000s, if I recall correctly. I don't recall if it actually got published anywhere. Despite the misleading title, it really is a poem about falling down stairs. Specifically, my brother and I were play-fighting at the top of the stairs and I threw a wild punch and lost my balance, teetering for just a moment before going ass over tea kettle and rolling down the stairs. I wasn't in any pain from the fall, but the wind was knocked out of me. That's why the lines near the end are broken up the way they are—to simulate how hard it was for me to breathe.

Just Like Falling Down a Flight of Stairs

They should bottle this stuff,
You feel
Every…

Gerald Dean Rice

Single…
Solitary…   5
Bounce.
Falling and landing
mouthfirst on a soft
Letter 'V',
Measure the lumps   10
on your head,
Test the tolerance
of the joints of your bones,
Bumpity-bump…
Bumpity-bump…   15
No one is there
And they won't be coming,
Spring your elbow's crick,
Feel the presence
of no landing,   20
Drift farther away
And further from the point
Buy one, get one,
You've got butterflies
in the head,   25
Little stars
behind the knees
And the walls hold their
hands behind their backs,
Bumpity-bump-bump—   30
Bumpity…
Dodge the nail pops
and creak out the
last drops of
struggle, before you   35
give way; (bumpity)
as you climb
Down, freefalling
into a dizzying hell
That whispers the   40

breath from your (bump)
lungs, crushed by your
Own terminal velo-
city, beating the
fight (bump-bump) right out   45
of you, tum-
bling along;
wheel (bumpity) barrow-
ing, until
you aren't   50
here, but
(bump) you are
here.

Gerald Dean Rice

I barely remember writing this. But I do remember wanting to have some promotional material for my experimental novella, Axe to the Face. I had all kinds of ideas for this, including writing a prequel series for the antagonist, Rat. Cole is the 'antagonist' of AttF, although I was being ironic in that he's largely ineffectual in the denouement of the story. This was supposed to inform the reader on the motivation of Cole. Honestly, I have no idea where I would have included this in the story.

This is Not a Baby

Donna turned the little car into the subdivision. Dave and Katie Lanergan were a lovely couple who had waited several years before their bundle of joy was finally delivered. Despite the unusual circumstances in which the child had come to her attention, t was kismet that he had eventually come into their lives.

She weaved through the new concrete streets, taking in the new sub with all of its small saplings and big houses. It was a warm, sunny day and the only thing disappointing about it was the lack of children playing outside. Donna saw only a little boy, sitting on his lawn, but he looked strange. He had to have been eleven and he was just lazily beating a yellow toy bucket with a toy hammer. He was much too old to be playing with something like that, but he never stopped as his eyes were locked on something far, far away.

That was just one weird child. She had Dave, Katie, and the baby to think about. What was his name? Donna must have been getting old.

'Twenty-nine plus' she liked to say when the subject of her age ever came up. She definitely didn't look like she was almost fifty. Thanks to uterine cancer when she was a teen, Donna hadn't been able to conceive. That was partially why she'd gotten into social work and mostly why she'd eventually turned to adoption placement as a vocation. She loved children and wanted to see every single one of them have a family to love.

Henry. That was what the couple had named him. Such an old name for such a young person, but it hadn't been her choice. Donna had seen some downright awful ones, though she would never say that to the parents. But no matter how terrible, Donna had never had an issue with remembering baby names. She could even spell them all too. The first baby she had ever placed almost fifteen years ago had been Manchester. Manchester had been a blue-eyed, ten-toed little angel, and her parents, Ricky and Myra, had been sending Donna Christmas pictures every year since. Every time she placed a baby with a family, she felt like she was an unofficial auntie. So odd that she couldn't remember little what's-his-shit's name.

"Oh!" she said out loud. Donna stopped the car right there in the middle of the street and crossed herself. She *never* swore, not even to herself, and was deeply embarrassed even though no one could have known. She considered herself only casually religious, and that type of language was fine coming from other people, but not her. She felt speaking a certain way meant being a certain way.

Donna checked her blind spots and her rearview mirror before proceeding. She could see the house up ahead on the right and was two miles below the fifteen mile an hour posted speed limit. She used her remaining time in the car to practice smiling, applying another coat of lipstick and checking her teeth in her visor mirror.

She pulled into the driveway and stopped behind a late-model Dodge Caravan. If she remembered correctly, Dave still drove the Challenger, though his wife was working on him to trade it in for something more family-friendly. Donna took a deep breath and let it out after she'd cut the engine. She grabbed her purse and her file folder, opened her door and climbed out. She had to resist the urge to stretch. Doing such a thing in public came off to her as…unseemly. She forced her long legs to walk up the driveway, noticing along the way that the two tires on the driver's side of the Caravan were flat.

As she rounded the walkway, she noticed all the curtains were drawn. Katie was a bit of a germaphobe and Dave was definitely an enabler. Anything his wife wanted, he either provided or acquiesced. She probably was worried about the baby getting skin cancer or something else ridiculous and was keeping the sun out. Donna would casually ask if the little fuck was enjoying the outside and she'd see what the woman said.

Donna stopped at the porch steps and pursed her lips. It wasn't as if she couldn't have walked up the cracked steps in her heels, but they just didn't look proper. But if she didn't take them that meant hiking her skirt and stepping directly onto the porch cap and that *definitely* wouldn't be ladylike. She'd been standing there for a good thirty seconds, deciding what to do, and her cheeks flushed once she realized anyone outside or peeking through blinds could see her just standing there like a buffoon.

She picked the worse of two evils and hiked up her skirt to just below her knees and took a step. Her face became even hotter when she felt the fabric of her skirt hug tightly against her bottom, giving someone a good view. Donna was embarrassingly shapely, with wide hips and a narrow waist and voluminous breasts that were always in the way. Because she'd never been able to give birth, these useless parts of her anatomy only served as reminders of how she was inadequate.

Donna didn't dare look behind her for fear she would see someone watching, instead taking a moment to regain her composure before ringing the doorbell. Katie was taking leave from her job and had been home for about two months now. The baby should have been sleeping through the night by then, which meant Mommy and Daddy had plenty of time to fuck each other's brains out.

Donna put a smile on her face and rang the doorbell. After a count of twenty with no answer, she rang again. They were probably bathing the baby or were upstairs taking a nap. They had a scheduled appointment at two, but new parents were always forgetting.

The door cracked open before she could ring a third time. A lone, brown bloodshot eye stared at her, wily brown hair draping across the column of face she could see.

"Hello?" Katie said as if she didn't recognize her.

"Hi, Katie, how are you?"

"Who? How do you know my name?"

Donna made a pronounced frown and put her fists on her hips. She cocked her head slightly at the woman and said in a mocking tone, "Don't tell me you've forgotten me, already! It's me, Donna Douglas, with the agency. We had an appointment, remember?"

Katie's eye narrowed then widened. The door swung open.

"I'm so sorry," she said, all but ripping Donna's jacket sleeve off as she pulled her into the house. "Please come in."

She shut the door and they were enveloped in darkness. And cold. It was seventy-two degrees outside, according to Donna's car, nowhere near hot enough to have the air turned down this low. If she were shivering this much after being in here for only ten seconds, what was this doing to the baby? And what was that smell? It was like dirty diapers, but it was a much more aggressive stench. Baby poo was supposed to be almost odorless. This smelled like a giant dog had taken a dump in here and that was saying a lot considering the cold had to have been staunching the smell.

She almost said, "What the hell?" to Katie, but the woman had a far-off expression, facing the great room. Donna heard some sort of scratching sound but had no idea where it was coming from.

"You want to see the baby."

Donna had no idea if that was a question or a statement of fact.

"Yes," she said. "Where is the little fuc—*guy*?"

Katie walked straight ahead. The floor was an obstacle course of broken toys, clothes, food wrappers, and other things. She stepped over the items in her path as if they'd been strategically placed and Donna almost tripped over a bent golf club she hadn't seen right in front of her. By the time she caught up with Katie, the younger woman was standing at the island in the kitchen. There was a knife and what looked like beets that had been sliced to hell and a large hunk of steak.

She wanted to ask where the baby was, but instead asked, "What are you doing?"

Katie was staring blankly at the refrigerator and Donna got the impression that this was where she'd been before Donna had rang the doorbell.

"Lunch," Katie said, grabbing the knife. "The baby's hungry."

"The baby?" Donna said, wondering what that had to do with anything on the island. "I don't hear him crying. Where is he?"

"He's right here." Katie didn't point or otherwise indicate where 'here' was and Donna approached.

When she had reached the other side of the island with Katie, she saw him on the floor. He was so big. The baby was only two months old, but he could have easily passed for eight. He was on his hands and knees, his bulbous head bobbing as if he were struggling to keep it up. One of his hands was working furiously at the floor and she realized the scratching sound was him.

"What are you…" The baby looked up at her and Donna gasped. He was hideous. "Shit," Donna said, then quickly corrected the expression on her face. "How *adorable*."

Katie sliced off a hunk of meat and dropped it on the baby's head. His leaden eyes rolled up, seeming to drag his head upright, and he stared at Donna. There was savage knowledge in the boy's eyes as if he had learned how to hurt things. The corner of his mouth lifted, but she didn't mistake it for a smile. There was anything but joy on that face.

One hand lifted, his body teetering for just a moment until he regained his balance, and those tiny little fingers deftly plucked the chunk of meat off his head. He stuffed it into his toothless mouth and it was gone. No chewing or slurping or savoring.

"Bah," he said, fixed on Donna.

Donna's eye twitched as if part of her didn't want to see this. The whole scene felt wrong. He was only two months—why was she giving him raw meat? Why had she left him alone on the floor to answer the door? Why was she letting him scratch the floor? And how had he gotten so *big*?

She pushed down her instinct to turn around and walk out. What this child needed—this *family* needed—was some assistance. Donna was certain one of the reasons Katie was in such disarray was because her husband was never home. And for this little fucker to be so gigantuous meant he must have some sort of growth disorder.

Meat from cattle on a constant diet of any number of hormones couldn't be helping the situation, either. Donna forced herself to walk over to the baby and scoop him up. Her back strained with the effort—he had to have been at least thirty pounds—but he surprisingly didn't stink despite the overfull sack that was his diaper. His eyes were slow in catching up to the sudden movement, but they gradually settled on her.

God, he was ass-end hideous.

Donna had a sudden sensation of bug legs crawling all over her and almost dropped him. He writhed in her hands like a worm, but she held onto him.

"This is not a safe place for a baby," she meant to say, but what actually came out was, "This is not a baby." She shook her head and corrected herself. "A safe place, I mean. And you shouldn't be feeding him solid food and raw beef, no less. You should kill him! I mean, you *could* kill him."

"This isn't beef," Katie said.

"Well, whatever it is," Donna said, placing him back on the floor as gently as she could. He went immediately back to scratching the same raw spot on the floor. "What is it?"

Katie gave a slow shrug. "Found it on the road. Brought it back home." It was then that Donna honed in on the stench permeating the air. The hunk of meat on the island was some poor animal's rotting carcass. She hadn't eaten anything with a face in almost nineteen years, and realizing what the smell was almost overwhelmed her. Donna wretched. The little bastard tilted his head up, his mouth open almost like he was hoping to catch whatever came out of her. Donna charged the sink just as lunch marched its way up and out.

She ran the sink, rinsing her upchuck off the stack of dirty dishes and hopefully down the drain. Well, no, not down the drain. Something was at least partially blocking it and water began backing up in the sink. Donna ignored it as best she could and plunged her face into the cold water. It was refreshing, resetting her to a prior, calmer self. Fuck the make-up, she could reapply it in the car.

How to get a hold of this situation? It wasn't the baby's fault, no matter what he was doing. He was just a baby. It was Katie and it was Dave. She would start with her because Katie was the one who was here. Donna turned the water off and faced Katie.

"You have to take care of this baby."

"Do you really want me to kill it?"

"Yes," she almost said, but forced it back. "No. Of course not."

"But you said I should—" Katie seemed in a trance.

"Never mind that. I…misspoke." Donna began smoothing her hands down the front of her skirt. It helped her to not concentrate on the rancid stink not three feet away from her.

"Look," Donna began, trying a different approach, "come sit with me." She headed for the couch, hoping Katie would follow. By the time Donna sat, the other woman had crossed into the great room. Katie still had that dreamy look on her face, but there was also a touch of confusion, like she was slowly waking up.

Donna put a hand on Katie's knee and felt a tiny charge of electricity. Katie blinked and stared at her as if she weren't entirely certain what Donna was.

"Donna!" She leaned forward and wrapped her arms around her. Donna could tell she was genuinely glad to see her and returned the hug. "Oh my—I'm a terrible mother." The smile on her face evaporated and she began to cry.

"Why? What happened?" Donna had been concerned before, now she was downright alarmed.

"I…" Katie began. She was wringing her hands in her lap and Donna put a hand on her wrist to make her stop. "I don't know if I can even say it!" She hung her head and fresh tears rolled down her cheeks.

"It's not Dave's fault," she said, changing the subject. Donna wanted to know what she felt so horrible about but didn't press. "I know you're thinking he should be here, to help out, but it's not like that." Katie looked up. "I told him to work as much as possible, to not be here."

"But why?"

Katie narrowed her eyes. "You see what this house looks like?" It sounded more like an accusation than a question. "It's him. He's…inside me. He makes me do things."

"Like the meat?"

"The what?" Katie's eyes widened in understanding. "Yes. He told me to cut it up and feed it to him. When Dave realized what he was doing, he wanted to do something, but the baby hurt him too."

Donna wanted to ask six questions at once but settled on, "How does he tell you to do anything? He's only a baby."

Katie shook her head. "No. Since the accident, Dave and I knew he wasn't a baby. I…dropped him on his head six weeks ago."

Donna's mouth dropped open, but she held her silence.

"I hadn't slept in almost seven days when it happened. I think I might have done it on purpose. I might have been trying to hurt my baby. I was warming a bottle for him and he was just screaming, like he'd been set on fire. I remember looking at him in my arms and he just…slipped.

"Dave was at work, so I had to take Henry to emergency myself. I picked him up and held him. I thought he was dying. The sound he was making was so hysterical. But then I looked at him, really looked at him. It was hard to tell at first, but he was smiling."

Katie was searching her eyes, looking for something. Maybe she just wanted to know it was okay to continue. Donna put a hand on her leg.

"Go on."

Katie looked at her and nodded. "When he came home, he was such an angel. For the first three days, he never cried, and all he ever did was sleep." She shook her head. "But then, all he ever did was cry. It was non-stop. No matter how much we fed him, it was never enough. Dave still had to work, so he slept downstairs while I did everything I could to keep Henry calm.

"I was exhausted and Dave tried to help out. As soon as he came home, he took the baby until about midnight so I could get some rest. But I wasn't tired from just lack of sleep. Henry has been draining me. I saw he was doing the same to Dave and when his project at work started taking up his time, he wanted to take vacation to be home with me.

"What Henry had been doing to me would have been done to Dave and I couldn't let that happen. I…convinced him to do his project. We always talked about putting an addition on for the baby and his project being a success could add to his bonus."

"I'm so sorry," Donna said.

"But it's okay because he's okay, right?" Katie smiled nervously. "I finally figured out how to keep him happy.'

The little shit had crawled over to them and was scratching at Katie's leg. She twitched but didn't move otherwise. She wanted to grab it by the arms and shake it until its neck snapped and it's brain rattled until it turned to mush. It should have been difficult to believe what Katie had just told her, but Donna had no doubt it was true.

She could feel inside of herself how she was different, how something subtle yet concrete had changed, and the only remedy would be to kill this child.

"Oh my God," she said. How could she think something so terrible about an innocent child? Her mind dialed back to the odd circumstances in which Henry had come to her attention. At the time, Donna would have thought it had been some sort of divine intervention. Hers had been the third agency contacted to place the child the hospital had taken into custody through safe harbor. Mars Robinson had been the first phone call at almost midnight. He had been getting dressed to leave when he had had a massive heart attack and died before opening his front door. Just after three in the morning, they had contacted Wendy Millsap who had died in a freeway crash en route to the hospital.

When Donna had finally gotten the call, she had just finished having breakfast. She worked out of her home office, and it was simple for her to turn to her computer and pull up her file of prospective parents. Simon and Andrew Macklin had already had a child placed in their home and Phillip and Edna Eastbrook weren't interested in a boy. That had left Dave and Katie Lanergan and the match couldn't have been more perfect.

"Dave should be here with you," Donna said. "You need to lean on each other in difficult times."

"No." Katie shook her head and let out a small laugh. "This is a little more than just difficult times. Something's wrong with that…baby. The whole neighborhood knows it." Donna's mind flashed on that lone child, 'playing' outside and how empty the subdivision had seemed despite how pleasant it was outside in the middle of the day.

"Can we call him?"

"*No.*" Katie fixed her with a steely gaze. "I don't want him…tainted by this." The baby was distracted by something that had just scurried across the floor. Donna watched him wobble-crawl on his way to investigate.

"Katie, you have a big baby," she said, watching him as he tossed aside broken toys and trash. "But that's not abnormal. And children are dropped all the time. I mean, look at him—" Henry had dug out a pink-eyed, albino rat, holding it aloft as it wriggled and squealed before shoving its head into his mouth and wrenching its body around until the neck broke—"he's…healthy."

Her last word trailed up like she was asking a question. The 'baby' slurped the rest of the body into its mouth and down its throat, again with no chewing. It looked back to its mother, a look on its face as if expecting approval. Donna didn't know when she'd begun thinking of him as an it, but she knew this was no human child. All those blanks surrounding its delivery to the hospital began to fill in with her worst possible imagining. He was an evil thing and it was even a sort of dark kismet that he had fallen under her provision and thereby into this home with two of the loveliest people she had ever met in her long career.

"Where…" Donna began, a sudden, haunting thought invading her mind. "Where is your husband?"

"I told you," Katie said. "He's at work."

Donna narrowed her eyes. "On a Saturday?" She knew it was possible that he could have been exactly where Katie had said, but she had to ask.

"Yes." There was a hint of uncertainty to Katie's eyes.

"Could you get him on the phone?"

"No." The woman shook her head like she was four years old. "I can't disturb him. His work is much too important."

"Then I'll call him."

"No, wait!" Katie put a hand on her arm as Donna began reaching into her purse.

"It's not as if he can get upset with me, Katie. We had an appointment."

"I know, but…I just don't want to drag him into this."

Donna turned more fully toward her. "Katie, he's your husband and this is your child together. He should be here."

The woman shook her head. "No."

"No, what?" Donna said, pressing. "You don't want him here or he won't come?"

"I *can't*."

"But what about *him*?"

Katie's gaze lifted and Donna could see the plea in the woman's eyes. Katie shook her head, her lips slightly parted and an expression as if she were about to start bawling.

Then she punched Donna in the face.

Donna was a tall woman. She wasn't fat by any means, but neither was she skinny. Katie was about five-two and a hair's breadth over a hundred pounds. Donna tumbled backward from sheer surprise. By the time she'd blinked the stars out of her eyes, she could feel the smaller woman crawling on top of her. Donna swung one arm wildly above her and felt the heel of her palm connect with Katie's jaw. Katie fell against the couch and immediately came at her again. Donna got her foot up just in time, planting it in Katie's stomach and shoving her away. She got to her feet, staying in a low crouch. Katie had fallen into the soft couch, tossing pillows out of her way before scratching at the air as she came on again.

"Katie, what are you doing?" Donna brought her forearm up when Katie sprang at her, connecting with the smaller woman's cheek.

One arm flopped over Donna's shoulder as the lights went out in Katie's eyes. Donna was ready to hit her again but felt the woman sliding away. She let her fall into a half-sitting position against the couch, almost like she was sitting on the floor to watch TV. Donna's hands were shaking as she leaned over and checked Katie's pulse. It was thudding and strong, her skin on fire. Donna was reminded how cold in there it was and shivered as she felt the smaller woman's forehead.

Maybe it was just adrenaline that was making her this hot, but Donna thought otherwise.

"That motherfucking baby," she said quietly, looking around. He'd crawled away somewhere and Donna had to find him. He was what had gone wrong in what had been a lovely home. She couldn't help but think she was partly to blame, but she knew that wasn't true. Donna was just one link in a chain of eventuality. Some divinely evil force had chosen this couple and was seeking to destroy them. Well, Donna wasn't about to let that shit happen.

"Heeeeenry," she said. She clucked her tongue, calling him like a dog.

"Aaaaaaaah," the demon-baby said from somewhere to her left. She looked in the direction of the dining room and she began heading that way. Donna realized she was creeping, like she didn't want him to know. She couldn't think of a sensible reason why. Yes, he was a big baby, much more adept than he should have been, and liked meat, but he was still a baby and Donna was a grown woman.

He couldn't hit her hard enough to cause damage, and if he had teeth, she could simply pluck him up by the scruff of his neck before he could bite.

She stomped the rest of the way into the dining room, scouring the floor around the table, then upended it. Nothing. She was just about to turn around and head back toward the kitchen when she noticed movement above her. It was too late to react by the time she looked up and Henry fell on her from the small chandelier.

His little hands were so *strong*. The blood pinched off where his fingers were dug in and her lips began to go numb as she plucked at his little iron grip. She could breathe but had to tell herself she was still getting air. She finally reached around his neck and pulled forward as hard as she could and hurled him across the room.

He smacked off the wall, and Donna felt the blood stream back into her head, her face throbbing momentarily with her pulse. Her scalp hurt, but she ignored it as her eyes began scouring the area where she'd thrown the little bastard.

Henry wasn't hard to find. He was about a foot away from where she'd thrown him, sitting up. At first, the choked sounds coming out of him struck her as cries because she'd thought the wind had to have been knocked out of him, but as she drew closer she saw him slurping down a long rope of her black hair. He laughed and clapped his hands.

"You little—" Donna said and charged. Her stride was perfect and his head didn't move. Donna caught the side of his face perfectly with the flat plane of the top of her foot.

His head bounced off the floor, and he slid about five feet, but he didn't cry out in pain. Instead, he made a drooly, 'squeeeee!' sound like he couldn't have been happier. Henry propped up on one arm and stared at her, thick saliva with rivulets of red roping down his chin.

"What *are* you?"

Donna charged him, seizing the baby by the shoulders and shaking him like an Etch-a-Sketch. Henry let out another choked cry of laughter and she spiked him like a football. There was a tiny whoosh of air escaping his lungs, but he turned over on his belly and crawled back toward her.

Was he enjoying this? Did he think she was playing with him? Momentary doubt clouded her mind before he sank the hard crescents of his gums into her shin. Donna yowled in agony and flung him off, sending him tumbling into the kitchen. She pursued, noticing again the running water in the plugged sink and the big hunk of meat Donna was relatively certain was Dave Lanergan. Demon Henry had just sat up again, and he was still orienting himself when she bent, seized him by the throat, and dunked him in the sink, splashing water everywhere. She'd lost her shoes at some point and made a mental note to look for them on her way out.

It was odd how she could be so detached, but Donna supposed it wasn't every day you met Satan's baby. This *thing* had to die because of the two beautiful people it had ruined and all the precious lives it would derail if it were allowed to live.

She heard Katie stumble to her feet in the other room but paid her no attention. This would be over in just a few more seconds, and Donna was certain she could take the much smaller woman a lot easier a second time if necessary.

But then she caught him looking at her beneath the surface of the water. His hands were on her arm, but he wasn't struggling, on the contrary, he seemed to be caressing her arm, like what she was doing was soothing him. Donna almost recoiled in disgust, but she forced herself to hold on. She stared into his eyes, really looking into him.

He was...he was *horrible*. But he was just a *baby*. She took him out of the water and held him before her, like she'd just been bathing him and was inspecting the child for cleanliness.

Henry belched and suckled a couple fingers. Donna opened her mouth to speak but didn't know what to say. Katie had finally stumbled her way to the island, and the two of them turned and looked at her. Henry grunted a laugh and looked at the slab of the man who was once supposed to have been his father. Katie blinked, her eyes focusing in a way they hadn't before since Donna had come in and she saw.

"Oh no!" she said, putting her hands to her face. She reached and clenched fistfuls of her husband's squishy, rotten remains. She pressed her head into them, sobbing loudly, and when Donna looked down, saw she was cradling the baby in her arm.

"Henry," she said, walking toward the door. She could feel him in her mind, but Donna was strong, yes very strong. She understood what had happened here and it would not happen to her.

She grabbed a blanket that was mostly free of filth and quickly wrapped him in it. So, he was evil. Donna had a feeling she could deal with that. No, she knew she could. He had corrupted Katie because the woman had been weak. She'd never struggled in life the way Donna had. She'd never had to fight. As she came to the door, an idea began forming in her mind how she could simultaneously foster his nature, but not fall prey to it. She could feel him groping around her mind and pushed him away. He'd been cooing but fell silent a moment before crying.

He wasn't going to have his way with *her*.

Donna shut the door behind her. She had a feeling the Katie and Dave thing would sort itself out on its own. She looked up at the sky, the sun still high. Henry had ceased crying and was suckling hard at his fingers, a look of deep concern on his face. He was still at the edges of her mind, but she had him fenced out.

She opened her car door and tossed him over the seat into the back. Henry bounced and began mumbling a moment later as she started the engine. Donna backed out of the driveway and pulled onto the street, humming a little tune to herself as she gave the Lanergan house one last look.

"We're going to be together for a long time, Henry. Can you take care of that?"

Henry giggled and flames exploded out of the windows.

"Good boy," she said. "That's a *good* boy."

Gerald Dean Rice

These are several poems I wrote while I was in college, somewhere between 2000-2006. There's a marked improvement from the stuff I wrote in high school (see the very end of this book if your masochism button needs pressing). I remember some of them or at least why I wrote some, but there are a few I have completely forgotten and have no clue what the meaning was supposed to be.

Her

Men hang off her
like bracelets,
Perfuming her air with
Compliments,

They thirst, first seeing her poured hourglass frame
Breathing out mint-scented lies
Cemented in 'casual conversation'
They adorn adult jargon
To inadequately dress up

Gerald Dean Rice

Teenaged desires

They dust her with lust
Their green speech
She desprinkles from her hair
With imperceptible shakes of her head

Even her walking away
They lap up with silverware tongues
Hanged about their necks,
She strides a melody
That dances their heads
Side-to-side,

Hooding their eyes
Their sunken faces lack foundation
To hold up malnourished smiles,
Struggling inside them is unremembered
Dignity, tugging them away
from animal lives
They trenchcoat hunched backs
Scuttling back in revulsion
At the company of their own kind.

Untitled #84

"Fuck you,
"You're here for rock
"bottom, you horror of a
"human being."
Loose the tide of agony,
Hot-palmed, upturned in supplication,
ready to wave off this flame
And belly crawl a Sisyphus path
To heaven. Old wounds—
Tattering the soul in retelling—
Healed, like jagged lines of unwritten poetry.
Fire taught trees yield the fruit
Of ash, learning hopelessness—
Mouthful by mouthful—
gray bitterness. The highway is
Long and fevered with never-
ending furnish of the sun,
Be selfish with your memories of water
The barefoot sizzle should remind you

Of what's been come for,
The angel on your shoulder slaughtered
With a wink of an eye,
The thing cooking inside you
Boils life from your eyes
And rolls it down your cheeks.

Give, my Pavlov Pretty,
When silvered tongues ring
In the bell of your ear.
Distance cannot shapeshift you
Fast enough to fake away the pain.

Bull In Cloud

The mines walk up onto plateaus
Children and cigarettes
Ignore me angrily

The plane follows a crescent of stars
So fast
Eagle the color of lightning

Wings joyous flaps
All night the
Sky has been streaking

A rocket arching up
My skin holds a nervousness the closing
Clouds freeze my brain

They promise
To stop me flat at a gate
Satellited and widowed a milk land

Winter Coats

Winter coats are great,
They keep you warm and all
But what's best is the fresh
Find of something you left

In the pockets for three seasons.
The ticket stubs expired coupons

and dignity slide on that coat,
Remembering earlier in the year
When bitter words escaped sweet lips
And you in turn, bit your tongue
And it slid, off your chin
Across the lapel, down the front of you,
Deposited quietly in your inside pocket.

Winter coats are great
Not like that frigid bitch
You can give them away
And start new with another one

Dopamine

He stunk of clean
Itching with soap
He hoped to scratch his way out
Into a new life in this straight world
He straightens his spine
And walked upright
Ditched his coward's tail
Praying to the gods of Upward Failure
In case he should stumble
He felt his stomach grumble
Full on a breakfast of promises
A champion for the schizophrenic
He is resident alien
Viewing the human homeworld
With medication-colored sunglasses
His schizophrenic regard for mankind
Marginalized
But it's too sweet a pill
For a bitter tongue
As he pounds the pavement
Shaking loose the dirt of opportunity
        from the sky
But he is still undomesticated.
Shying away from foreign helping hands
Fleeing to alleyway jungles
Resigns himself to woodland street corners
He has deforested his own heart yet again
And bared a barren soul
He takes off from the wavering mirage of Earth
Wrapping himself in the welcoming arms

of newspaper and detritus
To protect himself
From the sterile elements
He follows the whispers in his ear
As he clings desperately to the ideal
of monkey-less backs
Under a sky waxing
with _____ clouds
Whistling as he walks
In empty fields in his mind
Above ventricular tunnelwork
The rain has come again
But he smiles
Anchored against the flooding waters
By hands shoved deep into pockets
Locked around clozapine seeds
He will plant again.

Counting Mississippis

One Mississippi,
Two Mississippi,
Three...

We ride for hours until we reach
The land of rounded words,
Humidity nooses about our necks,
Choking the sweat from our bodies,
We sardine-stack into the motel room,
Hanging our heads beneath cool sink water,
A thin wet heaven
Inside of a moistened Hell,
My father notes the lone black chin hair
And with a laugh, lynches it from my white face.

One Mississippi,
Two Mississippi,
Three Mississippi,
Four...

We came from Michigan, Illinois, Ohio, Indiana,
Even Sweden
To the place where Greats stood
Before Grands stepped out of line
And it feels like someone is still holding our places

Gerald Dean Rice

As we return to those who stayed behind
And company with strangers with familial faces,
We cast our eyes like rods,
Fishing cousins,
Wishing cousins weren't
Missing cousins,
Listings cousins
'Til we count our way
Back to common ancestry.

One Mississippi,
Two Mississippi,
Three Mississippi,
Four Mississippi,
Five…

The day dips into a pool of black,
And moon glow milkens our eyes.
We do absolutely nothing
And embellish all night about it,
We fear sleep 'cause tomorrow waits with
Grandmotherly toasts and goodbye,
Our tongues loll with overuse
As creeping, unwelcome
Yawns toll at the end of conversation,
And our eyes tear over with sleep
We lay our heads down,
After giving the Lord our souls to keep,
But instead of counting sheep,
We count

One Mississippi,
Two Mississippi,
Three Mississippi,
Four Mississippi,
Five Mississippi,
Six…

To You

i thought of this on the fly
so I hope these misshapen words
hold the contour of what
i want to say

i pulled this from the air
hoping you could make out
these muddy thoughts
these velcro emotions
despite how many times
i fumbled, trying to give
this sticky heart to you

i wrote this in the nick of time
i stumbled
over every word
as I hurried home to you

Stay

Stolid, I watch you leaving,
Eyes conspire to betray hidden emotions,
Leaking tears like falling smoke signals,
Treasonous hands tremble in Morse code,
Communicating the words I hold
hostage, My body mutinies
And I am captured
On the tip of my tongue,
I walk the plank,
Holding onto words I want to say
I fall…
'Stay.'

Slipping Through

Passing by unseen
Leaving no trail of remembrance
Existing as a shadowed afterthought
Using only what fits into pockets

The eye bends around flesh
A craned neck to look over
A twilight stare sees through
Even the fleeting lines of fingerprints fading fast

To glide past; a silent
Threading through the interwoven fabric of civility
Becoming cousin to invisibility
Calling downwind home

101

Name withheld and no picture taken
Staining not the glass surface of society
An invited glance quite mistaken
To crawl beneath the skin of notice;
Living without hello or goodbye

Discomfort

You rest in a knot
Between my shoulders
You are pain's
Next-door-neighbor
Even though you only
Live in my head

You are the embarrassing
Words someone else said
And where i sleep
You are the lump inside my bed
I should kick you out, instead
I opened my door
Inviting you to my table
And even though you put

Carts before all the horses in my stable
I let you turn my silences awkward
And bring up the past
To keep me chaste
You tsk-tsk when I
Dare to risk
And take a firm stance
Against the possibility

Of chance
You take pleasure
In uncertain surety,
And the only thing
You assure me
Is probably, maybe

You convict me
For the company I keep
But maybe I'll learn you ill-fitting dance,
As i no tap to tap

Beneath six left feet.

Dirty Mind, Pt. II

Baby, I'm sorry,
But my mind's in the gutter,
I was wondering—do you give good brain?
C'mon, darling, stroke my ego
And let's exchange fluid ideas
You look like you can get down, but
Would you go up on me?
Sugar, I think very deeply
And my $E=MC^2$ all night long…
Am I turning you on?
Grab the hypotenuse
Dangling from the bottom of my triangle,
Pythagoras don't have nothin' on my theorem
Let's make theological exclamations
And repeated affirmations
Until…until…
Damn.
Premature conversation again.

Sleep

Baby, remember when we laid
In bed and taking a siesta was the last thing
We did?
Gaze deep into my red-rimmed eyes,
I may be well-rested
But I can't go on thinking another moment

Unless I get some sleep
Please, take your hand
And lay down with me
I've been waiting so long to dream
That every waking moment
Is an aching nightmare
Blue is the color of this dry-spell insomnia,

I try rocking myself to sleep, but,
Add up all six sisters and they don't equal you
It takes two to sleep properly
And I like the way you saw wood

Let us kneel like prayers before bed
Then we can spoon or do charitable work
In a foreign country.

Should I put on a nightcap before we cuddle up?
Let me get just a bit more of that nap,
We can snooze all night long
Or at least for forty winks,
Believe me, I can go coma deep

I'll wipe the sleep from your eye
And make you a cup of coffee
Or light your cigarette come morning,
If you would please
Do that thing that always
Puts my lights out.

Hit It

I sniff, then spit,
You don't know how many
Sheets of paper it took
To straighten these here lines

I wish I could say
They been cut by Chilean
Poets, but I had to
Steel it under my own name

Coking vowels and consonants
After I piled out a
Powder of letters
Then stamped, barefoot, on

Each and every word
And razor bladed
Divides between stanzas
But I admit,

I took a little for myself,
Unraveled one and
Whispered it out loud,
Rolled up George Washington

And blew my own mind,

Leaving you short
By one hit.

Gerald Dean Rice

I can't exactly put my finger on the genesis of this story. It's a definite departure from my usual, maybe more cerebral than I'm accustomed to writing. But it was definitely one of those, 'if I don't write it now I'll forget how to write it' kinds of stories.

The Drawer

They brought Leslie in right after some poor sap who'd left the interrogation room in tears. Maybe he'd been a fake out, maybe not, but letting her see him had been intentional.

She'd been on this ride more than once. No surprises so far.

The young bull of an officer standing by her gently nudged and almost toppled her over. She'd met more than a few guys built like him, and even when they were being careful, they were still lummoxes. Leslie stumbled forward half-intentionally and let him 'catch' her. Despite her grizzled interior, she was pretty and knew how to wield her beauty like a baseball bat.

Officer Stansman saw he was palming a handful of her he shouldn't be and his farm tan rinsed away in shock.

"Sorry, ma'am," he said, as she shifted a foot under herself to catch her weight. She stood on her own, making continued eyeball contact with him until he removed his other hand from her shoulder.

"Thank you," she said, sprinkling as much helplessness into her voice as she could. Good, wholesome, Christian guilt flooded his bloodless face and she knew she had him. This man would bring her one of the good pillows in her cell or give her an extra bag of chips with dinner. He wouldn't hit her or verbally abuse her. There were probably a half dozen other cops who would do who knew what, but this one was safe.

He gave her a six-inch buffer of no contact as he led her to the interview room.

"Take those off," the white-mustachioed man in the interview room said. She was surprised because she wasn't sure what the play was by taking off her cuffs. If she could move around, that made it harder to hit her with the phone book.

Leslie crossed the threshold, genuinely intrigued to know what was about to happen. This was a one-stoplight town, and the 'detective,' or whatever the man in the interview room was, probably also doubled as the town barber. They probably were going to keep her up until three in the morning.

She'd experienced some version of what they more than likely intended to do two dozen times over. But the dresser in the middle of the room was new.

Well, not *new*. It looked like Ben Franklin had signed the Constitution on it. It was different. For starters, it wasn't a table they could look across at each other. There were chairs to either side of the front and back, but it would be an awkward sit and even more awkward conversation. They wouldn't be able to see each other over it once she was sitting.

"Please," the man said after he'd stood and gestured to the other chair.

"All right." Leslie shrugged and sauntered over in her high heels. Her feet hurt. "I guess we're doing this." She knew what she was dressed as but preserved her dignity as she took her time and sat. The man looked about fifty or so, with blue eyes that cored into her passively. He was like a diamond tip that had been dulled over years of use. Maybe he wasn't as sharp as he'd once been, but if pressed, he still had plenty of hurt to dole out. Those eyes had seen things not located in a town like this. He hadn't grown up here, he'd retreated here.

She saw the two painted footprints on the floor before her and, just to be contrarian, spread her legs in her knee-length dress and slumped in her chair. Her posture had the desired effect when the man appeared to wince before returning to his chair. He still had that same sneer on his face he'd had since she'd walked in, though. Like he knew something she didn't and Leslie *definitely* didn t like that.

She was the kind of person unopposed to breaking a law or two if it suited her needs at that moment. Jail didn't matter to her. Getting beat up by some Podunk cop in a hoedown town didn't either. She had no official job to speak of or proclaimed residence. A night in a cell was free room and board until she stumbled over whatever was next.

"It goes easier if you keep your feet on the painted footprints."

"Oh?" Leslie didn't know why that was and didn't care, but she clapped her feet on the floor as if she were complying. She didn't know if this state was one where they had to stop talking to you when you asked for a lawyer and she didn't ask immediately just to hear what he was going to say.

There was an interminable silence between them that she didn't feel like putting up with and Leslie asked, "So what brings me here?"

"Ma'am, I have no intention of asking you a damn thing," the cop said. She took that to mean he was going to whip out the phone book at any moment and her gut clenched. "You're going to tell me everything of your own free will."

"Hm," she said, honestly curious how he was going to manage that. She had noticed he had no badge or gun on him. The ones who did that traditionally tried to 'good cop' her. This cop had a definite mean streak in him.

"Just start talking when you want it to stop."

Leslie wanted to ask what that meant, but she heard him slide one of the drawers of the dresser open. The room went black. She couldn't hear the low susurrus of the old building, and the bitter untaste of having not eaten anything for the last few hours was replaced with a nil blandness. Her elbows and knees tingled, and when she wiggled her fingers, Leslie realized she couldn't tell if her hands were still attached to her body.

"What the hell?" she said, or thought she did, but she didn't hear her voice. Not even in her head. It was like she was a grain of sand hurtling through the vast nothingness of space.

The drawer closed and she was back.

Leslie had the sudden sensation of being dropped into her chair, as if she'd been hovering above it a millisecond before, but to the best of her knowledge, she hadn't moved.

The old cop leaned around the dresser and looked at her. Just for a moment, then he sat up straight again.

She heard another drawer slide open.

Leslie felt every cell of her being pulled down as if they'd all been weighted by thousands of little anchors. Then she realized the sensation of being catapulted up. God knew where—her eyes couldn't keep track of the passing blank skyscrapers around her. All she could see through her periphery was a kaleidoscope of color, each hue transforming and coloring into a weight pressing on her mind as it passed.

And then Leslie had the empty-stomach feeling of weightlessness. She was alone—wherever the hell she was— immersed in a color she couldn't describe. It was as much blue as it was orange. It had a feel like the flat of a cold butter knife pressed against the back of her neck in a perpetual state of unexpectedness. When she breathed deep of the atmosphere, the synesthetic sensation brought the 156th decimal place of pi concrete into her mind. She put her tongue out to taste the pool of ether washing around her, and it was like being ejected from the womb of the sun, burning through cleansing heat but only dying because she had not gestated to term.

And then the drawer shut.

Leslie heard animal gasping and realized from the burn in her lungs and tingling lips that she had to have been holding her breath. She went on gulping air for another thirty seconds as she stared at the back of the dresser.

"What...*the hell*...was that?" Leslie finally managed to say.

"It's a shortcut," the cop said. He rose into a half crouch, scooched his chair around to the side, and sat again. "I had you figured as soon as Officer Braff brought you in. Just like I'm sure you have a pretty good idea about me. Neither of us belongs in a town like this. Am I right?" He put his elbows on his knees, leaning closer. "I know I'm hiding. And I have every reason to let you go on hiding too. But you have something that isn't yours. It needs to go back to the...individual who had rightful possession of it."

"You took the long way around saying I stole something." She was starting to feel more herself. "And what was that last part? That was a fancy way of saying 'owner', wasn't it?"

"Yeah. It would be. If I had meant 'owner'. But the individual you took it from was not the owner. The…item *has* no owner. It is simply in the possession of an individual, or it isn't."

Leslie wondered about this individual' business. She had taken it from the pocket of an old man. Well, she'd picked a bag from his pocket and that thing had been inside. She'd never seen anything like it, but it had to have been hella valuable.

"Did you know he was rude to his waitress?" Leslie asked the cop. Yes, he definitely looked like a youngish Charlton Heston, circa *Planet of the Apes*.

"What?" He looked at her curiously…maybe slightly annoyed his little parlor trick didn't have her bumbling and crying like a baby like the guy before her. Leslie was a little more resilient than he probably was expecting.

"The old guy. The…individual."

"Never mind about him." The cop sighed, his eyes drifting to a corner of the room. She didn't want to ask. The cop was seeing something a thousand miles away that probably didn't bear repeating. "You ready to talk?"

"I thought we were talking," Leslie said.

He sighed as if he were exhausted.

"All right. Time for part two."

She heard the drawer slide open and thought a millisecond too late to get out of the chair.

She was falling and not. Her body was stone while everything inside her plummeted into a bottomless pit, circling the center of her, vacuuming her surroundings into her pores with high-powered osmosis. Leslie opened her mouth to scream and the universe screamed into her every orifice.

And the drawer shut.

Beads of cold sweat as wide as dimes stood on her goose-fleshed forearms. Leslie's vision wasn't right. The cop, Tracy Oldham from what she could read on the ID in his wallet tucked away in his pants pocket, was flashing a penlight he'd bought a week ago in her eyes. She could have read the detail of the penlight had she wanted, but the microscopic amount of information at her visual disposal made her stomach queasy.

The entire sensation retreated just as she thought about his backstory, seeing only the trails of a sick and dying child, small in a bland white hospital bed, with an egg-shell pallor and attached to tubes.

Leslie's eyes focused to sharpen on the cop in front of her.

"You saw him just now, didn't you?"

She'd understood the question, but opening her mouth and responding wasn't automatic. It was as if the cogs and wheels of common pleasantries had rusted still. The cop—Oldham everyone called him, cop and crook alike—became diamond-sharp in her vision and she sat back in her chair.

"The boy…my boy…you saw him, didn't you?"

He gave her a wan smile and rose from his knee. Leslie realized that would have been prime real estate for a foot to the nuts, but the moment passed without her making a move.

"It won't be much longer, y'know."

Leslie had been moving her mouth for five seconds when she realized no sound was actually coming out. "Much longer for what?" she said aloud after clearing her voice. There was a slight niggle at the top of her throat like the beginning of a cold. She swallowed. "What do you mean?"

"Y'know," he said, wiping his hand on a kerchief a good five feet away.

She hadn't seen him retreat. She watched as Oldham twisted his hand around in the cloth and realized the taste on the tail end of her tongue was of his fingers. Had she lost consciousness and choked on her tongue? She pushed the thought away as fast as it came to her, something more pressing coming to mind.

"Wait, that stuff I was seeing—that wasn't real." She forced it into a statement.

"I used to think it was all black and white," Oldham said. He rolled his eyes up to the ceiling. "Life. Reality." He held his arms out and looked around. "All…this. Or if I thought about that sort of thing at all before I found things like—" He rapped his knuckles on the side of the dresser. "Now I see everything in various shades of grey. If you, this whole building, turned into mist, I don't think I'd be surprised anymore."

Panic bubbled up in Leslie. "Somebody did the thing with the drawers to you, didn't they?" She sat up in her chair, realizing who somebody' was. "It was you. You did it to yourself, didn't you?" She puzzled for just a moment before her brain shifted gears. "You know what? Don't really care. I'm done with this. I want a lawyer. Take me back to my cell."

"It's not that simple, Joan Danvers," Oldham sa d, sending a chill up her spine as he disappeared on the other side of the dresser again. He'd said her name. Her real-real name. The one she'd been born with before her mother had married her stepfather and changed it. With enough scrutiny, the fake ID she'd been arrested with would collapse, but that would take time. She hadn't seen a single computer newer than black-screens-with-green-font-old. Hell, she'd seen about four or five *word processors* on desks. "I to d you, you aren't technically under arrest. So far as the outside world is concerned, we're just having a conversation after which point you are free to leave."

"Free to leave, huh? Great. I'm out, Oldham." She stood and tried to take a step toward the door. Her foot was rooted to the spot like her shoes were in hardened concrete. Leslie lashed her arms about to throw herself back into balance.

She thought and tried to lift her foot out, testing her equilibrium again when her leg didn't move. Her feet slid together until they were atop the little yellow painted footprints on the floor.

"What the hell?" she was about to ask, but the drawer slid open.

Leslie tried to prepare her mind for some new existential challenge but found herself in the middle of a field with a man she didn't know. Except she did. She'd known this man for three years. They were in love. She'd turned him down the first time he'd asked her on a date and had regretted it as soon as she'd said no. Six months had gone by with him respecting her answer before she'd broken down and asked him out.

They'd barely been apart ever since. And here in the middle of nowhere but a place she'd been with him many times, she knew he was about to ask her to marry him.

And then with a push all over her body at the same time and the rush of wind that seemingly passed through her like a line of silk through a needle's eye, she was giving birth to their second child. Something was tearing inside her and the doctors would realize it late as she nearly bled to death.

Memories between the two events flooded the gap like a limb having blood recirculating into it. Leslie was on the verge of calling to her husband as a nurse laid her naked child on her chest.

The push and the rush came again. This time she was in another hospital, sitting up in. The preceding memories flooded into her mind and she recognized the two young adults standing at her bedside as the children she had given birth to and loved with unwavering fierceness. She remembered for a moment the brief affair that Phillip, her husband, had had as he stood on the other side of the bed, holding her hand with a longing that had faded and returned long ago. Leslie had fallen out of love with this man, but they had rediscovered the spring of their affection for one another despite how very nearly they had ended a twenty year marriage.

It took her a moment to understand why she was here and when that final gap closed, Leslie put a hand to her chest. The doctors hadn't taken her left breast yet, but that was why her family was here with her now. She took solace from the tears in Phillip's reddened eyes, a crashing tidal wave in comparison to the ripple of fear she felt. Leslie felt like the worry she was supposed to have had been lifted off her shoulders and hung on his.

The push and the rush once more. Phillip Jr. had married and moved two states away. He and his wife had a child of their own, a little boy Leslie had only met once. There was some issue between her husband and son and he'd stopped calling for a while. She was still giving the ice some time to melt before reaching out—too soon would hurt her husband, too late would hurt her son. Bonnie still lived in the city and she came over every Sunday for dinner.

Details were slower in filling in and she found her mind drifting back to the older ones that came in sharper for some reason. A middle-aged man came into the living room. He looked familiar and the way he smiled at her was so warm it was obvious he was happy to see her. Leslie smiled back and nodded, letting him sit next to her and put his big hands over hers.

Then she remembered this was her Phillip. He'd gotten so old and he had a cute paunch. Something in his eyes said he could tell she recognized him now and just after he began to lean in for a kiss, his face changed. It was like…like he was trying to reel back a mighty sneeze. His complexion changed to a deeper shade of brown. One palm against the back of her hand felt unnaturally clammy and warm compared to the other which remained a dry cool, the muscles in both twitching like she was shocking him with electricity where their skin met.

Phillip folded off the couch, timbering over and smashing his head on the edge of the coffee table. Leslie was calm and quiet as he sprawled on the floor, looking up at the ceiling. She scooched closer, giving her slow bones time to kneel by his side. She loved this man and should have been panicked, but it was as if whatever was going wrong with her—something some man with an old name was or had been doing, she wasn't really sure—was keeping her emotions dull.

Her husband had a gash about the distance of a finger's width above his eyebrow and blood pulsed slowly from it. His lips worked, spittle clinging to them and a long line casting from his mouth onto his cheek.

Leslie came closer once she'd realized he was trying to speak but only successfully managing to etch closer to death. She turned her head so the bell of her ear hovered inches from his mouth.

Then the drawer slid shut.

Leslie felt the flood of urine down her legs and cried out something nonsensical. She said the location of the item she had stolen—in a public trash can underneath the liner bag. She'd intended on going back for it tonight after they'd released her.

She didn't care about Oldham or any of this. The door to the interview room creaked open, and she ran, making random left and right turns, not recognizing or really seeing anything in front of her. Finally, she pressed open a door and was outside.

The sun was in the wrong place, like time had rewound. She couldn't have been in there more than two hours, but time had nothing to do with what she cared about. Leslie turned about to try to gain her bearings. The police station was at least thirty yards away even though she hadn't moved from the walkway after stepping outside, but the feet between where she was and where she was supposed to be had nothing to do with what she cared about.

Years of memories. Everything that had happened. Leslie held her hands up and clasped her hands into mock fists, running her fingers over the meat of her thumbs and the edges of her palms. This was her flesh, still with the glow of a youthly thirty year old and not an old woman. Despite the years she had grown old, despite the area she'd lived in she was confident was nowhere near here, the fact remained she was not old and was very much right here with children she had never given birth to and raised, and a husband she had never met.

But Leslie knew them just the same. All three in their own uniqueness, but still tied together, like three different colored strings of tinsel on the same Christmas tree, looping around and crisscrossing, but having their own origins and endpoints. She had loved and been loved by them, and that love had converted her, conveyed her throughout space and time.

Yet here she was. Before any of that. Right now. *This* was reality even though it felt less than real.

Leslie held that last memory, greyed and fogged, the slight tinge of metal in the air. The man whose love had waned and waxed again, who was so patient that he dared not kiss her until he saw she had recognized him again, who held her hand through childbirth, near coma, and in recovery after life-saving surgery. But the memory was like a water balloon with a hole poked in it. She'd seen it and known it was real, but it was gone. No cry to heaven or demand of any god would yield even the evidence of the moment's passing.

She closed her eyes and tried to immerse herself in that last moment, leaning close again so she could hear him. Even if it were only a whisper, those last words would have been enough.

Leslie couldn't remember ever hearing his voice.

The Locked Door *came about from a writing challenge at the end of March 2021. I'd never seriously considered writing a mystery—and I still don't think I really have, but it was fun to do and I wrote 700-something words in 20 minutes. The Detective Savine character intrigues me. And Captain Melvina Jones as his 'straight man' makes me seriously think about exploring both of them more. I am not British, nor is it my intention to make either character British or set at any time in the past, however the story kind of comes out that way.*

The Locked Door

They passed through the lobby, Captain Melvina Jones and the mysterious Detective Savine. He did not work with any government agency officially, but was occasionally used in s tuations other detective inspectors found more confounding than most.

They took a lift to the fourth floor. She had already explained the circumstances of the double murder and aside from a quiet, "Mhm," Savine had said nothing since.

The apartment in question was the first on the left after the elevator. Savine, in his awkward attempt at chivalry, stepped aside and gestured for Melvina to go inside first. He was beyond an odd man and made her feel not unlike an unreachable itch at the center of one's back.

He followed behind and Melvina immediately went to a window to stare at the street below. She did not like witnessing death so…fresh. She had done her duty insomuch that she had verified both man and woman—Mr. and Mrs. Thomas Willamette—had been chopped up like so much meat and were thoroughly deceased.

He began making sounds. At first it was like an, "Ah. Ah. Ah," every few seconds, then he began tapping something. She turned to look at him and his eyes flicked up to hers and then away. He seemed to shudder—not from the sight of the bodies in front of him, but from eye contact with another human being. He was tapping something beneath his overcoat. Something metallic. She guessed it was a canteen of some sort, but he didn't strike her as a man given to drink.

Savine stroked his grizzled chin and began a stroll in her direction. Had she wanted to touch him at all, she would have shaved that face of his and perhaps trimmed his wild, bushy hair.

"Melvina, my good friend, would you bother to stand in front of the door?" he asked.

She complied, more than glad to not only walk away from the man, but to also be closer to the exit of the room.

Savine walked to a wall and began casually walking the perimeter of the room. There was a painting of a child in a field hung in the center of the wall, but he paid it no more mind than the opal and striped wallpaper. Melvina thought he seemed lost in thought. He turned at the first corner, continuing his leisurely pace, head tilted slightly upward like he was looking at something on the far end of the ceiling.

He turned the next corner just as before, with his hands laced loosely behind his back. Savine seemed incapable of noticing anything. As far as Melvina could tell, the man's mind was a thousand miles away.

But then he sprang like a cat, seemingly at the corner itself. She had to blink several times before she could see what exactly he was grabbing. It appeared as though the perpendicular intersection of the walls was struggling in his hands.

Melvina turned her eyes away and then looked back. Then she saw it. Saw him. A man, his flesh and clothing—if he wore any—painted the same color as the walls. He'd even copied the way the light fell in the corner. Savine reared back with one hard and struck the figure someplace low. Whoever it was grunted and wrenched himself free, awkwardly running toward Melvina.

It was difficult to fathom the man—Melvina made sure to keep her eyes above his navel—had been impossible to spot as Melvina stepped forward, drawing her handcuffs. She planted her feet and stiff-armed him with the heels of her palms to his chest before grabbing the man roughly by the wrist and bending it until he had no choice but to submit to her authority and turn round. But what little fight he'd had was quickly drained as his play had been revealed before his intention and he must have known he was thoroughly caught.

Two young officers came into the room, apparently hearing the kerfuffle. Melvina passed the murderer to them, and they led the man away, covered ridiculously in opal blue and black stripes.

"Curse you," the painted man said.

"You have a nice day, Mr. Malko," Detective Savine said.

"How do you know who he is?"

"Dwight Malko." Savine finally looked down from the ceiling and at her, his eyes somewhere south of hers. "I figured it almost as soon as we came into the building. The post boxes have the names of the tenants corresponding to their apartment numbers. Mr. Malko, an actor and live exhibitionist, is known for elaborate body paintings in which he or whomever he paints appears to blend into almost any background. It's quite awe-inducing. You should see it sometime."

"Why did you tell me to stand by the door?"

"In case I could not grab him. I knew you would have been more capable than I."

Melvina shook her head. "Thank the world there is only one of you, Savine."

Gerald Dean Rice

I wrote this story in 2012 after moving to a new house around the same time my daughter was about to start kindergarten. I had to go to her new school with paperwork showing that we now lived in the school district. There's something eerie to me about empty schools and I remember two other parents hovering around trying to figure out where to go because there weren't any teachers around and I think the staff was still at lunch.

First Day

Brad climbed out of the car, paperwork in hand. The little school was a mix between old and new; the part in front of him looked like a more recent add-on, a brick rainbow-brown single story connected to a much older schoolhouse to his right.

He didn't know where to enter and turned toward the older part of the building, headed for the big wood double doors. Brad tried the right one, locked, then the left, also locked. There was a light somewhere inside and he leaned closer to peer inside when a bug on the window of one of the doors leapt off and flew past his cheek. Brad jumped back with a mix of disgust and fear. He'd had a deep phobia of insects since his brother had tormented him with them when he was little, tiny red ants in his hair, fat black ones dropped into him from the top bunk. He'd barely caught a glimpse of the one that had just buzzed him, but what he'd seen had been big and ugly. He looked up and behind him, hoping not to see it again and saw nothing but blue sky with great big tufts of white clouds floating lazily along.

Brad jumped again when he turned back to the door and saw several more bugs on the window he must have missed before. He scrubbed his palm against his pant leg as if he'd touched something slimy. Maybe it was because he'd touched something they were touching that made his hand feel gross. Brad quickly walked back the way he'd come, hoping he'd just missed the entrance and that the school wasn't actually closed.

It was the perfect temperature outside. He'd missed hearing what the high was supposed to be today, but it was a much appreciated reprieve from the ninety-plus degrees of a week ago. Brad was thinking maybe he could go for a walk with his wife and son around the new neighborhood later when a tallish slender woman with long dark red hair slow-walked past him. He looked to where he surmised she was heading and saw it. The door had just about been right in front of him when he'd gotten out the car and he'd missed it. Brad slowed his pace so he wouldn't overtake her and appear like some jerk in a hurry to be first in line. She was pretty in a slightly-too-much-makeup sort of way, in a loose shirt with multiple colored squares and jeans cuffed up to her calves. The way she stepped—her platform shoes going *clop-clop-clop*—made it look like she had tiny sharp pebbles digging into the soles of her feet.

He came up behind her, slowing even more as they entered the building and they came to an elbowed hallway. She went right and he followed. There was an open doorway and a row of windows to the right and another open doorway farther down. The hallway was brightly lit, but the office was dark. She turned left and right as if wondering if this was the proper place and Brad looked around too, not quite ready to speak or make eye contact. He spotted a name on the door, 'Mrs. Mars' and underneath that 'Office Secretary'. He checked his watch. 12:17. Had they gone to lunch?

"Maybe they stepped out for lunch?" the woman said. Brad turned her way and shrugged, as if to say, 'maybe'. He truly looked at her for the first time and added a couple years to her age once he spotted the tiny crinkles at the edges of her eyes. He paced down the hall some, craning his neck to look farther down. Brad wasn't certain, but from his perspective, there were classrooms that way. If there were any place to take his son's information for registration, it would be right here.

Clop-clop-clop went the redhead's shoes again and when he turned around she'd stepped into the office and the lights were flickering on. She turned her head left and right then peered around a corner.

"Hello?" She stepped back into the hallway, looked at him and turned for the women's room right next door. That sounded like a good idea to him so he walked to the men's room next over.

Brad sat his papers down on the edge of the sink and set about his business at the urinal. When he finished, he went to the sink and took two squirts of soap to lather up and regretted it, the stuff smelling more suitable to clean industrial machinery than human skin. The complementary whoosh came through the wall, signaling she was through as well. Brad finished, turned off the water, and took two tugs of paper towel, hoping this wasn't going to take much longer. He still hadn't had lunch yet and would need time to drive wherever before heading back to work.

The door squealed open on its hinges as he exited the men's and he saw the woman already in the hall. They nodded to one another and Brad figured he would see if someone was in one of those classrooms. He walked down the hall and through the open doorway, figuring he must have been crossing over into the older section of the building. The floor inclined slightly and the lights weren't on, but there was a lit classroom to his left with its door open and soft rock playing somewhere inside, Steve Perry melodiously advising anyone listening to continue believing.

"Hello?" Brad said, peeking in. At first, he saw nothing that wouldn't be inside a classroom. Tiny desks, tiny chairs, bookshelves, semi-inspirational posters on walls. There was a pile of construction paper strewn across one of the little circular tables and onto the floor and he spotted a pair of white gym-shoed feet pointing to the ceiling. Maybe somebody was taking a siesta on the job. Brad wouldn't make a fuss so long as he or she wasn't going to be Max's teacher. "Excuse me?" he said.

And that was when he'd heard the sound just below the screech of twin guitars on the radio. It was a sound he was so accustomed to hearing that his brains had almost boxed it away, labeled for the 'to be forgotten' section of his mind. "Reep-reep," an insect said. The fact that it was inside wasn't all that strange. Brad gave a clipped laugh at the completely ridiculous thought, but it had sounded like it was about ten registers too deep and who knew how many decibels too loud.

"Almost like it was a giant insect," he said under his breath. He stepped into the room, wanting to rouse the person under the construction paper blanket. But when he looked at the feet again and the mess on top of the person it just didn't look quite right. These could have been the feet of a mannequin, they were so still, and the paper was slightly steepled in an odd way. He couldn't see the top of the person's head but guessed that bulge would have been somewhere around his or her stomach. He thought it was much too big to be a beer belly.

"Reep-reep." He flinched. Whatever it was, was underneath the construction paper. Maybe it was the teacher—not sleep after all, but working out the kinks of some kind of a...class experiment? He quickly glanced around—this classroom didn't have any science equipment he could see. Maybe a lesson on nature?

Brad didn't want to be afraid. He felt stupid and lame for wanting to turn around and walk away. The redhead would ask and he would lie, but instinctually, she would know. His wife gave him that look, sometimes. Like she was looking at a little boy in desperate need of his mother.

"Hello?" he said more quietly than he'd intended. He reached down to grab the edge of a sheet of red construction paper.

He pinched it and moved it ever so slightly when he heard another, "Reep-reep-reep," and a thing popped out at the other end. Brad's eyes bulged and he froze, not understanding what he was seeing. It was as big as a medium-sized dog and looked *mostly* like a grasshopper, except it was reddish brown and seemed to have front legs like a praying mantis. Its antennae were pitched backward and almost as long as its carapace—that word had popped out of an ancient corner of his mind. It was turned away from him and for a moment, he assumed it was looking ahead. But then he saw an eye on the side of its head, dancing up and down, pointed in *his* direction. He broke eye contact with it, letting the corner of construction paper, which suddenly felt icky and dry, slide from his fingers and away from the body on the floor.

It could have been a man or a woman, Brad couldn't tell. The bug had eaten a giant hole that started below the eyes, taking the nose, mouth and throat—all the meat and bone gone back to the spine, leaving only parts of the gums and a few rear molars.

He was rubbing his hand on his leg again, eyes locked on the leftovers of human being—

"Reep-reep!" It hopped a three-point one-eighty, rising off a rear pair of legs to stand nearly chest height to him, rubbing its forelegs together like it was hungry for seconds. Brad ran out of the room then, snatching at the door on his way out. Let the redhead think he was a coward, he was going to drag her right out of here if he needed to. He'd just tell her there was someone with a gun or something so she would get in her car and drive away and he'd do the same.

But she couldn't run. There was a smaller version of the thing that had been in the classroom on her neck, apparently slapping her with its butt. That wasn't why she couldn't run—she was doing a fine job of thrashing about, bouncing off walls and flailing her arms like a millionaire tossing away free cash. No, had she been looking where she was going and had a clear path, she could have already been in the parking lot right now if not in her car, peeling out into the street. There were three of those bugs—maybe the parent bugs of the one stinging her—blocking the exit.

Brad barely broke stride as he backhanded the thing a little less than twice the size of his fist off the redhead woman's neck, grabbed her by the wrist, and jerked her by the arm, trailing her behind him into the men's room. The thing's body had felt stiff and smooth, like petrified leather. He made a silent promise to himself to scrub his hand and wash it in bleach if he got out of here alive as he pressed his weight on the slow-closing door to shut it faster.

"Reep-reep-reep!" one of the bigger bugs said, hopping to the door. It peeped its head in, cocking it sideways, the one conical eye shifting in all directions. Its forearms shot out, one grabbing the door, the other pressing against the edge of the frame and he felt it push back against him, the door almost coming to a stop. Brad crouched even lower and doubled his effort, the bottom of his chin almost on level with the top of its head. Had he been insane enough to have the inclination, he could have leaned over and given it a kiss on the crown of its head.

For a brief moment, he thought he might be able to catch its head in the door. That he might have been able to kill it—at least one of them—but at the last moment, it ducked out of the threshold. But it hadn't been fast enough, the door caught the hooked tip of one of its front legs, neatly snapping it off.

"Reeeeeeep!" it said. Brad pressed his back against the door and jumped when *something* punched the other side, moving it the tiniest of an inch. He closed his eyes and counted as high and as fast as he could—anything to get his mind off the things that would eat his face if they got through an inch-and-a-half of wood.

"What was that?" the redhead said. Brad opened his eyes, for a moment not registering the human being standing in front of him. She wasn't looking at him, alternating between rubbing at her neck over and over and looking at whatever she was getting on her hand. She had angry red splotches everywhere she touched that looked monstrous zits. "What *was* that?" she said again.

"I…don't know," he said. "I don't know what those things are. But they look like praying mantises."

"No." She turned and looked at herself in the mirror. "That was not a praying mantis that stung me. A praying mantis only has six legs." She sounded way too calm for someone who'd just gotten stung by a giant bug. She was still shaken, but in his estimation, not shook up enough.

"You might be in shock," Brad said, somehow hoping his diagnosis would be calming to one of them. He became aware of his own heavy breathing and forced his intake of air to slow, feeling briefly like he was about to suffocate in his quasi-panic.

"I want to say it was an arachnid," she said. "Except it had antennae." She turned and looked at him. "Antennae!"

"We need to figure a way out of here."

The redhead started examining her face in the mirror. She put two hands on her face and tugged at her cheeks, pulling the lower lids away from her eyes. She worked her jaw up and down and opened her mouth wide while flexing her hands open and closed rapidly. Brad listened at the door and heard nothing.

"Do you have a cell phone?" he asked her. The holster to his own cell had broken and he'd left the phone in the car, thinking he'd only be here a few minutes. The redhead was pinching her forearm and apparently studying the skin after.

"It had to be some sort of paralytic. Had to be."

"Do you have a cell phone?" he asked again. She still seemed to not be aware he was three feet away from her. Brad chanced it, pulling away from the door and putting a hand on her shoulder. She jumped back from him and made a face.

"What's wrong—" He searched her eyes and saw she wasn't quite there. Maybe she was in shock or that was what the thing's stinger had done to her. That 'P' word she'd said or whatever. Maybe it had gotten her high. Maybe that kept their victims from running or at least getting too far away. But he needed to get her back on script if possible. He needed her to focus on what was happening right now. "What was that you called it?" he asked. "A…paralytic?"

"Yes-yes." She nodded.

"What if it kind of gives you a detached kind of surreal feeling? Like whatever's going on isn't *really* happening? Y'know, like when you're asleep and you realize you're dreaming."

She pulled back and her eyes danced around as if she were considering. "Yes." She made a popping sound with her mouth. "Yes, that's it. That makes sense. I'm not afraid at all anymore. But just a moment ago…*yes.*"

She looked like she was climbing back into herself and Brad clapped his hands. She blinked and looked as if seeing him for the first time.

"Do. You. Have. A. Cell. Phone?"

She nodded and reached around into the purse still on her shoulder. It was so large, she could have easily smuggled a newborn baby in it, but she found the cell in a second or two and handed it over. Brad opened his mouth to say she could have tried it, but instead flipped it open. No bars.

He called 9-1-1 anyway. After a pause of a few seconds it beeped and the screen indicated the call could not be connected. He deposited the phone into his pocket and the redhead didn't protest. Brad would get the both of them out of here if he could, but if whatever was coursing through her veins made her seize up at the wrong moment, he'd have to leave her. There was no way he was not getting back to his wife and Max.

"We have to figure a way out of here," he said.

"Yes," the redhead said. He looked at her and saw she was way too focused on him. Like she was trying to see his pores. He grabbed her by the shoulders.

"What's your name?" he asked her.

"Paisley," she said immediately. She didn't appear to be blinking.

"All right, Paisley. I'm Brad. I don't know what's happened out there, but we both saw it with our own eyes. Giant freaking bugs. Out there. We need to get out of here and back to my car so we can get away. That cool?"

"Cool." She nodded absent-mindedly. Her eyes were so dilated there was only a thin green circle of iris left.

"I haven't figured it yet, but we have to make a way past these things. We need weapons. Something we can fight these things off with. Hopefully, they've moved away from the door, but we have to be prepared to fight. I think it's only a matter of time before they get in here. Any ideas?"

He took it as a no after she'd stared blankly at him for several seconds.

"You cain't just walk out the front door," a man said from one of the stalls. Brad jumped, but Paisley remained locked on him.

"Hello?" he said.

"I know a way…if you take me, I can show you." Brad walked over to the stall and slowly toed open the door. There was a man in a custodian's blue uniform with 'Ed' stitched on the nametag, clutching a mop. His head looked swollen and there were three angry red knots on his chin, forehead, and one on his cheek that almost made him look like he was smiling. The bites stood out on his pale skin like black polka dots on a white sheet.

"Who are you?" Brad asked.

"I'm Ed," he said as if that were obvious. "I'm the maintenance engineer."

"How do we get out of here then?"

"I'm blind," Ed said. "From those things—the baby ones—got me real good four times." He made a circle with his hand around his face. "Three times and once on my back. I ran for the doors next over, but there were a bunch of them. At least a dozen, I'm not sure now." Brad's blood ran cold. He hoped Ed was overestimating. "I guess I've been in here about an hour or so."

"An hour?" Brad asked. "Why didn't you say anything when I came in here before? We could have gotten out then!"

"I…I fell asleep. Sorry, I don't know. I'm just really tired." Ed took a deep breath and let it out as if to illustrate his exhaustion.

Brad pursed his lips. He looked Ed up and down and nodded. He was maybe in his late forties, stubble-headed with talon-like tips of a tattoo peeking from beneath his shirt collar.

"Okay. You're with us." There was no use in beating the man up now. It was done. "Can you walk?"

"Think so." He put his feet under him and groaned, planting the mop and hauling himself up with both hands wrapped around it. "Ooowee! That hurt. I'm achy all over." He held an arm out and Brad took it. "You think it's permanent?" Ed turned his head in Brad's general direction. "The eyes, I mean. Think they turned my peepers off for good?"

Brad spotted the little cross dangling off the string chain around his neck. "I don't know," he said. "I'll say a prayer." The older man nodded like it was enough of an answer and wrapped a long arm around Brad's shoulder.

Paisley was still exactly where he'd left her. For a moment he despaired. There was no way he could escape with a blind, limping custodian and a near catatonic woman. He hated the idea of having to leave either of them behind, but he knew he would if it made the difference between all of them dead and just him alive.

But Paisley snapped out of it when they came up beside her. Her eyes still had that faraway look, but her face seemed to have taken on the animation of an actual human being.

"So, are we going to make a break for it or what?" she asked. Brad smiled.

"Yes. Can you hang onto Ed while I take a peek outside?" Her mouth turned into a grim line, but she nodded. Ed put his other arm out and she put it over her shoulder. "Uh, Ed, this is Paisley. Paisley…Ed." They seemed to relax slightly after the introduction. Paisley smiled a little, but Ed's swollen face was unreadable beyond his stuck-on smile.

He scratched his salt-and-pepper head. "Pleased to meet you, Paisley." Brad noted his Ps came out a little like Fs. "In case the exit is still blocked, we make a right when we get outside, head down the hall, past the double doors and make a left at the end of the hallway. There's an emergency exit right there."

Brad thought that was simple enough to remember.

"Ed, I need to borrow your mop if I could." The older man cocked his head as if considering the request. He held t out for Brad to take, transferring more of his bulk onto Paisley's slender frame. She grunted and made a face, but seemed to bear his weight all right.

Brad took the mop and turned for the door. He didn't want to go out there, but he didn't want to drag out the constant feeling of dread coursing through him. He grabbed the handle, took a breath, and gently pulled the door ever so slightly open.

He could see nothing in the narrow sliver of the darkened hallway. Panic seized him for a moment, but then he realized the hallway probably had motion-sensor lights, which meant there was nothing moving out there. He let the door shut and turned back to Paisley and Ed.

"I think we're all clear," he whispered. "We'll go around the corner, out the door, and to the red Grand Am outside." Brad fished his keys out of his pocket and fixed his car key in his hand. "I'll drive us straight to the hospital and Paisley you can call 9-1-1 to let somebody know what's happening here."

She nodded and Ed licked his lips.

"I sure could use a drink of water, but I can wait if we're this close," the other man said.

"I'll buy us all a round of three dollar bottled water at the hospital," Brad said and all of them laughed quietly. "All right, let's roll."

They tucked in close behind him. Brad hooked a finger over the handle of the bathroom door with the same hand that held the mop. He held up his free hand and counted down from five.

After one he threw the door open wide and charged out into the hallway, the handle of the mop firmly in both hands, soppy business-end out. The lights came on and there were easily twenty of them choking this corner of the hallway, blocking the exit. Several of them reared up, their subset of forelegs scrabbling at the air.

"Reep-reep-reep-reep-reep!" they all said in unison. By the hind legs of many of them were tinier mantis-like creatures skittering about, left and right. They were more bright yellow than grey like the adults and he recalled that brief contact of leathery chitin.

"Ruuuun!" he shouted and one leapt at him. Brad jabbed it in the chest, sending it onto its side atop two others. There was a brief moment where he could feel those cone-like eyes sliding all over him and he dipped low, sweeping at as many of their legs as he could. He knocked several down and batted the slower young ones aside that didn't have the wherewithal to dance out of the way. But about three-quarters of the way through his swing a bigger adult dipped its head and grabbed the head of the mop in its massive mandibles. He felt the effort through the handle just before it bit the business end off.

Alright, then, he thought before taking a half step back and jabbing the thing in the chest with the now sharp spear. It made a high-pitched 'Ooo!' sound as he drew his weapon out of its body and instead of descending on him, the others piled atop the wounded bug. Brad wasted no time, turning to run after Paisley and Ed, who had managed to get ahead of him by a good fifteen yards.

The one he'd stabbed went 'Ooo!' three more times and went silent. He didn't bother looking over his shoulder to see them devour one of their own. Brad had no doubt they were faster than him and he ducked his head as he ran past the office windows and the relative few ahead of him on the walls, floor, and ceiling.

There were golf ball-sized dents in the door to the classroom he'd shut earlier. Brad caught up as they came to another 'L' in the hallway. He looked to the left and spotted the red exit sign and the orange-painted door. He pulled them along, but another mantis creature skittered out of what had to have been another open door to the same classroom. Its head turned—not in their direction, although its eye definitely turned their way. Brad took a wide stance, gave a few preparatory hops and threw the spear and it bounced off the wall, clattering to the floor. The bug skittered sideways, regarding the fallen stick on the floor.

Ed began a wild coughing fit as the bug faced them. "Is it another one?" he said.

"Yeah," Brad answered.

"Point me toward it."

"What? No."

"*Trust* me," he said. Brad chanced a look over his shoulder at the group at the other end of the hall. They weren't exactly chasing, but they had gotten closer. He pulled the older man away from Paisley, put his hands on Ed's shoulders and aimed him. Brad put his palms on his back and gave him the lightest shove he thought Ed could manage.

"Alright, you *sucka*," Ed began, getting into a half crouch and spreading his arms apart. "Come here! I got somethin' for ya." He took a few steps, snatched at open space when it hopped out of the way, then called over his shoulder, "Ay, call out the time."

Brad was about to ask him what he meant, but the man's meaning clicked into place. "Two o'clock." Ed turned slightly to his right and took another step forward. The bug hopped back a couple paces, turning its head to consider the human approaching it.

"Eleven." He turned and followed.

"Two."

"Midnight."

"Ten."

"One."

Brad and Paisley followed behind him, hand-in-hand, looking frequently behind them. Either the bugs were disorganized or they weren't necessarily after them because they only saw this one for the next couple minutes.

Ed stopped suddenly, pitching his head up and down as if he were looking around.

"I've been at this school nigh on thirty-three years." He dug a small knife out of his shirt pocket and unfolded the blade from the handle. It clicked in place and he held it aloft in one hand. "I know every nook and cranny in this place by now and there ain't nowhere a mouse or no other critter that didn't belong could hide where I couldn't find it. *Oh*, my back!" Ed drew in a sharp breath of air and Brad noticed for the first time the diamond of wetness that had started under the collar of his uniform that ended just above his belt line. Ed gripped the knife in his hand and when the bug bumped into the mop bucket as it backed away from him again, he leapt on it, wrapping his arm around the upper part of its body.

It tried to push him off with those upraised legs and Ed brought the knife up into the underside of its body.

"Rrrrp-rrrp," it said as he gutted the thing, thick green sludge saturating the sleeve of his uniform and slopping onto the floor. Its mandibles snapped at him, but blind or no, Ed was ready and yanked his head back just in time. He brought the knife around and buried it in the top of the creature's head and wrenched it down and out. That had to have been a killing blow, but its body bucked harder against him, finally freeing itself and scuttling away on all six legs straight into a wall.

Brad watched, rapt, until the awful smell hit him and he realized the others would be along momentarily. The exit door was just ahead and Paisley squeezed his hand and pointed. He nodded and they both went to Ed and grabbed him off his knees. They dragged him the remaining few feet and pushed the door open and were outside.

"Reep-reep-reep-reep!" came a chorus of bug voices deeper inside the building they heard over and over, all in unison. Brad saw maybe two dozen, but it sounded like many, many more.

"Not it," Ed said, sagging in their arms. Brad looked at him and saw the man had four punctures in his upper chest. So it had gotten him after all.

Brad jumped as the door shut behind them. "Alright. They haven't done anything yet." A bug the size of a German shepherd hopped toward them. Before they could move it jumped on Ed and sank the barbs to either side of its mandibles deep into his chest. Blood exploded from his mouth and his unswollen eye went wide. It wrenched where it fastened onto him until Brad felt something inside the man pop. Brad looked up and saw a team of them heading their way from the rear of the school.

"Leave him!" Paisley said, pulling on his arm. "Leave him!" He ran with her around the side of the building, passing the school's playground set. Insects—the regular ones—buzzed all around him, but he noticed they didn't really seem to be bothering her. He briefly thought about just continuing to run, but they crossed the parking lot to their cars. He'd forgotten the keys in his hand, but looked at them now and plugged one in the passenger door.

He opened the door, but Paisley only looked at him with that zombie stare.

"I can't go," she said.

"What? What do you mean?"

"It's Ed. He was bitten by those bugs and so was I."

"So what?" He shook his head. "We'll get you a shot or something at the hospital."

"They never came after you. You weren't bit."

He just stared at her.

"The paralytic wasn't just a paralytic. I think they laid eggs."

"How could you know that? You couldn't—"

"I *do* know. My back is starting to ache. And I guarantee you the eggs they laid in Ed…" She bit her lip. "They have them now. They *harvested* them."

"But the hospital—

"*No.* Just get in your car and drive away. 4520 Atkins. Call the police. Save my little girl."

He knew she would fight him if he tried to force her in. Brad nodded and got in the car, climbing over into the driver's seat after shutting the door.

She turned and headed for the door, wiping her cheek as she walked. Something in him screamed this was wrong, that he should have been right there with her wherever she was going. Paisley held something in her hand and Brad watched until he saw her unfold Ed's knife.

He thought of Max and his wife and his promise to make it home to them no matter what. He twisted the key in the ignition and the engine roared to life, the fear of the car not starting quelled in the pit of him. Brad hovered a hand over the steering wheel, but made a tight fist instead of honking the horn.

If the bugs' goal had been to kill him or lay eggs in him as Paisley had supposed then he had won. But as he pulled out of the lot, the car jangling across the sunken approach and onto the clean straight street, he couldn't help but feel like he'd won a far distant second prize.

This wasn't right. The hero was supposed to get the girl and save the day, instead it was her sacrificing herself to save him. Well, not really to save him, but he felt like one of them was getting cheated. He figured the hero—at least in his case—was supposed to make it home to the woman and the boy in time for dinner. That he was supposed to play and help with homework and put to bed. Not gallivant about, saving damsels in distress. But still, it didn't sit right with him. Brad hadn't even killed one of those things.

He looked up and saw the sky was dark with them. Swarms of insects like a washing tide. It chilled him that there were so many they made a mock night above him.

They peppered the air around his car. Another bug, a small one of a type he'd seen before, landed on the windshield. It seemed to regard him a moment and he hit the wipers, smashing it and streaking its guts across the glass before it could fly away.

One down.

I do not remember writing this story at all. Apparently, I wrote it about five years ago. I wish there was more to tell.

A Cup of Joe

Buster saw it roaming through the office, a white coffee mug clenched in its fist by the handle. Whatever the hell it was, it was doing a pretty poor job pretending to be human. For starters, the fact Buster noticed was a big sign. But the thing wore a suit, had a head of black hair trimmed neatly, two eyes, and skin. But other than that, there was very little that was *homo sapien*-ish about it.

Not that anyone else seemed to notice. Sarah and Vince waved to it and it held up its cup in response. Matt, Greg, and Tito didn't mind when it passed right between them in the midst of their usual, Monday morning *Game of Thrones* recap. And Tilly looked over her shoulder as it passed.

Buster was more curious than afraid and followed, slipping into the department before the door closed. It winked at the cute analyst on the other side of the cubicle partition straight ahead and continued on its way.

"How's it goin', Buster?" Kay asked, peering at him as he hung back by the door. "What can I do you for?"

"Oh, uh," he began, patting his thighs absentmindedly. "Y'know, I think I forgot the check request form on my desk." His eyes drifted back to the thing standing in the center between four cubicles, including Lana, the cute analyst. It stepped toward the heavyset woman whose name Buster could never remember and did something so fast he wasn't sure what he'd seen.

It had had something in one hand and held it up to the woman's face while putting its cup beneath. A dash of red shot out, and it quickly stepped back, putting the cup to its lips and tipping it back. It made loud, smacking sounds, made a face, then turned the cup upside down, pouring the rest onto the floor.

"So…you gonna get that request down here?" Kay asked, drawing Buster's attention back to her.

"Um, yeah," he said. "Yeah." Buster turned fully to her and smiled. "I'm sorry, I haven't had coffee; I'm just not right yet, y'know?"

The corner of her mouth pulled into a knowing smile and she said, "Mm-hm."

Buster didn't really like Lana, the pretty analyst, but a lot of guys did. He decided to let Kay think he was staring at her.

The creature looked around and decided upon Pete, the ever-widening analyst who looked like he'd probably explode out of his clothes somewhere around February if he kept up his current diet. He was a recent father, and Buster actually liked him, so it was with some reticence that he watched whatever it was as it reached for him and tapped him with that silver thing in its hand, pouring a little bit of Pete into its cup.

Apparently, it liked Pete. It made a great show of smacking its lips and sipping some more from its cup. Not that Pete seemed to mind. He leaned back in his chair and began speaking to the person across the aisle, an older Asian lady Buster didn't know.

He didn't hear their words, but when they both stopped as it put the silver nozzle-thing to Pete's skin again, the silence between them was jarring. Buster looked at Kay as if to ask, 'Are you seeing this?' but she had already gone back to her work.

It filled its cup to the top and pocketed its tap before holding the cup in both hands up to its nose and taking a deep whiff.

"Oh, man," Pete said and blinked. "I just got a little lightheaded. What was I saying?"

The woman across from him began to respond, but Buster didn't hear. He watched as the creature strolled toward him, opened the door and waved to Kay as it went out.

"See you later, Kay," Buster said absentmindedly, slipping out before the door shut.

Buster saw it several more times throughout the day, stopping in various departments and filling up on employees. It grew more careless with each refill, spilling as it filled its cup and stumbling a little as if it were getting drunk. When it filled up from Mark in Legal, it fumbled the cup and spilled half on its shirt and the rest on the floor.

It was sometime after lunch when he finally ran into the creature in the restroom.

Buster was finishing at the urinal when it came n, bloody cup in hand. It had a half smile on its face and nodded to him as it went to the sinks. He flushed and joined it, turning the faucet on with one hand and getting two pumps of liquid soap with the other.

"Say, are you new here?" he said to the creature.

It stiffened, blood coating its hands and shirt sleeves halfway up its forearms. It opened its mouth but didn't seem certain if it knew how to answer.

"Y-yes," it said, with a voice that was obviously fake. It was trying for Morgan Freeman smooth, but it came off as something far less secure. "I work in HR."

Buster snorted a little. Three women worked in HR, four if their intern was counted. It would have had to put on a woman's skin to pull off that lie.

"C'mon, we both know that isn't true. Where are you from?"

The creature had been intensely focused on the running water, rinsing the blood off its cup.

"Imlay City."

Buster shook his head.

"Did you come alone?"

It finally looked at him, fury in its eyes.

"We have an armada! We will destroy—"

Buster zapped it with his own nozzle and it evaporated into a dense gas hovering in the air where it had stood. He finished rinsing its cup and turned off the faucet.

"Nice cup," he said and turned back to the gas. Buster scooped as much of the creature as he could into it and it settled into a steaming dark liquid. He tasted as Randy from Treasury came in.

"Buster!" he said, making a beeline for the urinal. "How you doin', man?"

"Good," he said, wondering where the creature had really come from, wanting more. He slipped out before the door could swing closed. "Real good."

Another story I don't remember the genesis of. I think I submitted it to an online magazine that no longer exists but I'm not sure if it ever got published.

Perfect C

Joe didn't get it. The little red man constantly banged away on the piano, but no one seemed to mind. They all sat there while he used his big fists like hammers across the keyboard, knocking off black and white keys along with pieces of the wood frame.

Admittedly, Joe wasn't a big music guy. Music just didn't grab him the way it did with most people. Besides, the man was destroying the piano. Why was everyone just sitting there? Joe may have been a lowly janitor, but he should do something about this.

Sure, it sounded okay. Joe had heard classical before and this kind of sounded like it. The way all the people just sat around with serene looks on their faces to varying degrees must have meant they were enjoying it at least, but enough was becoming enough. Joe just couldn't stand around while the red man destroyed such fine craftsmanship. That piano was something he *could* appreciate.

He left his mop and bucket just before one of the legs fell off, taking his time to cross the large room.

"It's a blend of Chopin and Mozart," one older man said to the woman seated next to him. She nodded in agreement, swaying her head back and forth in time with the 'music'.

The little red man had a madman's focus, making himself even smaller by hunching down so his face was close to the keys. Sweat ran down his face and stained through the jacket of his burgundy tuxedo with tails hanging down farther than his dangling feet. His hands worked up and down, swinging high over his head before crashing down again on the keys.

Joe was close enough now to see the feral yellow of the little red man's eyes, a pink milky fluid spilling like tears. He regarded Joe for an instant without stopping his assault on the piano.

Joe stopped himself before grabbing the little red man. For a brief moment he felt unsure of himself, afraid even. He knew he didn't belong in here. Not with these kinds of people. Maybe they'd paid for the little red man to come in and do this. But he'd cleaned this piano before. Many times before over the years; there was no way the owners would want it destroyed like this.

And the little red man was obviously not normal. For starters, his head was so big—and round to boot—atop a child-sized body with thick, rough-looking fists with tufts of hair. Not to mention his red skin. It was the shade of a dark red wine stain Joe had had to clean out of the carpet in this very room during a benefit—he'd hated having to put on a black and white tux just to clean up so the guests wouldn't be 'disturbed'. His nose was also another feature that made him look other than human. It was long and hooked, dipping past his upper lip, appearing as though, had he desired, he could have puckered up and kissed the tip. The wispy strands of long jet hair were flying around his mostly bald head like a flag in a high wind when Joe grabbed his wrist after a cluster of piano wires snapped.

"That is enough!" he said.

The audience gasped.

Their reaction made Joe's gut clench. As sweat crept out above his upper lip, he felt as though he'd done something wrong. He let go of the little red man's wrist, wanting to clasp his hand over his nametag and run out of the room. The little red man grunted as he pounded out a last few notes on the baby grand before it collapsed.

The first punch turned his knee to the side. Joe didn't realize, but his long high-pitched scream was in a perfect C. By the time it was all over, the audience was rapt, giving the two of them a standing ovation as Joe lay in a bloodied heap.

Gerald Dean Rice

This was a short I wrote for a website. I don't want to give the name because I'm sure I'll get it wrong. I had big plans for this idea and I may wind up expanding on it. I think it's a novel idea that could make for an excellent screenplay with the proper execution.

Friend

The first blow caught Edgar completely off guard. Cindy's head exploded, and her body careened into him, sending them both over the back of the couch. He lay there with the sack of meat that was his co-worker a moment ago lying on top of him, blinking bits of skull out of his eyes and wiping blood from his face.

From back where they were, Marcia was screaming. The door closed. Her screaming stopped and, a moment later, began again even louder. There was another loud *thunk* followed by a thick spraying sound and she fell quiet.

Edgar thought he should be more panicked. They were both dead and the killer was still in here. He looked around, but his vision was still blurry. He didn't see anyone.

Then someone was standing over him.

Edgar twisted his head around to see the pair of work boots. He flopped Cindy's body up against the couch to get a better look and felt something cold, wet, and large press up against his cheek.

He held very still, feeling nothing but his heartbeat and the large metal thing the killer had used to smash Cindy and Marcia's heads on the side of his face.

"You don't have to do this." He sounded much too calm. He should have been begging, pleading, but this foreign monotonous voice he'd never spoken with before was the only thing that would come out of him. "I can help you."

Everything more than two feet away was blurry, but it looked like the killer cocked his head.

"Look, they—they had it coming. I work with them everyday—I'd know. You just did what you had to do. But me? No, you don't need to do that. I can be your friend."

The killer knelt.

There was a gray mask. Edgar couldn't see a seam or anything where it was affixed to his head, like it was a part of his face. But there were only two gaping black eye holes and a bigger one for the mouth. Kind of like an electrical outlet.

Everything else looked normal. Blue plaid shirt, rolled up at the sleeves, revealing well-muscled forearms on an otherwise thin frame and khaki pants with a sharp, ironed-in crease.

"You could use a friend, couldn't you?" Edgar's pulse slowed as Cindy's blood soaking into the carpet cooled beneath him. He put his hand to the handle of the killer's weapon and gentled it away. "I know I could." He rolled over onto his stomach and saw the killer's shoulders tense.

"Hey, we're all friends here. It's cool." He brought his knees up, slicking across saturated carpet, and stared into the eye holes of the killer's mask.

"I'm Edgar." He held out his hand. The killer looked at it. "So, what do we—"

The killer stood up, walked around the couch, and sat down.

Edgar looked at the back of his head, a wily mass of hair, and then to the door. If he were quick, he might be able to make it. He stood, and just then, those empty eyeholes turned to Edgar as the killer patted the back of the couch.

Edgar joined him, almost spilling over Marcia's half-headless body, splayed across the floor. An arc of red had splashed from the coffee table to the loveseat across from them.

"I can help you clean this up." The killer cocked his head again. "So, is this your last thing for today?" The killer checked his watch. "I mean, after this, you wanna grab a beer…or…*something*?"

No answer. Edgar was beginning to worry when the killer stood up.

"So, where we goin'?"

The killer looked at him. He shook his head. Edgar crawled backward on the couch, curling his legs up like a loaded spring.

"But I thought we were—"

The killer didn't move.

"Yeah. You're right. Hurry. You need to get out of here." Edgar laid on the floor and closed his eyes. And he listened to the killer breathe.

Gerald Dean Rice

In 2020, I was invited to participate in a horror gross-out contest. I'd heard of these and wanted to try it out. I came in 3rd place, I believe. Not bad for my first try. Warning: this story references peepee and poopoo.

The Old Hog

Granddad had to pee again. My pop had called me over to do it because he couldn't. He'd fallen face first into a toilet full of shit and broken his neck and was now convalescing in bed. I wasn't about to make the argument he should have gone to the hospital with a broken neck just like I wasn't about to ask for details as to how exactly he fell into said beshitted toilet.

My ma couldn't do it on account of her carpal tunnel. She'd never worked with her hands in her life and yet somehow, her hands at rest always looked like she was ready for a can of beer. Also, the fact she and my sister were women, and Granddad was starting to lose his marbles and was prone to grabbing a little ass if a woman was holding onto the old hog.

I'd done it once when I was a teenager when my father had been out of town on business. Granddad was living in the basement back then, same as now, and he'd been old twenty years ago.

I kissed my ma when I came through the door and waved to my sister as I headed to the basement. Granddad was good for two pisses a day, and I hadn't been around for the first this morning, so my sister had had to clean up the aftermath. No surprise she'd still looked green and freshly scrubbed as I came in.

"Hey old man!" I said, coming down the stairs. My pop would've kicked my ass even with a broken neck if he heard me call his father that. Half blind, neuropathy in his extremities, and he'd lost his senses of taste and smell in Korea, but Granddad's ears were still sharp.

"Get down here, you sonofabitch!" he yelled back at me. "My back teeth are floatin'!"

I strapped on the pair of gloves I'd brought with me and helped him stand.

"Those vinyl?" he asked.

"No," I said, confused. "Latex."

"I'm allergic. Take 'em off."

I was crestfallen as he quickly undid the zipper on his brown slacks. I don't know where to get pants like those, but they were like uniforms for elderly men. He let them drop to his feet, and there was that smell that dialed me back two decades.

"Get the bucket," he said.

"Huh?" I was frozen in the haze of old and ammonia smell.

"The bucket!" he shouted. "I can't just go right here on the floor!"

I saw the old Folgers can filled with his chew juice by his recliner and a pan over by the old Zenith television, but no bucket. I stepped over and grabbed the pan, put it between his feet and turned to him. The smell of liniment and tangy chew mixed with the stank of saliva slowly joined the nauseous bouquet. I tried tucking the horizontal island of flesh between my nose and upper lip over my nostrils, but the flavor in the air was like a weight on my tongue.

"You got this, old man?"

"No." He turned those rheumy, pearlescent eyes on me and raised a hand, opening and closing it like a lobster claw. "I can't grip no more. You gotta do it."

Everything got small and large at the same time. I felt like I'd stepped outside of my body and was standing next to myself. Nobody told me that. I wasn't ready to…I couldn't…

"So…so you need me to what…exactly?" I asked, my lips tingling, though that might have been from the poisonous levels of liniment vapor in the air.

"Well, *you* gotta pull out the old hog. Let me know when you got it aimed."

I hadn't intended to be anywhere near. The backsplatter…the steam heat…

"Hurry up. Once I stand up, the flood starts comin'!"

I didn't want to, but I weighed his demand against the Exxon-like cleanup my sister must have done earlier. I noted the warped appearance of the floor tiles all the way to the stairs, like they'd been *soaked* and had never settled back down right.

I turned my brain off as best I could and went for it, peeling the top of his boxers down from his clammy skin. He was pubeless and smooth as I reached in and it was…*soft* and malleable like one of those homemade stress balls.

"That's not it, sonny," he said. Every hair on my body stood up and screamed—I was sure that wasn't his sack *but what the hell was it?* "Up and over to the left."

I opened my hand and whatever I'd been holding expanded and filled the space between it and my fingers. I did as he told me and it was amazing how I'd missed it. It was—no pun intended—like going to the bush and not seeing any bushes.

Granddad had the collective penis of three average men. I could feel him going, and thankfully, the hose was as long as it was because I barely had enough time to aim.

The stream was yellow, but not urine yellow. It was a brilliant shade of pus, and as soon as it hit the bottom of the pan, it began brewing a foamy head like an Irish stout. There was something a little more solid than urine that provided an extra splash interspersing with the stream.

The smell wasn't a smell, it was two fists around my lungs. I gagged and Granddad slapped me across the back of the head.

"Pay attention to where you're aimin'!" he shouted.

I managed to look over, and dammit if I didn't see that Granddad had a Prince Albert, and he was sprouting from his additional holes. I adjusted as best I could, but there was going to be a mess. I was just mitigating the disaster as best as possible.

Gerald Dean Rice

As the hose continued unceasingly, I started looking around. The mottled skin of his penis and the scar tissue on it. Granddad had been in Korea, but his cock had been in its own war. And then it kicked into another gear. I had to readjust his aim again as the stream strengthened and the pan I was sure would be more than enough a moment ago was suddenly near to overfilling.

"No! Wait!" I shouted, the head of his flood beginning to bubble over the lip of the pan. I finally spotted the bucket he'd been referring to in a corner. It was easily three times larger than the pan I saw. In my panic, I let go of the hog and it began to whip all around like an unmanned fire hose. Without thinking, I stepped in front of him as if I could block it, and the pressure of the ammonia-rich, strangely warm—and slightly mentholated—urine almost knocked me over.

I dashed for the bucket, snatched it from the floor, and slid back to Granddad on my knees like I had just scored a game-clenching goal in soccer, my skin burning beneath the tiled floor. I was hosed in the face and held the bucket up, half to catch, half to collect, and it wasn't long before my arms were shaking because of the weight he was putting in it.

Finally, the stream began breaking, signaling he was coming to an end. I trembled in fear and near muscular exhaustion, my shoulders and upper back on fire as he kept going.

In place of shaking off, Granddad banged the anaconda against the inside of the metal bucket, surprisingly lithe through the hip, with fists propped at his sides like he was a superhero.

When he was done, I barely could hold up the bucket. I realized what we looked like. He was a piss-god and I was his lone congregant. I tried to lower it gently, but I cramped and off-balance, pitched forward, headfirst.

Common sense should have told me to have my mouth closed, but no. I dunked myself into Granddad's homebrew like I was bobbing for apples, my skin somewhere between numb and tingling. I whipped my head back when I felt his shaft slide down inside the back of my shirt and pulled Granddad down on top of me. He screamed, slapping those lobster claw hands on my shoulders and ears. His taint, balls, and whatever else he had stewing inside those boxers must have gone sliding over me just before I catapulted him halfway across the room.

My pop, broken neck or not, was going to kill me. I controlled my wretching as much as possible and got Granddad up again. Amazingly, he was fine.

He looked at me with those foggy eyes.
"I gotta take a shit."

Gerald Dean Rice

I remember getting this idea and banging it out in a day in a Starbucks (before the pandemic). I was writing it for an anthology and either I missed the deadline, it was rejected, or the antho fell apart. I honestly don't remember. This is a rarer story for me because it's largely bloodless, but I think it has a great degree of being unsettling.

One of Everything

Blue knew there was gon' be trouble as soon as that northerner came through the door. He didn't look right, just way too happy. Way happier than a man oughtta be at that time 'a day. He looked like the type to jump outta bed and say some foolishness like he was ready to seize the day with a hook of his arm and a wink of his eye and not another soul in the room. His suit was way too white too.

Blue was an early riser, but not by choice. He had to be here. Well, not here, but he needed a coffee and one of Merl's number threes to start his day right.

This fella looked like he was just grateful to be wherever he was. Obnoxious.

"Good mornin', gentlemen," the man said with what sounded like one of those northern Midwest accents. Maybe Ohio or Michigan. Blue had a cousin live uppere. Blue'd visited and hated every minute of it.

"Unh," Blue said.

Merl just stared at him, squeezin' that spatula like he was juicin' it. Merl had somethin' wrong with him. It took him a good while to process, especially if it was somethin' or someone he didn't know. Catchin' his head in a thrasher when he was fifteen probly didn't help none, and people typically hung the excuse on that, but Blue had been 'round long enough to remember Merl'd been off even before then. The thrasher sure hadn't helped none, though.

"Mornin'," Merl finally said, still starin' at him with those dead bug eyes. The stranger kept on starin' at him as he sat, like he ain't pick up on somethin' bein' off 'bout the house chef.

"You got a menu?"

Blue took offense at the man alterin' his speech like he was tryin' to appeal to them. Plus, the fact the menu was right there in front of his face. Merl took one clumsy step forward—he always looked set to fall over when he moved but usually kept his feet—and slapped his fat palm on the menu on the counter and slid it the four inches or so closer to the stranger.

"Oo, thank you!"

"Start ye off?" Merl asked.

The man's eyes rolled up and to the left as he sucked his lips into his mouth. "I'll have…coffee," he said. "Black."

Merl stood a moment longer, starin'. Then he turned and headed back into the kitchen, somehow the back of his shirt just as filthy as his apron. It was barely five in the mornin'. Blue had no clue how that boy could be so dirty already.

"My name's Harvey," the man said, spinnin' in his barstool to face Blue. "Harvey Denton." He held out his hand.

Blue's suspicion was roused, but unless he had reason not to, he could shake his hand.

"Benson Harvey," Blue said. "Everybody calls me Blue."

"Then I too shall call you Blue." They shook, the man's hand was supple but not moist, his firm grip but not overly so, like he was tryin' to crush Blue's hand.

"Pleasure to make your acquaintance." Harvey looked around, then settled his green eyes on Blue. "So, what are you having?"

Blue glanced at his half empty plate. "Bacon and fried eggs. Toast."

"Mm, sounds delicious."

Merl came chargin' out the kitchen too fast, cup in his giant hand and he slapped it on the counter. With the steam comin' off it, Blue knew it would take ten minutes before ol' Harvey would get a sip. The coffee maker behind the counter was broken and they had a big monster in the back that only brewed coffee boilin' hot.

The stranger looked at the cup with a blank expression before pickin' it up and chuggin' the whole thing in one go. Merl refreshed the cup.

Blue sat up, sure the man had just cooked his entire digestive tract. "Mister, you okay?"

Harvey sat the cup down gently, smacked his lips and looked at Merl. "Ahh, that was delicious. Best I ever had. Could you make me a number three?"

Merl stood just there for a goodly five seconds or so. Blue thought he saw a tinge of surprise on the boy's face. Hell, why did Blue keep thinkin' of him as a boy? They were the same age take a year or two. After his accident, Merl had stayed in the hospital long enough he had to repeat freshman year. Well, would have, 'cept after his accident Merl hadda go to a special school up in Arkansas to relearn how to do just 'bout everything.

"How do you want your eggs?" Merl asked.

"However *you* like them, my friend."

"Just do over easy," Blue said and Merl backed up into the kitchen.

He started knockin' around in there. As much of a clod he was in every other way, he was just as close to a ballerini as he could be in the kitchen. There wasn't nothin' he couldn't cook just as good as a Alain Ducasse, Pierre Gagnaire, or any of them other fancy chefs. When Blue's feet hit the floor in the mornin', the thing that really got him goin' was Merl's number three and a steamin' cuppa coffee.

"I am *fine*, how about you?" Harvey asked. Blue took a moment to realize the man was talkin' to him. He hadn't turned to address him.

"That coffee is usually pretty hot. You sure you didn't scald yourself?"

"I *like* it hot." Harvey slowly rotated to face him. There was somethin' not right about the man's face. He didn't have a freaky eyeball or nothin'. Just not right.

A minute later Merl was back with a plate. Another number three. That was the other thing about Merl. He was *damn* fast. He sat the plate down, and Harvey picked up a roll of silverware, unwrapped his fork and knife. He took care not to touch anything with his hands, scoopin' up all four slices of bacon and puttin' them between the eggs. He folded the eggs over and managed to shovel the whole thing up and place it on top of both slices of toast. Then he put down the fork and picked up the plate with his free hand, tipped it toward his open mouth and swept the food in with the fork.

It only took three bites and it was the most amazin' thing Blue had ever seen.

"Ahh, that was delicious. Best I ever had. Could you make me a number one and a number two?"

Merl's mouth opened and closed like he was 'bout to say somethin' and forgot. He took a step backward and stopped like he forgot where he was goin'. Then he disappeared back into the kitchen.

Blue wasn't really afraid at that point and didn't see any real danger in the man's odd eatin' habits.

Despite makin' twice as much food, Merl was just as fast as before and he popped out the kitchen with both plates and placed them down next to the one Harvey'd set aside. He prepared the food just like before, the number two havin' sausage 'stead of bacon, the number one havin' hash browns in place 'a toast.

Then one after the other, Harvey sucked food into his mouth same as before, gently replaced both plates 'n said, "Ahh, that was delicious. Best I ever had. Could you make me a number…"

Blue had stopped listenin', decidin' he'd seen just about enough. He had work needed tendin'. He stood and dug out his billfold and slid out a wrinkled twenty and dropped it next to his plate. He'd never been the type to waste food, even when he didn't like what he was eatin', but he really couldn't finish after what he'd just seen.

Merl came out with four plates. Blue estimated those were numbers four through seven, but he didn't even wanna look at 'em.

"Where you goin'?" Merl asked.

"I gotta get to the farm," Blue said.

Merl looked at his unfinished food and the money, then back at Blue.

"I cain't make change," Merl said. "Marsha don't let me work the machine."

Merl had a voice like somebody blowin' over an empty jug. He was six-foot eight, easy, and had to be near about three hundred pounds. But he always sounded like a frightened li'l boy when it came to the cash register. Blue was not without sympathy. He'd known him half his life and could tell it wasn't just the 'machine' scarin' Merl. It was also the reason why Blue wanted to leave right now.

Merl didn't wanna be left alone with the stranger.

He sat the plates down, left hand, right hand, left arm, right arm, bobblin' back and forth like a buoy. Blue's heart skipped when he looked like he was fixin' to drop the third one, the number six by Blue's estimate. But he stuck the landin' and no sooner were all four down then the stranger—he'd ceased bein' a Harvey to Blue by then…they did share a name, after all—began consolidatin' the food all onto one plate and foldin' and scoopin' until it was one large mess that shouldn'ta been good enough for the hogs, but a moment later…

"Ahh, that was delicious. Best I ever had. Could you make me a number eight, a number nine, a number ten, a number eleven, *and* a number twelve?"

Blue's keys fell out of his hand. This time, he was the one standin' there processin' after Merl finally went back in the kitchen. And true to form, Merl didn't take one second longer than he ever had makin' all four plates.

He placed everything in front of the man, carefully, and stepped back. The fear on his face was clear and Blue wondered if his own face looked the same. Merl glanced his way, then back as the growin' stacks of plates next to the stranger were about to rise again.

It was too disgustin' to watch. It was…unseemly. The stranger sucked the food down just as fast as before.

"Ahh, that was delicious. Best I ever had. Could you make me a number…" He looked confused. He'd gone through the whole breakfast menu. "When is lunch?"

Merl's eyes worked like his brain was gettin' hot. His lips moved like he was practicin' the words 'fore he actually spoke and Blue knew what he was fixin' to say and jumped in.

"Lunch ain't 'til ten-thirty," Blue said, hopin' this was the end of the show.

Harvey turned his head toward the pie case.

"I'd like a wedge of pie."

He waited for Merl to eventually bring over the whole thing. He lifted the lid and the stranger ate all seven slices.

"Ahh, that was delicious. Best I ever had. When's lunch?"

"Hey, pal, you payin' for all this, right?" Blue asked.

Harvey slapped a hundred dollar bill on the counter.

"I cain't work the machine!"

"It's okay, Merl." Blue had hoped the man could pick up that he was just tryin' to get him out. "Why don't you...why don't you make your lunch special?"

"Lunch special?" Merl asked. "But lunch ain't 'til ten-thirty."

"Yeah. The spicy one." Blue figured this guy had to be some kind of weirdo competitive eater. He probly could pack away one of everything. But Marsha's homemade hot sauce had sent many a man to his knees.

Merl seemed like he understood. He gave Blue a raise of his chin and disappeared into the kitchen again. It was a long seven minutes with Blue standin' there, watchin', the stranger just facin' forward, waitin' for Merl to come back.

Finally, he came out. It was a lone plate, piled high with spicy fried chicken, spaghetti, a handful of banana peppers, a bowl of chili, and cheddar-cheese cornbread with jalapenie peppers in it with a heapin' dollop of cha-cha on top. Blue folded his arms and smiled, feelin' a note of satisfaction as Merl sat the plate down and backed away like it was sittin' on dynamite.

The stranger hesitated for just a moment, like he was processin' what to eat on first. He picked up the bowl of chili, sat it down, skewered a drumstick with his fork, then slid it off. Then he dumped the cornbread in the chili, breakin' it up and swirlin' it around like he was tryin' to soak up as much of it as he could. Then he dumped it all over the chicken and spaghetti, stirred the peppers in with the noodles with his fork and began weavin' some sorta food envelope. It was amazin' to watch, and when he'd finished a minute later, he raised the plate and downed the whole works, bones 'n all.

Even though he felt like wretchin', Blue was in absolute awe.

"Hey, Mister," he said. "You okay?" Blue was even more concerned about the bones than the spiciness of the food and the stranger didn't look too good. He also realized with all that this man had eaten, he hadn't belched once.

"That was...delicious. Best I ever had," the stranger said. He sounded like he was chokin' on one of those bones. Blue thought he saw a bulge in the man's throat.

The thought the man was fixin' to die crossed Blue's mind and he couldn't deny to anyone that he'd been here. Everyone in town knew he had a number three six days a week at this time of the mornin'.

He took a step forward as the man's face turned red then crimson. Harvey stood still for a long moment. That was definitely a bulge. Blue hesitated to touch him but finally made up his mind when he started turnin' purple.

Then Harvey's complexion returned to normal and he said, "How's the fried apple pie?"

Merl cooked four up and then they were gone down his gullet, still steamin'. Right out the fryer, those were like molten lava, Blue suspected the skin on the roof of his mouth had to be peelin' off.

"You okay?" he asked for what felt like the millionth time.

"Absolutely!" the stranger asked, that cheeriness still in his voice. He spun toward Blue again. "I'm only here for a bit and I just had to stop by for a bite. We don't have eatin' like this at home!"

"And where is that?"

The stranger cocked his head to one side as if he hadn't understood the words. He opened his mouth and said somethin', but Blue was damned if he could make out what it was. The man stood, took a step toward Blue. Blue held his breath. This was the part of the horror movie where the monster took off its human face and started rippin' everybody apart and eatin' 'em.

He wanted to stand his ground and when he told the story to anybody after, he did. The man pulled a billfold out of his suit jacket pocket much the same as Blue's and tugged out another hundred dollar bill.

Harvey placed it on the counter next to Blue's twenty.

"Keep the change," he said, turned and headed toward the door. As strange as that had been, Blue hadn't forgotten about his money.

"Merl, I gotta get." He held his twenty up for the other man to see.

"I cain't work the machine!"

"I know, I know." He held out a calmin' hand. "I'll be back this afternoon to settle up with Marsha." Blue hoped she'd be here by then. Merl looked at the money, then back at Blue. The stress seeped out of him when the cash disappeared back into Blue's billfold.

He pushed outside, headed for his truck. Blue hadn't paid attention, but he hadn't noticed the man get into a car. There was some sort of soft green light comin' over the berm in front of his truck. Blue clenched his keys, his curiosity gettin' the better of him. He climbed the berm and spied the stranger walkin' a brisk pace about thirty yards ahead.

He was curious, watchin' a man walkin' like he had someplace to go when there was nothin' but an empty field—Dwight Hammersmith had already harvested the corn for the season. Blue followed, walkin' and joggin' 'til he was about ten yards behind.

Ahead was what looked like a big hole, a soft, glowy green stretchin' out of it. It had to have been a sinkhole, but so far as Blue knew, there wasn't water underground here. The stranger stopped at the hole and peered over. Blue was about ten feet away when he saw the man was hollerin' his guts out.

It figured. Blue nodded, ready to head back to his truck. He'd give ol' Dwight a call to let him know about his new hole. He'd be happy to hear about that. But then somethin' poked out of the hole. Blue did a double take and saw it was four wigglin' fingers followed by a sleeved arm.

A man in an off-white suit hauled himself up and Blue stepped over to assist. He was all kinds of surprised to see the man looked exactly like Harvey. He looked between Harvey One and Harvey Two, one brushin' himself down while the other was emptyin' out everything he'd just eaten.

"Buddy, you okay?" Blue asked Harvey Two, then felt somethin' on his foot. Another hand was reachin' out the hole and it was grabbin' onto his boot and pullin'. A third Harvey pulled up onto its elbows and began scrabblin' out.

"You know a good place to eat around here?" Harvey Two said.

"Yeah, I'm starved!" Harvey Three said as he got to his feet.

Several more hands began risin' out the hole. Harvey One had a last convulsion and stood there with his hands on his knees.

Blue began backin' up, not understandin' what he was seein' and wantin' no more of it. He estimated those were numbers four through seven, but he didn't even wanna look at 'em. They all stood, watchin' him, with more comin' up outta that hole every minute.

Harvey One finished and wiped his chin. "Hey, I know a place. Best I ever had!"

Just a conversation between my cat and me.

The Last Word (A Transcription)

Pedro: Meow.

Me: I'm on the phone.

Pedro: Meow!

Me: I'm on the phoooone.

Pedro: MEOW!

Me: I'm. On. The. Phone.

Pedro: MEOWWWW!

Me: I'M ON THE PHONE!

Pedro: …meow

Me (staring hatefully): I'm on the phone.

Pedro (hiding somewhere): Meow.

I wrote this story somewhere around twenty years ago.
Maybe a few years shy. It was just based on an idea going through
my head. I never did anything with it.

The Laugh

Milt wasn't funny. He hated to admit, but the brutality of the audience left no room for denial. He felt ashamed asking his uncle for the sixty dollars, and George had harangued him about his piss-poor routine to no end until he'd turned away, slinking out of the club.

He was tired of running away from life. Milt desperately wanted to be good at something, but he invariably failed at everything. He'd always seemed so promising at whatever came before the job, but the job itself tended to be his undoing. He'd been a great clerk but a terrible attorney. He had narrowly escaped disbarment and made no case to his firm as to why they shouldn't ask for his resignation. He'd been a great fiancé, but Laura had left him less than a year after they'd said 'I do'—coincidentally, right around the same time as when he'd stopped being an attorney. He'd been a decent amateur boxer, but he'd been knocked out cold by his sparring partner while training for his first pro fight.

Milt had to face it. He was a loser.

"You're a loser," Uncle George said for what must have been the fiftieth time as he waved around a wad of singles. George had verbally badgered him, clenching the cash in his pudgy fist as if he could guilt Milt out of taking his payment. If it weren't for his Aunt Thelma, Milt wouldn't have even gotten the shot to begin with. George hated him and had no problem making his feelings known at every turn. In the end, George slapped the cash down on the counter and turned to go back in the kitchen as he shouted expletives about Milt's dubious parentage.

Milt closed his eyes and bumped against the door. He'd been so bad at everything else, he just had to succeed at this. Even if it were the worst job on earth. This was his rock bottom. The cool night air felt good on his cheeks and he took a couple deep breaths to scrub his lungs clean of the thick cigarette smoke filling the club. Milt opened his eyes and stared at the moon.

"Maybe I should've been an astronaut," he said.

Someone laughed. He saw a man pushing an overfilled shopping cart down the alley. Milt stepped away from the door and down the two concrete steps. This was a dead-end alley, so he turned and followed behind the man.

"At least somebody likes my sense of humor. Maybe you'd like to hear my routine."

The disheveled man stopped in his tracks. The angle of the moonlight coming over the opposing building left him half in, half out of the dark.

"That was funny." The homeless man turned around. "Tell me another one."

Milt felt a sick niggle in his stomach, telling him it wasn't a good idea to be speaking to homeless people in moonlit alleys. Clearing his throat, he decided to use one skill he'd been at least fifty-fifty with: talking himself out of a fight.

"Did you hear the one about the masochist who got a divorce? He liked the beatings, but he didn't wanna be tied down."

The man laughed again. Hey, this wasn't so bad. Maybe he just had the wrong audience. But Milt thought his comedy career would be off to a bad start if he had to kick it off in soup kitchens.

"That was funny. A-another one." The man took a step closer.

"You ever notice people don't go crazy and do anything constructive? Mailman goes crazy and shoots up the post office. Next door neighbor goes crazy and eats blondes. Uncle goes crazy and rapes the dog—how come unemployed people don't go crazy and get a job? 'Honey, I went crazy and painted the house' or 'honey, I cleaned out the basement 'cause I'm *crazy.*' "

The man coughed up a chuckle. "That was funny. Tell me another one." Another step.

Milt took a step back.

"Uh, how about my cheap uncle who owns a bar?" Milt thumbed over his shoulder. "He's so cheap, even the water is watered down."

The man's hacking became thicker and more insistent. He sounded like he had ball-bearings rattling around in his lungs.

"Come on, buddy," Milt began. "That was a softball. I just made it up."

"Tell a...tell a—*cough-cough-hack!*—a-another one." Every time the man coughed, he shuffled closer.

The stench from the man was almost overpowering, even with several yards between them. Milt breathed through his mouth, the sickly air wafting over his tongue and tickling his insides. He was already past the door when he thought to run back up the stairs to try to get back inside.

The other man's catchphrase had degenerated into constant phlegmy hacking. He seemed like he was barely standing, but still he advanced on Milt. He didn't want to have to slug him, but Milt found himself balling up his fists, ready if he had to.

But before he could close the distance any farther, the man fell to one knee, his coughing becoming even more stressed. He put a hand to his chest and reached toward Milt with the other and Milt took a big unintended step backward. He was wondering what to do as the man fell over onto his side.

"Hey, Buddy, you all right?" Milt took a few cautious steps closer.

The man's coughing was worse now. He seemed on the verge of dislodging a chunk of vital organ.

"Pal?" Milt asked. "Hey, I'm gonna go get some help, all right?" The other man's eyes went wide and he began clawing at the air. Milt ran up the steps to the club's exit and banged away at the door. He could feel the music pounding from inside and knew he was just wasting his time. He looked around, considering what to do, and returned to the man's side.

"Look, I'll be back, okay? You just stay there." He turned and ran down the alley, leaving the homeless man's death-impingent hacking behind. At the mouth of the alley, he looked up and down Woodward and was surprised to see nobody. The streetlights were always out down here, but still, someone should have been around.

He had trained to become an EMT once, but giving that man mouth-to-mouth nauseated him even thinking about it.

He turned in the direction he would have to go home and began jogging. In his panic, Milt never considered going to the front of the club. Maybe there was a payphone nearby. Then he saw a man across the street in a burgundy jersey and matching kerchief tied around his head and sagging pants.

He came to a shuttered gas station with a payphone at the edge of the lot. He picked up the receiver and rubbed the earpiece off on his shirt before holding it up to his ear.

Why didn't I go back in the club? He jabbed in the numbers with his index and listened as the phone made clicking sounds before ringing. An automated message came on, informing him he would be placed on hold and put into a call queue. Milt felt edgy having his back to the man on the other side of the street, so he switched the receiver to his other ear and glanced across. The man was taking his time, but he had started to cross and was walking in Milt's direction. Panic scraped across the bottom of his stomach and Milt was about to hang up just when the operator came on.

"Nine-one-one, this is Sandy, what is your emergency?"

"Yeah, there's a guy in the alley. He's having a heart attack or something."

"All right, sir. There's—" The operator made a high-pitched squealing sound. "I apologize. What's the location!" Her voice rose into a hysterical laugh.

"Hello?" Milt asked.

She responded by bursting into an even louder series of laughs and Milt pulled the phone farther away from his ear.

"You lookin' for somethin'?" a voice asked behind him. Milt turned around and saw the man from across the street.

"Uhh, I uhh…I'm just calling nine-one-one," Milt said. "There's someone—"

The man began to laugh, low at first, seemingly surprised the sound was coming out of him, but as it rose he doubled over, tears springing from his eyes.

Milt looked at the receiver and back to the man. He didn't understand the wrong that was happening, but it was too much of a coincidence for two people in entirely different places to begin laughing uncontrollably for no reason. Milt gently set the receiver back in its cradle, cutting off the operator's cackling.

"Look, I'm just gonna go check on my friend, okay?" Milt said. "I don't want any trouble."

The man was half bent, laughing, his eyes locked on Milt. Not a drop of humor was in those eyes.

Milt tried walking past and the man stepped in front of him. He put his hands on Milt's shoulders as if he were trying to hold himself up.

"Look, I don't want any trouble, okay?" Milt felt his mouth running on automatic, imagining everything coming out of his mouth beginning and ending with the same two words. *Look, I'm bleeding a lot from all these bullet holes, okay? Look, I'm not a fan of man-rape, okay? Look, buy pork belly futures, okay?*

The man clapped his hands around Milt's neck.

He jerked back and reached for the man's wrists. The man's dry thumbs dug into his skin and flashing black dots popped into Milt's vision. He coughed and wrenched at the laughing man's iron grip.

Milt felt light-headed and his legs went out from under him. He fell backwards with the man still holding onto his neck. His head bounced off the concrete as everything was turning gray, then suddenly he could breathe again. Cold, clean air washed into his lungs, and as Milt took deep gulps, his vision returned. He rolled over onto his side and heard the man who attacked him laughing hysterically. As he slowly sat up, his vision returning, he looked and saw the man, tears in his eyes as he pointed at Milt, the both of them sitting on the sidewalk.

Milt struggled to his feet and backed away. Breathing came easier now and he ran as best he could in the direction he'd come. Back at the club, he saw a throng of people milling around the entrance.

It must be past two, he thought. Milt figured he could mingle into the crowd and be safe, but better still, he could get inside the club and try nine-one-one again. As he came closer, he noticed a few people watching him run toward them. One guy had a strange smirk on his face, but it was a woman, deeper into the crowd, who pointed at him.

And she laughed.

Milt's blood turned cold as he skidded to a halt. He took a couple steps back, unsure of what to do. The woman laughed even harder and slowly others turned to see where she was pointing. Others began laughing too.

Milt turned around and ran across the street. He looked over his shoulder and saw people leaving the comedy club and following him. They were all laughing.

He was almost running when someone surged out of the crowd, cackling. It was a woman in heels and a dress, and before she could get halfway across the street, she tripped and fell, sliding a few feet across the asphalt. The crowd seemed further amused, gathering around her. Milt could see their feet rising up and down, but she was obscured. He could hear the woman laughing above the rest, and her occasionally going, "Uh! Uh!" as they stomped on her. As soon as her voice died out, they turned back to Milt.

He ran.

They remained behind Milt for several blocks. For a while, he was certain they would catch him, but slowly he pulled away. His blood was fueled with fear and adrenaline, his lungs were on fire, and he felt at any moment his heart would explode out of his chest like a bomb. He finally made it to his building, half collapsing against the door. He fished his keys out of his pants pocket and steadied his hand as best he could as he unlocked the door. He stumbled in, gasping for air and collapsed on the floor of the lobby. Milt was glad no one was around; he would have been completely helpless.

He opened his eyes, realizing at some point he had passed out. He slowly rolled over onto his back and drew himself up into a sitting position. He tried twice to stand, but his legs weren't working like they should have. He finally made it to his feet, but his body was stiff, all the way up to his neck. He started for the elevator when he heard it ding as it settled on the first floor. He hurried as best he could through the door to the stairs, afraid to be seen. Milt was only on the second floor, he should have been able to make it.

Everything was quiet by the time he got to his floor. He crept down the slender hall, poorly covered with peeling pink wall paper, to his apartment and slipped in.

Safe.

He collapsed against the door, laying his head back. Milt listened to himself breathe and thanked the gods he was alive. He ambled into the bathroom, flipping on the sink and dipping his head into a stream of cool running water. He stayed there for at least a minute and then grabbed a towel. As Milt scrubbed his face dry, he flicked on the light switch. He dropped the towel in the sink and looked at himself in the mirror.

It was just a face. What had everyone gone insane over?

"What's so funny?" he asked. Milt shook his head, folded up the towel and threw it back on the rack. He felt the heat in his cheeks and neck and said, "What's so funny?" again. "What's so funny, huh? What? What?" He punched the mirror.

"Ouch!" he said, waving his hand furiously. He examined his hand, small specks of mirrored glass embedded in the index and middle knuckles. Blood beaded up from the tiny wounds and spilled down his hand.

Milt meant to reach into the medicine cabinet to take out the isopropyl alcohol, but he caught his splintered reflection in the mirror.

He had to admit, it *was* funny.

He laughed.

He never stopped.

Gerald Dean Rice

I wrote this story. I have no clue what was going through my mind at the time.

In the Butt

Neil followed her bulging hips as she swayed down the long narrow hallway. He'd promised his wife never again, but this woman was just too perfect to pass by. She was about five-foot three, maybe a hundred sixty pounds, a third of that in her ass.

At some point, his cravings had become undeniable. He was a married father who couldn't stop.

He bulk confessed now, copping every tenth time or so. Prostitutes, mostly, but he'd lay with just about any woman as long as she had everything back there.

Not that he didn't have standards. The goddess walking three feet in front of him had a small waist and shapely thighs, a must-have for Neil. He didn't go for the ones who had big everything. Neil also didn't care for big breasts, either. But an especially huge ass, well, what couldn't he do with that?

She was an ebony-skinned angel. Not that Neil sought out only women of color. No, he'd been with plenty of white women with a big back porch. Race was not a barrier he couldn't break through. All he cared about was how much she had and how quickly he could get to it.

She stopped at the door to her room, turned and gave him a knowing half smile.

"You ready, zaddy?"

"Y-y-yes." Neil didn't really care for daddy stuff, but the way this woman looked at him made the marrow in his bones rock hard.

Neil followed, shrugging out of his coat and hat. She had already taken off her skirt and something about her clothed upper body and mostly bare lower half made his mind spin.

He wrapped an arm around her small waist, drawing her in for a kiss. She turned her cheek to him.

"Sweety, not on the lips."

Neil nodded and put his lips to her neck. She tasted like almonds and a sprinkling of cocoa. She squealed, rubbing her hand up and down the front of his pants.

Neil moaned as her hand worked magic, gripping and twisting. He wasted no time, unbuttoning his shirt and chucking his pants.

She gave him another one of those smiles like she knew some mind-blowing secret. He began unlacing her shirt and unhooking her bra.

In truth, he didn't really care if she was naked completely. Just as long as he could have access to what he wanted, but he knew a woman wanted her whole body appreciated. She really was beautiful and this minor delay only increased his lust.

"What do you want me to do with it?" She gave him another squeeze.

"I want you to make it clap for me." He intentionally misread her question. Neil did not like blow jobs. At least receiving them. Maybe in his mind he was justifying pleasing himself as a means of pleasing them. To take pleasure solely felt like cheating. But then again, he didn't like Karen blowing him, either.

She stepped to the center of the room and began gyrating her hips and legs, her ample derriere shaking in a way that made his eyeballs feel like they would spring from their sockets.

Neil licked his lips subconsciously, grabbing hold of himself through his boxers. If he weren't hypnotized before, he definitely was now.

"I…need you," he said. "I need to be inside you. Right now."

She stopped her gyrations and looked at him over her shoulder. Her flawless skin was as dark as starless night, her eyes like two pits of coal. "Okay, zaddy." She made a show of turning around and walking back to him, her hips swaying in a way that made his knees turn to water. She pressed her body into his, his hardness pressing into her flat stomach. She had small breasts with large areola, and he scooped one into his mouth, rolling his tongue over her nipple.

"Mmm." She put her head back and moaned, drawing him close with those long fingernails. It was the first thing he'd noticed at the diner where he got his bagel and coffee every morning. For whatever reason, women with big asses liked fancy fingernails.

Neil reached around and grabbed two handfuls and felt himself spring free of his boxers. He slid slowly to his knees kissing his way down and pulling her panties with him.

She shuddered as he kissed her bald pubic mound. He hefted one well-marbled thigh over his shoulder, accessing the center of her. Her scent was spicy with a hint of a flower he couldn't place. Neil darted his tongue across her lips and felt her arch away from him slightly. He moved his hand back up to her ass and pulled her back.

He crouched underneath her as she gently tugged his hair between her fingers. He cupped his bottom lip, dragging it across her. As her moans grew louder, he concentrated on her clit.

Neil pulled it into his mouth, suckling like a baby with a pacifier while he massaged her expansive cheeks with his hands. She began tugging fistfuls of hair and calling out to him, saying, "Oo, zaddy, that's it. That's my spot!"

Finally, he could take no more. Neil stood, seized her by the elbows and turned her around. He marched her to the nearest flat surface, a bare shelf stripped of any paint or varnish. It was squat enough that he could bend her over it and her chest smacked hard as he pressed his palm on her back.

She wiggled her ass around, one final tease before he was inside her. Neil had two competing thoughts that almost took him out of the game before he'd properly started. He imagined his wife smiling at him with deep sadness in her eyes. He also realized he didn't know this young woman's name.

She wasn't a prostitute. Neil had learned all the dirty things women he liked liked to hear. He'd given her an ear full of it and she'd practically dragged him here.

He seized himself and glid inside, gasping sharply. She was so wet as Neil gripped her hips, angling so he could press deeper.

Her moans changed to audible panting as he gradually increased his pace, a tiny bead of sweat trickling from her tailbone across the wide curve of one ass cheek. Neil grunted, biting his lower lip as he thrust, pulling her into him with each stroke. She complemented his effort, throwing her ass back at him.

The thick scent of sex filled the air. Neil's hips clapped against her and he began sliding his thumb between her cheeks, readying to move into backdoor action. Something was off, though.

At first, he simply assumed he'd passed over her anus without feeling it. Not all girls were built the same. There was one he'd been with, a pretty pink-haired number, who'd been too tight, and he'd had to settle for regular sex. Neil popped his thumb in and out of his mouth and began probing between her cheeks again.

He kept finding his shaft where it was pumping into her. Was he already in her ass? It certainly didn't feel like it, but he leaned over so he could reach around.

"Oo, zaddy," she said as his middle finger slid between her, playing over a diamond-hard clit. He reached farther back and touched himself again.

What the hell?

It was like she didn't have an anus.

Then came the horrid crunch as his penis was torn free, blood spraying across her ass. Neil didn't immediately register pain as he stumbled backward, the pleasure center of his brain misreading signals and he immediately came.

His hips automatically bucked as a strangled scream tore out of him. He cupped a hand over his crotch, catching red, pearlescent semen. He felt lightheaded and stumbled over his feet as he fell on his ass.

Distantly, he heard her screams of passion, louder than his had been a moment before. There was more tearing and when he lifted his heavy head, he saw through half-lidded eyes, her vagina had dilated as if she were about to give birth. Her legs bent backward at the knees with thick pops and her feet rotated around.

As the thing approached, he could see the woman's head lolling around like an animal's tail.

"What the fuck?" he mouthed, the spicy, flowery scent even stronger as the thing stopped inches from his face. What had been a vagina just a moment ago was now, clearly, a vertically-slitted mouth.

The bare lips quivered as it reared up on what had been arms, the mouth widening. Neil had the briefest thought of Karen just before it completely enveloped his head and a moment later his shoulders.

Neil was helpless as it continued.

Gerald Dean Rice

I had this idea a while back to write a bunch of short horror stories. I don't know exactly what the intent was. It grew out of a few Z-Flash stories I was supposed to be writing for a publisher, but the idea lost its luster and I abandoned it. Dr. Hosack was the first one and was really fun and quick. I have a few more in mind that I may get to someday.

Horror Snippets

1.

Dr. Hosack's Original Account of the Burr-Hamilton Duel of 1804

Dr. David Hosack, physician of Alexander Hamilton at the time of his death, wrote his account of events in the aftermath of the duel between the two rival politicians, Alexander Hamilton and Aaron Burr, on August 17, 1804, more than a month after Hamilton had died as a result of his injuries. The prevailing reason for such a lengthy delay was that there was some debate as to what Hosack would be allowed to write.

In 1935, literary scholar Bennet K. Sage uncovered a box filled with various documents in a basement at Burmeister College. At first glance, he believed them unimportant until he recognized the signature of Dr. Hosack affixed to one. It appeared to be another draft of the events preceded by the duel between Burr and Hamilton and was dated July 20, 1804, nine days after the fatal duel that eventually claimed Hamilton's life. What could be read of the letter stated:

"The Colonel [Burr] never fired [at me]. Just after the second gave word, a wild man emerged from the bush. I had already given my affirmation when I caught site of him from the corner of my eye. At first, I mistook him for an African by his darkened skin. But he was not adorned as a slave, though his clothes were ragged. [Illegible] bit me and I screamed to the Colonel, 'Sh—[illegible]…to which, he fired, his shot landing in the man's side. Yet he did not fall, merely turning to him with those mindless eyes, then fleeing back into the bush…"

Only then did I begin scribing what my good friend had told me [illegible] moment his thoughts were sparse and inconcise. He claimed to have visions of relatives long past [illegible] demise would be short in coming. I also took note Hamilton no longer sweated. Believing him parched, I pinched the flesh of his arm, but he showed no symptom of dehydration. Again, [illegible] refused to eat.

The complexion of the facies in particular took on a pronounced paleness and there were several moments where I was certain he was no longer drawing breath. Again, I applied spirits of hartshorn [illegible] found his mouth clenched shut and unable to administer orally. Finally, I ushered everyone out of the room so that I may examine him privately. It is then he rose from his bed and attempted to attack me.

He was wild, but slow and perhaps blind; a milky layer [illegible]. I had fallen back from his attack and unintentionally barricaded myself inside by overturning an old oak desk. He advanced upon me and I still had my bag. I was left with no choice, I removed my scalpel and neatly slashed his carotid. A congealed substance not blood came out that I still cannot reconcile as a doctor.

[Illegible] burst through the door. They were in uniform, but I had never seen them black before. None of them wore rank. One aimed his musket and fired a single shot into Hamilton's skull, putting him down."

The college already had in its possession a half-finished journal of Hosack's secretary. One particular entry may shed light on why the doctor's letter was revised:

"At first I believed the man a potential patient. His eyes were bloodshot, his wig was not affixed properly on his head and there was an awfull scar across his face. He identified himself only as Sanford before storming past me and entering the goode doctor's examining room. The prior patient left quickly after, still replacing his clothing in the process. The door shut firmly behind this new man—I heard a considerable amount of yelling from the examining room, none of it Dr. Hossack's.

It was sometime later before either man emerged. All of the other patients had left. The man had a paper clutched n his hand and I caught sight of a pistol beneath his cowl before he exited. Dr. Hossack was covered with ink, appearing thoroughly out of sorts and dishevelled. He immediately took me aside and ordered me not to speak of the man's presents."

Before Sage could publish his findings, however, the newly discovered document and the journal disappeared. In his further research the only reference he could find to a 'Sanford' was a John K. Sandford, a lieutenant in the Revolutionary War who had allegedly been mortally wounded by a British soldier's saber.

2.

On January 30, 1911, the worst mining accident since the disaster in Monongah, West Virginia occurred in Frotua, Ohio. Two hundred and ninety-eight men and young boys were drowned when a black coal mine flooded from a rupture in the Allegheny River.

There were at least eleven known survivors, but considering many were migrant Italian workers with little command of the English language and a fear of authority, other survivors may have remained hidden for fear of punishment or retribution.

One known survivor, identified as Vincenzo Petrulli, chanted, "in piedi morti," as he emerged from the earth, which translates to "the standing dead."

In a statement to police that eventually aided in convicting Petrulli and the other survivors for the murders of the other mine workers, he described an explosion that initially killed about a dozen workers, the subsequent waters of the Allegheny River capturing all but about three dozen men.

"My brother," Vincenzo said, "I was holding his hand when the stream tore him away. I don't know how I wound up on dry land, but I asked St. Brendan to spare me one more time and went back in. But the water was too black and rising. The others pulled me free and we began searching for a way out.

"We heard them by the second day. Reason and our own echoes masked them. But it was the mine, and we had no light—solitude and dark inquisitors of all of us. We searched by hand until Carlo chanced upon a box of a few matches and we wound our shirts around some sticks to make torches. That was when we saw them, drenched in their clothes. Nunzio [Petrulli's brother] was there. Some of the others wanted to go to them, to help them. They seemed blind, but I warned them away. I knew that was not my brother."

Vincenzo's written statement is highly redacted after that point, but it goes on to state they found a secondary path leading out of the mine, but before exiting one of the miners ignited several sticks of dynamite, the explosion collapsing the narrow passageway and sealing in forever those who could not pull themselves free.

3.

Flint, MI – June 23, 2010

An earthquake in central Canada was felt across the border in states such as New York, Pennsylvania, and Michigan. In Flint, a city approximately sixty miles northwest of Detroit, the seismic activity was also felt when a two mile stretch of land cracked open.

"We were on our way to the bowling alley when it happened," Jim Butcher, a resident of Mt. Morris stated. "Everything just shook and we just stopped right where we was and just looked at it."

The 'it' Jim referred to was the two mile stretch of land that had just cracked open. The devastation churned up earth and street alike, including a large section of Corunna Road and cutting through Glennak Cemetery which is located there.

"A man climbed out," 87 year old Betty Harvest stated. "He was covered head to foot in dirt. I don't know, but he seemed upset."

Even though Chief of Police Montalvo Keye has stated there were no reported injuries or deaths as a result of the natural disaster, the unidentified disheveled man had been seen by several people.

"Yeah, Dirty Man was in there," a resident who wished to remain anonymous stated, referring to an abandoned home on Asylum Street, just north of Court. "We came home one night and saw him going in. A couple kids already went missing that week, so my husband called the police. But nobody ever came, so a group of guys got together and went in. My husband said he was in there and tried to bite him. They beat on him, but they left after my husband fainted. At the hospital, nobody would tell us anything. That was a month ago. Now the doctors won't even return my phone calls. And the police still never came to take a statement."

"Dirty Man killed my best friend," Ron Johnson, a teenager out of Grand Blanc stated. "We were urbexing one of the old GM plants over on Van Slyke. It wasn't even real in there. Maybe the plant had been closed a few months. We were about to leave when we saw him. He looked sick—I mean like dying. Bones and stuff were hanging out of his face. The back of his suit was split up the middle in the back. Weird. But my friend wanted to call 911 for him before we broke out. That was when he grabbed me. He was real strong. If you look at my wrist, you can see the scar from when he broke it. Compound fracture. Pete got him off, but then I couldn't help him. Dirty Man started biting him…and then he started eating him. It was all I could do just to run away."

The last sighting of Dirty Man was verified on August 3, 2010. Glenn Beckitt was driving west on Miller Road, a main street through Flint, when he struck a man he described as disheveled and filthy. EMS was quick to respond after he called 911 and the man bit off the finger of one paramedic before being subdued.

"They didn't know what they was doing," Pat Logue stated. "I mean, I been to the hospital before. I OD'd twice and I struggled both times. You don't punch the patient. That's how he got his finger bit off. He hit him. That's what he get."

All three local hospitals had no reports of anyone fitting Dirty Man's description being admitted or of an injured EMS worker.

4.

Name Withheld, Location Withheld—2004

(taken from the handwritten notes of a hospital employee, name redacted)
There's a ton of dead bodies in here. I don't know why, but a doctor slapped a clipboard in my hand and told me to take a head

count. Everybody's running around. A lot of people are hurt. A whole lot more are dead.

There wasn't enough room for me to stand out in the hall to count the bodies they were bringing in, so somebody else shoved me into this meat locker to count from inside. I think a plane crashed into a bus or something. People were saying stuff all at once, but I'm only catching bits or pieces. There was somebody else in here doing something, but as soon as she saw me, she must have thought I was her replacement and left.

Damn. Fifty. And from the sounds coming from the hallway, the day is still young.

There's some kind of ante-room in here with a whole lot more bodies in it. I started counting over. I stopped when I got to sixteen. There's this girl—I guess a girl, her body looks really young—except...she doesn't have a head. At first, I'm staring at this headless body, but then it hits me that I'm staring at a girl who couldn't have been eighteen even, and I feel all pervy. That doesn't even make sense to me because what kind of dude gets his rocks off by staring at decapatated (however you spell it) bodies of prepubescent (?) girls?

I heard the doors slap open twice out there. It's starting to feel crowd—

Oh shit. I swear to God, this girl's body just moved. My sides hurt. I laughed so hard. My mind is gonna play tricks on me if I don't get outta here soon! Maybe I need to step out for some air because her arm just completely fell off this gurney thing and it's just dangling now. I ain't touching it. The doors just slapped open again.

Okay, I know this sounds...reads (whatever) nuts, but for real the girl did just move. I was picking up my pen off the floor and her arm sorta...twitched. I'm no doctor, but it's probably like signals from the brain or something, right? Wait, she doesn't have a head. Okay, how the hell does that happen?

All right, I just stepped out in the hall and tried to flag down a doctor to come take a look. The only person who even remotely looked like a doc was this Pakistani guy, except he was crying and screaming in Pakistani, and he wasn't moving from that spot. I grabbed an EMT and he about slugged me when I touched him. I thought he was coming when I told him what I saw, but when I rushed back in here, he wasn't behind me.

The girl is really moving around now and it's getting more than a little creepy. Her arms are shaking and she keeps making fists and then shaking again. At first, I thought it was like a seizure or something, but I think she's in pain. I mean, I broke my toe once when I was a kid, and it hurt really bad, right? But I knew I couldn't just reach down and grab it 'cause it would hurt worse. So, I just stood there, hopping around on one foot and waving my hands around until my dad got me to the hospital. Almost like she's waving her arms around.

How bad does it hurt to get your head cut off?

I got the guts to take a step closer to look at the wound. I mean, I assumed her head was cut off, but I didn't really look-look. I don't know how to describe it—it looks like a clean cut for the most part, except at the back where I can see part of her spine and a fist-sized piece of meat (ugh!) hanging off it.

Dammit! She grabbed me. I don't know if she felt me or what, but she reached out and grabbed my arm. I barely shook her off. She was strong. The doors just banged open again and I th nk I'm outtie. I mean, I need the job and all, and I'm sorry, but this is just a temp job.

There's another gurney just in front of the doors with something about the size of a bowling ball under a sheet. I don't know if it's just my eyes or what, but I saw it move. My bad for not picking up the girl from the floor, but I ain't waiting around for all these other bodies to start skipping around.

We did an extensive search for plane crashes in the year 2004 but could find none that had crashed into any buses. There were three fatal bus crashes reported in that year, but one was a bus carrying only senior citizens, and the other had only one death. The third was a passenger bus passing through Virginia at the time of the crash. We received no responses to several Freedom of Information Act requests and a PR representative who wished to remain nameless declined to comment.

5.

The Eighth Bad Omen

As Taken from a Written Statement of an Outcast Informant of Sahagún

Several years before the arrival of the Conquistadores, there were allegedly seven omens that predicted their coming. From temples catching fire to a strange woman wailing in the street, whether these events actually predicted anything is debatable. But the Eighth Bad Omen as originally described to Bernardino de Sahagún, the Franciscan scholar and author of the Florentine Codex, found its way in and then promptly out of the text chronicling Aztec history.

"Their three bodies washed ashore in the morning," the unnamed informant stated. "They had the markings of warriors and looked as if they'd died in battle. An elder told us there had been a battle between two clans not far away. We bundled their bodies to burn them in honor of Tonatiuh after nightfall.

"We had just begun to gather for the ceremony when we heard a call. A woman was running through the village, screaming that her sons had been killed. But instead of finding us under attack by a neighboring clan, the warriors who had washed up on the shore were walking through the village, killing every man, woman, and child within reach. They still had the weapons tied to their backs for the funeral, but they were using their hands to break the arms of the ones attempting to get away and their teeth to tear their throats.

"Yaoquizqueh closed in to engage them, but stabbing them through with tepoztopilli harmed them none. They tried their quauhololli, but that only drew them closer, and the strange ones tore their flesh as well.

"The men who survived retreated if they could. Otherwise, the strange ones would gather and tear at their flesh until they died. One yaoquizqueh had managed a macuahuitl, and with one mighty swing, he took the head of one of the strange ones. He might have taken another, but the men who had died battling them began rising and surrounded him before he could fend them off.

"By sunrise, the few of us remaining began to come out. The yaoquizqueh and the strange ones lay on the ground, none of them moving. We quickly made a pyre and burned them all without ceremony."

6.

Faster

Aaron Flyte was a jerk and he deserved to die. Andy would have described himself as seething as he drove the man who was blackmailing him to the nearest ATM to empty out his account. He had no clue how he was going to explain this to his wife, but it had to be done.

Andy's wallet was in Aaron's lap. Aaron had picked through it, removing cash and the debit card to the account Andy had so foolishly used for his paycheck and the erroneous funds that had made their way there as well.

Had he been able to wish for a person's death, certainly he would have done so upon Flyte. It would have been better had Aaron simply turned him in once he found out what Andy had been doing. It would have been a relief of sorts.

The lies had been long and enduring. Once Andy was thoroughly hooked, he honestly expected someone to tap him on the shoulder and say something to the effect of 'gotcha', but it never happened. No one ever came. It got easier and easier and Andy began to take more and more. By the time Aaron came along, Andy was so deep he didn't know where the lying ended and where he began.

"How long have you known?"

Flyte looked at him with that all-too knowing smile. "Long enough."

Aaron let his hand hang out the window in that way people tended to do when they seemed to be relaxing on a drive in a way Andy had never been able to do. He had an enduring childhood phobia of a vehicle or some stationary object cleaving off his hand that kept all parts of him securely inside his vehicle.

Actually, it wouldn't be too bad of an idea if—

"Holy geez!" Aaron screamed, yanking his arm back inside the car. Andy glanced over and saw one hand firmly locked around his wrist. He didn't get too good of a look, but it almost looked like two fingers were missing from Flyte's hand.

Andy slowed for a light that had just changed, the cars in front of him surging back into the bloodstream of traffic.

"What the hell happened?" Andy asked.

"Turn around. You have to go back. You have to go back!" Aaron was on the point of hysteria. Andy saw the panic in a man's eyes just before pressing the gas again to keep up with traffic.

"Stop the car? Why?" Andy could feel a rising sense of superiority, though he didn't understand why.

"Please," the other man said. "My fingers. They fell off."

Andy felt more curiosity than panic. "Really?" he said. "Let me see." He reached over without looking and grabbed Aaron's wrist, holding it up to see. Aaron's thumb and middle fingers were missing.

That was funny and Andy coughed a laugh before he could stop himself.

No, eff you, Aaron.

Andy shoved the man's arm away, feeling him waning like a balloon with a fast leak.

"Please, stop the car and let me out. Let me get my fingers!"

"Sorry to break the bad news to you, Aaron," Andy said. "But your fingers are at least a half a mile back. On the off chance they didn't get run over or scooped up by some critter, you'll never find them. It's windy out there and those fingers probably rolled all over the street."

"Oh, sweet Lord, I think I'm going into shock!"

"I'm surprised you're not already. Hey, how bad's the bleeding?"

"I'm not…it's not…bleeding."

That was odd, but Andy didn't really care. He stomped on the gas and weaved around a little Toyota in front of them.

"My ear!"

Aaron's agony was like manna. Andy wanted more. The speedometer crept up to fifty and Andy gave it a little more.

"What are you doing?"

"What have you been doing to me for the last two weeks, Aaron? What just happened to you is the least you deserve." Andy gave the man a sideways glance before pumping the brake to keep from rear-ending a white pickup.

"Tell you what. You want to go get your fingers? Get out. Get out right now. You'll probably break an arm, maybe your tailbone. But people will probably stop for you and then you can get your fingers."

Andy began swatting at him, then shoving him into the door. Sure, Andy was wrong for what he had taken, but he hadn't caused anyone direct harm. The company could go for years and never know the difference. Hell, they probably would never know if it weren't for someone like Aaron who wanted to ruin everything. Andy had already begun the process to stop himself. It was like an addiction and he'd already planned his own intervention. He was going to quit.

But if Aaron had had his way, that could never happen.

Andy blew through a red light, several honking horns trailing after them. His speed crept back up to forty.

"Oh, God, my *teeth*."

His words sounded looser, like his tongue wasn't caged firmly inside his mouth. Andy chanced a few seconds for another look. Almost all of the uppers and lowers on the left side of his mouth were gone. A few of them were sitting on Aaron's pant leg, strikingly white against the dark blue of his jeans. The man sneezed and the rest that had come loose that were still in his mouth *clinkled* across the dashboard and windshield.

Andy laughed.

It was the first time he'd had a laugh like that in probably months. It felt *good*. By the time he got his eyes focused and back on the road, he'd scraped bumpers with a blue Grand Am. The driver screamed something at him he didn't understand and that made him laugh even more. And when he laughed the second time, he hit the gas again.

They were doing sixty now.

"My arm!" Aaron's elbow was resting against the door at an odd angle and the smile felt glued to Andy's face.

"I'm gonna go for seventy," he said. "I've never driven that fast off the freeway. What do you think?"

Aaron was babbling incoherently. He pulled at his tongue with his intact hand and it flopped into his palm. They flew past one of the branches of Andy's bank.

"I didn't want to stop at that one," he said. "No drive-thru." Aaron was making a high-pitched sound, like a deep-throated screaming tea kettle. There was a red light ahead of them with cars four deep stopped at the intersection. Cross traffic had just begun moving, but Andy could beat them.

He stomped on the gas, jumping into the incoming traffic lane. A car that had just rounded the corner drove onto the sidewalk to avoid them, the driver honking like he was communicating in Morse code. Walls of traffic closed in from either side, one of those trucks with the tall, compact trailers rigged to it large in the passenger side window.

Andy's tires chirped and the car leapt. Both men slammed back against their seats as the car fishtailed out of the intersection, weaving into a lane. Andy screamed in victory, crushing the dome light of the car with his pumping fist.

"Come on, Aaron, how *awesome* was that?" he said.

The two men met eyes and he could see they were on opposite emotional ends. That was panic he was looking at. Abject terror. He let off on the gas—

Just as everything above Aaron Flyte's chin fell into his lap.

It wedged between the man's legs, mostly upside down, nothing visible above the bridge of his nose. The empty cavern of his mouth seemed a perfect fit for the lump of a wallet merely an inch or two away.

But of course, Aaron had no need of his wallet anymore or the precious debit card inside. Andy snatched it away.

It didn't even cross his mind that what had just happened was bad. He rolled down his window, finally taking his foot off the gas. He put his elbow up, feeling the stiff wind against his arm.

Hey, why not?

Andy put his hand up, his speed slowing to sixty, fifty-five. The wind felt nice between his fingers.

At forty-nine miles-per-hour, his index flew off. It didn't hurt and Andy didn't immediately notice. He was at forty-four and down to a ring finger and index left before he saw something was wrong.

"My fingers!"

He stomped on the brake to turn around and his hand fell off. It landed on his thigh like it was about to try for second base. Andy screamed, his foot coming off the brake.

A car honked past, far too close and he looked around. Traffic was coming fast and in a panic, he hit the gas. The car jetted back up to fifty and pressure in his nub eased.

Andy cradled his wounded arm to his chest, despite not being in actual pain. He kept the car between forty-five and fifty, a long stretch of road ahead with no traffic lights. He didn't know how long he could go without stopping and the bravery he'd experienced just a few moments ago was all used up.

What would happen when he came to a red light?

It didn't seem like Andy was going to get the chance to find out. A police cruiser eased out of an abandoned gas station and injected into the stream of traffic behind him.

Andy knew. He just knew. Even as he hoped it wouldn't, he knew the siren was going to come on, that the cruiser would flash its lights. His only question was what he'd do about it when it happened.

When people have been married a long time, they tend to learn each other's ways, methods, and desires without direct communication. Maybe they know how a person will react to a situation, what meal they would order at a restaurant, or how they might answer a question. This is the extreme end of that.

The Ends of a Sentence

Jon sat at the kitchen table, finally ready to kill his wife. He'd had nothing but time to study her the last fifteen years since he'd retired, and in the last two years, he'd come to the realization he was going to do it. It wasn't that she'd had the affair. Martha had never told him, but he'd seen the signs. Jon had had his own affair or two. It wasn't that he suspected the boys weren't his. They'd turned away from him even before leaving the house.

It was that now, after all these years, she was going to leave him.

Martha set a glass next to his bowl. If she had her way, it would be the last time she'd ever do that.

"Do you know how much I love you?" he said.

She turned and stared at him.

"Well, of course, I know you love me."

"No. I said do you know *how* much I love you."

She leaned against the sink and folded her arms.

"No," she said, a smile playing across her face. "How much?"

"So much that I can tell you you used too much salt in the soup." He dipped his spoon and slurped a mouthful. "*Exactly.*"

"Aw phooey, you always say I use too much salt."

"Right. You have for years." Jon nodded. "You've been doing a lot of things for years."

"Now, what's that supposed to mean?" She dropped her arms to her sides.

"Nothing. Just that we've been married forty-two years. You get to know a person after a while. You can predict them, know them in a way they may not even know themselves."

"Oh really? What am I thinking now?"

"Now? Oh, any number of things, I'd guess. Mainly of which, what exactly your husband is up to."

"Well, you didn't have to be a mind reader."

"It's not mind reading. And I'm not joking." Jon took a long drink from his glass. "I know you."

"I see you're feeling cryptic today. Well, I've got things to do."

Jon smiled. Martha shook her head. He took a folded sheet of paper out of his shirt pocket.

"Honey, could you read this?"

He could tell he'd upset her by the way she stood, but he merely held out the scrap of paper until she came over and snatched it from him.

She unfolded it.

"'I've got things to do.' Jon, what is this?"

"That's what you just said."

"I just—oh, Jon, if you're going to claim you know me so well, you'll have to do better than an expression I use all the time."

"Point taken." Jon shrugged, the smile still on his face. Her eyes danced all over him.

"Eat your soup. What are you up to?"

"Nothing, really."

"I'm meeting Lois for bridge soon. I need to get ready."

'Bridge' meant she was going to see *him*.

Who the man was intending to take his wife away was the only thing he didn't know. It tore at him just as if someone were tearing off his arm. She would deny it and they would descend into an argument or she would simply admit and defy him to do anything about it if he confronted her about it. Both options would widen the gap between them.

So, killing her was the only way he could keep them together. After she was gone, he would follow shortly after—he had something waiting in the basement for that. But first, her.

"I don't want you to go to bridge. Stay here with me."

"And what will you do with me?" she asked. "Take me dancing? Write me poetry? Sing to me?"

Jon looked sheepish. She knew he couldn't do any of those things. It had been so long since he'd tried anything like that, but wasn't love supposed to be beyond all that? They still managed intimacy, which he thought was pretty good considering his condition and his sixty-seven years. He knew she'd say something like that, but he didn't have any defense for it.

"That's what I thought." Martha's voice shook him out of his thoughts. "I'll be gone about three hours, and when I come back, we can snuggle together and watch TV like you like."

He let her go upstairs and get cleaned up, letting his mind roam while she was out of the room. If he let her go to that other man, then she would be that much further gone, that much more not his, the tear that much deeper. He felt it like a pain in his neck as real as the glass in his hand. Jon wondered if he would have this same resolve now if he were in front of the man stealing his wife.

"Well, I'm going," she said once she came back downstairs. "Stay awake if you can, but if not I'll see you for breakfast."

"Martha?"

"Yes?" She turned to him.

"Would you look beneath the fishbowl on the mantle?"

"I need to go, Jon. I'll see you."

"Martha, please. Just a moment."

She sighed, made a show of dropping her head and stalked over to the mantle.

She slipped a scrap of paper from beneath the fishbowl. She looked at it, crumpled and uncrumpled it and looked at her husband.

"Jon, what's the meaning of this?"

"What does it read?"

"You know what it reads. How did you—"

"I told you. I know you. I love you."

"And this is the way you show me how much you love me?"

"In a way, yes."

She walked back over to him. "All right, I'm piqued. How did you know I'd say that when I got to the door?"

"It's easy now. I'd say it was around when I retired when I started to notice your patterns. You know, how you react in certain situations. The things you do, the things you say. After so many years I realized it became…repetitive."

"Are you calling me *boring*?"

"No-no, anything but. I've always been fascinated by you, Martha. Since the accident I've had more time to watch you." Jon put a hand on her hip and tried to draw her in. She held still.

"You're mad," he said.

"No, I'm not."

"Yes, you are. The way your eyebrows smush together and how your mouth is fixed. I knew you would be."

"Okay, so now I'm mad. You planned all this to upset me?"

"I didn't *want* to. It was kind of unavoidable."

"'Unavoidable?' Jon, what are you up to?"

He smirked but didn't find any humor in what he was about to do. Jon stood and slowly walked over to the cabinet over the refrigerator.

"Jon!" Inside, he'd left a notbook last night.

He turned to the first page and began reading to his wife. Martha's mouth dropped open as she listened in horror to him recount everything they'd both said and done since he'd entered the kitchen until now.

"Give me that!" She snatched it out of his hands and began leafing through the pages. "How long did it take you…to do this?" she asked once she was done.

"I couldn't sleep last night. I came down and started writing. I guess…an hour or so?"

"Is there something wrong with you? With your brain?"

He laughed. "No. Why would you ask that? Martha, don't you know how much I love you?"

She looked at him like he'd just walked off a spaceship.

"Don't come near me," he said.

"What?"

"That's what you were about to say. You were thinking it."

"I said no such thing!" Martha slid a foot back, the notbook slipping from her fingers and slapping onto the floor.

"I know. I said you were thinking it."

"Jon, *stop*."

"*You're scaring me*," they said together.

She put her hand to her mouth and Jon mirrored her. He took out his pen and pad from his shirt pocket and began scribbling.

"I can't—I can't—" she began.

He tore off the tiny sheet of paper and held it up for Martha to see.

'I can't, I can't,' Martha said again, backing away from her husband.

She fled upstairs, crying uncontrollably.

"Martha!" he called out to her. Jon knew but couldn't bear to follow to see what was about to happen. A second later, he heard her slip, hit her face on the stairs, and tumble back down.

By the time Martha reached the bottom step, she was dead. After a minute or two, he pushed himself over to her, to see what he'd done.

Those blank eyes stared at him.

Jon would have liked to have thought if he could have expressed in words how much he loved her, it would have made a difference. But he knew that she was just as set in her way as he was in his and there was nothing that could have been done to stop what she was going to do. He pulled himself out of his chair, kneeling with her, stroking her hair, and arranging her arms and legs so she'd be comfortable. Jon kissed every corner of her face, over and over, trying to commit the dimensions of skin to memory with his lips, allowing himself the briefest of whimpers as he held her.

After a while, he got up and went to the basement door. He paused long enough to rub the dull ache at his neck. It was already receding. Jon looked at the notbook on the floor before going down.

There was so much more he would have liked to have written in there.

Gerald Dean Rice

This is my first attempt at a vampire story. Though it is bloodless, for me it taps into the power dynamic between victim and victimizer. The vampire in this story is the undead embodiment of gaslighting. There's a whole novel for this tale, I'll get around to writing it eventually.

Do Not See Me

Jimmy sat in the back of the cruiser, waiting for the cop to take him in. They'd had them dead to rights. He wasn't sure what he would have done with that gun even if he'd had the time. But this guy, this police officer, was some kind of magician. He'd appeared out of nowhere and all but plucked the gun right out of Jimmy's hand.

He hadn't even noticed until the cop's hand was on it. Jimmy had panicked, felt himself reflexively squeeze—both his fingers and his guts—but the officer must have put the safety on with a bit of sleight of hand. Fire had raced across Jimmy's cheek and he spilled across the floor. His eyes rolled around in his head like pinballs as he'd heard the cries of the woman he'd been holding hostage. There was gunfire coming from the other room and that was either the guys shooting or being shot at.

Jimmy lost consciousness but felt himself being hoisted up, out of the inky blackness and by the arm, and though he couldn't see, knew he was being moved by the wind on his face.

But wind didn't make sense unless he was flying or something. Jimmy hadn't felt his feet on the ground but didn't have awareness of his extremities at all. He was more or less in a numb, grey area. He'd fully come-to in the back of the cruiser with these cuffs on.

There was an officer sitting in the front.

"Morning, Sunshine," the piggy said, meeting his eyes through the rearview mirror.

Jimmy said something, realized it was completely unintelligible, shook his head, and tried again.

"You the one that hit me?"

"The one *who* hit you," the cop said, correcting him. "And yes."

Jimmy forced a smile, though the ache in the side of his face went up a peg. "You're gonna hear from my lawyer. You violated my Constitutional rights when you put your porky mitts on me. Don't you know anything above the collarbone is off limits?"

The cop's eyes went wide and his eyebrows shot up. For a moment, Jimmy thought he'd scared him until he saw the crinkles at the corners of his eyes and realized he was smiling. He adjusted the mirror so Jimmy could only see his mouth. Yeah, big ol' toothy grin. Smug bastard. Jimmy made up his mind right then if he got the chance to headbutt him, he would.

"Jimmy." The cop shook his head, the mouth weaving in and out of the mirror. "Constitutional rights are for *humans.* You're no human. You're trash. Nobody remembers trash. Did you know you pissed yourself after I knocked you out? Me and Sylvia had a *real* good laugh after that."

That pissed Jimmy off. He didn't like being made fun of, dammit. He *was* a big deal.

Be cool, he told himself. *Be cool.* He looked down at his handcuffs, forcing the hard truth of his situation into his brain. He was cuffed. He was going to jail. They would take his freedom, but nobody got to take his pride.

He sniffed, smelled nothing and leaned forward and sniffed again. Jimmy had been in the sweltering heat of a building with no air conditioning for seventeen hours before he wound up in here and he stunk. But he didn't smell like no peepee.

"I did not," he said, flicking his eyes back up to the rearview. The cop shrugged. Jimmy looked at the back of the man's head. It was like this person and the piecemeal rectangle he saw in the mirror were two different people. For a moment, he got a weirdo feeling like when he climbed up too high and looked down. Jimmy blinked and it was gone.

"What's the matter? Still a little woozy?" A hand rubbed the chin underneath that mouth. "Maybe I hit you harder than I thought. You might have a concussion. Wanna go to the hospital?"

"*No*," Jimmy growled.

"Serious. I could have broken your brain or something. Might want to get that checked out by a professional."

"I'm fine. Can you take me to jail now? What are we waiting for?"

"Eight forty-seven."

Jimmy had no idea what that meant and had no intention of giving the cop the satisfaction.

"What's your name, anyway?" he asked. "So I can tell my lawyer who hit me when I sue."

The cop turned around for the first time, a slow, deliberate maneuver, and stared at him. For a moment, it was the most alien thing he had ever seen. There was absolutely no life to his features, Jimmy was looking at the head of a mannequin. A smile broke across the cop's face but it looked *too* animated. His face twitched in places Jimmy didn't know there could be muscles. His ears wriggled as his lips parted. The declining light of the day danced in his eyes, age lines deepened at the corners of his mouth and he could have tucked pencil erasers into his well-deep dimples.

"You can call me Bruce," the cop said. "Because I'm the boss."

And that's when Jimmy heard the music on the radio that had to have been playing all along. It was "Pink Cadillac", the only Springsteen song Jimmy had ever been able to stand. The Boss was really twanging it up with that pseudo-southern by way of New Jersey accent, and as Jimmy twirled the words in his head—not what Bruce the cop had said, but the tone and depth of his voice—he knew he was in trouble.

Bruce had some kind of accent. Or rather, a lack of one. Jimmy guessed he was American, but Bruce could easily have been somebody from somewhere else who'd practiced the foreign accent away to sound like anybody else in this country, but in actuality, not like anyone at all. Kind of like that blonde chick who was in all the movies nowadays. Charlie-something or other.

But there was something else about Bruce too. Maybe it was the hair that was a little too long or in the set of his face or how he seemed supremely confident in some secret Jimmy would never be able to guess, but it was clearly there. Jimmy had been arrested somewhere south of twenty times in his lifetime and all of those cops had had something in common that Bruce did not. Maybe it was a looseness of manner, though several of them had tried to get buddy-buddy, giving him the off-the-record pep-talk, particularly in his younger years.

Bruce was no cop. And at 8:47, Jimmy would find out exactly what that meant for him.

But it begged the question, how had Bruce come with the other police officers? When they'd stormed the building, clearly he'd been there, otherwise Jimmy would not be here. He looked out the windows of the cruiser. They were at least fifty yards off from the building, parked in the growing shade, a few stones' throws away from the nearest police car.

"Where are you taking me?" Jimmy asked Bruce. He wouldn't have believed it possible, but the horizontal hold on Bruce's already wide smile widened, his lips tightening as if they would split in their middles.

"I'm gonna eat you," the man in the front of the cruiser said matter-of-factly. "Split you up the middle and gobble up your insides. Poke out your eyeballs and pop 'em like grapes between my teeth. Tear off your limbs and let you watch me drink you down."

Jimmy's reflex—per usual—was to be combative. He was about to say, "I can't watch you tear off my limbs if you already poked out my eyeballs," when something told him to hold his tongue. It was the absolute conviction in Bruce's tone. And perhaps the hot plastic non-smell of his breath. Sure, the guy *could* be a cannibal, but more than likely he was just some sadist trying for a scare. Considering Jimmy was handcuffed and at the man's complete mercy, he figured it was appropriate to be scared. The possibility of actual murder at that moment was a minor thought for him, but it was still on the list.

"What are you gonna do to me?" Jimmy's voice was much smaller than he would've intended.

"I just *told* you," Bruce said. He threw his head back and gave a hardy laugh. Maniacal or no, it didn't seem like the proper time to do that, but maybe that was the point for a maniac. To be inconvenient. It wasn't like anybody made an appointment to be kidnapped. He pressed his nose against the hard mesh separating them and flicked the tip of his tongue in and out through one of the holes. That hot plastic non-smell almost burned in Jimmy's nose. "I'm gonna eat you."

Jimmy pulled back against his seat, his mind racing to the blank period between when he'd been in the building and winding up here. Had the police given him to Bruce? Were they trying to cover the whole incident up? There had to be a reason, this just wasn't right. There had to be a way out. Bruce turned around in his seat.

"Right now," he began, readjusting the mirror, "you're thinking something like 'how the hell do I get myself out of this?' You're wondering who the hell the psycho you're locked in the car with is and how did he get you. Something like that. Probably how you're not that bad a guy and what you don't deserve and blah-blah-blah-blah." Bruce held up a hand and flapped the four fingers against his thumb. "Well, I don't need to tell you, life is unfair. Bet nobody needs to teach that girl you had the gun on, either. Or all the people you robbed. Or hurt. Did you know four of her friends died because of you people?" Bruce shook his head, disgust plain in his voice. "And what would their parents say? Do you deserve to be right here with me or with them?" He inclined his head in the general direction of where the police were. Jimmy's blood ran cold at that moment.

"How did you...how did you get past them?" Jimmy dared to ask.

Bruce turned around again and his face was entirely different. The eyes were darker and weren't set in his head the same; the ridge of bone above them had even reoriented, becoming sharper. His cheekbones had risen, given him a mildly Asian appearance, and his skin had turned almost blood red. Bruce didn't look inhuman so much as he looked like he'd traded ethnicities, but the effect was terrifying in a manner Jimmy couldn't quantify.

"You should have an idea how this all went down by now." Somewhat-Asian Bruce gave him a look. Whether it had just appeared or Jimmy had only now noticed it, Bruce's smile had one particular tooth—a canine—digging into his lower lip. Bruce spoke without moving his mouth, looking like the lid of his rage was barely contained beneath his skin. "You didn't see me because I didn't want you to. I caught your eye across an incredible distance—a pretty fine trick even for me—and I told you the same thing I told all those cops I walked right by: 'Do not see me.'"

Gerald Dean Rice

The next five poems I wrote back in college; probably sometime in 2001, relatively close together. I won an award for poetry with one of these while I was a student at Mott Community College. This first one is my 'sexy Frankenstein' poem.

Petite Morte

My poor broken angel, buried in the yard,
Eternity to tend the lush greens,
purples and reds of your garden.
A twin engine of lust half-winged,

My over-brimming passions drowned you out.   5
Two fingers to your soft bruised throat,
Confirmed the look in your tender eye.
That accusing stare that becried your crumbled heart,

When only a moment before, I swear
Was filled with your undying lovingkindness.   10
Yea, the day is forever long that you left behind,

And all the darker the rest thereafter;

Choked I am from your presence.
Oh woe! for your beauty is consigned for alway to the microscopic beast
That scavenges and picks   15
And chooses and chews and—

What is it?
That unfamiliar scratch upon the door,
From a stranger hand.
A monster's sight behind thine knowing eyes! 20

Oh, beloved creature,
Take mercy upon me,
Where I was excess,
Leave me unmolested,

For more than filth,   25
And slime separate us.
The very walls of life and,
Death are our barrier.

Leave not your stiff kisses,
Upon my lips, O raised horror,   30
Nor your degenerate stain upon my door,
Grant me not the sounds,

Of dirty utterances,
No, I say! Speak not!
But instead I hear your soul-raking reply, 35
As you reach for me 'most tenderly,

"I didn't," you say on,
"I didn't."

Bitter Poetry

I whet my pain with each waking day
Elusive time already slipped my grasp
An old man staring harshly at me in the mirror
All because of you.

My poem was only a   5
Fledgling mote in your universe

A quiver; thrown
As if absent-mindedly turning to brush away an

Errant speck of dust from a shoulder
I fell to my knees and crumbled on that day without even knowing
       10
That stroke of your pen
May as well have been my heart

Hate and love did their dance inside me
As your words were read aloud
My cowardly scrawl fled my paper after   15
Leaving me to read from a blank page

Those beautiful words
That crawled inside me
And rotted
Eating away   20

Until pen and paper turned to foreign objects
And I could no longer communicate with them.
It would have been better if I'd
Turned from the mountain

To look back at you   25
I would've burned to grains of salt
And the high whisper of those words
Would have spread me throughout the world

My Eyes are Like Hummingbirds

my eyes are like hummingbirds
fleeting and flitting
never resting
in constant motion
outpacing sound   5
scenting everything there is to see
these eyes like hummingbirds
know no chains
a blur in a holding pattern
my brown hummingbird eyes   10
fly high into the sky
momentarily scorched by sun
temporarily blinded in flight
catching your attention

then gone from sight   15
a peck of thigh
curve of hip
swell of breast
pouted lip
off in the distance are   20
brown hummingbird eyes, like mine
when underneath cilia -edged blankets
they aspire to the highest treetops
brushing the floor of the sky with floss wings
drowning in rainbow pools   25
in a flower of black, they
flutter back and forth
aftertasting the briefest sips of glances, these
hummingbird eyes, light brown, quite fine.

Before You Left

Before you left, a fire throbbed to life.
The smoke took over all the rooms upstairs
Moving into the bedroom first.
I tried to put it out myself

But fistfuls of baking soda couldn't stamp it out   5
I needed the extinguisher, but you never told me where you put it

"I'll take care of it," you'd always said.
And I was happy to believe it.
The flames beat a path around the house
But you went through like they weren't even there 10

I can't breathe now because you're gone
Why can't you at least come back to beat out these flames?

I try coping with the fire,
Thinking maybe I can just sleep on the couch
But it crowded me out even there.   15
I go to the movies,

Do some shopping
And the fire still pulses when I come back.

The more room I try to give it, the more it takes
Until there just isn't any more room for me at all. 20
I hurt my wrists something awful trying to put out the flames

The fire won't let me go, but it isn't letting me stay, either.
My friends drum up support, saying

The day's too nice,
But when we go out, I pound out thoughts of   25
my house. (These bandages really itch)
I come home and see the roof ablaze.

I lay down in the vestibule with a handkerchief over my face
Listening to the flames thump against the wall and my eyes tear up
still.   30

I've been burning so long
These flames would be bearable
If only I could, but
I…

I just can't…
                                   35

Seem to…

Breathe

About Your Poem

At first I thought your poem was a little silly,
A firebug holding a book of matches with talk about

Heartache of someone too young to love,
But then its wild fire lit in my soul,

And wisps of that desire signaled the kindling catching inside me.
                 5
I struggled to keep my breath, but

Was overwhelmed with inhalation and
I fell. As I lay there, thinking about your poem the

Pain of it scorched my lungs. I tried
To cry out, 'I will love you!'   10

But the words just wouldn't come.
I shed internal tears to douse the flames

Gerald Dean Rice

Your poem set inside me,
But on it raged. My heart stammered inside me

And I died. Life passed me by as I read your poem, 15
But even then it wasn't done with me.

Your poem lifted me,
Carried me away to safety,

Its unrequited love resuscitated me,
It cracked a rib as it pumped on my chest.   20

I gagged, realizing I had not dreamed

That it was really there, but slowly,

Your poem backed away from me.

I wanted to be immolated again,
But it snuffed me, turned its back on me   25

It left me there, barely standing,
Running so fast I couldn't follow

Leaving me for another.
I wanted to scream, 'Come back to me!'

As at the same time I wanted to tear at its eyes for leaving,
                    30
But I had no voice.

Your poem took all that was inside me and burned it down
Then huffed a cold wind, blowing the ash away and leaving me
hollow.

I wrote Is that Weird *in 2019, hoping to submit it to Jordan Peele's Monkeypaw Productions for his reboot of The Twilight Zone. By the time I had a working draft, the site had been closed to submissions.*

Is That Weird?

ACT ONE

FADE IN FROM WHITE

1.   INT. FUTURISTIC-LOOKING HOME, ALL IN WHITE
                    1.

A man and woman awake in a spacious bed. There's a large blank wall that blinks open onto a panoramic view of a beautiful, mountainous landscape as the woman slowly sits

up and stretches. The man smiles and reaches an arm
across her legs, pulling himself closer to kiss her on the hip.

                    Norman
          Good morning, sweetness.

                    Abby
          Hey.

                    Norman
          Last night got pretty intense,
          didn't it?

                    Abby - smiling
          You tell me.

Norman shrugs and looks a little embarrassed for a moment.
He sits up in bed and hangs his feet out. As soon as they
touch the floor, a pair of fluffy flip flops form over his feet.

              Norman - looking down in half
                    surprise
          Wow. They really think of
          everything here.

                    Abby
          Isn't it wonderful?

Norman shrugs and stands, stretching once before he begins
shuffling toward a wall. A section of it lifts into the ceiling and
he continues to the kitchen.

                    Norman
          I'm making coffee. Want some?

Abby slumps over and burrows into her and Norman's
pillows.

                    Abby - muffled
          I thought you'd never ask.

He shakes his head, standing in front of what he assumes is the coffee maker. He hesitantly pushes a button, then another. The coffee maker jumps to life with electronic noises and Norman stares at it. An electronic emoji face appears on the display and a message asking how strong he'd like his coffee.

> Norman
> You want regular or, uh, decaf?

Abby sits up and gives him a harsh stare.

> Norman
> Right.

He presses a few more buttons and coffee begins to sputter out of the coffee maker. Norman scrambles for a cup and catches most of the liquid. As he cleans up, something flashes on the display. He stops to look, and for just a second, he sees his own face looking back at him.

> Norman
> That's weird.

> Abby
> It's not tea, is it?

> Norman
> No. I…I just saw myself in the coffee…thing here.

Abby saunters over, pretends to look interested, then hip checks Norman out of her way, taking the coffee cup just as it finishes. She takes a long sip and lets her head fall backward.

> Abby
> Better-better-better-better.

> Norman
> Look at it. Did you see—

>> Abby - holding out a hand to
>> silence him.

Wait-wait.

>> (beat)

Okay, go.

>> Norman - pointing

Right on the display here. I saw
myself.

>> Abby

So, the thing has a camera or
something. Everything does
nowadays.

She presses two buttons and restarts the coffee maker, deftly
stepping around Norman and grabbing a cup from the
cupboard and placing it beneath. She steps to the fridge and
removes a carafe of milk and places it on the counter next to
a sugar bowl. She presses a couple buttons on the fridge,
and two danishes generate in an inset that she places on
saucers, handing one to her husband. The coffee finishes
pouring and she removes it and pours in milk and spoons in
sugar and stirs it. Norman reaches and Abby sips it before
handing it over. As the cup passes between them, we see the
coffee is green. Norman sips.

>> Norman

Ahhh.

They walk to the window, eating, and stare out. The
mountains are just as beautiful as they are harsh, sharp and
steep.

>> Abby

I can't wait to get out there.

>> Norman

You really wanna go out there?
I mean, it looks so…dangerous.

>> Abby

>I know, right? I'm gonna hop in
>the shower.

She pops the last piece of danish into her mouth and pats
him on the butt before leaving the room. A moment later, the
sound of water turns on. Norman goes on looking outside for
another moment. He waves his hand in front of the window
and it turns back into a solid wall.

2.   INT. STILL INSIDE THE HOUSE
                    2.

Norman turns at what sounds like the clearing of a throat.
Norman looks around before going to the front door and
waving a hand in front of a small screen in the wall next to the
door and an image appears of the front porch. No one is
there. He turns at the sound of a cup breaking in the kitchen.

>   Norman
>Honey?

He stands silently for a beat, then heads back to the kitchen
to see the broken cup on the floor, his green coffee splashed
across the tile. A little circular robot comes out of the wall and
begins cleaning up the mess. He opens his mouth to call out
to his wife again when the doorbell rings. Looking annoyed,
Norman heads back to the front door. This time, when he
waves a hand, he sees two men, dressed in what looks like
suits made of clear plastic trimmed in red, one man hiding
behind the other.

>   Norman
>May I help you?

>   Stranger 1
>Ah yes, we have an urgent
>matter we need to speak to you
>about. It's imperative we speak
>to you urgently.

>   Norman
>What is it?

Stranger 1 hushes the man hiding behind him, then turns back to the door.

>   Stranger 1
>   We need to speak to you.
>   ASAP, probably?

>   Stranger 2
>   Now! Tell him now.

>   Stranger 1
>   Sooner is best?

>   Norman
>   Fellas, my wife and I are on
>   vacation. We really don't need
>   any vacuum cleaners.

Norman turns to see the automated cleaning robot has followed him and is cleaning up something else.

>   Norman - to himself
>   They kind of have that handled
>   already.

>   Stranger 1
>   That's…that's very good. We,
>   uh, we aren't selling anything.
>   That includes vacuum cleaners.
>   But we do need to speak with
>   you. Need I remind you that it's
>   urgent. Imperative. Over.

>   Norman
>   I believe in the Flying Spaghetti
>   Monster. I'm a Pastafarian. I'm
>   not looking to switch religions.
>   Can you just get lost?

The first stranger blinks several times and shakes his head.

> Stranger 1
> I'm a Pastafarian as well. Okay.
> Thank you.

He turns around, and the second man behind h m yells something, but Norman waves off the monitor before he hears it. Someone on the other side of the door hits it once and Norman stares at it.

> Norman - under his breath
> Try me, weirdos. I'd love to call
> the cops.

He waits a moment and, when he hears nothing more, nods in satisfaction and heads toward the living room. He picks up a remote control, and before he gets to the couch, a disheveled man with wild hair and a long beard jumps on him, knocking him down on the couch. It is the second stranger, dressed in a raincoat suit as well.

> Stranger 2
> Now you listen to me, dead
> man. You're gonna stop
> whatever it is you've been doin'
> or I'm gonna eat your face!

He shakes Norman violently and wraps his hands around his throat. Norman stares in horror and surprise as he is bounced off the couch cushion.

> Stranger 1
> No, no, no, no!

Stranger 1 runs over and pulls Stranger 2 off Norman. Stranger 1 shakes a finger at Stranger 2.

> Stranger 1
> You know violence is not an
> allowable first resort. C'mon, we
> have rules to follow here!

> Stranger 1 - to Norman
> I'm sorry. That was totally
> wrong of Norm. He apologizes
> too.

> Stranger 1 - to Norm
> Isn't that right, Norm?

Norm stalks back and forth hurriedly like a pacing animal.

> Norm
> Yeah. Sorry.

> Stranger 1
> Norm…

> Norm
> You're right. You're right. Sorry.
> I'm sorry.

Norm looks at Norman, pleadingly.

> Norm
> I'm sorry. Sorry to you. You too,
> Vic. Aw, man, bring 'er in.

They hug briefly.

> Stranger 1
> My name is Vic. This is my
> companion Norm. We need to
> talk to you about something
> extremely important. Uh, is now
> a good time?

Vic and Norm slowly advance on Norman and he retreats from them until he falls over the back of the couch.

> Norman
> Stay away from me. I-I'll call the
> cops.

             Vic - laughing nervously
No. No. There's no need for
that. Nobody is going to hurt
anybody.

             Vic - looking at Norm.
Anymore. From this point on.
We're all gonna be <u>fine</u>.

Norman rubs his neck.

             Norman
Get out of my house.

             Vic
Uh, it's not your house. You
said it yourself, you're on
vacation.

Norman looks quickly around.

             Norman
How did you even get in here?

             Vic
Well, it's interesting you ask
that. I—

             Norman
Nevermind, get the hell out.

Norman stands and heads toward the phone in
the kitchen.

             Vic
Um, please don't do that.
Please—

Norman picks up the phone and dials. He turns back to see
the two men are gone. As an operator picks up the call, he
looks around.

Norman

Hello?

He waits a long moment then hangs up.

Norman

Abby!

Norman charges into the bathroom barehanded and, realizing this, looks around and grabs the first makeshift weapon he sees—a plunger. Abby turns off the shower and slides open the door to see her husband standing poised with the tool, holding it like a batter at the plate.

> Abby - wiggling her eyebrows
> You here to clean the pipes or
> my clock?

> Norman
> Did…somebody just come in
> here?

Abby looks around conspiratorially as she grabs a towel. She peeks out of the bathroom and steps in close to her husband.

> Abby - waving him in to whisper
> in his ear
> About thirty seconds ago a
> crazy guy came in waving a
> plunger around.

She leaves him standing with the plunger in his hand.

> Norman - calling after her
> I got the plunger after I came in
> here.

> Abby
> Tomato, tomato. You gonna
> hurry up and take me or what?

She drops the towel wrapped around her.
Norman drops the plunger.

FADE TO BLACK

3.   INT. BEDROOM
                    3.

Norman lies in bed as Abby gets dressed.

                    Norman
            I just don't understand. There
            were two guys. I swear there
            were.

                    Abby
            Honey, that just doesn't make
            sense. How could anybody but
            us be in here when this whole
            place and the grounds are only
            coded for us?

                    Norman
            That's just it. I don't know.
            Maybe they were hackers?

                    Abby
            Hackers who just wanted to talk
            to you? Sweetie…

She shakes her head and reaches over to pat
his arm. He pulls away.

                    Norman
            Don't do that. Don't diminish my
            experience.

                    Abby
            I'm not. I'm just asking you to
            question for yourself. What did
            they look like? How were they

dressed? How did they get on
the grounds, let alone in the
house?

                    Norman
I...don't know.

                    Abby
Have you even taken your
medication today?

        Norman - sounding dejected
No, not yet.

                    Abby
See?

                    Norman
It can't always be my...illness,
Abby. I feel <u>fine</u>.

                    Abby
Of course, it can't.

Abby sits next to her husband and puts a hand
on his cheek.

                    Abby
But maybe it might have been
this time?

Norman rolls on his side away from her. She
leans in and kisses his back.

                    Abby
Aw, honey. I'm gonna go for a
run. You just stay here.

                    Norman
You're not going out there, are
you?

He points toward the big window that Abby has
reopened.

> Abby
> No, no, no. I'm just going
> around the grounds here. I'll be
> less than an hour.

She pats him on his ribs.

> Abby - in a mock New York
> accent, adjusting an imaginary
> tie
> Clean yourself up and have on
> somethin' pretty by the time I
> get back and I'll take yez out for
> egg creams, y'hear?

> Norman
> I'd like an egg cream. Okay.

His wife leaves and he rolls onto his back. A moment later
comes the hush of the door sliding open and shut.

> Norm
> That was a thing to behold.

Norman sits up in bed. He opens his mouth to speak right as
Norm's disembodied head hovers into view. Norman
screams, pulling the sheet up to his chest. The rest of Norm's
body appears next to Vic. The two men quickly approach the
bed, shushing him.

> Norman
> What do you want? Are you
> ghosts?

> Vic
> No. Although—

Vic pauses to think for a moment.

                    Vic
        No. We are not ghosts.

                    Norm
        The thing you did. You know at
        minute twenty-three.

He kisses the tips of his fingers and blows.

                    Norm
        God, the style, the technique.
        What a thing to behold!
        Magnifique!

                    Vic
        We weren't watching. The
        whole time. We're still very
        sorry about that, though. Right
        Norm?

                    Norm
        Oh yeah, right, dude. Totally
        sorry. Totally. Vic, you want to
        talk to him about that thing
        now?

Vic pauses for a long moment.

                    Vic
        Oh yeah. Yeah. Okay, where
        was I? I got it. We are from
        different dimensions.
        Something is happening that is
        destroying entire dimensions
        throughout the multiverse, and
        we traced it to this universe,
        more specifically to you.
        Specifically. And we need you
        to stop if you would, please.

Vic claps his hands together.

                    Norm
        Is that it? Seems like there
        should be more of an
        explanation.

                    Vic
        I know. I suppose if I
        understood it better myself, I
        could give him all the science
        on it, but…

Norm holds his hands up in mock surrender.

                    Norm
        Oh, spare me. I fell asleep the
        first time.

                    Vic
        I know, right?

They laugh briefly before Vic turns back to Norman.

        So, you believe us?

                    Norman
        Are you ghosts?

                    Norm
        Looks like somebody is having
        a vapor lock.

                    Norman
        Are you haunting me? What do
        you want? Are you seeking
        vengeance upon me? Do you
        need me to avenge you to
        somebody else? Who do I need
        to avenge upon to send you to
        the great beyond?

                Norm - half smiling

Dude, it's not that deep. We just
need you to stop destroying
universes and killing billions
upon billions of people. Simple.

Vic
I didn't want to tell him like that.

Norm
I know. I just thought it was
better to rip the band-aid off.

Norm mimics ripping off a band-aid in the air.

Vic
We agreed, though, Norm.

Norm
Vic, bro. You're right. Sorry.
Sorry, man. I been tramplin' all
over your deal all day. Bring 'er
in.

They hug briefly again. Norman's eyes go
wide. He points at them.

Norman
Wait. You're Vic and Norm?

Vic - smiling
Yeah.

Norman looks confused.

Norman
Norman and Victor. My first and
middle names.

Norm
I think somebody's startin' to
catch on.

>   Norman
> You <u>are</u> figments of my
> imagination.

>   Norm
> Oh.

He thinks a moment.

>   Norm (CONT'D)
> Look, you were almost there.
> The reason we have your first
> and middle names…

He gestures as if urging Norman to finish his
sentence.

>   Norm (CONT'D)
>   …is…

He gestures again.

>   Norm (CONT'D)
> …is because we're you. We're
> <u>you.</u>

Norman looks confused.

>   Norman
> I'm a figment of my
> imagination?

>   Norm
> No!

>   Norman
> I'm a ghost?

Norm looks annoyed.

>   Norm
> No—dammit. We're <u>you</u> from
> another dimension.

> Norm - smiling.
> I'm from Earth 2367 and Vic is
> from—uh, uh.

He snaps his fingers.

> Vic
> Earth 0069.

> Norm - laughing
> Sixty-nine. Yeah.

Vic checks a big, strange-looking watch on his
wrist.

> Vic
> Oookay, it's been approximately
> an hour and thirty-seven
> minutes since first contact. I
> think it's time for phase two.

> Norm
> You really think so? I thought I
> was connecting with him just
> now.

> Norman
> Phase two?

Norm shrugs.

> Vic
> Tori, You can come out now.

4.   INT. NORMAN'S BEDROOM.
                4.

After nothing happens for several seconds, Vic
looks down at his watch again.

> Vic

> Crap, I didn't even have the
> thing on. C'mon, Vic.

Vic begins to press buttons on the watch, and when nothing happens, he slaps it several times. A holographic display pops up, filled with several different columns of numbers, letters, and other symbols Norman doesn't recognize. Vic slaps at it a couple more times and the text changes. He carefully pokes at a symbol and the hologram vanishes.

> Norman
> Are you guys from outer space?

> Norm
> You're just <u>so</u> close.

> Vic
> Tori, can you hear me?

> Tori
> I hear you just fine.

A woman saunters into the room. She is tall, strikingly beautiful, and she stops just inside the doorway and puts her hands on her hips.

> Tori
> I'm Tori. I'm you from Urdu
> 4749. I believe you call it Earth
> here, right?

Tori's voice is sultry and deep. She wears her hair short and sharp, like something from the 80s.

> Norman
> So, in your universe, I'm a girl?
> Sorry, <u>woman</u>. Prove it.

Tori pulls up her jacket, exposing her upper body. Only Norman doesn't turn away.

                    Tori
I got this scar when I was
eleven. I believe we were riding
a bike, as you would call it?

                  Norman
I don't understand. I have that
exact same scar.

                    Vic
Right. See, even though we're
all from different universes, we
all have similar convergence
points where we do or have the
same things happen to us.
Once the council identified you
as the source, it was simple to
backtrack throughout the known
universes and find greater
variants of you to make contact.

                  Norman
Greater variants?

                    Vic
I'm glad you asked. Greater
variants have a higher number
of convergence points in
common with a being in a
particular universe and are far
less likely to come to a
paradoxical apocalypse. A
paradoxalypse, I like to call it.

                    Tori
You promised you wouldn't say
that.

             Norman - nodding
I don't get it.

                Vic - sighing

> If only there were some means
> of consolidating the time it takes
> to make him understand.

Vic and Tori slowly look up at the camera. Norm is trying to appear thoughtful with his thumb and forefinger beneath his bearded chin. He looks up and sees Vic and Tori and tries looking in the same direction.

FADE TO BLACK

ACT TWO

5.   INT. KITCHEN
                        5.

Norman sits at the counter with the three versions of himself. He and Tori both have a cup of green coffee. Norm has one, but he eyes his suspiciously.

> Norm
> Okay, I don't get it.

Everyone glances at him.
> Norm
> How is this coffee? It doesn't
> look or taste like coffee. 'Cause
> it's brown where I'm from.

Norman looks back at Vic and Tori.

> Norman
> So, you're saying something I'm
> doing is destroying universes?

> Vic
> Right. It probably isn't
> intentional. I mean, I don't know
> you, but I know me, and if I
> were destroying billions of
> people in the blink of an eye, it

definitely, most likely wouldn't
be on purpose. I'm pretty sure.

                    Tori
Whatever it is you're doing, we
have to stop it. By whatever
means.

She pats the blaster at her hip, glaring at Norman and he
looks around nervously. The front whispers open and closed.

6.   INT. KITCHEN
                          6.

                    Abby
Honey, I'm home!

Norman turns back to his guests and sees they've all
disappeared. His mouth drops open and he stands just as his
wife enters the room.

                    Abby
Ooo. Coffee.

She picks up the cup Norm was drinking from. Norman raises
a hand to stop her just as she drinks.

                    Abby
Somebody here?

                    Norman
Um. No. Why?

Abby gestures to all the cups on the counter.

                    Abby
All the cups of it?

                    Norman
Because I was thirsty?

Abby eyes him suspiciously.

Abby
Is there anyone else here?

Norman
No?

Abby
Okay, blink once if you're being
held against your will.

Norman's eyes widen in surprise. Abby leans over the
counter and stares at him as he struggles not to blink.

Norman
Okay, I'm ready to talk.

Abby
Maybe I don't want to hear it
now. Maybe I want to
enjoy…breaking you.

Norman blinks several times.

Norman
I just want it noted, I blinked
three times, not just once.

Abby
So, you're being held against
your will by three people?

Norman
What? No, I never said—
blinked that.

Abby
Oh? How many people then?

Norman
Zero. Zero people. I was
hallucinating just before you got

                    here. I made coffee for all
                    my...hallucinations.

                              Abby
                    And one of these hallucinations
                    wore lip gloss?

                              Norman
                    What?

He looks down at the cup Tori had and looks back up at
Abby.

                              Abby
                    So, one woman and two men.
                    Now to figure out what they
                    want—

Abby leans over the counter and takes another
sip from the cup.

                         Abby (CONT'D)
                    —with you...

                              Norman
                    No. No woman. No men.

She walks away from him, stripping off her clothes and
dropping them along the way to the bathroom.

                              Abby
                    I'm going for another shower.

                    Norman - calling after her
                    Do you want to go out today?

                              Abby
                    Really?

The water turns on in the bathroom. Norman makes a face
like he is regretting what he is saying.

                    Norman
          Yeah. I thought we could hit
          that nature path. Maybe get
          some lunch first.

                    Abby
          I'd love that!

7.   INT. LIVING ROOM.
                    7.

Norman looks around suspiciously, hurriedly picking up her
clothes. He points accusingly and randomly, warning the
visitors away. The shower turns on and he tosses her clothes
into the bedroom before coming back to the open area.

             Norman - whispering loudly
          Where are you guys?

All three of them appear in front of him. Norman jumps back
in surprise.

                    Vic
          Sorry about that. We have to
          minimize our impact in this
          universe. She's not supposed to
          know we're here.
          Paradoxalypse and all.

                    Norman
          Okay, I didn't sign up for any of
          this. The only options you're
          giving me are letting my wife
          think I'm crazy or hide people
          she already knows have been
          here.

                    Norm
          I vote tell her.

He raises his hand and looks to the other two.

                    Tori
          Norm!

She pushes his arm down.

                    Norm
          Sorry, she's really good. I figure
          it's only a matter of time before
          she figures out the whole thing.
          Confess now and <u>totally</u> give in,
          I say. She might be able to help
          figure out what he's doing.

                    Vic
          Okay, I'm not saying no to that.
          But no for right now. We have
          to abide by the rule book and it
          clearly states we have to go
          through a process to figure out
          between us what he could be
          doing to exterminate the lives of
          billions.

Vic turns to Norman, holding his hands out.

                    Vic (CONT'D)
          Do you have thermonuclear
          devices of any kind?

                    Norm
          Do you have one of those
          snowy things that have a town
          in them, except yours has a
          whole universe?

                    Norman
          You mean a snow globe?

                    Norm - nodding
          Yeah.

                    Norman

No.

> Vic
> How about the thermonuclear
> devices? Any of those?

Norman shakes his head.

> Norman
> No.

> Tori
> We could just skip to the end
> and say we did this part.

> Norman
> What's at the end?

> Tori
> We just kill you.

> Vic
> Okay, I'm not saying no to that.
> But no for right now. That would
> be a major change to an
> unincorporated universe and we
> have to go by the rules. Um,
> could you give us a detailed list
> of everything you do on a daily
> basis?

> Norman
> I don't know. I mean, I don't
> really write that stuff down. That
> would be weird.

> Vic - looking offended
> Oh, well excuse me.

Norman counts off on his fingers.

> Norman

Okay, I sleep. I eat. I-I go
number one and number two…

Norm
You number…what is that,
exactly? I mean, we obviously
have counting in my universe,
but what do you—

Tori
He means eliminate waste.

Norm makes a confused face.

Norm
Eliminate waste? Why do you
need two numbers?

Norman uses both hands to gesture to the front and then the
rear of his body.

Norm
Now I'm confused.

Vic
Don't you go poopoo and
peepee?

Norm
No! Only birds do that. I'm not a
bird. When I go, it's one big
gooey glop. You guys are
freaks.

Norman
But you're human. How could
you—

Norm
Look. Vic already told me where
he's from, humans evolved from
apes.

He laughs and rolls his eyes, pointing toward Vic with a thumb. Then he gestures to himself.

                    Norm (CONT'D)
               <u>We</u> evolved from the Great
               Slime Bush and apes went
               instinct three thousand years
               ago because they were stupid.
               Very stupid.

                         Tori
               Extinct?

                    Norm
               Yes. That's what I said. Instinct.

                    Tori
               No. You mean extinct.

                    Norm
               Yeah, I normally say what I
               mean and I did this time too.

                    Vic
               I think I get it. 'Instinct' and
               'extinct' are probably the same
               word in his universe. Hey Norm,
               what's that steamy Sharon
               Stone movie with Michael
               Douglas?

                    Norm
               You mean <u>Basic Extinct</u>? Oh,
               so steamy.

                    Vic
               See?

                         Tori
               Or he could just be dumb.

                    Norman
          So how do you <u>know</u> I'm the
          one destroying universes?

Tori presses a button on her own big watch. What looks like a
solar system pops up on her holographic display. Norman
leans forward and watches the graphic as a massive ball of
energy appears, intensifies, and the planets in what he
assumes is a solar system similar to his began peeling away
like sandcastles caught in a high tide. Finally, the sun itself
expands and everything turns white. After the light fades,
there is a massive, ugly hole where the sun used to be, and
all the stars begin winking out.

                    Tori
          This was my universe. Three
          days ago, it was destroyed, and
          all but seven souls were
          salvaged. The Council had
          already been attempting to
          track down the genesis of these
          attacks, coming closer after
          each one. They were finally
          able to identify this universe as
          being the source, and after the
          last one two days ago, they
          were able to trace it to you. The
          only reason I survived was
          because I was with an envoy
          that was in the middle of
          interdimensional negotiations
          with Universe 3333.

              Norman - awestruck
          I'm so sorry. What can I do?

                    Vic
          Yeah, if you don't mind, if you
          could just list everything you do
          on a daily basis, we could start
          to whittle that down and maybe
          be on our way.

Vic hands him a pen and pad.

                    Norman
          And Abby can't know?

                     Vic
          It wouldn't be preferable. The
          more interference we cause
          here, the closer we come to
          destabilizing your universe. The
          aforementioned paradoxalypse.
          Because you're an
          unincorporated universe,
          there's all kinds of limitations on
          things we're able to do here.
          Ooo, do you do this?

Vic begins to pat his head with one hand and
rub his belly with the other.

                     Vic
          Or this?

He begins rubbing his head with one hand and patting his
belly with the other. Norman shakes his head.

                    Norman
          What kinds of limitations?

                     Vic
          Oh, I don't know. The cure for
          cancer.

Tori folds her arms and rolls her eyes.
                    Tori
          Psh. You don't have the cure
          for cancer.

                     Vic
          True. True. But 4959 does and
          it's simply a matter of peace

accords being signed before the free flowing exchange of knowledge and technology. So, we practically have it now. It's just about the same thing.

                    Tori
Except for the terrorists who blew up your moon.

                    Vic
I feel like we're getting lost in the weeds here. A little bit. The point is, there is information whether <u>shared</u> or not that is within the <u>shared</u> multiverse that could potentially be <u>shared</u> with this one once they are incorporated. Here, look.

Vic digs out a small, colorful object and sits it on the counter in front of Norman.

                    Norman
What is that?

                    Vic
It's a Quezza.

He stands back, looking self-satisfied.

                    Norman
What's a Quezza?

                    Vic
It'd be too hard to explain it to you.

                    Norm
You told me it's a child's toy.

                    Vic

Okay, yeah. It's a child's toy.
My point remains, however. It's
something you don't have here
that we—all of us—could share.
          (beat)
You don't have these here,
right?

                    Norman
Uh-uh.

                    Tori
The point is, we need you to
start writing out your daily
routine.

                    Vic
Right. Yes, do that first.

Vic reaches over and picks up the Quezza and puts it back in
his clear plastic pocket. Norman picks up the pen and studies
the blank page.

                    Norman
Well, if I start with this morning,
I woke up, had coffee, took a
shower—

                    Tori
You can skip anything you've
done so far this morning.

                    Vic
How do you know that?

                    Tori
Because he hasn't destroyed a
universe today.

                    Norman
Okay, can we stop saying I'm
destroying universes? I'm not

comfortable with that. Besides, I
don't know that I'm doing that. I
certainly don't feel like I am.

He writes something on the page.

                    Norm
I don't know if we need to race
over the stuff he's already done.
But I mean, maybe he can list in
detail some of the more choice
events from this morning. So
we can, I dunno, read it over
the trip back and file it.

                    Vic
C'mon, Norm, will you focus?
Although Norman making
sweet, sweet love to his
beautiful and very lithe and
Olympically flexible wife was
very arousing for everyone who
saw, I'm sure he doesn't want
to give us a detailed play-by-
play along with the sensations
going through his body at the
time.

Vic turns to Norman.

                    Vic (CONT'D)
Unless you're totally cool with
that.

Norman looks horrified.

                    Vic
Okay, we're going to put a pin
in that while you complete your
otherwise daily list.

                  Abby - calling from the
                       bathroom
          You ready to go?

She walks into the room fully clothed, running her fingers
through her still wet hair. Norman's companions have
disappeared again.

                     Abby
         I'd like to hit that trail before
         lunch.

                   Norman
         Um, sure. Are you sure you're
         up to going?

                     Abby
         I am. And so are <u>you</u>.

She sidles up to him and they kiss before she
looks down at his notepad.

                     Abby
         What's this?

                   Norman
         A…grocery list.

                Abby - suspicious
         Really?

She snatches up the notepad before Norman
can get to it and reads it.

                  Abby - aloud
         'One. Grocery list'. 'Two. How I
         make sweet, sweet love to my
         wife'. Honey, what kind of
         grocery list is this?

                   Norman
         An unfinished one.

Norman wiggles his eyebrows at her and she pulls away.

>   Abby
>   No, no. I know you. You'll keep
>   me in bed all day if that means
>   you don't have to go outside.
>   We're going.

>   Disembodied Voice -
>   whispering
>   Nuts!

>   Abby
>   Say again?

>   Norman
>   Nuts? I mean, I just wanted to
>   make sweet, sweet love to you
>   because it's on my grocery list.

Abby puts her arms around Norman's neck.

>   Abby
>   Well, nobody said you couldn't
>   after we have lunch.

They kiss again.

ACT THREE

8.   EXT. NATURE TRAIL
>   8.

A blazing red sun sits high in the blue sky. A winding trail stretches as far as the eye can see with alien vegetation to either side of the path. What passes for birds on this Earth fly around with translucent wings and feathers that look like diamonds.

>   Abby

It's so beautiful up here.

Norman
Yeah, it is.

They kiss. Norman looks nervous.

Abby
So where are your friends?

Norman
My…who?

Abby
Your friends. The people you've
been talking to?

Norman sputters. Abby kisses him again.

Norman
I don't know what to do here.

Abby
What do you mean?

Norman turns away from his wife.

Norman
I really don't know what to do.
You said too much interference
is a bad thing. But isn't this
interference in a way too?

Abby - laughing
Norman, you don't have to
pretend there's anybody
around. I have eyes. But I heard
you talking to someone while I
was in the shower. Is there a
surprise or something?

Norman looks at his wife again.

> Norman
>
> I really don't know what to do
> here. I mean, I could tell you,
> but it could be bad. I'm not
> supposed to say.

> Abby
>
> It is a surprise!

Abby does a happy dance. Then she starts
poking and tickling Norman.

> Abby
>
> Come on. You know you're
> gonna tell me. I practically know
> what it is now.

Norman backs away, looking worried.

> Abby
>
> Are you feeling okay? You look
> a little green. When did you
> take your medicine today?

> Norman
>
> I forgot. I'll just take it when we
> get home. Maybe we should go
> back now.

> Abby
>
> Not so fast. I know you, and as
> soon as we get back, you'll be
> all over me, and we won't set
> foot outside for the rest of the
> day. You've made it this far and
> you can go for a little bit longer.
> We'll head back in a half hour.
> And you can tell me all about
> my surprise.

They trudge on for a while longer through a montage of sceneries. They even have to remove their coats when they come to an area devoid of snow and desert-like in appearance. Both point at different things as they stop occasionally until Abby points at a row of cactuses.

>   Abby
>   Who's that?

Norman looks to where she's pointing.

>   Norman
>   You mean the cactuses?

>   Abby
>   No, the guy standing behind the
>   cactuses.

Norman looks again and sees the wily head of Norm who slowly stands and begins waving. His hair is barely restrained by a tie at the back of his head.

>   Norm - shouting
>   Hello there!

He walks toward them, an unnaturally wide smile on his face.

>   Norm
>   Ho, fellow travelers. I see you're
>   enjoying this fine…weather
>   we're having. It's so…typical for
>   this time of year.

>   Abby
>   Hi. Isn't it wonderful?

>   Norm
>   Indeed, it is.

>   Abby
>   Have you been to the caverns?

>   Norm
> No, not yet. Not yet. Planning to
> go, though.

Norm puts his hands on his hips and looks around. Then he hooks a thumb over his shoulder.

>   Norm
> Say, my friend and I were
> hiking—y'know, toward the
> caverns—and he fell down and
> hurt himself pretty bad. He can't
> walk. Do you think you could
> help?

Abby looks concerned.

>   Abby
> Absolutely! I'm a doctor.

Norm's face turns surprised.

>   Norm
> Oh, wait. You're the doctor? Not
> this man whom I've never met
> who may or may not be your
> husband?

>   Abby
> No, I'm the doctor.

Norm puts his hands up to stop her from walking.

>   Norm
> Wait. You really shouldn't
> come. My friend's really sexist.
> And he's not injured real real
> bad. Besides, you don't even
> know me. I could be a serial
> killer. Just let your husband

come. While you wait here all
alone in a strange place,
completely devoid of any
danger whatsoever.

Abby eyes him suspiciously.

                    Abby
        Are you a serial killer?

Norm looks her in the eyes.

                    Norm
        Yes. <u>No</u>!

Norm shakes his fists in frustration and grits his teeth. He
looks off in the distance.

                    Norm
        I'm actually…between jobs.

Abby looks around.

                    Abby
        All right. What's going on here?

                    Tori
        We are trying to stop your
        husband from extinguishing all
        life on Earth.

She walks out from behind a row of orange
bushes.

                    Abby
        And who are <u>you</u> now?

                    Tori
        I am from another universe.
        And we actually do need <u>your</u>
        help. Vic has been injured. I am
        a doctor, but his physiology is
        strange to me.

Abby folds her arms and pauses for a long
moment.

                    Abby
          Okay, let's go.

Tori leads the three of them past wild vegetation via a small
footpath to where Vic lies on his back. He's obviously in
agony but tries smiling when he sees them approach.

                    Tori
          I am actually a version of your
          husband from my universe.

                    Abby
          What?

Tori stops walking. She turns slowly and looks
at everyone.

                    Tori
          Didn't you all tell her?

                    Norm
          No, we were kind of hoping to
          avoid elling-ta the ife-wa.

                    Abby
          I understand Pig-Latin.

                    Tori
          I don't. What did you just say?

                    Abby
          He was hoping to avoid telling
          me what's going on.

She turns to Norman and puts her hands on
her hips.

                    Abby

Are you cheating on me?

           Norman
<u>Now</u> you think I'm cheating?

           Abby
Up until now, this little secret
game of yours has been cute. I
thought you were trying to
coordinate some sort of early
birthday surprise for me, but it's
something else. What the hell is
going on?

Norman looks far off into the distance and puts
a hand to his mouth.

           Norman
Birthday…

He shakes his head and looks at his wife.

           Norman (CONT'D)
As far as I can understand,
these three people are
representatives from different
dimensions sent by a United
Multiverse Council, or UMC, to
ascertain what, if anything, I
might be doing to disrupt
numerous incorporated
universes, causing billions of
lives to be lost. At least that's
what I got from their
explanation.

           Norm
That's pretty much it. Y'know, in
basic layman terms.

           Tori - nodding

Yeah. That'll do for an initial
explanation.

                    Abby
So, you believe there's
something my husband is doing
that's causing the disruption of
universes. Why should we
care? I mean, what's our buy-
in?

                    Tori
If he doesn't stop, we'll have to
kill him.

                    Abby
But how do you know you
haven't tried that already?

                    Norm
Because we just got here this
morning?

                    Abby
Sure, but you are all versions of
my husband, right? How do you
know there aren't other versions
of him—you—from another
multiverse council, traveling
around doing the exact same
thing and causing the very thing
you're trying to prevent right
now?

Tori and Norm look at each other.

                    Norm
Because we're not?

Abby folds her arms.

                    Abby

How many universes have been
destroyed so far?

Norm looks at Tori.

> Norm
> I'm not sure.

> Tori
> Three hundred sixty-two.

> Abby
> And how frequently does this
> happen?

> Tori
> Approximately once per day,
> give or take.

> Abby
> Okay, so this has been going
> on for a little under a year. So,
> you need to know something
> my husband may be doing that
> he started almost a year ago.
> Right?

> Tori
> In theory.

Norm slaps Norman's arm.

> Norm
> Hey man, your wife catches on
> fast. Whoa, you okay there,
> buddy?

Norman's forehead is covered in sweat and his
eyes are distant.

> Norman

I don't feel so good. I think I
need to sit down.

Vic - from a distance
Is anybody going to help me?

Norman sits down abruptly and Abby rushes to
his side.

9.   EXT. STILL AT THE NATURE PATH
                9.

Abby
Honey, why didn't you take your
medicine?

Tori & Norm
Medicine?

Abby dabs Norman's brow with his shirt and feels his pulse.
She holds his hand, a look of concern on her face.

Abby
When was the last time you
took your pill?

Norman
I'm not sure. Yesterday? Maybe
the day before?

Tori
What is the nature of your
husband's illness?

Abby
He has seizures. It's
neurological? He was
diagnosed around this time last
year.

Tori
A year ago?

> Vic - from a distance
> Guys?

Abby looks at Tori.

> Abby
> You don't think it could be this,
> could you? It only affects <u>him</u>.

Vic finally crawls over and lays a hand on her arm.

> Vic
> We really don't know what it is.
> How can we help?

> Abby
> He needs his medicine. Could
> you?

She looks around at the three strangers.

> Abby
> Could you go back and get it?

> Vic
> Uh, why do you think we've
> been there?

> Norm
> Yeah. Watching you in your
> most intimate of intimate
> moments? That would just
> be…<u>creepy</u>.

> Tori
> Where is his medication?

> Abby
> It should be in his luggage?
> Um, what he used to bring his
> clothes in?

Tori nods and looks at Norm. The two of them head back.

> Vic
> So, what's your story, pretty lady?

Abby looks at him and his sly expression turns pained.

> Vic
> Oh, such pain!

He rolls onto his back and grabs his leg.

> Abby
> What did you hurt?

> Vic
> My ankle. I think I might have broken it.

> Abby
> Let me look at it.

She gets to one knee and begins to examine.

> Abby
> I just need to take your sock off.

> Vic
> Oh, no. Don't do that. I'm sure an over-the-sock examination would be perfectly suitable.

Abby strips off the sock, holding onto his calf.

> Vic
> Well, that was way less painful than I was expecting.

She grasps his foot and sees his toenails are painted silver. Vic shakes his head.

>   Vic
>   Painted toenails are perfectly
>   normal in my universe. Not a
>   big deal at all.

Abby smiles and leans closer.

>   Abby
>   No, they aren't. But Norman
>   likes to paint his too. It looks
>   like you've got a sprain.

She gets up and drags him by the legs to a boulder half in the ground.

>   Abby
>   Keep it elevated and we can all
>   go back together.

>   Vic
>   Is he going to be okay?

>   Abby
>   Yes. His medication helps to
>   reduce the amount of episodes
>   he has, but it's something we
>   know how to deal with when it
>   pops up. He'll probably sleep
>   the rest of the day once we get
>   back to the house.

Abby looks at her husband's prone body. She smiles wanly.

>   Abby
>   Looks like you got your way,
>   sweety.

>   Vic

You said it's neurological?

                    Abby
Yes.

                    Vic
I'm a neurologist. As it
happens…

Vic props up on one elbow and digs into his fanny pack,
removing a blister pack of pills.

                    Vic
Give him one of these. In my
universe, we're pretty good at
curing neurological
dysfunctions.

Abby takes it and looks it over.

                    Abby
But we have no way of knowing
how it would match up with his
physiology.

                    Vic
Yeah, that's not a problem. That
pill is good for pretty much all
life on my planet. All life with
brains, I mean.

                    Abby
And how would I know that this
isn't the thing that triggers this
cataclysmic event?

Vic rolls his eyes.

                    Vic
Because the council has ruled
out every other universe. It's
only coming from here and it's

only coming from your husband.
For all we know, this could cure
him <u>and</u> fix our problem. And if
it doesn't work, the entire thing
flushes out of his system with
very few side effects. Maybe a
little diarrhea.

Abby nods and examines the blister pack.

> Vic
> Look, if it were a trick, this
> would be extremely convenient,
> wouldn't it? Tori's got a blaster
> gun. I mean, she could have
> vaporized the both of you, if
> killing you was all we were here
> for.

Abby looks between him and the pills. She finally pops one
from the pack and goes over to Norman. She gives him one
and helps him wash it down with her water bottle.

> Vic
> Wow. A traveling container
> specifically for liquids? That's
> <u>amazing</u>.

Norman opens his eyes, blinks several times,
and sits up.

> Abby
> Honey, are you okay?

Norman looks around like he's seeing where
he is for the first time.

> Norman
> I feel…<u>wonderful</u>.

Norman gets to his feet. He stretches, touches
his toes, jumps in the air.

Abby - looking at Vic
Is this normal?

Vic - smiling confidently
Ma'am, since when is feeling
good bad?

Abby
Since you just told me that my
husband might be destroying
universes and I gave him a pill
that makes him not act like
himself!

Norman wraps her up in a hug and spins around. His eyes
are huge. He kisses her and sits her back down. He goes
through the strange bushes, and Abby follows, concern on
her face.

Abby
Honey, are you all right?

Norman
I'm better than all right. I've
never felt this good in my <u>life</u>!

Abby
But can you sit down for just a
moment? Let me look at you?
You just had one of your spells.

Norman
I can't imagine ever feeling like
that again.

He rubs his hands up and down his arms. He begins jogging
through the foliage and Abby pursues, quickly falling behind
as his pace quickens.

Norman

I want to see the cliff. I'm going
to drink in the sun!

                    Abby
        Norman! Norman! Wait for me!
        Wait!

She loses sight of him but keeps running. Abby breaks out of
the vegetation and comes up quickly on a jagged cliff.
Norman scoops her up just as one foot dangles over the
edge.

10.   EXT. CLIFF'S EDGE
                    10.

The sun is just barely over the mountains, the sky a mix of
pink and burgundy atop the snowcaps. Norman and Abby
stand on a well-worn, old path that looks like not many people
have been on recently.

                Abby - breathless
        Oh God. Norman.

He is beaming and appears to be the picture of health. He
kisses her and she relaxes. Norman turns toward the edge.

                    Norman
        I love you. Isn't it beautiful
        here?

                    Abby
        Y-yes. How are you feeling,
        Norman?

                    Norman
        Like I never want to sit down
        again. I feel like I've missed out
        on so much! Can we come back
        here next year?

                Abby - smiling weakly
        Sure?

Vic finally crawls out of the vegetation. He is scraped up and his clothes are torn.

> Vic
> See? I told you it would be fine.
> It's all good. I think I sprained
> my other ankle, though.

There is an electronic hum behind them and all three people turn to see Tori aiming her blaster at Norman.

> Tori
> Step away from him, doctor.

> Abby
> No!

She steps in front of Norman.

> Tori
> I am authorized to vaporize you
> both, if necessary.

> Abby
> Then do it. I won't just let you
> vaporize my husband.

> Vic
> Uh, Tori, I just told her it's all
> good. His seizures are the
> cause and I had the cure.

> Tori
> You don't know that.

> Vic
> It was the only thing we hadn't
> ruled out.

> Norm

They're so steamy, though. Are
you sure we need to vaporize
them, Tori?

Tori
We are nearing the estimated
time for when he'll do it again.

Norm
How about I give him his pills?
His pills keep him regulated.
Right?

Abby
Right. Yeah, they do.

Norm tosses the pill bottle and Abby catches it. Norman takes
them from her and tosses them over the edge.

Abby, Vic, & Norm
What the hell are you doing?

Norman
I don't need those anymore.
Look, Tori, I've never felt like
this in my entire life. I'm cured. I
mean, whatever it is I was
doing, I haven't been doing it
forever. It's like I've hit a reset
button on my whole life!

Disembodied Female Voice
Estimated Paradoxalyptic Event
in thirty seconds...

Tori
I have to do this. I'm sorry.

Vic
But you could be killing an
innocent man. You don't know
that he's still dangerous.

                              Tori
              Billions of lives are at risk.
              Billions, Vic.

She looks back at Abby and Norman.

                              Tori
              I'm sorry. We just can't risk it.

                    Disembodied Female Voice
                    Estimated Paradoxalyptic Event
                    in twenty seconds…

She aims at Abby and Norman again.

                              Tori
              You won't step aside?

                              Abby
              No.

                            Norman
              Don't shoot her! I'll move.

                              Abby
              Norman, no. No. I won't let you.

Norman picks his wife up. She struggles until he puts her in
front of Norm who holds onto her.

                    Disembodied Female Voice
                    Estimated Paradoxalyptic Event
                    in fifteen seconds…

                            Norman
              Okay, I'm ready.

                              Tori
              Sorry about this.

Just before she squeezes the trigger, Vic pulls on her boot, causing her shot to go wide, zapping the tip of a mountain and causing a huge explosion and avalanche.

                    Disembodied Female Voice
                    Estimated Paradoxalyptic Event
                    in ten seconds...

Tori kicks at Vic.

                              Tori
                    Let go of me!

Norm lets go of Abby long enough to join in the fight. He grabs Tori's gun arm, and she tries to fling him off but manages to fall on her side on top of him. Norman dances left and right as the blaster waves around. Vic gets on top of her but is punched in the face by Norm.

                              Vic
                    Whose side are you on?

All three of them have a hand on a part of the blaster, but Tori is clearly overpowering the two men. She squints and manages to aim roughly at Norman.

                    Disembodied Female Voice
                    Estimated Paradoxalyptic Event
                    in five...four...three...

The ground in front of him disintegrates and everyone stops. A giant cloud of dirt is tossed into the sky and rocks and clumps of earth fall all around them and into the foliage.

                              Abby
                    Honey!

She rushes to the edge, a huge, u-shaped divot where he'd been standing just a moment before. She gets on her knees and screams. The three visitors rise, dusting themselves off. Vic limps over and they stand behind Abby.

>   Disembodied Female Voice
>   Estimated Paradoxalyptic Event
>   is now…Estimated
>   Paradoxalyptic Event is
>   now…Estimated Paradoxalyptic
>   Event is now…

Tori slaps her watch and the voice ceases.
She re-holsters her blaster.

>   Tori
>   I am sorry that had to be done.

Abby pulls up fistfuls of grass as she cries. She finally stifles
her tears, rising and whirling on the three visitors.

>   Abby
>   This is all your fault. You came
>   here unprepared. You took the
>   easy way. You didn't see him
>   as a person. A husband. A
>   human being. You played a
>   numbers game and took away
>   the man I love. How do you
>   know I won't figure out a way to
>   do on purpose what he did by
>   mistake?

As Abby speaks, a figure emerges behind her. The dust
continues to settle and Norman begins coughing.

>   Abby
>   He's right behind me, isn't he?

All three visitors smile, nodding eagerly. Abby turns and
embraces her filthy husband. She kisses him, pulls back in
revulsion, kisses him again.

>   Vic
>   He's alive!

He tries to do a little dance and almost goes down in pain.
Tori pulls him up and he leans on her. The three visitors
embrace while Abby and Norman embrace. A moment later,
all five of them embrace.

11.   EXT. OUTSIDE THE FUTURISTIC-LOOKING HOME ON A
BRICK PATIO.   11.

The group all sit around in deck chairs surrounding a pit.
They've all set aside plates they've eaten from and are either
drinking beer or wine. Norman sits in a lounge chair with
Abby sitting on the arm stroking his head.

                    Norman
            So, when do you guys have to
            head back?

Vic checks his watch.
                    Vic
            Oh, anytime now. Council cast
            a pretty wide window in case
            we needed to um, clean up.

Abby notices Norm and Tori holding hands.

                    Abby - smiling
            Is this okay?

                    Tori
            Yes, it is, actually. I mean,
            we're not siblings. It's more like
            doing it yourself rather than
            someone else doing it. Besides,
            I don't have a world to go back
            to.

                    Norm
            Yeah. It's like discovering your
            body all over again. Except now
            you've got <u>boobs</u>.

Vic stands.

                              Vic
            We probably better get going.
            Paperwork and all that. Dinner
            was great, guys.

                              Tori
            And I apologize again about the
            blasting.

                              Abby
            Don't worry about it. It's just
            another story to add to a
            wonderful trip.

Tori stares at her.

                              Abby
            That we'll never tell anybody.

Tori manipulates her watch while Vic does the same thing.
Abby leans over and kisses Norman, and they both stand.
The couple hug all three visitors in turn. Tori and Norm hold
hands and smile at one another.

                              Tori
            Ready?

                              Norm
            Yes, my sweet love.

The two are sucked into a ball of light about the size of two
basketballs. The light zips into the sky and is gone in a
second. Norman stretches.

                              Vic
            You know, this might go a long
            way to getting your universe
            incorporated. I wouldn't be
            surprised if I'm not back here
            soon offering you an
            ambassadorship.

Abby
Oh. Okay.

Norman walks to the edge of the deck, looking over the mountainous landscape. Abby shakes her head, truly surprised that her husband is outside at all.

Vic
It usually starts with a visit like this. Well, not like this but—

Norman's body pulses with light and shoots a high-intensity beam into the sky for half a second that ends with him stretching and yawning. Vic's mouth hangs open.

Abby
Is something wrong?

Vic
He just…he just…

Norman
You okay, Vic?

Norman saunters back over.
Vic
You just…you just…

Norman shrugs.

Norman
Expended the balance of my corporeal excess energy wastes. Sure, I could have gone to the bathroom to do it, but it's just the three of us here.

Vic
Yeah but…yeah but…

Abby looks Vic in the eyes and stares at him a moment.

> Abby
>
> I just did it yesterday. Do you do that differently where you're from?

Safe was taken from a book of short stories I'd started called Men in Chairs. *I had a few stories in mind, but not enough for a whole collection. I may still write the others; this was the only one I completed. If you read a short story of mine in the future where it involves a man in a chair, more than likely it was intended for that collection.*

Safe

Charlie hit him again, knocking a trail of blood, saliva, and teeth out of his mouth.

"Got anything to say now?" he said to the man.

Jimmy didn't point out to Charlie how the man hadn't cried out in pain from the blow or any of the ones that came before it. Hadn't begged for mercy at any point throughout the long, cold night. Nothing they'd done had remotely come close to getting him to say or do anything they needed in the last four hours.

Jimmy needed him to give up the combination to the safe. They'd managed to haul it to this abandoned warehouse but didn't have the tools to get it open. But this man, this was the person who knew how to get it open. And uncooperative had been the word of the day.

"Just tell us…tell us already," Jimmy said, frustration bubbling to the surface again. He was tired of hurting this man. Jimmy's hands ached from gripping tools used to pull out fingernails, clip off pieces of finger, and extract teeth.

The man was older, fifty or so, baldheaded, and pudgy around the middle. His salt-and-pepper mustache had a wedge of crusted blood the width of two fingers dividing it in half. One blue eye had started to puff up from Charlie's heavy-handed blows.

"No," the man said, his clear and steady eyes locked with Jimmy's. The younger man looked away. "I have no reason to. I'm dead either way, right?"

Jimmy opened his mouth to say, 'no', but realized the man must have already known the answer. "Gimme *something*." He sat sideways in the folding chair across from the man, resting his head on his palm and running a middle finger across the lines developing on his forehead. "I promise we'll let you go."

He wouldn't have believed himself.

"Really? After the two of you have done all this to me, you would just let me walk out of here with the six fingers I have left if I just gave you the combination?"

The man was smart. Smarter than probably Jimmy knew.

"Hey, smart guy," Charlie said, reading his thoughts. "You weren't smart enough we couldn't find you." He slugged the man again, rocking his head back so hard Jimmy thought Charlie had broken his neck. There had to be a way around this, some way to set things back. Jimmy looked at the safe, willing the numbers to come to him. There was a bad idea locked in there. Of course, they couldn't let him go; the fact he'd seen what was in there was enough, but killing him wasn't the difficult part.

Jimmy managed a smile. It crawled up his cheeks but stopped a million miles from his eyes. He hoped it looked scary, but the man smiled back, freezing Jimmy's lips in an angry rictus.

"Gimme the numbers," Jimmy said, picking up a pair of bloody pliers from the tray next to him. A crescent of toenail was stuck to the business end. The man's eyes went wide and he exhaled sharply, his cheeks puffing out like a cartoon animal. Good. He was afraid.

He mumbled something.

"Say again?" Jimmy said.

"Three-three-one-six," he whispered rapidly.

Jimmy's heart rose, but just as quickly fell again. Charlie strode over to the safe and began spinning the dial once more. Even before his partner turned to him and shook his head, Jimmy knew it was a lie. The man had the look and feel of someone who was afraid and had the certain knowledge they would hurt him badly, but he had a tell. A real obvious one, too. It had taken three erroneous combinations, but Jimmy had finally picked up on it. Every time he gave them a series of numbers to try, he half winked with his left eye. Maybe he knew he was doing it, maybe he didn't, but Jimmy saw.

He growled his frustration at the man tied to the chair and stalked over to him, putting a foot in his chest and shoving him onto his back, ripping the IV out of his arm. The man coughed furiously, trying to get his wind back when Jimmy stood over him, daggers in his eyes. He needed to get back to Drea before this all went to hell, if it hadn't already.

"Give me the numbers. The real numbers, cocksucker. Or I'll…I'll…" He was running out of steam, mid-threat.

"Let me help. You'll take a hammer to my toes. Or you'll break my shins. Gouge out my eyes." His left eye had closed—the tell one—from Charlie's last punch.

Jimmy lifted the chair back on all four legs and began putting the IV line back in his arm.

"You know, that's really good. Keep me hydrated so I can take more punishment." He looked around as much as his bonds would allow. "I've been doing a whole lot of bleeding."

Jimmy put his hands on the man's shoulders. "What's it gonna take, huh? How bad do you want me to hurt you before you give me what I want?"

The man looked up and met Jimmy's tired gaze with his good eye.

"Suck my dick," the man said and laughed.

Jimmy slapped him across the mouth. He reared back to punch him and the man laughed harder. Jimmy dropped his arm and stalked away. He was playing them. How could he wield so much power when he was the one tied down?

"This is gonna be one nice last ride for me. I'm wondering how this is gonna pan out for you, though." He spat a gob of blood. "Outside of what you have tied down in this chair, you don't have anything on me. You have to hurt me to hurt me. But you? There's a million ways they're gonna get to you without even laying a finger on you. I saw it, you know." Jimmy's eyes flicked to the safe again. "I could have told you that was a bad idea. It really doesn't matter whether or not I give you the combination. By virtue of what you took not being where it's supposed to be, they're gonna know it was taken. Do you have any idea the shitstorm you put—what—a dozen other guys in because they knew about that? And something like that, they send *the* guy. I mean, you two have been impressive so far, but the guy they're gonna send?" The man attempted to whistle with his busted lips. "I hear he doesn't leave any marks. Who knows what he does—I hear the coroner doesn't even know what killed them half the time."

"I heard 'a that guy," Charlie said.

Jimmy shushed him quickly, the fear in the other man's voice probably fueling the man tied to the chair.

"I hear that sometimes they find guys sucked dry like empty beer cans, with no cuts or nothin' on 'em. Like some kinda vampire or somethin'."

"Like some kinda vampire," the man repeated, mocking Charlie's pseudo-New York thug accent, looking away from him and back to Jimmy. "See? He's heard 'a that guy."

Now this was getting to be too much. "Shut up," Jimmy said.

"No, serious." The man nodded rigorously. "I hear this guy studies this kind of stuff. It's not that the two of you aren't any good, but he's a pro. I bet he could get me to sing in a few minutes' time. But what about you? I mean, they're so much there." He looked Jimmy up and down. "You got that wife of yours, those little girls…"

"Shut up!" Jimmy took two big steps over and hit him upside the head with the flat of his hand. "Just shut the fuck up right now."

"Ay," Charlie said, putting a hand on Jimmy's shoulder to nudge him aside. "Lemme take a crack at 'im." He began taking off his jacket, making a show of flexing his bulky, muscular arms.

"Looks like this is getting *serious*," the man said. "Jimmy, he's taking off his jacket. What's he gonna do after he takes off his jacket?"

Charlie tossed the jacket on the floor, his breath pluming in the frigid air. He grabbed the pliers from Jimmy's hand and pinched the tip of one of the man's remaining fingers. Charlie smiled as he curled the man's finger backward, the sound of several bones breaking like pencils. The man stomped his foot several times, grimacing and clenching his eyes closed.

"You know what happens after I break the finger, right?" Charlie whispered.

The man nodded, his voice a tight whisper. "You cut it off."

"Yeah, and then it goes in the can with the others." Charlie looked down at his handiwork, wriggling the pliers back and forth, the man squirming in his chair. Charlie's mouth hung open like he was particularly impressed with what he was doing before his eyes flicked back up. "You're right. We are gonna kill you. But it can take three days for you to die or you can be dead in three minutes. It can be more pain than you could ever dream of or it can be just you goin' to sleep and never wakin' up."

The man began to laugh, but it came out as coughing.

"You don't...*have* three days."

Charlie's face went white and he took a step back, letting the pliers fall. He gave the man a right hook that made the chair teeter dangerously for a moment before slamming back down.

"I already told you what it's going to take to make me talk. Jimmy, your idiot friend here fails to understand something very key, but I think I know you well enough to know you've seen it. This isn't working. It isn't going to work. You have no...no *theme* here. There's no reason for me to buy in. Pain, no matter how enduring, is only temporary, and the two of you have butchered me to the point where I don't care if I walk out of here. I prefer death. Your little hodge-podge method of skipping around all different parts of my body has left me looking like a chew toy. The man who's coming for you—the both of you—will be very *succinct.* You won't be able to get underneath what he's going to do to you. It'll be agony. I'd probably have a massive heart attack or something, but two young bulls like you will last and last."

Charlie hit him again. And again. And again.

"Wait." Jimmy put a hand on Charlie's shoulder. "You said you already told us what it's going to take. So, if you don't care about us hurting you, what do you want?"

"Jimmy, what the fuck? I'm about to break this guy. Just lemme—"

"Hold up." Jimmy nodded at the man. "Spill."

At first he thought the man was shaking, like he was having some sort of mild seizure, but then he raised his head, blood trailing from his nose and open mouth. His top front teeth were gone when he smiled. The missing ones Charlie hadn't knocked out, Jimmy had wrenched out of his head. His laugh rose to a conversational volume, tears streaming from his eyes. Jimmy and Charlie looked at each other.

"I told you. Suck my dick. You both can do it."

"The fuck you say?" Charlie slapped him upside the head. He back- and forehanded him a couple more times as the three words sunk in for Jimmy. Despite laughing, he'd been serious.

"Charlie, stop hitting him."

"What?" Charlie turned back, winded and bloody-knuckled.

"I said, stop hitting him."

"You can't be takin' this bullshit serious. He's fuckin' with us." Charlie raised a meaty fist. Jimmy grabbed his wrist.

"Don't hit him again."

Charlie yanked his arm away. "You're not even thinkin' about this. We're gonna break this guy, get the shit…get it back where it belongs, and be back in bed in time for corn flakes."

Jimmy wished it could be that simple. Nothing they'd done had remotely come close to breaking the man. They'd hurt him. Hurt him as much as Jimmy knew how short of putting a bullet in his brain, but it was like somewhere beneath the pain he was *enjoying* this. Like part of him looked forward to whatever was going to happen next.

"Charlie, he's not going to break. And we don't know if there's any time left. My family could be dead right now and your mother—"

"Fuck you, don't you say it—" Charlie was pointing an accusatory finger at him.

"They could be doing God knows what to her right now. We need to save something from this. As much as we possibly can and every second that passes is a second wasted."

"Now, there's a man you can reason with," the man said. "He recognizes an untenable situation when he sees one."

"Who are you?" Jimmy said. "Why are you doing this? If you know you're dead anyway, why not just give us what we want?"

"Because what's in it for me?" His one eye met Jimmy's and he knew there was nothing that the two of them could do to break him.

"Well, that ain't happening," Charlie said. "I don't know what kind of gay stuff you're into, but nobody here is gonna get your rocks off. Save that shit for after the road trip to hell."

The man's eye swiveled over to Charlie. "You've never been a smart boy, have you?"

"Let me show you something." Charlie stepped in quickly, then before Jimmy knew what was happening, he was gouging out the man's good eye, swearing and grunting as he worked.

The man howled in pain as Charlie twisted the metal object in his eye socket, one hand atop his head. Jimmy was paralyzed until Charlie stepped back, pulling a long, stringy, bloody mass with him.

"That'll teach you, fucker," he said.

"Shit, Charlie, what did you do?"

"I took back control. And if I'm gonna die, I'm gonna do it on my feet—not my knees." Charlie's stare was all fire as he looked at Jimmy. "You're right, we don't have much time. Anything could be happening to our families right now."

"Charlie, what would you do to save your mother if you knew she would die?" Jimmy grabbed his friend by the shoulders. His voice was a harsh whisper. "You'd do anything, right?" Charlie's mouth was a grim line, but he said nothing. "Look, if we—"

"We?" Charlie threw his hands off.

"If I do this and he gives us the combination and we make it out alive, wasn't it worth it?"

"And what makes you think that, huh? All night, we been draggin' this guy through hell and he ain't breakin'. What if you suck this guy off and he just laughs in your face?"

"Then we kill him. We kill him, make for our families, and try to get as far away from here as possible. Nobody has to know—"

"I'll know. *You'll* know. You wanna have that shit on your brain for the rest of your life? Fuck that. I say we both die like men. Let's shoot this guy in the face now and hit the road."

Hot tears boiled over from Jimmy's eyes. Flashes of his wife and daughters in agony as everything they'd done to this man reflected on their bodies. He quivered as the images overtook him.

"I can't let that happen. I can't let that happen to them," he said. He looked at Charlie and grabbed him by the throat. Charlie's eyes went wide and he slapped at his hands. By the time he started striking Jimmy to get him off, his strength was already waning. Jimmy's arms burned, but he squeezed even harder. This was his friend, but he had to save his family.

"Just go to sleep." His voice was pinched and high, barely a whisper. He shook Charlie's stiff body, still trying to fight him. "Just fucking sleep."

Something in his friend's neck crackled beneath his thumbs. Jimmy blinked away tears and stared him in the face. Charlie's eyes were blood red. He still had a look of surprise on his face, his mouth fishing open and closed as he tried for air that couldn't get past his lips.

Finally, Jimmy let go, letting him slump to the ground.

"I wish you didn't have to do that," the man said, looking at Charlie. Something about his face looked genuinely sorry, the bloody remnants of his ruined eye clinging to his cheek.

"Shut up." Jimmy swiped at his tears with a numb hand, succeeding in slapping himself in the nose. His throat ached from the dam of emotion walled up inside him. "Give me the numbers."

"No." The man smiled. "After."

"Damn you." Jimmy dropped to one knee and began fumbling with the man's pants. He had to pause while he waited for the circulation to return to his fingers and even then it was difficult to get them down with the man being strapped to the chair. Jimmy had to settle with them at the knees.

The man was wearing a pair of tighty whities and Jimmy laughed so hard he choked. He didn't know what was funny about them or what he'd even expected but couldn't help himself. He rolled over onto the floor, his laughter rising until it echoed off the walls. By the time he'd composed himself, his stomach and back muscles hurt. He crawled on his hands and knees and sat directly in front of the man.

"So, this is it." Jimmy looked up at him, finally sober. "Can you even tell me why?"

"I don't know," the man said, suddenly looking unsure for the first time. Funny, how torture hadn't done a thing to unnerve him, but being questioned on his demand for fellatio did. "I always had this…vague bucket list of things I'd like to experience before I die. A blowjob from a desperate man was always a far-fetched one, though."

Jimmy nodded. He pulled at the lip of the underwear, dragging them over the man's hips. His semi-erect penis sprung out, slapping against his stomach. He was half afraid to touch the uncircumcised thing, looking like an ill-stuffed sausage, Jimmy's eyes bugging as if trying to jettison his head away from this man's genitalia. But he was going to have to do a whole lot more than touch.

It looked ten times bigger than it actually was. He wouldn't let himself look away, his stomach doing something that felt like the complete opposite of hunger. Jimmy felt the saliva building up in his mouth like whenever he was about to throw up, but he forced the mutinying muscles to relax and swallowed.

Swallow. *Jesus*—would he have to do *that*?

Jimmy forced himself to stare at it—to contain it in his mind. It wasn't a venomous snake. It was just a pin. Hell, Jimmy's was bigger. He tried to shrink it down in his mind. To make it less threatening.

Jimmy wanted to look at the man, to ask how long he needed to do this. But he'd been on the receiving end of many of these and didn't want the mental picture of what he would look like, turning his eyes up at him in such a supplicant position. He wondered if having the man exposed like this would have been the answer to getting the numbers out of him, but he couldn't risk the man withstanding the torture and then being completely uncooperative.

He placed his hands on the man's thighs and closed his eyes. Jimmy mouthed his wife's name, trying to imagine he was her—to move like she moved. He had to channel something to get him past the next few minutes. God, he hoped it would only take a couple minutes. His stomach lurched again at the realization that if he didn't do it well, he might not get the end result.

Jimmy looked around like a man about to be hung, waiting for a last second reprieve. He shook the thought from his mind, resolved to do this as well as he possibly could. Dammit, he would make it through this. He opened his mouth, rolling onto his knees, and leaned in.

Several red holes bloomed in the man's chest, the roar of a gun behind him. Jimmy felt the shots buzz overhead and instinctively fell to the floor, lying as flat as possible. The man's remaining eye bugged, and his tongue lolled like he was trying to lap up a last breath of air before he slumped over, lifeless.

"No!" Jimmy screamed. He looked around and saw Charlie with the gun in his hand. His friend smiled at him, dropping his arm.

"Couldn't let you…" Charlie said.

Jimmy wished he had murdered his friend. Charlie had just doomed Jimmy's entire family. He got up, checked the side of the man's neck for a pulse. There was one weak beat and then…nothing.

Jimmy looked between the two of them. In that moment, if he could have killed his friend to resurrect the other man, it would have been a happy exchange. In his desperation to save his family, he would have traded anyone else's life on the planet, especially Charlie's.

Jimmy took out his knife. Charlie looked at him but didn't move. He still had the gun but spread his arms as if welcoming Jimmy to finally kill him. He hadn't used the gun when Jimmy had been choking him and it would probably be a better way to die than whatever was coming.

Jimmy turned to the dead man in the chair. He quickly began cutting off his clothes. They should have done this from the start. Maybe demoralizing him more may have had a greater effect. The man had been right, though; they had come at him in a haphazard fashion. Jimmy had never tortured anyone before. Sure, he'd killed men, but to intentionally drag out someone's death had been completely foreign to him before this morning.

He had his body completely stripped in minutes and began looking over the naked corpse. Maybe he'd tattooed or written the numbers somewhere on his body. That only made sense if the numbers had significant personal value, but it was all he had to work on.

"Check his ID," Charlie rasped, sitting in a chair. "Maybe it's his date of birth."

Jimmy found the pant leg that held his wallet, feeling numb all over. He read the numbers, his heart fluttering at the shred of hope. There was a shadow over half his face, an imperfection in the photo, making it look almost like he was winking. Jimmy just knew it was a sign, and as if on cue, the office door burst in, and about a dozen men with guns flooded into the room. Charlie spun, the gun tumbling from his hand. Two men had him pinned to the floor a second later. Jimmy instinctively put his hands up, still on his knees.

Another man walked into the room, his hands shoved into the pockets of a grey trench coat. He wore glasses, but that was the only thing distinctive about his face. His whole head was bald, eyebrows included. He could have been anywhere between thirty and sixty. He could have been anybody. Jimmy knew this was the man, the one who would extract every piece of information from him.

"Get him out of here," he said, looking at Jimmy but pointing at Charlie. Even his voice was unremarkable. But the men scooped Charlie up, dangling him between them by the shoulders. The two holding him up by the arms looked at this new man as if asking, 'And then what?'.

"Put him on the treadmill," he said. "Run him until he dies."

Those five words chilled Jimmy. Somehow, that was worse than anything he'd thought to do. The thought of being active in your own murder sounded awful in a way that made Jimmy want to beg them just to shoot his friend. They dragged Charlie away, and Jimmy swallowed, wondering what horrible thing was in store for him.

He clenched the knife in his fist. Everyone left the room, save for the man in the trench coat. The man's weighty gaze on him felt hot and Jimmy couldn't move until the man turned to examine the hodge-podge tray of tools they'd haphazardly thrown together. Jimmy quickly got to his feet but wasn't sure what more to do.

The man took off his coat. He had on an oversized white polo shirt and khakis, both wrinkled. It looked like he had on whatever clothes were available. Jimmy took a step forward but stopped when the man began taking off his gym shoes.

What the hell was he doing?

As far as Jimmy could see, he wasn't armed. The man had to see he had a knife but didn't seem to care. Jimmy took another step forward, bracing himself to kill this man. There were others just outside, but he would fight to the death if he had to.

At least, he thought he would.

The man didn't look worried as Jimmy approached.

"Sit down."

Jimmy looked at the chair between them.

"No," Jimmy said heartlessly. He was easily sixty pounds bigger than this man, he could have taken him.

The man began unbuttoning his pants. He dropped them and began working on his shirt.

"Let's hurry up and get this done with so you can get back to your wife and little girls. I've convinced our friends there's no need to bring civilians into this unless you make a fuss."

Jimmy sat.

The man stood in his underwear and socks. He went back to his trench coat and took a container out of his pocket. He put the container on the tray, opened it, then took his teeth out and put them inside. He then began opening and closing his mouth, sticking his tongue out and pointing it in all directions.

Was he stretching? Why was he stretching?

"What are you gonna do?" Jimmy asked.

"You're going to tell me where it is. We can dispatch with the notion you don't know what I'm talking about?" He asked the question in a way that didn't sound exactly like a question.

"It's in the safe," Jimmy said, nodding. "It's in the safe."

He didn't know what this man intended, but he knew he didn't want to be touched by him. The man looked over at the safe, then swiveled his head back to Jimmy.

"I believe you. Tell me the combination?" His hands played over the tools.

The thought of them or any part of the man coming in contact with Jimmy seemed like the worst thing in the world.

Something in his tone made it impossible for Jimmy's panic-stricken mind to conceive a lie. He wanted to tell him the truth. Everything. Why he'd taken what was in the safe, how he'd even known about it. Who he'd paid to get access to it. But the combination—

Because he couldn't form the words to tell this man what he'd calmly demanded, Jimmy just shook his head. The man, regarding the corpse slumped to the point of falling out of the chair, turned back to him and nodded. Jimmy was shivering but was otherwise paralyzed.

The man's expression didn't change. He smeared a thick coat of what looked like petroleum jelly on his lips from a small container he'd taken from his pocket and opened his mouth wide, working all the facial muscles below his nose.

"We'll see. Take off your pants."

This was originally supposed to be a story I'd ghostwritten for a publisher that shall remain nameless. Not because of any potential contract violation to do with this particular tale, but I actually did go on to write a three or four part story for them, got paid for it, and the thing has never seen the light of day. I wrote this before I knew all the guidelines they had and subsequently, they didn't want this first iteration.

The Beast

She leaned over him and held out a hand.

"You okay?"

"Yeah," he said after a moment and looked up at her with the deepest brown eyes she'd ever seen. Kittie had been partnered with this man for almost three years now, but it was as if she were seeing him for the first time.

"What?" he said.

"I…nothing. Let's get you up." Abbott smiled and took her hand, knowing too well he was too big for her to really pull him. It was all she could do to keep from being yanked off her feet with him pushing himself off the sidewalk. They crashed softly into each other and she could feel the length of him, all muscle, from his chest down.

"Sorry, K. I let him get away."

"Are you kidding me?" She looked him in the eye. "I'm just concerned about you."

He looked the way the purse thief had run as if he could still chase him down. He looked at her.

"Me? Ah, nuts, I'm fine." He took a big fist and wrapped it on his skull. "It'll take a lot more than a lucky punch to put a dent in this melon."

"Let me take you to the hospital, just to get checked out."

"Nah. Couple Tylenol and I'll be right as rain."

"Then at least come inside and sit down for a minute, okay?"

He shrugged and followed along.

She sat him on the couch and pushed the remote into his hand. Abbott eased back as if he belonged there. He was long and lean and she had to scoot the coffee table back to accommodate his legs.

"Comfy?"

"Yeah," he said. "Hey, don't you need to cancel your credit cards?"

"Nah. I don't carry any. I just have the one I use for emergencies and that stays in my underwear drawer."

Sheesh. Had she just said that out loud?

"Oh." He looked away. "Okay."

"I'll just call the Secretary of State Monday morning to see about getting a new driver's license. Guess it's a wash for the cash."

"You know you could file a police report."

They both laughed. The likelihood of her money being returned, even if they caught the thief, was practically nil.

She left him there while she went to the bathroom for Tylenol. She looked at her hands and saw she was still holding one Salvatore Ferragamo. She'd thrown the other at the thief after getting back to her feet. God, why were her hands shaking? She was a cop!

Because cops weren't supposed to get robbed, that's why. Cops were supposed to catch crooks, not the other way around. She looked at herself in the mirror and forced her hands to be still.

Makeup was still okay. The tear in her black Diane von Furstenberg dress was minimal. Hell, anybody who saw it might think it was intentional. If she wanted, she could still make the dinner date with Duane.

Who the hell was she kidding? The only thing Kittie wanted to do right now was crash on the couch, order a pizza, and have a beer or two. She could even snuggle up to Abbott and watch the Pistons.

Where had that thought come from? She opened the medicine cabinet and took out the bottle of pills. She popped it open and shook out two for her partner. He was a great guy and all, but not for her. He was tall, handsome, looked like he worked out like a maniac, and was one of the sharpest detectives in the precinct. But he was her partner and, worse yet, a widower with two kids. So far as she was concerned, that was three strikes: a co-worker, married, and kids. Well, he wasn't technically married, but she knew he wasn't over Kelly. No way in hell did she want to get wrapped up in all that.

Kittie blocked out this line of thought and charged out of the bathroom. She tossed her lone shoe into her bedroom, not wanting to throw it away, but there wasn't anything she could do with it. She went into the kitchen, grabbed a glass, and filled it with water from the tap.

"Hey, Abbott, I got you some Tylenol," she said, walking back into the living room.

He was still sitting in the exact same position, but he'd obviously moved. He had a glass filled to the brim with amber liquid and was casually sipping at it.

"Okay, thanks," he said, looking at her and holding out his hand. "I found a glass of water in the liquor cabinet." He held the glass up to her in a mock toast. She was half annoyed that he'd just welcomed himself to her kitchen, but more so bothered that he was drinking.

"Abbott, you can't drink with Tylenol. It's bad for your liver."

"It is? What about with Flintstone's Chewables? It's what I give the girls."

Kittie laughed. She'd met Abbott's daughters and there weren't too sweeter little girls on the planet.

"You know what? What the hell?" she said and went back to the kitchen. She dropped the two pills into the drain, picked up the phone and dialed Duane's number.

He was a hell of a nice guy, and while she had enjoyed their first date, he wasn't what she needed tonight. That beer and pizza was sounding better and better.

"Hello?" he said after picking up on the second ring.

"Hey, Duane, it's me," she said.

"Oh, hey. I'm walking out the door right now. I'm looking forward to seeing you tonight."

"About that," she began. "I'm not going to be able to make it. I was just about to get in my car and I got mugged." She figured the truth was the best possible thing she could tell him, but it still felt like an excuse. As nice a guy as Duane was, he was so *boring*. His workday was boring, his hobbies were boring, his conversations were boring. Other than his car, a blood orange SRT Viper TA, there wasn't a thing about him she found interesting. Kittie had thought at the time that she needed someone more normal and she had powered through their first date. Maybe putting herself out there for someone was exactly what she needed. Kittie had been on the shelf for the last year-and-a-half and she could use a guy to at least 'knock the dust off'. Just not Duane.

"I'm so sorry," he said. He sounded let down. "Do you want me to come over?"

"No, I'm fine," she said a little too quickly. She imagined sitting down to eat with him and flinging herself out a window just to get a little excitement going. "Just a little shook up. I already called it in and I'll fill out a report in the morning. I'm more embarrassed than anything." She thought a little creative lying here would help soothe his thoughts.

"I really don't mind. I could head your way. You said you live in the city, I could be there in less than half an hour."

"Thanks, but no. I think what I really need right now is a long hot bath and bed." That didn't sound awful at all, but she wanted a little food first. Hold the Duane.

"Well, okay. I'm a little disappointed, but I understand."

I understand. That was probably what bothered her most. He was just *so* understanding. There was no fire in him. His politics were straight down the middle. He agreed with both sides and thought the best thing both parties could do was compromise. Nothing upset him. Nothing got under his skin. Which got under Kittie's skin. She'd contemplated stabbing him through the hand with her butter knife just to get a rise out of him, but he'd probably just say, "I'm sorry you feel that way."

They said goodbye after he made her promise to call him later and hung up.

"Okay, so who wants pizza?"

"Meeeee!" Abbott said excitedly.

He was never that animated and the childish glint in his eyes told her the alcohol must have been having an effect. Kittie dialed from memory and ordered their usual, and in a half hour, the delivery guy was at the door.

She paid him after Abbott had scraped the bottom of his wallet when Kittie realized she hardly had any money around the house. The kid frowned when he counted the money and saw his tip amounted to a couple drops of gas for his car. Kittie went to the fridge for a couple more beers. She had already had one and Abbott had caught up with her after finishing his Jack and Coke.

"So, what did you come over for?" Kittie asked as he flipped through channels. The Pistons weren't playing tonight.

"Oh. I got the Beast case file. I wanted to show you something."

"Did you catch a break? Anonymous tip?" They'd inherited the case from Detective Archie Biggum, who'd promptly retired after having a massive heart attack two days ago. The man had been on the job thirty-five years and not a day had gone by that he didn't have a coney dog with everything. The fact he survived the heart attack wasn't that amazing, it was that it had taken so long to happen.

"No-no. Nothing like that. I...I forget now." Abbott rubbed his head in that same way he'd done a million times before when he was frustrated, but all of a sudden it was sexy for some reason. She opened the pizza box and dived in for another slice, trying to distract herself.

"Hold it!" Abbott shouted and turned to her with a napkin. He shook it out then made a show of tucking it into the top of her dress. "You're going to get pizza sauce all over your dress."

"I don't care, Abbott. I hate this dress." She had paid over a hundred dollars for the dress for some reason. Even though she hadn't really liked Duane, she had still wanted to look nice for him, and all the outfits in her closet hadn't seemed good enough at the time.

"But it's so pretty," Abbott said.

"Then *you* wear it."

He made a show of looking her up and down and electricity raced down her spine.

"Nah," he said. "Too short for me. It would show off too much leg. Oh, I remember now. What I wanted to come over to talk to you about. The case—"

She held up a hand, and she must have been a little drunker than she realized because she hung her index off his top lip.

"Not tonight," she said. "I don't want to talk shop."

Abbott's eyebrows went up.

"I must have hit my head or something because it sounded a lot like you said you didn't want to talk about work."

"Yeah, I don't. So what?"

"Uh, remember Samantha's t-ball game?"

Kittie did. She'd tracked Abbott down to talk about a case they were working on. It had been the first time she'd met his then wife and the relationship had definitely gotten off on a bad foot. Kelly was shorter by about five inches and lighter by twenty pounds, but the woman had been poised to kill. It had been all Abbott could do to keep his wife from going full honey-badger on her that day and it had taken a long time for Kittie to get into her good graces.

But eventually, the two women had become close. They'd hung out many times without Abbott. Kelly had even begun referring to Kittie as Abbott's work wife. She felt the tiniest pang of guilt for feeling what she was feeling for the husband of the woman she had grown to deeply care about.

Then she kissed him right under the nose.

"What?" Abbott said, his eyes suddenly wide.

She hadn't meant to do anything but show genuine platonic affection with the gesture, but something in the air had changed. He stood.

"I'm so sorry, Abbot!" she said.

"I gotta go," he said, grabbing his jacket. "Thanks for the pizza and all."

"But you haven't eaten any yet. Besides, you're too tipsy to drive."

"I'll be fine. I'll walk."

She stood and took a step toward him, her hands out.

"Please." His voice was a whisper. He turned to fully face her as he fumbled with the zipper of his jacket. Kittie saw the tremendous bulge in his pants, but rather than recoiling in embarrassment, she stepped even closer.

"Abbott, I'm sorry." She could see how upset he was and all previous thoughts had been pushed back.

"No-no, it's fine. It's not you. It's—" He opened his hands and let the two halves of his jacket fall open. "I can't zip up my jacket."

She realized what had happened. Kelly had told her she always kissed her husband goodnight. She'd called him her big baby because he insisted he couldn't go to sleep unless she'd kissed him in that spot right underneath his nose. Then she recalled how disheveled he'd been in appearance since his wife had passed. Kittie wondered for the briefest of seconds how long it had been since her partner had gotten a good night's rest.

In a blur of motion, he had his arms around her. His mouth

was hot against hers and she was kissing him back. She'd put her hands up reflexively when he'd charged her, but now let one fall away. A tiny gasp escaped her lips and a second later a small grunt escaped his as she fumbled inside his pants and found him.

He swept her hair away from her face and went to the long cord of her neck, kissing gently and firmly at the same time. She'd tugged him out of his pants and he was so hot it felt like he was burning her palm. She kept stroking back and forth, twisting her wrist as she came to the head, his breathing coming faster and faster.

Abbott pulled the straps of the small black dress and the bra with him as he worked downward. She had to let him go for just a moment to take her arms out, the dress puddling at her feet as he took a nipple into his mouth.

She began moaning as his tongue flicked up and down, then moved to the other breast. Back and forth, back and forth as she pulled furiously at him. They'd almost made it back to the couch when she felt him begin to quiver and he hardened even more in her hand. His hips began to buck and something hot splashed her thigh.

Kittie burned with disappointment. They were well past the point of no return. There was no regret, no guilt in her for what she wanted at this moment. She squeezed him, searching his eyes.

Abbott scooped her up and they both laughed as he shuffled his feet with his pants around his ankles. He kissed her.

"I'm sorry, it's just been so long." He sucked on his bottom lip, making her ache for him even more. "Too long." He stood her up and swept the dining room table clear, pushing two chairs to the floor in the process. She'd assumed he was done, but now she understood he was just getting started.

Abbott lifted her onto the table and slid her underwear off. She arched her back and grabbed onto the end of the table, waiting for the steely hardness that had just been in her hand a moment ago. But what she felt instead was small, soft, and wet, dabbing at her clit and sliding down.

"You don't have to—"

His hands lifted her thighs and then his mouth was all the way on her. His tongue went inside her, curled, and slid back out. He did it again and again, so slowly, each time, giving her a feeling in the pit of her stomach like everything had frozen and then thawed.

"More," she begged. She wanted to feel him, all of him, but he was torturing her with each second he wasn't inside her. What he was doing was delicious, but it was like throwing a cup of water on a blazing fire.

He let her legs fall on his shoulders and then one big hand was on her breast. He kneaded it first and then began pinching her nipple. She felt his body shift and then his mouth fastened on her clitoris. The sensation was more immediate and then a second later he slipped a finger inside her. Kittie kicked the air and hit him with her foot. For a second, she thought she'd hurt him, but he continued lashing her with his tongue while sliding his finger in and out in slow, agonizing fashion.

Her body was on fire. Kittie didn't understand how he could be so restrained. She liked to be in control and tried to sit up and push him back. But he held her down easily with only one hand while he did exactly what he wanted.

"Please-please-please-please-please," she began saying as his tongue and hands picked up speed. He was hitting three different places like a well-oiled machine and she realized suddenly she was climaxing. For a moment she was weightless. She felt herself cry out but couldn't hear.

She came back to her senses, and she sat up shakily, seeing Abbott sitting on his butt. Kittie couldn't remember the last time she'd orgasmed with another person involved.

"You're pretty strong when you cum," he said. She looked down at him and saw he was still standing at attention.

"More," she said and slid off the table. She straddled him and, before he could speak, slid him inside. She began riding him, slow for a moment, but then gradually built in speed. Kittie found the angle she liked and kept it there, raking her fingers down his chest and rippled abs. She didn't remember him unbuttoning the shirt and didn't care.

Abbott pitched his head back and moaned. Now they were the well-oiled machine, Kittie pumping her hips and Abbott rocking into her as she came back down. She cradled his head into her breasts as she leaned over him and he licked whenever her nipples came within tongue's reach.

She felt him lengthen inside her and dug her nails into his shoulders. Her back stiffened as her climax began anew, and a long moment later, he began heaving underneath her. Kittie collapsed on top of him, drained and breathing heavily, the smell of their sex thick in the air.

Abbott was gone in the morning. As far as she could tell, he hadn't been here in a while. They'd made it back to the bedroom where, a few orgasms later, they'd finally collapsed into unconsciousness. She peeked one eye at the alarm clock and with her muddy morning calculations figured she'd gotten about five hours sleep. That was a lot for her.

Kittie rolled slowly out of bed, muscles in her back, legs, and stomach sore in a way she hadn't felt in a long time. Try as she might, she didn't feel bad about last night and didn't want to. So 'it' had finally happened. Abbott wasn't the type to spread what they'd done around the office, even though it wasn't like the other detectives in the bullpen weren't already teasing them. Detroit's *Finest,* they said in describing the two of them whenever they were together. As far as anybody else was concerned, they'd been sleeping together before they'd been partners.

Then her heart did skip. Abbott wasn't here. Did he regret what they had done?

She dropped to the floor in a plank position and went through her basic yoga routine. It had always helped clear her mind of the horrible dreams she almost always had at night and she used it now to try to get perspective on what had happened.

He wasn't ready for this, was he? Had she used him?

Even now, all he ever talked about was his wife. Almost every day. How he and Kelly used to go to this place, how the girls looked so much like their mother, how he'd seen a movie in a theater with her.

Oh, God. He wasn't ready for whatever this was. He was still dating his dead wife.

She finished her routine and quickly got in the shower. Kittie's jet black hair had a tendency to get long if she didn't get it cut at least every other month and just to her collarbone was a perfectly manageable length for her. Easy to wash, style, and wear professionally so that she looked like a woman, but not too girly. Her fellow police could be harsh critics.

She dressed in an all-gray pants suit with a salmon top. Her hair went into a pony and she put on the silver necklace with a cross her father had given her over twenty years ago. She'd never gotten around to having her ears pierced and that had suited her just fine. It was one less thing for her to do before she left every morning.

The place where she always got her coffee was two buildings down and about ten feet away from the bus stop. Kitty made it to the stop with thirty seconds to spare before Marty pulled up.

"Good morning, Marty," she said as she boarded. Kitty had been using the bus system in the city for as long as she could remember. She had a car but couldn't imagine taking it instead of the bus.

Marty smiled and nodded to her as she passed him and found a seat in the middle. She sat across the aisle from a boy who couldn't have been older than thirteen, who was stealing more than casual glances her way. She stretched, making sure he could get a good look at the badge on her belt. When she glanced at him a moment later, the boy was sitting straight in his seat, eyes forward.

Kittie exited the bus and pitched her empty coffee cup in a nearby trash bin. She stretched her long legs and made quick work of the two blocks to get to her precinct. Kittie went in the main entrance, pushing her way through the turnstile and into the lobby. She waved and said hello to officers and fellow detectives, walking around the metal detector and waving to Arnie on her way to the elevator.

Dread filled her as the elevator rose. Thoughts of her and Abbott on her mind. Ultimately, she decided she really only wanted to get laid and that had happened. Abbott wasn't boyfriend material, he was husband material, and she wasn't looking to be anybody's wife. But he might want to start dating.

"Ugh," she said aloud.

"'Scuse me?" The older man in the elevator with her looked her way, his trim salt-and-pepper mustache matching the remaining hair on the sides and back of his head.

Mildly embarrassed, she raised her eyebrows and asked, "Hm?" as if she didn't know what he was talking about.

Kittie worked Homicide, her goal ever since graduating from the academy. She was six months ahead of her goal, having made detective in just five years, and was well on pace to becoming a lieutenant in the next five. She was ten-percent ahead of average in cases closed and was eyeing fifteen. Kittie was a great shot and kept herself in peak physical condition in case she had to hawk a suspect down, which had happened on several occasions. She hated losing.

By the time she'd reached the bullpen, she'd already made up her mind. There was no way she and Abbott were going to be together. It was bad politics to date a coworker. It undermined her amongst the higher-ups, worse, amongst her peers. It might have been different if they were in different divisions or cities. Besides, she respected him as a cop. There could only be conflicts with that if they were in a relationship.

Kittie rounded a corner, expecting to see him at their shared desk. Instead, she saw Arthur Key, the OCI investigator who'd been dogging Abbott for the past two weeks. They'd been chasing a suspect on foot when she'd tripped and gone down while he'd continued pursuit. She'd only been down a second and had fought through the agony of a twisted ankle, gaining ground as best she could. But Abbott and the suspect were both fast. The only reason she'd caught up to them was because of the gun shot. She'd found them in an alley, the suspect bleeding out while Abbott holstered his weapon. At the time, he hadn't claimed the shoot was righteous, but he hadn't needed to. Not with her. But the suspect had lived just long enough to complain and his family had filed a grievance as well as taking their story to Channel 8.

In an age where cops were caught on camera shooting people to death for no justifiable reason, any shooting by a cop was held suspect. The fact she hadn't been able to verify her partner's account had made her feel like she was letting him and the whole team down.

"Mornin', Kittie," Key said, half his ass on her desk. He slowly stood, his orange and red tie sliding off his leg. It clashed horribly with his dark grey suit, but then again, so did his slicked back red hair, receding at the corners. And so did his face, a shade so pale he was almost translucent.

She didn't bother telling him to address her as Detective Ball because she'd tried that tactic on more than one occasion and he'd ignored it. It was obvious he wanted her, but she wanted no part of him. She just wanted him to leave her partner alone. Currently, Abbott Carmichael was on desk duty until this whole affair was clear.

Kittie slid past him, careful not to let any part of her touch any part of him, despite him leaning in at the last moment before she sat. She made a show of shuffling through haphazardly placed papers on her desk before finally looking up at him.

"He's not here right now," she said to the investigator.

"I can see that." Key lifted his Styrofoam cup to his lips and took a prolonged sip as he scanned the bullpen and beyond. "He's here. Probably hiding somewhere. Figured I'd wait for you to come in. See what you're up to."

She had just closed a case with Detective Raphael, the

patriarch of the bullpen. He had forty years on the job and had made it clear he had no intention of retiring. Ever. Raphael was across the narrow aisle from her, busily pecking away at his computer keyboard, glasses perched on his nose. She could tell the man was making a show of not looking her way, not because he was afraid of having the OCI investigator talk to him—Raphael was long past being afraid of anything, he had the battle scars of three marriages behind him to prove that—but because he was well aware of the time he'd put in and how the framework would be made to force his retirement if he slugged the guy. So, it was the best situation possible to just pretend the OCI investigator and all their ilk were not visible on any spectrum that he could see.

"I'm up for a case, I'm second on three others." She owed him nothing more than a professional response.

He leaned in close, his back hooking like a snake. "You seein' anyone, Kittie?" Coffee breath in general wasn't pleasant, but on Key it was something on par with soil from a disturbed grave. Kittie could feel the tickle of an eye watering and smiled.

She held her face a long moment until Key stood up.

"Y'know, things aren't going so well for your partner." OCI wasn't supposed to discuss an ongoing investigation, but then again, he hadn't said exactly what not going well meant. "I mean, look at this desk." Key gestured.

Kittie's was typically messy. She described it as an asymmetrical system that allowed her room for extra-cranial thinking. Meaning she kept her desk messy so intuitive leaps could come more naturally—complete bullshit magical thinking, but it usually kept the passer-by critics of her lack of organization at bay. Abbott's side of the desk was always immaculate. Three years in the army had taught him that. Even now, his three small picture frames of his wife and children were neatly bordered at the divide between his space and hers. His two-tiered wire basket had only a few sheets of neatly ordered papers. His stress ball was in its place where he left it every night, at the center. But beneath it was a manila folder, its contents spilling out of it like it had been tossed from across the room.

"Look at this mess!" Key ran his thumb and forefinger over his handlebar mustache, seasick green eyes floating back to her as he smiled.

"Investigator Key, I do have work to do. If you need a time for us to meet on premises regarding OCI's investigation of my partner, please coordinate that with my captain so proper arrangements of my schedule can be made." She had to specifically say 'on premises' to discourage him from asking her to meet at a restaurant. She'd made that mistake once and he'd taken that as license to grope her leg. There was full deniability on his part, though, as they were the only two witnesses of said grope at the time.

"No-no." The smile dropped from his eyes, leaving him with an expression akin to a sneer. "I'll catch you later." He turned to go. "Make sure to tell your partner to turn his phone on."

No sooner had he disappeared into an elevator, no doubt to harangue another cop, than Abbot reappeared. Cofield was with him, the bullpen's other female detective. She was pretty, taller than Kittie by an inch, with red lipstick on a wide, expressive mouth and eyes that glittered like diamond chips. She wore a white scooped necked blouse that showed off her ample cleavage, the only part of her with any curves, and a red skirt and heels that were not conducive to running down suspects.

The two were laughing as they came into the bullpen and Kittie felt a sting of jealousy that had never been there any other time she'd seen them together. She sat down across from Raphael and he sat across from Kittie.

"Good morning, Kitten," Cofield said. She was the only one who could get away with calling her that. Kittie actually did like her, they'd even gone to a couple bars after work together.

"Morning." Kittie spun in her chair to face Abbott. She felt her gut hardening as if expecting a blow. Abbott was suddenly deeply engaged in the file that had been strewn across his desk.

"Morning," he said back.

The bullpen's other three detectives came in and they all spoke. Kittie logged into her computer, all the while stealing glances at Abbott, hoping to catch him looking at her. His head was bowed and he was so still it almost looked meditative.

"G'mornin', boys and girls," Captain Oliver said, suddenly there. They all greeted him. He pointed to Kittie and Abbott with his index and middle fingers. "Can I see you two a minute?"

She liked her captain, but Kittie hated being pulled into his office. She always felt like she was going to get scolded or something, even when she knew she was about to get some sort of commendation. The three of them filed in and the captain sat behind his desk, picking up a steaming mug of coffee in his mighty fist. Captain Oliver had to have been hovering somewhere around fifty, but he was the most muscle-bound person she had ever met in her life.

"This Beast thing just got real," he said before they'd even sat. "Shut my door." Abbott was closer and he pushed it closed. "Our auditor on the inside just took a nosedive off the eighty-fifth floor night before last, as you know. We need somebody new on the inside." His coal black eyes swiveled between Abbott and Kittie. He pulled a manila folder out of a drawer and slapped it on his desk. "I just got a preliminary psych work-up from the FBI on this guy. He likes beautiful women, he likes to have them under his thumb, he likes to make a show of killing them. I won't beat around the bush with this. Thanks to a few new resources, we have the opportunity to put somebody on the inside to get a different view of this."

He looked squarely at Kittie. "I apologize for what I'm about to say, Detective Ball, but you are, by Western standards, attractive. Under the right circumstances, beautiful. Again, I'm sorry."

"You want me to go undercover? I'm not an auditor."

"No, but if I'm not mistaken, you minored in computer science at Kettering University."

"Yeah."

"I've already spoken to some of the tech monkeys around here and I've been assured that it's just a matter of jargon. And they can teach you that."

"I'm second on a couple cases, I don't know if—"

"We can spare you. You just cleared the only case you were primary on. I need you in tomorrow morning."

"I got the job? I mean, don't I need to go through the interview process with the—"

"Already taken care of. Human Resources Director is the wife of the Assistant Chief. She's been vetted up and down, knows the situation and wants this killer and thief caught as much as the DPD does."

Kittie shrugged. "Okay then. How much does it pay?"

On their way back to the bullpen, Kittie finally did catch Abbott's eye. He was looking at her, but she didn't know how to read his expression.

"What?" she said.

"I don't know. I mean, we need to talk about last night, but I don't know what to say."

She wanted to throw her arms around him and kiss him at that moment and felt herself consciously restraining. What the hell was going on with her? This had already been decided.

"I know what you mean," she tried to say blandly, despite her racing pulse.

"I mean, I like you—as a person—I just don't know if I'm ready."

"No. Yeah." She shook her head, then nodded like a teenager. He'd been more than ready last night and the brief flash of memory of what they'd done made things tighten inside her. "I totally get that."

"I haven't *been* with anyone since Kelly. I don't know what came over me."

Kittie realized that nothing had come over him except her. Maybe sex had been somewhere rattling in the back of his brain, but she had made it happen. He didn't know how to not make sex compatible with love and there she was with her chick boner, bashing him over the head with it.

Kittie nearly felt sick, realizing she'd used him.

But was that all it was?

"I get that. I don't want you to feel guilty." *She* felt guilty, especially at the thought of letting him blame himself.

"Hey, what's Detroit's *Finest* talking about now?" Detective Georges said. Kittie felt her cheeks flush and thought Abbott's eyes had gone wide.

"We're being redirected," he said.

They were free to talk about their undercover assignment with the rest of the bullpen, considering two of them were going to be the primaries. Abbott was going to be her point of contact while she was under.

"Poor you," Raphael said after Abbott had explained what was going on. "You get to dress up like a civvie and catch the bad guy 'cause yer perty."

"Hey, I don't like it any more than anyone else," Kittie said.

"Hell, I'd go, but my tits don't sit up the way they used to."

"And you got an ass like two bags of nickels," Georges said.

Everyone laughed and Kittie looked at Abbott again. He was looking at her, but his eyes were also a million miles away. She'd been so sure about how to handle this and a few fumbling words exchanged between them and she was like a confused sixteen year old.

The question had to be asked despite her better senses. She didn't know but had to figure out for herself and fast.

Could she be falling in love with her partner?

I wrote this way back when Medium *was a hit show on NBC. They had a program back then for a writing internship of some kind (they may still have it, I'm not sure). I wrote this as my entry, but the network canceled the show before I got the chance to submit. I still think it's a pretty solid teleplay, though.*

Medium: Company

INT.   A large white room, perhaps a warehouse, with fluorescent lighting in its high ceilings.

Allison is wearing a red and black dress with her hair curled. It is cold. A man leans against the wall on the other side of the room and she slowly approaches him. He has blond hair and blue eyes and is dressed in a black tuxedo with the tie undone around his neck. Yellow light pours across his face from the open door next to him.

> **Man** – with mist coming from his mouth
> I'm burning up.

INT.   The Dubois bedroom. Morning.

Allison awakes. The phone is ringing. She picks it up.

> **Joe**
> Hey. I can't sleep.

> **Allison**
> You're in luck. I just woke up. How's Chicago going?

> **Joe**
> Eh. The booze is watered down and the strippers are skanky. How are the girls?

> **Allison**
> Ha-ha. I miss you too. The girls are fine. Ariel got a B on her history test.

> **Joe**
> Why'd you wake up?

> **Allison**
> A dream.

> **Joe**
> Oh. A dream-dream or a dream?

> **Allison**
> What does that mean, a dream-dream?

> **Joe**
> You know. A dreeeeam.

> **Allison**
> One of those dreeeeams, huh? Well, they're all dreeeeams.

> **Joe**
> What was the dream?

> **Allison**
> Well, I was naked in the middle of the desert, burning—

Joe
Okay. So far—hot.

Allison
I could hear my skin cooking. I could even smell it. But that wasn't the bad part. There was something…coming. But the only thing I could say was, 'It's the rain. It's the rain,' over and over again. I had another one after that but I forgot it. Think that means something?

Joe
Did you smell like chicken?

Allison
What? Joe, I'm serious!

Joe
And sometimes a cigar can be just a cigar. Carl Lewis probably went for a stroll around the block just because. Siskel probably went out on a movie date with his wife, and Jeff Gordon probably goes out joyriding on occasion. Just because you have a dream about burning up in the desert doesn't mean you're going to burn up in the desert.

Allison
It doesn't have to mean I'm going to burn up in the desert. Maybe someone else died in the desert. I haven't had a dream that wasn't connected to something else in a long time. Hey, what s that noise in the background?

Joe
Some zombie movie. It's got Ving Rhames in it.

Allison
Zombie movie?

Joe
Yeah. That's why I can't sleep.

Allison
Then why don't you turn it off? You hate horror movies.

Joe

I'm into it now. I might as well finish it. Oh, that's the other thing—there's a slim chance we might wrap up early. I'll let you know. And if it's more than a dream, I'm sure it'll hit you over the head sooner or later. But you shouldn't worry about it. Not yet.

Allison
I know. I love you, Kurt.

Joe
Love you, Goldie. Bye.

INT.   The Dubois station wagon. Later in the morning.

Allison stops in front of the school. Ariel and Bridgette unbuckle their seatbelts.

Allison
Okay girls—kisses.

Ariel and Bridgette lean over to their mother and give her a kiss on the cheek. Bridgette gives her a second kiss.

Ariel and Bridgette
Bye, Mom.

They climb out of the station wagon and shut the doors, running to the school building. Allison looks in the rearview mirror at Marie in her child seat. Allison turns to look directly at her daughter and sees the blond man from her dream, but looking ill, seated in the back. Allison starts but keeps her composure.

Allison
Who are you?

The sunlight catches in his eyes as he looks out the window. He looks at Marie, then at Allison, confused.

Man – fanning himself
It's hot in here. Can you turn the air up?

Allison – whispering

Who are you?

The man tries the handle, but the door doesn't open.

Man
It's too hot. Please—the air.

Allison turns and flicks the air on full blast. She turns back.

Allison
Who—

He's gone.

INT.   The D.A.'s office. Morning.

Smiling, Devalos shakes hands with a youngish-looking dark-haired man.

Devalos
All right, Gordy. See you on the fifteenth.

The man nods at Allison and continues out the door.

Devalos
Good morning, Allison.

Allison
Good morning, sir. I got the word you wanted to see me.

He shuts the door.

Devalos
Have a seat, please.

Allison sits.

Allison
I sense a deep troubling within you.

Devalos smiles briefly, unbuttoning his suit jacket as he sits.

Devalos
That was Gordon Corralos. He's the family attorney for Vander Henderson of Henderson Construction and close friend of the mayor.

Allison
And what does Mr. Henderson need above and beyond what this office provides for the good people of Phoenix?

Devalos points his finger at her like a gun and makes a sound with his mouth, indicating she's hit the nail on the head.

Devalos
Apparently, Mr. Henderson's daughter went missing some time in the night. Routine stuff.

Devalos opens a manila folder in front of him on his desk and flips through it.

Devalos
While Mandy is your standard issue party girl, she's a type one diabetic—insulin dependent. Mr. Henderson is very strict with his daughter's medication because of her truant nature, and when he awoke this morning to find her still out and her insulin still in the refrigerator, he panicked. He tried her cell. Of course, she didn't answer, and ever since then, he's been pushing every button possible to find her.

Allison
And I suppose there's a reason why the DA's office is assisting in a police matter.

Allison looks through the pictures.

Devalos
Mr. Henderson is close personal friends with a one Art Monkhouse who is Mandy's godfather. Mr. Monkhouse is the sole proprietor of a series of home improvement stores in the Midwest and rumor has it he's looking to expand into Arizona. Mr. Corralos left no mystery about it regarding Mr. Henderson's and Monkhouse's appreciation and how it would be shown in the city of Phoenix if Ms. Henderson were to be found safe and sound.

Allison
And you're asking me to see what I can see so we can recoup Mr.
Henson's—

Devalos
Henderson

Allison
Henderson's daughter as soon as humanly possible.

Devalos
You must be psychic.

Allison
It comes, it goes.

Devalos
Can you have something for me by lunch? It'll help my ndigestion for
when the mayor rams this thing down my throat. I'm certain that's
where Mr. Corralos is headed now.

Allison
I'll talk to my people. Of course, this'll cost you.

Allison rises and stacks the pictures before putting them in the file
and picking it up.

Devalos
The usual four million deposit in your Cayman account?

Allison – standing in the doorway
You must be psychic.

Devalos
Allison.

She stops and looks back at Devalos.

Devalos
Thank you.

Allison

Gerald Dean Rice

> Just doing my job, sir.

She steps back in and looks at him.

Allison
Are you all right?

Devalos
Yeah. Sometimes it just helps to work a little magic when you have someone who really can.

INT.   Allison's desk. Afternoon.

Allison reads through the information in the file Devalos gave her. Detective Scanlon walks over to her desk.

Scanlon
Hey.

Allison
How's it going, Lee?

He sits on the edge of her desk.

Scanlon
Eh. Did the DA give you that thing today?

Allison looks up from the file.

Allison
Oh, you mean the missing girl thing? Working on it right now.

Scanlon
By the look on your face, I'm gonna guess you don't have anything yet.

Allison
No. Anything on your end?

Scanlon
No. I was hoping you'd be my compass.

Allison
So far, everything's a dead-end. Hopefully, no pun intended.

Scanlon
Hm. Think maybe a change of scenery might help? How about I grab us some lunch?

She checks her watch and sighs.

Allison
Apparently, I owe Manuel four million dollars.

Scanlon
What?

Allison
Inside joke. Thanks, but no. I brought a lunch. I might go sit on a bench outside, take in some fresh air.

Scanlon
The big man's really keyed up over this one.

Allison
Yeah, I got that too. I don't think it's entirely over the whole pressure from the mayor thing, though. I think there might be something else going on with him.

Scanlon
He'll work it out. I'll see you around. Must obey the tummy.

Scanlon pats his stomach, rises and leaves.

EXT.   A small park surrounded by small office buildings. It is warm and sunny.

Allison sits on a park bench by herself with her daughter's lunch pail next to her. She's eating a sandwich when she begins ooking around as if she is sensing something.

Allison – raising the sandwich to cover her mouth
Hello?

Gerald Dean Rice

She looks around from her seat.

Allison
Is anybody there?

The man from the car earlier that morning places his hand on the back of the park bench Allison is seated in. He hunches over and looks at her. His eyes are red-rimmed and his nose swollen-looking.

Man
Man, it sure is hot today.

Allison looks at him.

Allison
Yeah. I guess.

He looks at her, surprised.

Man
Hey, it's you again. I know you. I was out…<u>somewhere</u>.

Allison
Yes, me again. And you are?

Man
Uh, Neil. Sorry, I'd shake hands, but I have this summer cold.

Allison looks around again. She sets her purse next to her feet.

Allison
That's okay. I don't need any more colds with three little ones at home. Why don't you have a seat?

He sits and wipes his nose.

Neil
Oh, sorry, you're eating.

Allison
Trust me, when you're a mother you become immune.

Allison takes another bite of her sandwich.

Allison
So, what brings you out here?

Neil
I was just passing through. But come to think of it, I meant to tell you
something.

Allison
Tell me what?

Neil
Something about a woman? You're supposed to be looking for her,
but you're not. That makes absolutely no sense, I know.

Allison
And what is this woman's name?

Neil
That's funny. I don't remember. Starts with an M?

Allison
Can you describe her?

Neil
Blue eyes, blonde hair. More like yours than mine. I can almost
picture her face, but not quite.

Allison
Do you know who she is?

Neil - shrugs
Couldn't tell you.

Allison
How do you know about this? Where…are you?

Neil
What do you mean? I'm right here.

Allison

Gerald Dean Rice

I can't really break this gently to you. You've…passed. Right now,
you're in a 'transitional' phase until you've resolved something in
your life. You're somehow connected to this missing girl, and maybe
to get that resolution, you need to help find her.

Neil – looking confused
Passed? I'm not dead.

He laughs nervously and stands up.

Neil – backing away
I think I've made a mistake. Um, you take care of yourself and enjoy
your lunch. Sorry.

Allison
No, wait!

He runs behind a narrow tree.

Allison looks around without seeing him anywhere. Scanlon is
walking back to the building when he sees Allison and stops by.

Scanlon
If I weren't worried about making a bad joke, I'd say you look like
you've just seen a ghost.

Allison looks up at him.

INT.   Back at Allison's desk. Afternoon.

Allison is still pouring over the file Devalos has given her. She has
the yellow pages, various documents and an encyclopedia spread
over her desk. Her desk phone goes off and she answers after a few
rings.

Allison
DA's office, Allison Dubois speaking.

Muffled Male Voice
I'm coming to get you, Barbra. What are you wearing?

Allison

Sorry, you have the wrong number.

She hangs up. The phone rings again before she can return to her paperwork. She picks up.

Allison
DA's office, Allison Dubois.

Joe
Hey, you hung up on me.

Allison
Who? Oh, I'm sorry, honey. I didn't recognize your voice. What's up? I'm really swamped right now.

Joe
I can't believe you completely trampled my *"Night of the Living Dead"* reference. Now really, what do you have on?

Allison
Uhh, ten-inch heels and saran wrap.

Joe
Whoa, they really relaxed the dress code there. What are you swamped with?

Allison
Working on a VIP MIA. Why?

Joe
Well, the math emergency has been averted, and I'm on a plane right now getting ready to fly out of O'Hare. Any chance you can come out and play hooky with me?

Allison
You're coming home? That's great. I've been missing you. Oh, I don't know if I can make it, Joe. I'm going to be here pretty late. In fact, Ariel is staying over with a friend, and Bridgette and Marie are at the Beaudreau's tonight.
Devalos walks over.

Allison

Gerald Dean Rice

Joe, hold on.

Allison – to Devalos with her hand over the phone
Hey boss.

Devalos
How's everything going?

Allison
I had a little visitor while I was sitting outside having lunch. Might have something to do with our girl, might not. I'm waiting on him to show up again.

Devalos
Yeah, I was thinking about that. We got a little reprieve—the mayor's on vacation for the next two days. So why don't you go ahead and get out of here? The office is the wrong place for you to do your thing. Take the file with you.

Allison
All right. You sure?

Devalos
Absolutely.

Allison
Okay, well I guess I'll see you in the morning.

Devalos nods and begins walking back to his office. He stops momentarily and looks back at Allison.

Devalos
Tell your husband I said hello.

Allison nods back to him and removes her hand from the phone.

Allison
Joe—

Joe
I heard. I'm on American West, arriving at 3:40. Can we do dinner and a movie?

310

Allison
A date? That would be perfect. I can't remember the last time we
went out. But shouldn't we pick up the kids?

Joe
Well, we don't <u>have</u> to tell them.

Allison
Deceitful. I won't tell my husband if you don't tell your wife.

Joe
So, I'll see you soon?

Allison
Absolutely. I love you, Brad.

Joe
Love you too, Angelina. Bye.

EXT. Sky Harbor Airport. Afternoon.

Allison pulls up to the curb and Joe is waiting with two pieces of
luggage. She pops the trunk and he throws his things in and hops in
the front passenger seat. They stare at each other across the small
space between them, stone-faced, before Joe breaks character,
leans over, and pulls Allison in for a kiss.

Allison
(looking concerned after feeling his forehead)
Are you all right? You feel kinda warm.

Joe
Well, we have been apart for three days.

Allison
I'm serious. You might be coming down with something. Maybe we
should just go home.

Joe
No, no, no. C'mon, this is like a once in a lifetime opportunity—the
moon and stars are in alignment. We are going to spend time alone

together, even if it kills me. If you want, we can split the difference and just go to dinner.

Allison
All right. But if you start feeling bad, we go straight home.

Joe
You got a deal 'cause I'm as fit as fiddlesticks.

INT. A restaurant called Outshooters. Waitstaff shuffle back and forth in bright-colored uniforms with hats, and there are several families at surrounding tables. Joe sips at his soft drink more often than he eats as he and Allison sit across from each other in a booth. Allison looks up from her plate and sees the distant look in her husband's eyes and the sweat on his forehead. He looks up and notices her staring.

Joe
You know, as many times as we've been here with the kids, I never realized how annoying the waiters' uniforms are.

Allison
Yeah, they are a little on the bright side.

Joe
No wonder I'm losing my appetite. I think I'm turning epileptic.

Allison
Joe.

Joe
Okay, they're not that bright. (takes a deep breath) It's this dry heat, you get used to the temp in one place and then you gotta adjust all over again—(whispers) okay, my tummy hurts.

Allison
Okay, let me get the waiter over here to box this up and we'll head home.

The waiter comes over. The nametag on his shirt reads "Ned."

Ned
(His tone too chipper) How we doin' over here, guys?

Joe turns to get up, throws up on the waiter, and slumps back down in his seat. An expression of horror comes over the waiters face, but he continues smiling.

Allison
Joe!

INT. A hospital room. Joe is hooked up to an IV, lying in a bed wearing a hospital gown and covered up to his chest in white sheets. Allison stands by his bedside.

Joe
I feel fine. You didn't have to make a scene out of it.

Allison
You mean like you blowing chunks all over the waiter?

Joe
How long are you gonna hold that over my head?

Allison gives her husband a look.

Joe
Look, any minute now, the doctor's going to come in and say it's probably something I ate. It's probably just gas or jet lag. Or gas from jet lag. Or jet lag from gas.

Allison
Joe, don't joke. What if it's something serious?

Joe
Then maybe God'll be laughing while he smites me.

The doctor walks in. Her name tag reads "Dr. Ravesh." She straps on a pair of latex gloves. She turns down the bed sheet.

Dr. Ravesh
Good evening, Mr. and Mrs. Dubois, my name is Dr. Ravesh, I'm the attending. Mr. Dubois, I just want to check your stomach really quickly. How are we doing tonight, Mrs. Dubois?

Dr. Ravesh begins feeling around Joe's stomach.

Allison
A little shaken up to tell the truth.

Joe
Not me, I feel pretty good. It's not every day a guy gets (grunts) poisoned by his wife. I feel special.

Dr. Ravesh
Does he do this quite frequently?

Allison
Oh, you mean joke inappropriately when he's frightened? Yes. You shouldn't be joking anyway, Joe. I saw this thing on TV about a spy who was poisoned with this radioactive dust.

Joe
First, spies are cool; second, don't talk about my S-E-C-R-E-T-I-D in front of the D-O-C-T-O-R.

Allison makes a face. The doctor takes off her gloves and they both look at her. She turns and winks at Allison so Joe can't see.

Dr. Ravesh
Bad news, Mr. DuBois. You're going blind and deaf.

Joe
<u>What?</u>

Dr. Ravesh
See? Mrs. DuBois, your husband is going to be fine after a little routine surgery to remove his appendix. We're going to move relatively quickly now, but don't be alarmed; we always like to get those out ASAP before they can become problematic.

Allison
So, he's going to be okay? I mean surgery?

Dr. Ravesh
Yes. And like I said, this is very minor surgery. We'll have him back to you in a few hours, but we do have to operate immediately.

Allison
Yes, yes. Absolutely.

Joe
Hey, don't the deaf and blind get a say in any of this?

Dr. Ravesh
I'll let your wife tell you no.

Allison folds her arms and looks at him.

Allison
No.

Dr. Ravesh
I'll be right back. I just have some forms for you to sign.

The doctor leaves and then nurses come in to prepare Joe.

Joe
Helluva way for us to spend date night, huh Jane?

Allison stands, watching Joe. She reluctantly steps closer to him and grabs hold of his outstretched hand.

Allison
Yeah, Tarzan. You're gonna be okay, though.

Joe
Actually, I was going for Chevy Chase on the Weekend Update with Jane Curtin on SNL, but I like yours better.

Joe squeezes her hand and covers it with his other.

Nurse
Mr. DuBois, we're going to take you to the OR now. The doctor should be back shortly, Mrs. Dubois.

They wheel Joe out of the room and Allison follows until the elevators. They take him in and she stands in front of the doors a moment. She turns and walks back to the room to get her purse. Two doctors

315

precede her into the room and stand by the second bed in the room. They talk quietly to each other while looking over his chart and checking his monitoring equipment. Allison steps closer for a look. Beneath all the tubes, she recognizes the man from her vision, his face swollen and bandaged. Allison gasps.

INT. Hospital waiting room. Allison is within eyeshot of Joe's room and sitting down. There is an older woman with two very young children and a heavyset man with an arm cast up to his shoulder. Detective Scanlon walks in looking disheveled given the late hour.

Scanlon
Allison!

Allison
Detective Scanlon. I'm glad you're here.

Allison stands up and hugs Scanlon. He looks mildly uncomfortable and pats her back once.

Scanlon
I'm sorry, I was a little groggy when you called. What are you doing here again?

Allison
Joe has appendicitis and got sick while we were out to dinner. He's in surgery now, but they put him in a room with a guy I've been 'seeing' around. His name is Neil something. I couldn't write it down right then; his doctors were in the room.

Scanlon
Is he conscious?

Allison
No. Coma. He looked like he'd been beaten up pretty badly.

Scanlon
All right. I'll speak to someone at the nurse's station and call around. See what I can find out. And you think he's got something to do with Devalos' thing?

Allison

I don't know. Maybe. But at the very least he's connected to something.

Scanlon
Okay. Gimme a minute.

Scanlon goes over to the nurse's station and speaks to a young, heavyset brunette. He takes out his notepad and writes after she does something on the keyboard of the computer next to her. She picks up the phone and cradles it between her neck and shoulder as she types and a moment later a doctor comes over. They don't talk long before he comes back.

Scanlon
All right. Nurse said the only ID he had on him had the name Neil Gershonowicz. He was unconscious and non-responsive. They found him in the back of an old junker someone left in the hospital valet. They don't know if he has any family or not, so no one's been contacted and they haven't filed a police report yet. He has multiple lacerations to his face and neck but what they're more concerned about is the heat stroke.

Allison
Heat stroke (Allison's eyes dart around).

Scanlon
What? Anything?

Allison
Maybe. So, what do we do now?

Scanlon
Well, <u>we</u> don't do anything. You sit here and wait for the good word on your husband. I'll follow up at the station and see what this guy's history is and if he has any relatives. Hopefully, we can place him in our girl's proximity. Hopefully, whoever did this to him didn't have the chance to do it to her. Did you call Devalos?

Allison
No. Not yet.

Scanlon

317

Good. Don't. Let's see if this turns into anything first. I'll see you.

Allison
Thanks for coming so fast. See you.

Allison walks over to a vending machine and ponders the selections. She begins feeding quarters into the machine, when she feels someone behind her.

Neil
Fancy meeting you here.

She looks around and sees everyone within earshot is asleep.

Allison
Listen. I want to apologize about earlier. I'm kind of…weird that way, and it can come off as abrasive.

Neil
Don't think twice about it. Obviously, if you're here, you must be under a deal of stress. I've said goofier. I'm Neil.

Allison
Allison.

She holds out her hand for him to shake. He stares at it, nervously.

Neil
Sorry, I'm a little germ-phobic. So, who are you here to see?

Allison
My husband. Appendicitis. And you?

Neil
A friend of mine. Heat stroke. They should be letting him go soon.

Allison
Wow, heat stroke. Is he from out of town? What's your friend's name?

Neil opens his mouth to speak, but the older woman with the little boy yawns loudly and stretches, distracting Allison from Neil. When she looks back, he is gone. She turns and makes her selection from the vending machine.

Later.

Allison is watching television in the waiting room when Dr. Ravesh returns. She looks concerned and Allison stands to meet her.

Dr. Ravesh
Mrs. Dubois—

Allison
Is everything okay? Did the surgery go all right?

Dr. Ravesh
Your husband did fine through the surgery, but there was an unexpected complication.

Allison
What? What?

Dr. Ravesh puts a hand on Allison's shoulder and her other on her arm and guides Allison to a seat.

Dr. Ravesh
He had a mild reaction to the anesthesia, just as the surgeon was wrapping up.

Allison
How mild? What does that mean?

Dr. Ravesh
Your husband is in a light coma.

Allison
Coma?

Dr. Ravesh
He could awake in ten minutes or in a few days. However long it takes for him to work the anesthesia out of his system, but he is in no immediate danger.

Allison
I need to see him. Can I see him?

Dr. Ravesh
In just a moment. This is almost like he went on a bender and just needs to sleep it off, but I want to assure you, Mrs. Dubois, that your husband will be fine. I need to go see the nurses, but I will be right back just as soon as they bring your husband down to take you to him.

Allison
I need to call my girls. I need to call work. Are you sure he's going to be okay?

Dr. Ravesh
Scout's honor. Now relax, Mrs. Dubois.

INT. The Devalos kitchen. Morning.

The Devalos residence is quiet except for Manuel straightening his tie in between bites of dry toast. He turns on his cell and it buzzes immediately. Manuel dials his cell one-handed and puts it to his ear. We hear scratches of Allison's voice as he pops the last piece of toast in his mouth and shuts his briefcase. He hits a button on his phone and flips it shut, grabs his suitcase, and heads toward the front door. His wife, in her night clothes, meets him at the stairs.

Mrs. Devalos
Good morning, sweetheart.

Devalos
Good morning.

They kiss and she wipes away a piece of toast from his mouth.

Mrs. Devalos
Did you take your shot?

Devalos
Yes, I took my shot.

She undoes his tie and starts it again, lingering as she does so.

Devalos
Hey, what's the protocol for giving a man flowers?

She looks at him with a confused expression.

Devalos
It's Allison's husband. He had emergency surgery last night—he's fine, but apparently he went into a mild coma from the anesthesia.

Mrs. Devalos
Oh my. Is everyone okay?

Devalos
Yes, but do I get him flowers? It just seems kind of—I don't know—strange.

Mrs. Devalos
You men are so complex and silly at the same time. I'm just a girl—I would. Tell you what, if it seems so weird, then just send the flowers to the Dubois family. No doubt, Allison will get them and let her interpret any way she likes.

Devalos
I might have married you for your body, but I'm glad it came with a brain.

Mrs. Devalos
Yeah, I'm pretty hot.

They kiss. Devalos' cell rings.

Devalos
See you tonight. On time.

Devalos walks out and she shuts the door behind him.

INT. Police Headquarters. Morning.

Detective Scanlon flips through some files on his desk as he waits for DA Devalos to pick up.

Devalos
Devalos.

Scanlon
Got some news.

Devalos
Go ahead.

Scanlon
Allison put us on to a Neil Gershonowicz last night. He's in the hospital; it doesn't look like he's going to make it. Somebody roughed him up pretty bad and left him in the sun so long he had severe heat stroke. Dumped at Phoenix Memorial two nights ago. Your standard ne'er-do-well, a couple sheets' worth of B&Es, petty larceny, destruction of property, etc.

Devalos
So far, you're not scratching my itch, detective.

Scanlon
I know. This kid is small time. For the past three months, however, his record is clean. Squeaky clean. I spoke with his PO last night and he told me Neil had moved into an upscale apartment and was driving an expensive Mercedes Benz.

Devalos
I presume he was teetering on the edge of parole violation, but again, so what?

Scanlon
Well, as it turns out, Neil's wealthy benefactor is a Karl Debussey, Jr. The car is registered in his name and he's on the lease to the apartment Neil lives in. I couldn't find any connection to Karl Debussey and Neil Gershonowicz until, by chance, I pulled up a picture of Debussey, Senior and Junior. Get this: they're twins.

Devalos
Please tell me there's a connect to my kidnap.

Scanlon

As multi-millionaires go, the Debusseys are as close to being next door neighbors as you can get with the Hendersons. Our girl and Debussey Junior went to high school together.

Devalos
All right. Keep digging. I want to know as much as possible on both of them ASAP o'clock. I'll take care of interviewing the Debusseys after I review. Oh, and I'm sending Allison's husband some flowers if you'd like your name on the card.

Scanlon - looking confused
Flowers?

INT. The Dubois kitchen.

Allison sits at the head of the table with her daughters seated next to one another. Outside the kitchen window, a man on fire waves, trying to get Allison's attention.

Man on Fire
Hey!

Allison looks at each of her daughters from oldest to youngest. The man's shouting makes her lose count.

Allison
One…two…three…

Man on Fire
Hello?

Allison – looking confused
One…two…three…

Man on Fire
Anybody? Anybody?

INT. Joe's hospital room.

Allison sleeps in a chair by Joe's bedside. Their daughters come in with a brunette-haired woman around Allison's age behind them.

Ariel
Mom?

Allison snaps awake and turns to her daughters. She holds her arms out to them and they rush to her.

Allison
Babies.

Allison looks up to the woman with them.

Allison
Thank you, Cynthia.

Cynthia
Oh, Allison, don't mention it. Are you okay?

Allison
I'm fine. (She turns to her daughters). And your father's going to be fine too. The medicine they gave him to put him to sleep for the surgery just made him a little sick.

Marie
Daddy's got a tummy ache?

INT. DA's office. Late morning.

Scanlon knocks on Devalos' office door.

Devalos
Come in.

Scanlon
I just emailed you everything we have on Gershonowicz and his twin brother. We swung by the apartment, but there's nobody home. Karl Debussey, Jr.'s birth certificate lists Karl Debussey, Sr. and Laura Debussey as his birth parents.

Devalos
Why would millionaires give a child up for adoption?

Scanlon

Don't know who Gershonowicz's parents are. Maybe he and Karl Jr. just look a lot alike. He grew up in an orphanage, so we're going to need a ton of subpoenas to get to everything we need. I don't know if it makes any difference, but Laura Debussey is Karl's second wife.

Devalos
Unfortunately, we don't have the time for all the legal wrangling to get a look at the documents we need. I'll have to make a shortcut.

Scanlon
What are you going to do?

Devalos
I'm going to ask Mr. Debussey. He knows me: I tried him for murdering his first wife.

EXT. Outside the Debussey residence. A cool, slightly windy afternoon.

Devalos stands at the front door, briefcase in hand. He has shown up unannounced to have somewhat of an element of surprise when either Debussey opens the door. He has a young blonde ADA with him with a pair of thick-framed glasses too sharp for her ovular face. He rings the doorbell. After a minute, a blond-haired man in his late teens or early twenties pops his head out the door.

Karl
Yeah?

Devalos
Mr. Debussey, my name is Miguel Devalos, and I'm the Maricopa County district attorney, this is Assistant District Attorney Pauline Fisk. Could I have a word with you inside?

Karl
What about?

Devalos
Neil Gershonowicz.

Karl
Man! (he looks around) C'mon, c'mon.

INT. The Debussey Living Room

Karl paces nervously back and forth. Devalos and Fisk sit calmly on the couch watching him.

Devalos
What can you tell me about Mr. Gershonowicz?

Karl
He's my brother.

Devalos
And how did you two meet?

Karl
Fate. (pours himself a drink. Devalos and Fisk look at one another but say nothing). I mean, what kind of father would hide his son from his own brother?

Devalos
That's not exactly an answer. Under what circumstances did you two happen across one another?

Karl
I told you (drinks down the entire glass). Fate. I walk into Starbucks and we bump into one another.

Fisk
Did you ever stop to consider that Gershonowicz may have followed you?

Karl
No. He was already there when I got there.

Devalos
Mr. Debussey, are you aware that Mr. Gershonowicz has been in the hospital since Monday?

Karl
Yeah, well. I found him like that. All swollen and red. I thought he was dead. I rushed him to the hospital, but then I thought, if my

father knows I know about him, what's he going to do? I mean, everybody knows he killed my mother. Maybe he'd kill me too. Maybe he was the one who did that to him.

Fisk
So, you think your father did this. Do you have any idea of your father's whereabouts between Saturday night and Sunday morning?

Karl - laughing
Clever girl. Trying to get the angst-filled teen to spill the goodies on his daddy. See, I said, 'Everybody knows he killed my mother' so that's not in dispute and no one can do anything about it now. I might hate my dad, but I <u>love</u> my dad. Besides, if, per se, he hypothetically were to kill someone, he'd never do it himself. And to answer your unasked question, I was just getting to know Neil. There was a huge gap between us that we were just starting to fill in. I'd given him my apartment and my car; I had no reason to kill him. And if I did, I certainly wouldn't have dropped him off at the hospital.

Devalos
You went to school with a Sandy Henderson, correct?

Karl
(looking confused) Uh, yeah. What about her?

Devalos
She's a witness in an unrelated case. Have you seen her?

Karl
(lights a cigarette) Not since graduation day. What she do this time?

Devalos
What makes you think she's done anything?

Karl
Oh, you know old Sandy. Into a little of this, (sniffs and wipes under his nose with the back of his index finger) a little of that.

Devalos
And I take it you're familiar with that side of her?

Karl

Gerald Dean Rice

Me? No—I believe in good clean living (raises his refilled glass
before downing it).

Devalos
I see. Well, I thank you for your time. If you recall anything about Ms.
Henderson, here's my card. Call anytime.

Karl
Hey, wait, is Neil gonna be okay?

Devalos
I don't know, Mr. Debussey. Last thing the doctors said was it was
touch-and-go. You might want to get out there as soon as possible.

EXT. Outside the Debussey residence

Fisk
How honest do you think he was?

Devalos – taking out his cell phone
I have no idea. It was difficult to get a bead on him in his current
state.

Fisk
Speaking of which, Debussey's only eighteen.

Devalos
I know. And if he cares at all about his brother, he's going to be
leaving any minute to get to the hospital. Debussey doesn't know his
brother's already brain dead. I'll have a black-and-white ready to take
him into custody as soon as he steps off the property. We'll get some
coffee into him, and while he's in the middle of getting the hell scared
out of him, we'll take a DNA sample off the cup.

INT. Interrogation Room at police headquarters.

Karl Debussey sits in the interrogation room with his head down on
the table. Scanlon walks in with two Styrofoam cups and sits one
down. An officer stands behind him at the door.

Scanlon
Here's a coffee.

Karl
Yeah.

Karl takes a sip and makes a face.

Karl
Ugh. This is black.

Scanlon
Oh, you don't like it that way? Sorry about that. Let me get you another.

Scanlon takes the cup and hands it to the officer behind him.

Scanlon
Jeffries, could you put some cream and sugar— (to Karl) cream and sugar?

Karl
Yeah. Whatever. Can we just get this over with? I think I have a hangover.

Scanlon hands Jeffries the cup, both of them carefully avoiding the lip. Jeffries leaves.

INT. The viewing room adjacent to the interrogation room. Scanlon and Karl Debussey are inside.

Devalos and Fisk watch Jeffries leave the room.

Fisk
Now we figure out what we already know. The trouble is how we tie any of it with our missing girl or what happened to Gershonowicz.

A detective walks in with a file. He hands it to Devalos

Devalos
Thank you.

Devalos skims through it.

Devalos
Apparently, Neil Gershonowicz was raised in an orphanage. Birth mother had him at home and disappeared soon after he was born with no other family to speak of. And according to his birth certificate, he was a single birth.

Fisk
A woman who abandons her baby—I wouldn't necessarily be inclined to believe she was telling the truth about him being an only child. Maybe she sold one of them to Debussey and he didn't want the other one.

Devalos
Maybe he didn't know about the other one.

A fortyish woman in a well-tailored skirt suit bursts into the room, followed closely by another man and two officers.

Debussey Sr.
You let my son out of there _right_ now, dammit.

Devalos and Fisk turn. Fisk waves the two officers off and they leave.

Devalos
Mr. Debussey, your son is being held for interrogation for the assault of Neil Gershonowicz.

Debussey Sr.
He didn't do it. You people are just persecuting him like you did me.

Devalos
Mr. Debussey, I assure you, your son will not be charged with anything unless evidence suggests his guilt. Currently, we are in the process of investigating and will make a determination when all the facts are in.

Jen Fowler
Jen Fowler. I'm the family attorney for the Debusseys. I'd like to see my client.

Devalos

I don't see why not, but he hasn't asked to see an attorney. He's old enough to make the determination on his own.

Fowler
You're pressing your luck, Mr. Devalos. Mr. Debussey was found not guilty of murder way back in 1990, yet this office has a penchant for harassing him, present company included.

Devalos
I might be inclined to agree with you if Assistant District Attorney Fisk and I hadn't seen Mr. Debussey's son consuming alcohol with our own eyes. Despite an ongoing investigation, he's only being charged with consuming underage.

Fowler
Nevertheless, the questioning stops now.

Devalos steps over to the window and flips a switch.

Devalos
Scanlon.

Scanlon looks back at them, rises and leaves. He comes into the room with Devalos and the rest.

Devalos
Detective Scanlon, this is Karl Debussey Sr. and his attorney Jen Fowler.

Scanlon
Okay. Mr. Debussey, at this time, your son is being charged with being a minor in possession. We will need to speak to you regarding how he acquired the alcohol.

Devalos jumps in.

Devalos
But we would be willing to overlook charges against you or your son in this matter if you would be willing to cooperate with us in a separate investigation.

Debussey

Gerald Dean Rice

What investigation?

Devalos
If you could fill us in on your relationship with Neil Gershonowicz.

Fowler
Hold on—Mr. Debussey does not know a Neil Gershonowicz, and if by chance he does, he is not affiliated with any criminal enterprise—

Scanlon
Save the spiel, counselor. Neil Gershonowicz is your son's twin.

Debussey
A twin? My son doesn't have a twin.

Devalos
Take a look for yourself.

Devalos opens a folder on the table and takes out a file with arrest photos of Neil along with his record.

Debussey
My son has never been arrested.

Devalos
That's not your son. That is Neil Gershonowicz. Right now, he's on life support at Phoenix Memorial in a coma he may never wake from. And before you say your son doesn't know him, Neil listed his address with his parole officer as the same apartment your son is living in.

Debussey gets teary-eyed.

Debussey
He's…dying?

Devalos stares a moment.

Devalos
Quite possibly. I'm sorry to inform you in such an…impersonal manner. You <u>do</u> know Neil Gershonowicz?

Fowler
Mr. Debussey has been under a great deal of stress. You'll have to excuse us.

Debussey
I want to go.

Fowler
Excuse me? What?

Debussey
To the hospital. I want to see my son.

Fowler looks back at Devalos as he ushers him out of the room.

Fowler
We'll talk. In the meantime, I'll send someone from my office to pick up Mr. Debussey's son, unless you're actually charging him?

Devalos
By all means. There's time for that later.

Mr. Debussey and Fowler leave.

Scanlon
You're just going to let him go?

Fisk
Sometimes you throw back the little fish so you can catch the big one.

Devalos
The way I see it, either Mr. Debussey knew he had another son and was helping to hide him or Karl Jr. was hiding him all on his own. Either way, I don't think he had anything to do with it. The trouble is, the deeper this rabbit hole goes, the farther we get from our missing girl.

Scanlon
If there even is a missing girl.

Devalos

Gerald Dean Rice

Your doubts are noted. In the meantime, get back in there with Mr.
Debussey.

Scanlon
We still waiting for the lawyer?

Devalos
I don't see that we have to right now. He didn't ask for one. His father
did. I'll call in an hour or so. In the meantime, see what you can get
out of him. I need a result on this fast.

INT. A kitchen in the early morning hours.

Two women struggle with each other, the shorter one strangling the
taller one from behind. Blood is smeared on the floor and the tall one
struggles to get her feet under her. She falls, slipping out of the grip
of the other woman, but quickly rebounds. Winded, the two women
stare at each other like wild animals. The short one lunges and the
tall one punches her in the face, sending her into the counter and
knocking over a host of seasonings and kitchen utensils. The short
one picks up a knife and spins, slashing through the air. The tall one
jumps back and then dives for the knife hand. They struggle, and
when the short one pops free, she is off balance, slides across the
bloody floor and falls throat first into the island in the center of the
kitchen. The tall one stares as the woman writhes on the floor
choking to death.

Ariel
Mom!

Allison wakes. Her daughter stares at her.

Allison
Was I sleeping?

Ariel
I thought you were choking. You sounded like a wounded animal.

Dr. Ravesh enters.

Dr. Ravesh
Good afternoon, Mrs. Dubois. How are you?

Allison
As okay as can be expected. How much longer is Joe going to be
sleeping?

Dr. Ravesh
It won't be long now. His levels are all back to normal. He should be
awake any time. In fact, he may even hear you now. Mr. Dubois—
four very pretty ladies are here to see you. Don't you want to get up?

Joe shifts in his sleep.

Dr. Ravesh
See? He'll be up soon. Go ahead—talk to him.

Dr. Ravesh steps back and Allison and Ariel get closer. Arie has a
hand on his leg, Allison holds his hand.

Allison
Joe? We're here, Joe.

Ariel
Time to wake up, Daddy.

Bridgette
Yeah, time to get up, sleepyhead.

Marie
Sleepyhead!

Joe moans again, shifting. He opens his eyes slightly, appearing as if
he is looking at no one in particular.

Joe
Sandy…

Joe closes his eyes.

Allison
Joe? Joe! Girls, go get the nurse or the doctor. Tell them he just
woke up.

Gerald Dean Rice

Allison takes Marie and puts her in her lap while Ariel and Bridgette run from the room. Allison leans in close and begins shaking Joe's arm.

Allison
Say 'Wake up, Daddy!'

Marie
Wake up, Daddy!

Allison
Time to wake up, Joe.

Joe opens his eyes again. He seems to focus on Allison and Marie a moment.

Joe
Hey, girls.

Allison
Hey, how are you feeling?

Joe
I'm tired.

Allison
What do you mean, you're tired? You've been sleeping for two days.

Dr. Ravesh comes in right behind Ariel and Bridgette.

Dr. Ravesh
That's because a coma isn't the same as sleep. Your husband is going to need his rest. You could probably use some of the same. You look exhausted.

Allison
What do you say, girls? Now that daddy's okay, do you want to go get something to eat and go home? We can come back in the morning.

Joe begins snoring.

Allison
So, he'll be able to come home soon?

Dr. Ravesh
Oh, absolutely. You'll have him home probably sometime tomorrow afternoon.

Allison
Thank God. Okay girls, let's give Daddy a kiss.

They each kiss Joe and Allison holds Marie up to kiss him.

Marie
Daddy has stinky breath.

INT. Hospital.

Karl Debussey Sr. takes long strides down the hall as his attorney, Ms. Fowler, follows closely behind. Debussey walks by a woman and three young girls and she looks at him a moment before continuing on. He walks past a sleeping man and over to Neil Gershonowicz's bed.

Debussey
Jen, go get the doctor. I need a moment. And tell him I want my son in his own room.

Fowler
All right, Karl.

Fowler leaves. Debussey tentatively touches the edge of the bed, staring at Neil's bandage-wrapped head.

Debussey
I should have known. I should have known.

He steps around the foot of the bed and comes closer. He barely notices the blonde-haired woman returning for something by the bed next over. Debussey kneels, clenching Gershonowicz's hand, and weeps. He almost doesn't hear the woman leaving the room.

EXT. The hospital parking lot. The Dubois station wagon.

Allison picks up her cell phone and dials the DA.

Devalos
Hello?

Allison
Mr. Devalos, this is Allison. I was just visiting Joe and an older man came in to see Gershonowicz. He seemed to be pretty upset that he was in the hospital.

Devalos
That would have been Karl Debussey—we think he's the father. What's your…professional opinion of him? Would you say earnest?

Allison
Definitely. I don't think he knew I was even in the room and he seemed pretty distraught. I didn't catch the impression he was pretending.

Devalos
How's your husband doing?

Allison
Good-good. He just woke up as a matter of fact.

Devalos
That's fantastic news.

Allison
Listen, I think I'd like to take tomorrow off too, but I can definitely stop by the office in the morning. They may be releasing Joe.

Devalos
By all means, take all the time you need. See you in the morning.

Allison
Good night, sir.

INT. Devalos' office.

Devalos sits at his desk, going over information Scanlon has given him. Gershonowicz's birth certificate lists Jean Franka as his mother. Devalos looks through a different file and pulls out a W-2 form for Jean Franka that lists Karl Debussey Sr. as her employer.

Devalos
The plot thickens.

Devalos picks up the phone and dials a number off a card on his desk. A sleepy voice can be heard on the other end of the line.

Devalos
I need to speak to your client tomorrow. I am inclined to nct press charges against him in the Gershonowicz matter if he is completely forthcoming regarding any information to do with Mandy Henderson...Okay...9:00 a.m. it is.

INT. DA's office. Morning.

Devalos and Fisk are seated across from Karl Debussey, Sr. and Jen Fowler. Fowler's nose is red and she has a bandage on her forehead.

Fowler
Please excuse the bandage. I started coming down with a cold last night, sneezed a little too close to a wall and...

Devalos
All right. Onto business: Mandy Henderson.

Debussey
What about my son?

Devalos
Uh, which one?

Debussey
Neil. What are you doing to catch the person who did that to him?

Fowler
We talked about this. Karl—

Debussey
Don't tell me to wait, <u>Jen</u>. I have a son who is about to die and I've never even spoken to him before.

Devalos
So, he is your son?

Fowler throws up her hands.

Debussey
Yes. Absolutely. And he's getting the best care possible.

Devalos
Well, Detective Scanlon will be able to provide you with any detail regarding the investigation; however, it is ongoing, so there may be details he can't discuss. In the meantime—Mandy Henderson.

Debussey – looks at his attorney who nods
Just a girl my son knew in high school. We hear things occasionally, but I try to ignore teenagers as much as possible, so I don't know.

Devalos
Can you vouch for the whereabouts of your son, Karl, two nights ago?

Debussey
Well, I know he went to a party, but he was home by 12:30. I mean my house. He still stays there occasionally, even though he has his own apartment. And if you're asking, I was working out of my office on the phone with Tokyo until two in the morning.

Devalos
I see. Well, thank you for your cooperation, Mr. Debussey. I'll send in Detective Scanlon.

Devalos and Fisk leave the room. Scanlon is waiting just outside and he walks up to the two.

Scanlon
That was quick.

Devalos

I don't have time to baby-sit dead-ends. Debussey has an alibi that needs checking, but I don't think he had anything to do with Mandy Henderson's disappearance. In the meanwhile, give him an update on Gershonowicz, and let's connect the dots between them.

Scanlon
I'm on it.

Devalos and Fisk walk away and Scanlon enters the room with a file. He sits and opens it.

Scanlon
Mr. Debussey, I'm not going to beat around the bush here. Your son's birth certificate lists him as a single birth and your former wife is listed as his birth mother. Care to explain that for me?

Fowler
We were under the impression this would not be an interrogation, rather a sharing of information.

Scanlon
The fact that Mr. Debussey isn't in handcuffs right now is evidence of the district attorney's good faith.

Fowler
Handcuffs for what?

Scanlon
Fraud for one. How many forms for insurance, registrations, and who knows how many government documents, including a birth certificate, have you filled out for your son with false information?

Debussey
I can explain that (takes a deep breath). Laura and I tried for years. It was very important to us both to have our own—we both were only children. But in the end she just…couldn't. We eventually agreed on a surrogate. Laura found her. We kept it quiet—we fully intended to pass the child off as ours. Laura even bought pregnancy pads to give the impression she really was expecting. The time came and…the girl gave us the baby and she left. Obviously, she was pregnant with twins, but I swear to you, had I known—I would have combed the ends of the earth to have him.

Scanlon
And who is this surrogate?

Debussey
I don't remember now. Some foreign exchange student, probably back in her home country now. What about my son, Detective? Where do you stand on finding the person who did this to him?

Scanlon
To be honest with you, Mr. Debussey, your son, Karl, is our only suspect.

Debussey
That's ridiculous—my son was taking care of him. He had no cause to try to kill him.

Scanlon
He also hid his brother from you. Obviously, there are some things he doesn't want you to know. It could be they had a fight or a falling out, and maybe Neil attacked Karl, and Karl hurt him defending himself.

Debussey
I don't believe that. He…he liked to party, sure, but you can't find a sweeter kid.

Scanlon
Take a look for yourself (Scanlon slides the file over). Neil Gershonowicz had an extensive juvenile record.

Fowler takes the file and scans through it.

Fowler
Conceded, but answer this, detective—if Karl was defending himself, what cause would he have to hide it? It's to my understanding that Karl kept the relationship with his brother hidden because he was afraid—and pardon me, Karl—of what his father would do to Neil after what he'd heard his father had done to his mother.

Debussey makes a sour face at Fowler.

Scanlon
So, it's not self-defense. I doubt it was jealousy over women or money. Neil didn't have either of those.

Debussey
So, isn't it obvious that it couldn't be Karl?

Scanlon
Maybe. Mr. Debussey, who did you say handled the details behind finding this surrogate—you or your wife?

Debussey
My—my wife. Yes.

Scanlon
You're still living in the same home you did back then. Do you think it's possible she may have kept a record you may not have known about?

Debussey
Anything is possible, but I doubt it.

Scanlon
Well, with your permission of course, we'd like to search your home. We won't be looking for anything connected with anything else. We'll be specifically looking for a record that can tell us anything about who this surrogate is.

Fowler
Detective, I'm confused. I don't understand, even if you find out exactly who his birth mother is, how that has any bearing whatsoever on who attacked him.

Scanlon
And only one-third of the people in this room have any experience whatsoever with things of this nature. We find your sons' birth mother and perhaps we find a blackmailer who contacted Karl and connected him with Neil. Perhaps we find someone she knows who does have a tendency to do what was done to Neil. Perhaps we find a reason to believe your son didn't almost kill his brother.

Debussey

Everyone was quick to believe…I had killed my wife. I'd already been married twice before, I was ten years older than her, there had been rumors about us separating in the papers. To the casual observer, Laura was a speed bump on the way to my next failed relationship. But every woman before her paled in comparison, and every woman since has been a bitter reminder that she is never coming back. She would have wanted Neil as much as I do. Her heart would be breaking as much as mine is. We were a match, Detective. In every sense of the word—I knew her inside and out. I've hated on sight, every single person I came across with a badge for putting me through the disgrace of a trial that pointed the finger at me for her murder and by the grace of God I wasn't convicted. To this day, I have spent a great deal of my fortune to find her killer, and I've never spoken about it. As much as it burns me, if it means finding the person who left our son for dead, my door is open.

INT. The Debussey basement.

Scanlon and team of detectives and officers search through boxes in Karl Debussey's basement. Fowler is overseeing when Scanlon gets a phone call.

Scanlon
Yeah.

Devalos
Anything yet?

Scanlon
No. We're turning up empty. There's some interesting stuff, but per your agreement, we're overlooking anything that doesn't have to do with our boy.

Devalos
Okay, I'm headed over to the hospital to pay my respects. Keep me posted.

The line goes dead and Scanlon puts his phone back on his hip.

INT. The hospital. Afternoon.

Devalos hurries down the hall to Joe Dubois' room, carrying a large bouquet of flowers in a vase. He steps in the room to see Joe eating a small bowl of applesauce, but otherwise alone.

Joe
Oh. Hello.

Joe looks at the flowers, holding his spoon in midair.

Joe
Are those for me?

Devalos looks mildly uncomfortable.

Devalos
Good afternoon, Mr. Dubois. Uh, yes. I'll just...I'll just set them...set them here.

Devalos sits the bouquet on the tiny stand next to Joe's bed, but they hang over into the side of Joe's face. Devalos tries scooting them over, but there just isn't enough room, and he winds up placing them on the floor.

Devalos
Is Allison around?

Joe
Yeah, she and the girls just went to the cafeteria to get something to eat.

Devalos looks around the room.

Devalos - nodding
So...appendix.

Joe
Yeah.

Devalos
Did they...did they have to give you a transfusion for that?

Joe

No. At least I don't think so.

Devalos
I had my adenoids out. I was…around fourteen, fifteen.

Joe
If it weren't for the coma, this would have been pretty tame. I'm probably going home today.

Devalos
So soon? Wow. HMOs.

Joe
You're telling me. You should see the injury I got that had me in the hospital for three weeks. I tore my back all to hell—it's a miracle I can still walk.

Devalos
See this right here (Devalos pushes back his sleeve)? Compound fracture—broke it in history class of all places. It looked like I had a stick of chalk sticking out of my arm. My hand looked like it was on backwards and the <u>blood</u>!

Joe
Blood? You should have seen my face after the school jock found out his sister asked me out on a date. He got me in the two places that bleed the most—my nose and my ear. I still can't hear right out this one.

INT. The hospital hallway down from Joe's room.

Allison and the girls are bringing back lunch to have with Joe. They turn into the room and see Devalos with his tie undone and his shirt half-unbuttoned as he's leaning in and showing Joe, who's sitting up, something on his neck.

Devalos
Just barely missed the jugular—look at that.

Allison
Sir?

Devalos
Allison!

Devalos stands up and begins buttoning up his shirt.

Devalos
Just talking old war wounds with your husband.

Allison
Should we leave you two alone?

Joe
Your boss was just keeping me company.

Bridgette
You brought my daddy flowers. That was sweet.

Devalos
Yes, well, it was on the way and I was already headed here because
I needed to speak to you, Allison.

Allison
Certainly.

Allison kisses her husband before turning to walk out of the room
with Devalos.

Ariel
Mom? Can I still borrow your phone?

Allison
Right. Yes.

Allison takes her cell phone out of her purse and hands it over to
Ariel.

Allison
And remember—keep it under a half hour. You're burning a hole in
my minutes.

The three of them leave the room, Allison, Devalos and Ariel, the last turning in the other direction from the first two. Marie hands Joe and Bridgette a flower from the bouquet.

Marie
These are pretty, Daddy.

INT. The hospital hallway outside Joe's room.

Allison and Devalos walk slowly down the hall.

Devalos
So, any new sensations?

Allison
I don't know. It might not be connected to anything, but I had this dream…there were two women…struggling. There was blood on the floor. It was slippery. One of them grabbed a knife, they wrestled for it and then the other one fell and hit her neck on the island. Does that connect with anything?

Devalos lets out a long sigh. He gestures to his neck.

Devalos
The injury you're describing and where it happened…it may have some bearing in the long run with Neil Gershonowicz, but it certainly muddies the water right now. Feodora Ellerman was Karl Debussey's housekeeper back in 1989. She was killed from a blow to the neck so severe it dislodged two vertebrae that severed her spinal cord. The coroner said she laid there, paralyzed, and suffocated to death because her throat had been crushed.

Allison
Why do you have such a long memory on this one?

Devalos
I was still an ADA back then and this was my case. We tried Debussey for double homicide, but the lack of two bodies was a stumbling block. The case resulted in a mistrial, and Debussey led an all-out campaign that painted DA Michaels as being on a witch-hunt during the next election, and no DA after has had the guts, the remaining evidence, or a combination of the two to go after him

again. Myself included. I may not be psychic, but I think I have a
clearer picture as to why the police never recovered a body.

Allison
What are you thinking?

Devalos
That Laura Debussey isn't as dead as she's supposed to be. And
that Feodora Ellerman is more than likely Karl and Neil's mother.

Allison
You still don't seem very happy about that.

Devalos
Well, it's one step closer to a case solved, but it doesn't have
anything to do with Mandy Henderson.

Allison
Mandy Henders—the missing girl! I've had absolutely no luck. Maybe
the bad news is she isn't dead?

Devalos
There seems to be a growing consensus on that and I may be
inclined to agree. I may have an idea on how to bring this thing to a
head.

INT. The Dubois household.

Joe and Allison sit on the couch together, watching the news. A female
reporter is reading a story with a picture of a heavyset older man with
a grayish beard.

Reporter
Construction and real estate mogul Vander Henderson was admitted
to Good Samaritan Medical Center early this morning after suffering
what doctors are calling a massive heart attack. Henderson recently
unveiled plans to build a forty story building here in Phoenix and
owns a chain of home improvement stores throughout the country.
Doctors list his condition as guarded.

Allison
So that's how he's going to do it.

Joe
Do what?

Allison
Mr. Devalos thinks Vander Henderson's daughter went missing-in-action all on her own and he figured a way to flush her out.

Joe
Ohhhh, the old massive-heart-attack trick. Mine was better.

Allison
Yours was—come here. Let me snatch out those stitches if it was just a trick.

Joe
Omigod, no. Dr. Ravesh said she'll sign my booboo.

Allison
Shut up so I can kiss you, Gene.

They kiss and lay face-to-face on the couch.

INT. Good Samaritan Medical Center.

A young, semi-disheveled young woman and her boyfriend hurry down a long hallway. He drags behind her and she rounds into her father's room. DA Devalos is sitting in a chair, speaking with her father, who is fully-clothed, sitting on the bed.

Mandy
Daddy? What's going on here?

Devalos turns and sees her and her boyfriend, who looks exactly like Karl Debussey Jr.

Devalos
That is a very good question.

INT. Police headquarter's interrogation room.

Karl

I keep telling you, I'm an only child.

Scanlon
When we had you in here before, Karl, you indicated that you barely knew Mandy Henderson.

Karl
What do you mean 'before'? I've never been here. I've only been in the country for a few days.

Scanlon
Then where's your passport?

Karl
I was robbed not long after I arrived.

Scanlon
Right. Do you really expect me to believe any of this, Karl? Your brother's dying in the hospital and I'm two hairs away from throwing you in a cell and charging you with attempted murder. Your father's lying for you and the best you can do is you just got here in a phony Swedish accent?

Karl
My father is dead. And my accent, it isn't Swedish. It's Norwegian. Look, let me call my mother—she'll tell you.

Scanlon
What's your full name?

Karl
Karl Allen Montrose.

Scanlon looks up at the window. Devalos stares intently from the other side.

INT. Scanlon's desk.

Karl dials a number while Devalos and Scanlon listen in. It rings a few times before going to voicemail.

Karl

I don't understand, my mother keeps her phone on her all the time. Even throughout the night she leaves it on.

INT. A large white room, perhaps a warehouse, with fluorescent lighting in its high ceilings.

Allison is wearing a red and black dress with her hair curled. It is cold. A man leans against the wall on the other side of the room and she slowly approaches him. He has blond hair and blue eyes and is dressed in a black tuxedo with the tie undone around his neck. Yellow light pours across his face from the open door next to him. Salsa music plays softly in the distance.

Karl – with mist coming from his mouth
Care to dance?

Allison steps into his arms and they begin to dance. She continually tries to see into the room with the yellow light, but the angle is wrong. It is difficult to hear over the music, but at first, it sounds as if two women are struggling and then just one woman's voice, yelling at someone. As Karl brings her back up after a dip, Allison feels another man behind her. She turns to him.

Karl
Mind if I cut in?

INT. The Dubois bedroom.

Allison wakes up. She gets out of bed, hobbling.

Joe
Did I do that, Betty?

Allison
I slept wrong on my leg and it fell asleep. Sorry, Hulk.

Joe - yawning
Hulk smash.

Allison
I have to call the DA. I just figured something out.

Joe
Congratulations, Jessica.

Allison makes a face.

Allison
Who are we going for? Jessica Rabbit?

Joe
Ohhh, that was Jessica Fletcher—Murder She Wrote from 1984 to 1996.

Allison
I never watched that show. She wasn't married.

Joe
She had a thing with Magnum PI.

Allison
Did not.

Joe
How would you know? You didn't watch.

Allison
I'll have you know, Magnum PI was my boyfriend, and we were deeply in love with each other.

Allison dials and whips a pillow at Joe with the other hand.

Joe
Ohhh! My complete and total lack of appendix—how could you?

INT. Devalos' car. Morning.

Devalos speaks to Allison through a hands-free device while driving.

Devalos
I see. Well, I guess we'll need to meet with Mr. Debussey again. You'll be in today? All right—see you soon.

Devalos touches the earpiece, disconnecting the call.

353

INT. A conference room at the DA's office. Afternoon.

Devalos, Allison and Scanlon sit across from Karl Debussey Jr. and Sr. and their attorney, Jen Fowler. Devalos slides a file over to Karl Debussey Sr and he opens it, seeing photos of the crime scene from where Feodora Ellerman's body was discovered.

Devalos
Recent evidence has come to light that you were not responsible for the murder of your nanny, Feodora Ellerman, and for that, this office submits its humblest apology. But recent evidence has also highlighted who did and this office owes no apology for charging you with that person's murder.

Karl Debussey, Sr. looks nervous as well as his attorney. Karl Debussey Jr. looks confused.

Devalos
Our forensic accountants recently commenced pouring through your financial records and they've found a dummy corporation out of the Netherlands by the name of Kelly, Incorporated—your wife's mother's maiden name. Unless you are prepared to reveal her whereabouts right now, we will be freezing all your liquid assets, as well as obtaining warrants to search the premises of every home or office you own and charging you with a list of crimes the length of my arm.

Karl Jr.
Dad, what's he saying?

Devalos
Your father didn't kill your mother, son. She's alive.

Karl Jr.
What? That's not possible—

Devalos
It is. Worse yet, we have every reason to believe she is the one who killed Neil Gershonowicz.

Karl Jr.

Killed?

Devalos
He died at 2:20 this morning.

Karl Sr.
Oh no.

Devalos picks up the phone and hits 0.

Devalos
Send him in.

The door opens and Scanlon escorts Karl Montrose into the room.

Karl Jr.
But you just said—

Allison
It's amazing how your father isn't surprised in the least to see his other son, Karl Montrose.

Karl Jr.
Dad. I'm confused.

Karl M.
What is…what is going on?

Scanlon
My apologies—let me introduce you to your father and brother, Karls Debussey Sr. and Jr.

Devalos
Allow me to illuminate what we believe is going on here. In 1989 Karl and Laura Debussey paid surrogate Feodora Ellerman for a child Karl fathered with her. Feodora gave birth to triplets and, considering her unexpected good fortune, saw a blackmailing opportunity, considering the Debusseys wanted to keep the true origins of the pregnancy secret. One night, Feodora showed up to collect. There was an ensuing struggle where Mrs. Debussey was injured, but only Feodora was killed. Mr. and Mrs. Debussey schemed for her to flee the country with the second child, not knowing of the third, leaving

Gerald Dean Rice

Debussey to take the fall for his wife and nanny's deaths. There was
enough muddied evidence for Mr. Debussey's team of lawyers to
hang a jury and periodically, subsequently, he would make 'business'
trips to visit his wife and other child. Sound about right?

Karl Sr. stares wide-eyed at Devalos.

Karl Jr.
Dad, you didn't do this. You couldn't have done this. Dad!

Allison
We figure Feodora left some kind of note with Neil, who grew up in
an orphanage and eventually sought you out. Somehow, he found
your mother and was blackmailing her and probably would have
eventually blackmailed your father.

Fowler
This is unsubstantiated, but let's say if any of this is true, what are we
talking about for my client?

Devalos
Well, this office is willing to concede that perhaps we were a little
zealous in the initial prosecution, and we are willing, with full
cooperation, to agree to a plea deal that would involve no prison
time. Hindering prosecution and he pays whatever state and federal
fines involved with the filing of fraudulent documents. But any
deception as to the true whereabouts of Mrs. Debussey will not be
tolerated.

Karl M.
My mother killed my brother?

Allison
We believe so.

Fowler
Can I have a moment with my client?

Devalos
No. This deal expires the moment I get out of this chair.

Fowler whispers in her client's ear. Karl Sr. nods.

Karl Sr.
We were supposed to meet at our place in Scottsdale tomorrow.
She'll be on the 12:15 flight in the afternoon.

Karl Jr.
All this time, I spent hating you for the wrong reasons. When I
actually should have been hating you and her.

Karl Sr.
Son, please.

Allison
Karl, I know you're angry right now, but I know you loved Neil in the
short time you two had with each other. Perhaps your brother
(gesturing to Karl M.) is your second chance.

Everyone but the two younger Karls get up and leave the room,
leaving the two of them to sit and look at each other across the table.

INT. Devalos' office. Afternoon.

Allison comes into Devalos' office and sits down.

Allison
You wanted to see me, sir?

Devalos
Yes. As you can imagine, I've been under a good deal of stress the
past few days. But as you might have guessed, it's been more than
about Mandy Henderson.

Devalos sighs and slides a file over to Allison.

Devalos
This was in my mailbox Monday. My wife hasn't seen it, thank God
and hopefully she never will. I feel embarrassed to be asking and
humiliated that whoever this is would do such a thing, but I need your
help.

Allison begins to open the file.

Devalos
Before you do that, I just want to inform you, those pictures are very graphic in nature involving three people, one of whom was my daughter. They haven't asked for any money, but in my line of work, I know it's only a matter of time, and there are probably many more photos like those. (Devalos gets choked up) I have to find them before they can wreak any more havoc on my family than they already have. My wife and I barely survived our daughter's suicide. The only way I can make it through this is if my wife never finds out about it. I'm…begging you. Whatever you can do.

Allison
Absolutely. I'll let you know as soon as, y'know.

Allison puts her hand on the file to pick it up and Devalos covers it with his.

Devalos
Thank you.

INT. The Dubois kitchen. Early morning.

Allison sits at the table, eating an apple and reading through a file. The house is very silent. She hears a creek outside and ignores it at first until she hears it again. Stepping to the window, she peers outside and sees nothing. When she turns to go back to her chair, a man on fire is standing in the middle of the kitchen.

Man on Fire
Do you have time now?

INT. The Dubois bedroom.

Allison awakes with a gasp.

I used to write a ton of poetry years ago. I was a part of a poetry group in Detroit where we shared works in progress and stuff polished as best we could. I have this weird thing where I can't (typically) write poetry and fiction at the same time. It's either one or the other. This poem was sparked from a relationship that began and ended in 2020. Someone I fell deeply in love with who never came close to feeling the same about me. This is my own version of goodbye.

Hope You Missed Me While I was There

I don't like that I love you still,
Even after you erased me a second time,
I hope what was left of me
still stains your mind.
You scrubbed me empty
and discarded the rest,
Left me broken
while you remained clean,

Gerald Dean Rice

Went back to be held by an old pair of arms,
Refreshed lips to kiss,
While I turned into a ghost
and haunted my own life,
Chained to my bed
Washed away by sunlight
A corner filled with the shadows
of spoiled joy,
The love in me like an eraser,
Consuming me,
Until I am
gone.

I actually thought of this story years ago and it was one of those I abandoned because I didn't know where to go with it. I don't know where that version of the story is or what I named it. I'll probably find it in some random file somewhere.

DWD

Officer Lebend hauled himself out of his patrol car, hitched up his belt, and sighed as he lumbered toward the silver Cutlass Supreme he'd pulled over.

"Three more hours," he said. The flashing red and blue lights on top of the cruiser gave him mild nausea and he held up a hand to shield his eyes as he stepped ahead of his own vehicle. The flashing yellow hazard lights on the rear of the Cutlass were more soothing and the pounding in his head eased.

He walked casually up to the divide between front and rear windows on the driver's side. The driver had already placed his license and registration in the open window, and Lebend shook his head, seeing what was behind the wheel and wishing he'd just let this one go.

"Do you have an idea why I pulled you over tonight?" He leaned over and did his best to peer into the dark interior without really seeing. To do no more than due diligence and keep his remaining sanity intact. The driver had his hands at ten-and-two and there was no one in the passenger seat. When they were alone, it wasn't so bad. But when there was another body—or kids in the backseat—that was about as much as he could take.

He pulled his mind away from a horrible memory and concentrated on what was in front him. Three more hours and he was done.

Seat belt on, obviously no drinking involved. Hopefully, license and registration checked out and Lebend would let him go without a citation. He plucked the two cards from the window and resisted the urge to flee back to his cruiser. The red and blue blinded him a moment and he had to look to the street to get his bearings back. He sat and closed the door behind him, his back and palms clammy. He sat the cards on the dash and began rubbing his hands on his pant legs as if trying to scrub the film of *something* off.

Lebend had to talk himself down from just putting the cruiser in gear and flooring it out of here. Mostly because 'here' was everywhere he went. They were everywhere now. In businesses, houses, cars. There was nowhere Lebend could escape *to*.

Not that he had any reason to escape. Pat had left a year ago—gone to Windsor—and Lebend hadn't joined him. He would always love Pat, but he was just so afraid. Every day, all day, all night. The fact there were more of them every day had been bearable while Lebend had had someone to bear it with, but now that he was all alone...

And people were no better. Everyone, including him, wandered wherever they went like ghosts. Lebend was wraith-like in appearance too. He was six foot four and had been a husky two hundred eighty, but he'd stopped stepping on a scale when he'd gotten close to two hundred pounds and had only been getting thinner since.

He had to get his mind off himself. Not that the occupant of the vehicle in front of him would mind however long it took to run a license, but that was when he felt closer to the idea of joining Pat. Lebend snatched up the license and opened the CODEX system on the dash computer. He entered the last name, Sanders, first name,

Kenneth, and picked the one matching the driver's license he was holding from the list.

One ticket in the last month for the same thing Lebend had pulled him over for. Ticket paid, no points. He shook his head. This was a complete waste of time. He took off his hat and ran a hand over his slicked, thinning hair. Lebend clapped the hat back on and blew out, his breath curling in the cold night air.

The door felt gigantic, Sisyphusian, as he curled his fingers around the handle and pulled it open. It felt like an uphill climb as he walked back to the car.

Lebend forced a smile into his voice, although it wouldn't matter to the driver. He did it for himself. "I'm gonna let you off with a warning, Mr. Sanders," he said. "But you have to get your speed up. Match the flow of traffic." He laid the license and registration across the threshold of the door, half in, half out. A light breeze licked the registration, blowing it into the air, and it fluttered like a single butterfly's wing to the ground.

He bent to pick it up, and when he was upright again, Lebend grit his teeth together so hard he could feel them moan like a chorus of tiny voices reverberating throughout the bones of his skull.

Mr. Sanders was looking at him—those unblinking eyes, that ever-wide smile, skin like a charred, disarranged jigsaw puzzle. Lebend's hand seemingly acted on its own as he flicked the registration into the car, and his feet slowly pulled him toward the street, then changed direction toward his cruiser.

He was down on one knee with his back turned, vomiting onto the gravel, as the engine to the Cutlass revved to life again, and the vehicle crawled away. Lebend dared to look over his shoulder, taking a small degree of solace that Mr. Sanders was going away, his hazards still blinking.

Lebend put one hand into the gravel, making a fist in it as if to hold the earth still beneath him. As if he could stop the world from moving for just one moment. He missed Pat and wanted nothing more than to be with the one person who could console him through the rest of his life. But he was afraid of what the man he'd loved for the better part of twenty years had become, so he felt stuck in between. Lebend had to do something.

"Three more hours," he said and wiped his mouth as he stood.

Gerald Dean Rice

I've had some iteration of this story stirring around in my head for a long time. I believe I started it and stopped and this was another one of those that needed to simmer before I could finish it. This might be a mild homage to Draculas *by Joe Konrath and others.*

Satans

"Now y'all know there's gon' be some satans in here," the fat man on the raised wooden platform said. "But most of em's just gonna be regular ole souls escapin' hell. Don't make no mistake about it, ain't none of 'em s'posed to be up here. Shoot 'em. Shoot 'em all."

John hadn't hunted since he was a little boy and this was one helluva reintroduction. Ed, his future father-in-law and a big man who defied his age somewhere north of seventy, smiled at him, the double barrel shotgun laid across his forearm, broke open.

"Just stick with me, son. It'll be just fine."

John didn't trust the man's smile. Ed had gotten him nice and liquored up before bringing him out here and now had him sitting on a horse, holding a shotgun. What had seemed like a big joke was turning into a sobering, surreal nightmare.

"This…isn't real, is it, sir?" John asked, leaning over to whisper to Ed. The older man just smiled at him, the butt of that unlit cigar tucked in the corner of his mouth, and clapped him on the shoulder. "Is it paintball or something?"

As if in answer, the fat man undid a tie on a sack containing whatever was strung up from the big tree the wooden platform was built around. Another man stepped onto the small platform and helped, but he moved back to let the fat man, a good foot shorter than the second man, yank off the sack.

It looked like a big, red dog. No. It didn't. It definitely didn't look like anything John had ever seen before. The hindquarters, if that were what he was looking at, were dog-legged and hoofed. One leg looked like it might have been broken by the way it hung. The creature had an emaciated waist, the hip bones protruding to either side of the stock of a spine that disappeared into a concave-stomached torso. Its wiry chest was like a man's with black nipples, like two exclamation points atop its red skin.

The arms were much longer than the legs and were muscled, not unlike a man's, coarse hair covering the forearms, hanging from broad, sagging shoulders. The hands were massive too, with nails as black as its nipples, the fifth and sixth fingers on the ends of either hand much longer than the others.

It had stumps of horns that apparently someone had sawed off. It looked like a man's head, complete with a pointed vandyke, but its mouth was affixed with a kind of permanent smile, and there was a glitter of light dancing in those almost pearlescent large yellow eyes, making them look like they were following John around.

He didn't see any seams of it being sewn together from different animals and couldn't imagine what animal the human-looking parts must have come from. But he couldn't accept what he was seeing as real, couldn't process it. It was like the pictures he'd seen of the dead 'bigfoot' stuffed in a freezer. His eye hadn't been sophisticated enough to tell what was wrong with the picture, but that hadn't made him any less certain it was fake.

"This gets official come sundown, as all y'all regulars know. Now lookin' around, I see a lot more new faces than last year. Vern brought his nephew, I see. Wendell's boy is finally here. Happy belated, by the way. That's good and that's prob'ly bad too. Y'all know why." John didn't know why and he desperately wanted to ask.

366

"A few may pop out before the sun sets alla way. Consider those practice. Feel free to 'warm up' if it pleases ya."

John looked around at all the men on horseback. He'd spotted a few who looked as nervous as he was, but he could hardly count any of them as allies. He was bewildered and still didn't think any of this was real.

"Any questions 'fore I send y'all in?"

"Do we need a license?" someone ahead of John asked.

The crowd laughed.

Someone fired a pistol. "There's your license!"

The crowd laughed even louder. Some hooted and one person whistled.

The fat man let the crowd continue for a moment before holding out a hand for them to settle down. "Now that's enough," he said. "Bow yer heads for the prayer."

John continued looking up long enough to see the fat man pick up a bible as he got down on one knee and laid his open hand on an old shotgun.

"He biddeth me go to him and see, for I was invited to come. Then he giveth me a book of *Jesus'* inditing, to soldiereth me the more freely to come; and he said concerning that book, that every jot and tittle thereof stood firmer than heaven and earth. Then I asketh him what must I do when I come unto ye; and he told me I must entreat upon my knees, with all my heart and soul, the Father to reveal him to me. Then I asked him further, how I must make my supplications to him; and he said, Go, and thou shalt find him upon a mercy-seat, where he *has* sitteth for all of eternity to give pardon and forgiveness to them that hath been sendeth. I told him, that I knew not what to say when I came; and he bid say to this effect: God be merciful to all as sinners, and make them to know and believe in Jesus Christ; for I see, that if his righteousness had not been, or they have not faith in that righteousness, they are utterly cast away. Lord my God, I knoweth thy mercy, that thou art willing to bestow him upon such a poor sinner as they are—and they are sinners indeed. Lord, take therefore this opportunity, and magnify thy grace in the salvation of these souls, through thy right-hand weapon. Amen."

Several men repeated the last word but their 'amens' were swallowed up with more hoots and whistles. Some of the horses knickered and neighed as the energy all around turned up.

"Now, what say y'all get out there and get to sendethin', y'hear?" The fat man raised a starter pistol and fired, and men began hollering, eager as they rode their horses into the forest. John couldn't stop staring at the 'satan' strung up on the platform before him.

"Ed, is that thing real?" He had a difficult time processing what he was seeing because it looked like it was made up of several different formerly living creatures, including human. And those eyes. As his horse shuffled around nervously, he would have sworn they really were following him.

Ed's smile was a mile wide. "Son, you're about to find out for yourself. C'mon." He spurred his horse on and was a good twenty yards ahead before John thought to follow.

The setting sun had turned the sky a bruised yellow-purple. John clutched his shotgun, a Cimarron 1889 Hammerless 20". He'd never held one of these numbers before tonight. There were plenty of shells in either of his overcoat pockets and his future father-in-law had shown him how to break it open and load it.

The two men rode in silence, John watching Ed to gain an idea of what he was supposed to be doing. Ed stayed low on his horse, reins in one hand, shotgun in the other. No one had fired a shot in the ten minutes they'd been in the forest. Even though John had seen the 'satan' as the fat man had put it, he had no real conception of what they were supposed to be hunting.

"Ed!" John whisper-yelled. "Ed!"

The other man turned in his saddle.

"This…this isn't real, is it?" Ed just stared. "I mean, this is some kind of hazing thing. Right? We're not really gonna shoot people."

Someone emerged from a collection of trees about fifteen yards ahead of them. John could see the person clearly, but other than being small, there wasn't much he could make out.

Ed sat up and aimed. John was still not believing any of what was happening as they approached the figure. John wanted to shout for him to look where he was going, but that would have breathed life into the idea that there was any degree of seriousness to anything that had happened so far tonight.

And then Ed shot the figure.

The blare of the shotgun turned his blinders off as whoever it was crumpled.

"Oh my God," John said. Ed trotted over to the body and peered over at it.

"No matter what you do, don't get off your horse until you're sure," Ed said. "You can always just—" He took out his revolver, a long-barreled silver number, aimed, and shot the man in the head.

John was even more revolted, as if shooting an already dead body was worse than a living, breathing person.

But they were escaped souls from hell, according to the fat man. And all the men who had willingly rode into this forest on horseback were supposed to be holy appointees somehow, even though he was certain a good deal of them were certifiably drunk, as they meted out righteous justice.

John wanted to believe the quasi-crusader explanation of why they were here instead of believing his future father-in-law had just murdered somebody right in front of him.

As if the shot from his revolver had begun whatever this was in earnest, more shots followed in the distance. John looked around as if he could see the bullets, his personal sense of safety becoming much more acute. Every year during hunting season, there was always a story about some hunter getting shot by another hunter and they at least wore those high visibility vests. John and everyone else he'd seen were dressed in dark trench coats with nothing but a sliver of moonlight to see by.

"Look," Ed said, pointing to the body. John looked again and saw the body had begun melting.

"What the hell?"

"Their bodies are just vehicles to carry their damned souls around. Most times, any shot is fatal. Head or heart is fastest." He looked around. "They're easy. They just want to get out of the forest. It's those damnable satans you have to be wary of."

"Satans?" John asked, as if he hadn't seen that thing strung up.

"They'll attack anything that moves. Souls, deer, *us.*"

"What? You're telling me those red things will kill us if they can?"

"Oh, absolutely." Ed began riding again and John followed. Several moments passed between them, an occasional gunshot or shotgun blast in the distance. John finally placed the smell in this forest, like something burning had been doused with rancid water. Ed finally smiled. "I'm just pulling your chain a little. There's about sixty or so men out here hunting. Maybe, *maybe,* there's that many souls and ten satans on the high end."

"Has there ever been more than that?"

"My first year. There were probably thirty. If it hadn't been for Crowden, we would have been in serious trouble. He was a military man, gathered us all together, and we pushed back."

"What do you mean, 'pushed back'?"

Ed shrugged. "Well, there were so many of them. Back in those days, we easily had over a hundred men on the hunt. Those satans killed at least two-thirds before we got back in control."

John shook his head. "So they were killing people and you all *stayed*?"

Ed stopped and turned to him. "Son, we have a holy charter. There *is* no running."

"I don't—I don't get it. Why would you *choose* to do this?"

"Because we can't let them out. Any of them. *Especially* the satans."

"What happens if they do get out? I mean, has that happened before?"

"Every once in a while," Ed said after a moment.

"What do they do when they get out?"

Ed held out a hand to silence him, sniffing the air.

"You smell that?"

"Smell what?" Beyond the constant soggy-burnt scent hanging in the air, he didn't smell anything.

"It's kind of a skunky smell. Sulfur. One of 'em's close." Ed broke open his shotgun and replaced the empty shell.

John gripped his shotgun, his palms sweaty. "How will I know?"

"You'll know. You'll see their eyes first. They glow."

Someone screamed. At least, John thought it was a man's scream, it was so high-pitched and *pained.*

"Let's ride," Ed said and kicked his heels.

John urged his horse on as well, ducking to avoid branches whipping his head and face. He yanked on the reins to keep the horse on the path as it ran alongside a shallow creek.

Ahead, a man was face down on the ground, his long coat thrown over his shoulders and head and a *thing* crouched over him, peeling long, pink-red strips from his back as he weakly clawed at the earth. There were studded peaks of white sticking out of his back that might have been the man's spine, but John couldn't be sure from this distance.

As they rode, Ed leaned forward and shot, splintering the bark of a tree a few yards away from the monster. John shouldn't have known what it was. It was different from the dead satan on display for all to see not thirty minutes ago but still similar in its wrongness.

The satan leaned back on its haunches, taking a moment to fold a strip of flesh onto its thin, outstretched black tongue. Its head was anvil-like, bulbous and wide with horns like thick, curled fingers wreathed around its crown. Ed's second shot cut into the earth next to it, catching the creature's attention as it swallowed.

It rose and John saw it had a pair of heavy breasts that fell to its waist. Its skin glistened in the moonlight, its teeth about the size of pea pods as it seemed to be smiling at him. It looked at him as his horse came to a stop. He was unnerved that it had noticed him.

"John, get off that horse!" Ed shouted.

He was about to ask why when his shoulder went numb and his horse suddenly dropped. It went straight back, like it had sat on its hind legs before folding over onto one side. The taut muscles between John's thighs were suddenly limp and weighted, like the buoyancy of life had just fled the animal.

John tasted copper on his lips as he was still processing the last few seconds. There was hair in his mouth and he spat on instinct, reaching to pinch the strands of horsehair off his tongue. Something hot crept into the outer leg of his trousers and he realized he had an unobstructed view in front of him.

The horse's head was gone.

Something thick crunched behind him, much too close. John shivered even as his body warmed from the blood soaking into his clothes. There were several shots and then the blast of a shotgun.

John finally registered the pain in his shoulder. Another man yelled and someone or *something* grunted. John lay frozen until somebody tapped his shoulder.

"You 'live?"

John nodded then, "Yes."

Two men pushed the dead horse off John's leg and Ed helped him up. John remembered pissing himself in second grade, one leg unnaturally warm and wet. This was a nightmare version of that.

"Did it get you?" Ed asked. John stared dumbly at him until he slapped John's cheek. "Did it get you?"

"Nuh...no," John said. "I dunno." He looked at his shoulder, afraid to move his arm. Ed stepped closer and poked his gloved fingers into a hole in his long coat. He grabbed John's wrist and raised his arm, working it like some machine part like he knew what it was but not what it did.

"It's still attached," Ed said and clapped him on the back. He turned to the man standing behind him. "Thanks for the assist. This is my girl's boy, John. I'm Ed."

"Passel," the man said. The two stepped toward each other and shook.

"What happened to your horse?" Ed asked.

"That satan," Passel said, pointing somewhere behind him. "Ambushed us both. Killed my horse and frightened Alex's off."

"Alex?" John said.

Passel sighed and trudged over to the fallen man with his long coat over his head. He was still alive, still trying to crawl away from a monster that had already been slayed. He covered the man's wounded back with his overcoat, exposing the man's scalped skull.

He had to have been in immense pain, but his eyes were blank, like he was looking at something in another county.

"What do you want to do with him?" Ed asked.

Passel sighed and knelt, placing the barrel of his pistol to the wounded man's head. He shot and John yelped.

"You just killed him! You killed him!" John pointed at the dead body as if the man hadn't understood what he'd done. Ed seized him by the shoulders and gave him a shake.

"Calm down." He looked over his shoulder at the other man as he holstered his pistol. "I'll handle this. You wanna?" He nodded in the direction of where the body of the satan lay. "Listen to me, son." Ed stared at John until they locked eyes. "That man was about to die. Worse yet, if he died as a result of the wounds that satan inflicted on him, his soul would have gone to hell. What Passel did was a mercy."

"You don't know that. You don't know that!" John felt a tear trail down his cheek.

"I *do*. Now breathe with me. Calm yourself down. Don't think about any of it." Ed took a deep, slow breath and John mimicked him as best he could. They went on like that for a good thirty seconds, and surprisingly, John did feel calmer.

"He...really would have gone to hell?" Out of the corner of his eye, John saw Passel kneeling by the satan, digging at its body with a big knife.

Ed nodded. "I had to do the same thing for my best friend back in '84. Trust me, you don't want to know what it's like to be tormented by a stolen soul." Ed's eyes went distant for a moment.

"We'd better get movin'," Passel said.

"You wanna go back?" Ed asked John, waving a hand through the air. "No judgment."

He did want to go back. But he felt a surge of...responsibility. If things like what had been eating on that man were out here and he knew about it...could *do* something about it...

"No." John shook his head. "But what about my horse?"

"I got a coupla coconut shells." Ed gestured to the satchel on his horse. John smiled. "Just stick close. 'Sides, Passel's puttin' it on foot too."

John retrieved his shotgun and examined the barrel, bent in the middle.

"Take the shells and leave it," Passel said. "It probably kept the horse from breaking your leg when it fell on you."

They'd been walking for a good ten minutes when John asked, "How do we know where to go?"

"We follow the trees," Ed said from atop his horse. "This is your first time in here, but you come often enough you'll start to see the pattern."

"Pattern?"

"How the trees are grouped," Passel said. You don't memorize where you are, more you get an idea of where you are by how the air sounds passing through the branches. The thickness in the air. The whole thing has a feel to it. Sometimes, the forest whistles like it's tryin' to get you to notice somethin'. The best way to get lost in here is to try to learn your way around by sight." Passel tapped an index to his temple to drive the point home.

A young man and a little girl in tattered clothing emerged from behind a tree.

"Please, sir. We're lost," the young man said. He rested a protective hand on the little girl's shoulder. They were both in tattered clothes and were visibly filthy even in the moonlight.

John was opening his mouth to speak when Passel fired. The little girl fell, and the boy, who looked twelve at the oldest, backed up until his back was against the thin tree behind him.

"Zodi!"

John felt as though he were detaching from his own body as Passel pulled his knife out, an open-mouthed, toothless smile on his face.

John's sudden vomiting was the only thing that broke him away from what Passel did to the boy. He believed what he'd been told, but he couldn't help but see a child. John could only imagine he was going to move onto the little girl's body next and went into a shell before Passel could begin on her.

"You shouldn't be in here," Ed said. He shook his head, disapproval all over his face. "This isn't for you." He leaned over and held out a hand from atop his horse and John pulled himself up. He loved Ed's daughter and wanted to marry her more than anything. That was the only reason he'd come on this ridiculous 'hunting trip'.

Would Kate be disappointed in him? Would she leave him? Did she even know about what her father did in this place?

"No," John said. "I'll stay." Passel sauntered back over to them, wiping his blade on his trousers and carrying something weighty and small in a sack. John didn't want to look at the bodies to see what was missing. "I'll be fine." John drew himself up, hoping he appeared to be drawing strength from a reserve Ed probably didn't believe he had.

"I think I could handle it better if we were killing those…other things."

Ed raised an eyebrow. "Really?" He smiled. "They are harder to kill and there aren't as many of them."

"So, they're harder to find?"

He shook his head. "Finding them is pretty easy." He pointed somewhere beyond Passel.

"How do you know where to find them?" John asked.

"There's a center to this place. That's where they come out. They're concentrated there." Ed called over to the other man. "Passel, you up for a little extra danger?"

"Absolutely," he said as he reloaded his pistol and clapped the cylinder back in place. Then he flung his arm out, aiming at something in the distance and fired.

"Damn," he said. "Missed."

"What was it?"

"Not sure. I think one of those scuttlers."

"Scuttlers?" John asked.

"Half and halfs," Ed said. "I'm sure our friend Passel is mistaken. Scuttlers are a kind of urban legend in this forest. Half demons bred with the damned and supposedly worse than satans 'cause they'll kill and eat anything. But like I said, urban legend."

"I wouldn't be so sure about that," Passel said. "It couldda been one."

They headed in the direction Passel had fired, and a moment later, they came across the ruined body of one of the damned, just as it had begun liquifying.

"Can't take anything out of that one," Passel said.

There were more gunshots in the distance, but John noticed they were sounding farther and farther away.

"Does anybody else go this far in?" he asked.

"Only the crazy ones," Ed said. John looked up at him and thought he saw the glean of impending vacancy behind his eyes.

"Have either of you gone there before?"

"A few times," Passel said. "Never killed anything, though."

"Once," Ed said but didn't elaborate.

"Grab that lantern," Passel said.

"What, you see it?"

"Not sure." Ed took the lantern and held it out to Passel, but the man had already begun advancing ahead of them, shotgun in hand.

"I'll take it," John said. He'd been shown how to use the lamp and knew its purpose. It was a ward against evil and should have offered a level of protection for whatever was in its light. They passed a row of overgrown bushes and John barely kept from yelling at the pair of dark eyes staring at him.

There was the rapid cracking of a revolver and then Passel yelling, "Comin' your way!"

John spotted it immediately, but Ed was still scanning. He wanted to point it out to him but didn't want to distract him, hoping Ed would see it in enough time. He brought his shotgun up too late and was knocked off his horse.

John turned and held his lantern out, hoping the light would scald the creature, but it scowled and brought club-like fists down on top of Ed. The man screamed as loud as the sickening crunching of his bones. John was frozen next to the horse as the red thing stood up straight, disturbingly thin and at least a foot taller than him.

Hate-filled eyes locked onto him and it took a step forward. It looked like something not accustomed to walking upright. The horse chuffed and shuffled but stayed put. John gripped the handle of the lantern tighter, not thinking to draw any of his weapons as the satan drew close.

The lantern was either having a minimal effect or the creature was taking its time. It was less than three feet away from him when John finally thought to draw his pistol. It felt limp in his hand, lighter than air and just as inconsequential.

As it reached a rail-like arm for him, the horse k cked, catching the satan high on its torso and knocking it to the ground several feet away. John thawed, aware he had a weapon in nis hand, and he rushed forward and aimed, shooting it twice in the face and then in the heart.

"John!" Ed said a few feet away. He had drawn up on one arm, his face dripping with mud. He helped him upright, and despite the older man not screaming, it was obvious he was in a tremendous amount of pain. Ed leaned heavily on him as they walked back to his horse. Passel was waiting for them and helped him make a sling for his broken arm.

"We won't be able to do anything about the broken ribs," Passel said after they had checked him over.

They helped him mount his horse, and the man said, "He won't be able to ride alone." John nodded, and Passel mounted in front of Ed. John stayed close to the horse, his shotgun clutched in one hand, the lantern in the other.

Passel said, "We need to get Ed out of here for medical treatment."

A strong part of John was up for the fight, but Passel was right. Ed could have internal bleeding. "Maybe we could drop him off and come back."

"That's the fightin' spirit, son," Ed said and coughed, groaning like he was being gut-punched.

A long-haired man darted past them but tripped before he could get out of sight. John rushed him as he was getting to his feet and aimed.

"No-no-no!" the man shouted before the blast of the shotgun took off everything above his collarbone. His body crumpled as John resisted the urge to fire a second time.

"Finish it," Passel said, holding out his knife by the handle. John had his own, but it seemed to mean something more that the other man was giving him his knife. John looked quizzically at him. "You'll know what you're looking for when you cut him open."

He nodded and John took the knife and went back to the body. He knew if he hesitated, his nerve would flood out of him and he plunged the blade into the torso and yanked up. Gore poured out of the cavity that wasn't reminiscent of anything in John's scant knowledge of human anatomy and the smell was like old mulch.

"Dig around in there. Quick, before it gets away." John fished inside with the knife, parting a mass that could have just as easily been a liver or a large clump of leaves. The flesh yielded in a way that didn't feel natural, although the closest John had ever experienced was slashing his brother's arm with a kitchen knife by accident when they'd called themselves sword-fighting as children. The peak of something glowing caught his eye and without realizing, John thrust his hand in and grabbed something spherical and cold.

He stood, holding it as the body turned ashen. John suspected if he touched the remains, they would have collapsed like standing ash. Passel was holding that sack he'd had before and John dropped the glowing ball inside.

"Good work." Passel cinched it closed and nodded to him.

They continued for what felt like a mile to John's feet until they heard the crackle of distant gunfire.

"Must be something big," Ed said.

John looked at him and saw the shine of sweat on his forehead.

"I hope they killed it," John said. He sniffed the air. "I smell a fire."

"Me too." Passel said.

John continued sweeping back and forth ahead and behind, certain something was going to come at them any moment.

He was ready when something did. John saw the blur of red falling toward them from a tree. He got his shotgun up in time and hit the satan center mass. Most of its upper body disintegrated, but there was enough left that, when it fell on the horse, the animal spooked and reared back on its hind legs, throwing the two men.

Passel and Ed hit the ground hard and John turned with his shotgun trained on what was left of the satan's body still twitching on the ground. He looked around before he approached the two men, Ed moaning in pain.

Passel dragged himself up, but Ed was disturbingly still. John knelt beside him.

"My back!" Ed said. "My back's broke."

"Get up," Passel said.

"I can't, dammit. I said my back's broke!"

"We're surrounded. Damn things are all over the place."

John scanned around. He couldn't see anything at first but then spotted three pairs of fiery red eyes. He wondered how many more Passel saw.

"This is just like '84," Passel said.

John broke open his shotgun, plucked out the empty shell, and replaced it.

"Oh no," Ed said. He tugged on John's pant leg to get his attention. "Prop me up on that rock over there."

"I don't think I should move you," John said. Ed shook his head.

"Son, nobody's comin' in here to rescue me anytime soon. Especially if there's nothin' left to be saved. Hurry up and drag my ass over there and gimme my pistol."

John got behind him and sat him upright. His upper body felt sickeningly loose and the older man whimpered. John had never heard him sound so…frail.

"Wait-wait-wait," he said and fished inside his long coat. He took out a big silver flask and unscrewed the top. He took a long pull and nodded. John dragged him the five feet to the rock and propped him up as best he could. Ed had managed not to scream, but he had tears in his eyes when John was done.

"Pistol. Gimme." He sounded exhausted and his gray face was shiny with sweat. Ed had been the picture of health as long as he'd known him, but now he looked every minute of his age plus ten years. John took it from the holster and wrapped Ed's sweaty hand around it. "I'll cover you best I can. Let's get you back to my little girl." Ed took another long pull from the flask.

"How many?" John asked Passel.

"I don't know. All of 'em." The man shook his head. "Aim for the lower body. Satans'll eat their own. Count your rounds when you use your pistol. Save the last one for yerself."

"What are they waiting for?" John asked.

"They're toying with us. Sometimes, you can win the battle with intimidation alone. But they don't know me. I al*ready* shit my pants." Passel drew his pistol, aimed, and shot one between the eyes from fifteen yards.

The trees around them erupted in unholy cries as satans of all shapes charged them. John couldn't hear anything beyond the roar of blood in his ears. He shot at one and somehow missed and then hit it with the second blast but still not enough to take it down. John switched to his pistol and caught three in a row with shots to the face and neck.

Passel had moved several feet away and was wielding his shotgun like a club, bashing a barrel-chested satan upside the head. It toppled into another and he had his pistol in the second one's mouth and firing in a fluid motion like the move had been choreographed. Another satan behind him reached, and Passel crouched, reversed direction, and came underneath, flipping it over him in a kind of fireman's carry.

John fired a second shot between the eyes of one of the satan's he'd shot already, a thing with a long, snake-like neck and narrow, furry shoulders. It went down, and two others fell on it, ripping it apart. He barely ducked the satan with fists as big as cinder blocks as it swung at his head. It was about to crush him with its other hand when its head jerked back and it fell over. He didn't take a second to look over his shoulder at Ed. John quick-loaded his pistol and jogged backward out of the reach of a satan with claws as long as its fingers.

Ed winged it with a shot and it turned to charge him. He missed with a second shot and it was about to dive at him when John clapped shut the cylinder, aimed and fired. It was like a hand had picked the satan up and dragged it across the ground where it came to rest at Ed's feet.

The older man didn't take a moment to thank him, instead dumping out his shells and thumbing in more cartridges.

John gut-shot another satan, and it exploded in a ball of flame, knocking him over. There were small fires all around and he realized tiny flames were licking him too. He rolled around, slapping at himself until they were out and got to his feet. Several satans had been knocked down, but they didn't seem otherwise hurt, rising and coming for him again. John took careful aim and took down two more before he had to retreat away from three others.

He didn't know where Passel was, hoping the man was still alive. John tripped over a tree root and fell flat on his back. A massive, armless satan leapt on him. It was shaped like a sweet potato, with an eye to either side of a line running the length of its body.

The line began to split open at the top and the smell of rotten fruit poured over him. The only thing keeping him from gagging was the sight of razor-sharp teeth inside the cavernous mouth as it zippered open.

John wrapped his legs around it and squeezed as hard as he could to keep the mouth closed. The satan made some sort of frustrated chirping sound as he dug his knife out of its sheath and began plunging it into the creature's side over and over again.

He finally reversed his grip and brought the knife up and stabbed the thing in the eye. It screamed as dark, viscous fluid spurted into the sky, something cold like motor oil with metal shavings leaking into the inside sleeve of his long coat. John twisted the knife, wrenched it out, and the scream abruptly ceased.

He saw a pair of legs and got up on the balls of his feet, prepared to leap.

"Hold it," Passel said. He'd lost his long coat but still had on his hat.

John stood and looked around.

"We barely made a dent," he said.

There were at least two dozen satans in the trees.

"You still got your pistol?" Passel said.

"Yeah," John said.

"Let him go," Ed said.

John turned. "What?"

"He heard me."

"I think your old friend might be losing it," Passel said.

"No. I was suspicious of you as soon as I laid eyes on you. You didn't have no horse. What sealed it was you mentionin' '84. Only three men came out of there alive and two of the are dead."

"Aw, hell." Passel dropped his shotgun and stood up straight. He chuckled and turned around, smiling. "I figured I'd just tenderize you a little before supper, is all."

"You can't have him. You can have me, though."

"Maybe I don't want you. Maybe it's him I want. Maybe you're too old and stringy."

"Want in one hand, shit in the other," Ed said and gritted his teeth through a short coughing fit. "Either you send him home or I kill him right now." He pulled the hammer back on his pistol and aimed at John. "What is your name, anyway? The *real* one."

Passel pinched the brim of his hat. "Passa-el. I've been living in this forest since '84. Well, '82, actually."

"John, you get. Once you see my Selma, she'll know what happened when she sees I'm not with you. She doesn't know everything, but she knows enough. Take care of Kate."

"I can't leave without you," John said. "I'll carry you."

"Ohhh, shit. Don't make me laugh!" Ed coughed twice more. "I can't feel anything below my chest, and I'm pretty sure I got a punctured lung, to boot. Even if you could carry me, they'd be all over the both of us. No, the best bet is for me and my new friend here to have a nice little palaver while you walk on out of here. Just make sure you give me a bunch of grandbabies."

"But there are others. Maybe they might come—"

"They ain't comin' this far in. I suspect my new pal walked us right up to the center of this forest while I wasn't lookin'. Nobody but fools come this deep." He turned his eyes to Passel. "Where is it? The hole you crawl out of?"

"Just over yonder," Passel said. He took a step backward.

"Don't you move one more step. I don't know if I'm dyin' or not, but I got enough smoke in me yet to put one through you where it counts." Then he spoke to John. "Go on and no more fuss outta you. This is the only way one of us walks outta here. Kiss my girls for me. Tell 'em I love 'em."

John couldn't figure another way and finally said, "Yessir."

He walked past Passel and the satan that might have put on a man's flesh chomped the open air between them. His chilled breath smelled like burnt hair and house dust. "I wasn't going to eat the both of you. Probably just nibble on him 'til he went bad. You should stick around. There's a lot more to the forest than you know. *Come with us.*"

"Ignore 'im," Ed said. "Keep the moon to your back." A satan popped out of the shadows just ahead of John and it fell after a report from Ed's pistol. "You keep them dogs on a leash."

John's heart hammered as he passed by three satans, one of whom had a wide, flat head with four fish-like eyes on top. He wanted to shoot one of them, but looking around, he knew he didn't have enough bullets to finish the fight.

It took tremendous will not to look behind him once he was past all the creatures. Two teenish-looking girls and an old man with one leg moved away from him and John shook his head, trying to tell them without words that he wasn't interested in hunting them.

He kept walking for what had to have been five minutes until he heard what sounded like the high-pitched squeal of a hog and a single pop.

Ed's horse stood by a stream ahead, dipping its head for a drink. John approached it slowly and it made a low sound as if he'd startled it. It took some effort because his shoulder was incredibly sore, but he finally mounted, exhaustion flooding him as soon as he was off his feet.

"Let's go home, girl," he said and the horse turned and began a modest trot in no particular direction he could discern. John wished he had gotten some of that water before riding off and patted around for a canteen.

He found that satchel. Each one of those globes were about the size of a baseball. John's mouth went dry. He didn't know what to do with them. He passed another lost soul, a woman who tried hiding behind a tree even skinnier than she was. He let her go, too tired to even think about shooting anything.

The only thing he could think about was the next three hundred and sixty-four days. He was coming back next year. He was coming back for every one of these he could get.

Gerald Dean Rice

I wrote this short somewhere around 2002 from a writing prompt. I think it was the word 'keepsakes' but I'm not sure. A few other writers took the challenge—wherever it came from—but I don't think this story has seen the light of day.

Keepsakes

George stared at that stupid potted plant. He plucked his thumb out of his mouth and saw fresh beads of red. The pain was unbelievable when he'd tried to pull that thing from the windowsill.

He stood and approached it, wondering how it had rooted to that one spot. Carol would have enjoyed seeing this. Running off the way she had, she hadn't meant to do anything but hurt him. She was always so selfish.

George had gotten his revenge, though. Carol had left everything behind. Her clothes, jewelry, her cat, Gus—everything. He'd taken his time, destroying it all. George relished the pain of Gus' claws raking his arms for the last time right before he'd gone into the dishwasher. The platinum pendant went on top of the pyre of her clothes.

"Friggin' Robby Keller," he muttered as he examined the potted plant. "What he have I don't?" There were tiny razor thin barbs edging all the way around the saucer beneath the pot. George sucked on his thumb again, carefully circling his other hand around the top of the pot. Those barbs had hurt so much he'd stumbled over his own feet trying to get away from them.

"'He listens to me,'" George said, mocking her voice. "'He cares about me as a person.'" He tugged on the pot, but it didn't budge.

"What the hell?" he said. He gave it two more tugs, wrapping his wounded hand around the other and put his knee onto the cabinet face for leverage.

The plant had been his special project. He'd been ready to chuck it as far as he could when he'd decided to do something different. Instead, he poured everything in it he could find. Bleach, mouthwash, spoiled milk, and beer—anything, so long as it wasn't water.

The damn thing hadn't died, though. It didn't grow, either. It was always looking like it was ready to bud, but that was exactly how it looked the day Carol had brought it home.

"What is it?" he'd asked her, annoyed.

"I don't know, but it's exotic!" she'd said, looking excited. Carol was always into 'exotic'. That's why George had to waste so much money on jewelry. She was so inconsiderate she'd even waited until he'd slipped the engagement ring on her finger before telling him no. Before telling him she was leaving him for Robby Keller. He could take care of her the way she deserved to be taken care of, she'd said. He knew how to treat a woman, she'd said. He was a real man, she'd said. Her bags were already packed—when George had seen them he had assumed she was going to visit her mother again.

The things she'd said to him then. George knew he wasn't the brightest man or the best looking, but he didn't deserve how she'd made him feel. He didn't even want to think the words she'd said, they burned him so.

George was aware of his imposing size. His mother had always said how he had to be careful with people and Carol being as small as she was, he'd known better, but...there was only so far a guy could be pushed. He immediately regretted it after, wanted to run after her when she'd fled the room, but was too afraid of what he might still do.

He heard her screaming and knocking around in the kitchen, probably destroying it, but as soon as the anger rose up in him to run downstairs, he would see that wounded face again. He couldn't take that face again. George had sat and wept.

It wasn't long before the noise stopped. George didn't have his watch on, but he didn't think it'd been that long. He could have blacked out for a little while. He did that sometimes when he got angry.

"Carol?" He'd called after her, creeping downstairs, afraid to face her. "Carol, I'm so sorry. I didn't mean to hurt you. I understand if you want to leave me." He didn't understand why but knew that was the kind of stuff a person was supposed to say to get people to accept an apology.

Of course, she was gone.

"Of course," George had said.

"Of course," he said now, reminiscing. He felt himself bristle with anger and pulled one more time as hard as he could, and it seemed to give somewhat, but George would never know for certain because in the next instant the barbs extended to spikes, impaling George's hands.

He pulled his hand free and fell on his butt for the second time, holding his hands up as the blood flowed freely down his forearms. He blinked twice, the pain radiating to his elbows.

Thump. George looked at the cabinet door by the sink. *Thump.* There was something in there, bumping against the door. George got up on his knees, cradling his hands to his chest. He shuffled to the door and pulled it slightly ajar with an aching finger. He saw a few golden strands of…something and pulled it open slightly farther. The wedge of light revealed more golden strands. He could see something round and glistening on the surface, but the thing in front of him was a mass of parts to him. It was slow n becoming a whole.

"Carol?" he said, yanking the cabinet door open.

Carol's head lolled out of the cabinet, skin shriveled in patches and one remaining eye sunken and fogged over. The other socket was a hole, the artery hanging loosely over the cheek. There were a few straggling strands of her blonde hair left, clinging to her paper-dry scalp. Her lower body was gone and what was left looked picked bare.

"Carol, no," George whispered. His mind raced as tears filled his eyes, wondering when he had done this. His hand was cradling the back of her head, propping her up.

Thump. Carol's head fell free from George's hand. He scooted away from the other cabinet door and slowly pulled it open.

Thick green tentacles burst from behind the door and wrapped firmly around George's calf. His bones cracked as they began to pull. George screamed as they relentlessly drew him in, slapping a hand above the door and pushing. George's shoulder crunched and his clenching muscles began to give way. He caught sight of the potted plant above the sink one last time before he was pulled in. A bud had burst open, a flower reaching for the ceiling. It was the most beautiful thing he had ever seen.

His body shook as his muscles began to give way, the tentacles wrapping around his thighs and waist. The plant lifted him and pulled him in except for his arm and head. He cried out one last time before his face smashed with a sharp crunch and neck and shoulder were nearly torn off as he was drawn in. His fingers hooked the cabinet door and shut it behind him.

*This is an essay I wrote while I was a student at the University of Michigan *coff*coff*Flint*coff*coff*. I thought I'd lost it because I hadn't read it in a really long time. This was early to mid-2000s. Seinfeld had ended its 9 season run a few years before, so I thought writing this would still be relevant.*

Gerald Rice

ENG 252

Collage essay

Nothing Would be Nicer

A hole would be something. Nah, it was nothing. And it got bigger. And bigger…
      —Rockbiter, The Neverending Story

> Mike, I did nothing. Absolutely nothing and it was the best time of my life.
> —Peter Gibbons, Office Space

In the beginning God created the heavens and the earth. The earth was without form and void, and darkness was upon the face of the deep; and the Spirit of God was moving over the face of the waters. And God said, "Let there be—"

"Yo, Jehovah!" Jupiter shouted, bursting in Jehovah's room. "Me and the guys are tossing the javelin around. Wanna come?"

"Can't you see I'm in the middle of something here?" Jehovah, said, dropping the hammer and chisel onto his tablet.

"Aw, that'll hold. C'mon, we need another guy."

"Did you ever stop to think that maybe there are more important things than tossing the javelin? I mean, don't you ever get tired of this white background we're in all the time? Wouldn't you like to have things like up and down? Or a tree to lay down in the shade?"

"What's a tree?" Jupiter replied.

"It's this 'living thing' I've been working on. It grows out of the ground and feeds on sunlight and rain."

Jupiter just stood there, his face blank.

"Ah, never mind. This was a dumb idea anyway. Who's playing?"

"Oh, uh, Pluto, Apollo, Mars, Athena." Jupiter threw his arm around Jehovah's shoulders as they walked out. "Watch out for her, though; she is way too competitive. Hey, could I have that hammer when you're done with it? My nephew's birthday is coming up and man would that be a nifty gift."

Something for nothing. Isn't that the epitome of what Americans want? We are a zero-percent-interest-no-money-down-no-payments-for-six-months society. When was the last time you actually read the user agreement to anything you signed up for on the internet? We don't want to know. Or we don't want to do. We walk the path of least resistance in as many avenues of our lives as possible. So long as we don't have to think. Some businesses know this and take advantage. Take car insurance for example. You're paying for 'in the event of…' But in the meanwhile, you give them money, they give you…nothing. And we employees aren't exempt, either. We do the same job year and year out, sit at the same desk and work with the same people. But every year, we want more money for doing no extra work. What's wrong with that? you might ask. I have no idea.

I'd like to take this paper down a notch from all that thinking nonsense. Sure, I could write a paper on Americans and how a sense of entitlement has warped our culture from what can be seen on our televisions to how and what we drive. I could write about how we let things slip past us, like being charged full price for a can of peas on sale, but I don't wanna. That would require work. Like hours of it. What with the researching and the outlining and the interviewing. Who needs that?

Think of this more as an 'end of the day' paper. You know, when it's been a long day, you're tired and just want to zone out in front of the tube for hours. Zone out in front of this paper. There are no 'salient' points here. Put that highlighter away. No, you won't need to read that last line again. Nothing to make you pause and go 'hmm' to yourself. Set your brain on cruise control and relax in your seat, feeling the stress of the day slide off you and—well, you get the point.

INT: Lobby of a church.

Two men dressed in black sit together on a wooden bench. Other people are standing around at random, talking with one another.

JASON: Did you get the card?

GERRY: It took forever, but yeah.

JASON: What—you close your eyes and pick one out. One-two-three, you're done. That's what I always do.

GERRY: Greeting cards are so...impersonal. And that's the other thing—you don't want to call it a death card, but isn't that what it is? I mean, greeting card isn't exactly apt. It's like, 'Congratulations, your son is dead!'

JASON: What are you gonna do, write your own?

GERRY: I just may do that.

An elderly employee walks by, passing out obituaries and hands one to Gerry and Jason. Jason begins to thumb through his copy.

JASON: Look at this obituary. It's ridiculous.

GERRY: What?

JASON: Four pages, that's what's wrong. They couldda condensed. Some of this isn't necessary.

GERRY: Like what?

JASON: Like insurance salesman? Everybody has been an insurance salesman.

GERRY: Well, I haven't. Have you?

JASON: Well, no. But I know people.

GERRY: C'mon, John R. was a great man.

JASON: A great man? Martin Luther King was a great man. JFK was a great man. I knew John R., and I assure you—not a great man. Did you know he used to scalp the next-in-line tickets at the Secretary of State?

GERRY: So, he's guilty of a few things he's not proud of. He made good. They did name a street after him, after all.

JASON: Enough with the street named after him, already. A fluke. I could get a street named after me, and I certainly am not a good guy.

GERRY: You certainly aren't.

JASON: I'm a scumbag.

GERRY: No argument from me.

JASON: And there are no tears in this guy for John R.

GERRY: If you hated him so much, why'd you agree to do his eulogy?

JASON: Sometimes, Gerry…the fates smile down, even on me. This is my opportunity for revenge. I'm gonna expose him for the fraud he is.

GERRY (smiling ruefully at Jason): Man, am I gonna enjoy when you melt down.

JASON: Trust me on this. There's no way I can lose.

GERRY: And yet, you always find a way. You see, there's no way a normal man could lose. You sir, are apart from the rest of us mortals.

JASON: I assure you. I will not fail.

A tall man in a dark blue suit approaches. He has a ponytail and is smiling.

AARON: J-man, is that you?

JASON: I'm sorry?

AARON: Hey, man, good to see you!

He picks up Jason and hugs him for an extended period. He puts him down and turns to Gerry, extending his hand.

AARON: Aaron Hitler. Nice to meet you.

GERRY: Aaron Hitler?

AARON: That's the name. Don't wear it out (*laughs*).

GERRY: How do you two know each other?

AARON: John R.'s my cousin. I would come and stay with them during the summer. The three of us used to hang out together.

JASON: I remember you! **(Jason stands up and sees how imposing Aaron is and sits back down).** I've spent years in therapy from those summers. Gerry, their idea of 'hanging out' was tricking me into coming up into John R.'s tree house and then dangling me over the edge by my ankles.

AARON (smiling as he looks off in the distance): Happy days, happy days…

JASON (suddenly angry): Happy! Jason is gettin' angry!

AARON (looking confused): I gotta go. You're harshin' my mellow. Nice meeting you, Gerry.

GERRY: Yeah, you too.

No other treatment is proven to work better than Notatol.

- *Notatol works the first time, every time*
- *Notatol works to improve your quality of life*
- *Notatol works fast*

I'm intense. Intense in the courtroom and on the court. So when I began slowing down, I spoke to my doctor he recommended Notatol. It got me back in the game and now I count on Notatol because it works. With Notatol, I feel like my old self again.

Men taking nitrate drugs, often used to control chest pain (also known as angina), should not take NOTATOL. Men who use alpha blockers, sometimes prescribed for high blood pressure or prostate problems, also should not take NOTATOL. Such combinations could cause blood pressure to drop to an unsafe level. You should not take NOTATOL if your doctor determines that sexual activity poses a health risk for you. Men who experience an erection for more than four hours should seek immediate medical attention. NOTATOL does not protect against sexually transmitted diseases. The starting dose of NOTATOL is 10 mg taken no more than once per day. Your doctor will decide the dose that is right for you. In patients taking certain medications such as ritonavir, indinavir, ketoconazole, itraconazole, and erythromycin, lower doses of NOTATOL are recommended, and time between doses of NOTATOL may need to be extended. In clinical trials, the most commonly reported side effects were headache, flushing, and stuffy or runny nose. NOTATOL is available in 2.5 mg, 5 mg, 10 mg, and 20 mg tablets.

Remember, your doctor or healthcare provider is the single best source of information regarding you and your health. Please consult your doctor if you have any questions about your health, your symptoms, or your medication.

INT: The viewing room of the church.

Gerry and Jason are seated next to each other. All pews are filled and there is a large crowd standing in the back.

JASON (whispering): I'm nervous. I can't stop my hands from shaking.

GERRY (whispering): Calm down. You'll do fine tearing down a modern day hero.

WOMAN: Shhh!

JASON: You think I'm doing the right thing? I-I could always make some nice stuff up about him, couldn't I?

GERRY: Nah, at this point you'd be betraying yourself not to stick to your guns.

JASON (a little too excitedly): You're right. I'm gonna get up there and just go for it.

WOMAN: Shhh!

JASON: Sorry, ma'am. (*Whispering again*) My lips are dry. Give me some of your lip balm, Gerry.

GERRY (*looking disgusted*): My lip balm?

JASON: C'mon, c'mon! The usher is coming for me. I need something to keep the guck outta the corners of my mouth.

GERRY: Oh, all right. (*He hands over his lip balm. Jason goes over his lips several times very quickly and stops suddenly, slowly turning to Gerry.*)

JASON: Is this eucalyptus? I'm allergic to eucalyptus.

Before Gerry can answer, the usher walks up alongside Jason and puts his hand on his shoulder.

USHER: Sir. It is time.

Jason slowly begins to stand, but he is clearly apprehensive. The organ music swells as he is led down the main aisle to the pulpit. Everyone is looking at him and Gerry is watching with a puzzled stare.

JASON (speaking low as his throat begins to close): I'm not ready. It wasn't supposed to happen like this. Curse you, John R.!

The usher leaves Jason behind the pulpit and Jason stares blindly into the crowd. His eyes are puffy and teary as if he has been crying, and his lips are swollen and red. The music dies down and everyone waits for him to speak.

GERRY: Ugh, this is not good.

WOMAN: Shhh!

GERRY: Sorry. (To himself) I knew you wouldn't let me down.

Jason tries to force the words from his throat, but they won't come. He looks down at John R.'s open casket and sees his body there. He appears to be smiling at this angle and Jason tries to scream.

JASON (managing to force sounds out that sound like whimpering): Nn prrpss! Nn prrpss!

Life•Family•Health•Beauty

With Nu•Clear that is exactly what you get. Nu•Clear promises nothing and gives everything. Drink Nu•Clear, and infuse your body with an explosion of purity. You will be radiated and re-energized for a new day. You and your family deserve Nu•Clear. For life, for family, for health, for beauty. Nu•Clear.

So in conclusion, take only what you give. Read your labels and contracts. If the cashier at the 7-11 tries to use the change from the take-a-penny, give-a-penny thingy, slap it out of his hand, grab him by the collar, and tell him you'll be having none of that as you shake him until he has a mild case of whiplash. Ask the perfume lady at the mall how much you owe her when she sprays you with a sample and offer to take the guy who let you merge into traffic out to lunch so you can thank him properly. What will all this do, you might ask. Will it change the world? Will it help me live a longer life? To which I would reply, 'Good question, I don't know, and perhaps'.

Bibliography

http://www.bibleontheweb.com/Bible.asp

Gerald Dean Rice

http://www.Notatol.com/consumer/common_questions/Notatol_questions.htm

Bits list:

1. Jupiter and Jehovah
2. Gerry
3. Notatol
4. Gerry
5. Nu•Clear
6. Obituary
7. Card

*I made this last story last for a reason. I wrote it way back on October 30th, 1990. I was in 8th grade and we all had to write a story. I was 13 and already a horror fan and so I came up with a story where my entire class gets slaughtered. It is terrible. Hopefully, it's good-terrible. I'll leave it to you to judge. I haven't corrected it in any way from the handwritten pages I transcribed it from. Oh, Mrs. Carter is a woman who actually existed—she was my next door neighbor growing up and there was something creepy about her. I've incorporated her into two separate stories, this one being one of them. *Okay, side note—I had to correct the spelling errors and at* least *some of the grammar.*

Boogieman

Once, on a sunny day in Highland Park, the students in a school called Ferris. They had all decided to visit the old Carter mansion after school. They wanted to see who would chicken out and run home first. The dare was, whoever could last in the mansion until the next morning was the winner.

Rumor had it that once every Halloween, Old Lady Mrs. Carter would rise from her shallow grave somewhere in her house with a giant sickle.

It was 7:00, the time they all decided to meet at the mansion. Sam, Camilla, Kevin, Andrew, etc. were the first to arrive. Rodney came a few minutes later.

It was an old rundown home in desperate need of a paint job with a giant hole in the roof.

By 7:31, they were all there, and inside, it was pitch black. They began to explore.

They found the master bedroom and it was large and dusty. They explored all the other rooms and were done by 8:17. Some noticed all the rooms were linked together. By 8:35, they had finished telling ghost stories and somebody remembered something they had heard. All people have a boogieman behind them. No one could see him because he hides in the shadows. Out of sight. But he couldn't hurt anyone unless he had a body.

Boom! They heard a noise downstairs. No one could agree who would go downstairs to check it out, so they all went. They were downstairs in the kitchen when they heard it again. It was coming from the cellar.

"Who's going to open the door?" someone asked.

Others were too terrified to move.

Eddie yanked the door open and ran downstairs. He ran back upstairs and his skin had turned to a pinkly white.

"Mrs. Carter's grave is down there!" Eddie said.

"Would you get off of my back!" Kevin yelled.

They all began to creep downstairs, looking for the shallow grave. Jamie had his mouth open and got a mouth full of spider webs.

"Eddie," Camilla said, "there's nothing here but a hole in the ground."

"I swear she was buried right there!" he said.

A cold hand touched Sam's shoulder and she turned around and punched who she thought was Kevin in the face.

"Sorry, Kevin. You shouldn't have scared me."

Somebody started breathing heavily on Samantha's neck.

"Would you stop playing, Kevin?" Samantha asked.

"I'm over here." Kevin waved.

Samantha turned and saw Old Lady Carter. She screamed. Old Lady Carter stuck her long nails through Samantha and threw her corpse into the boiler room.

Marty, Michael, and Johnny ran into the bathroom, only to be swallowed by boa constrictors. Kevin ran to the window. Old Lady Carter cut off Dwayne's, David's, Sarneshia's, Kwontrel's, and Natashia's heads at the same time.

Kids began to crawl out of the window. She grabbed Eddie by the head and broke his neck. Just as Camilla was crawling out of the window, Old Lady Carter stuck her sickle through her back and stuck in the wall.

Little Andrew and Larry are hiding in the corner.

Larry said, "Who are you!"

"I'm the Boogieman and I've come to get you!" Old Lady Carter said, peeling Camilla off of her sickle.

Andrew screamed as something trickled down his leg.

The Boogieman laughed as he poked their eyes out and plucked them away.

They were running through the yard when the Boogieman said, "I'm coming to get you,"

Tamieka, Latoya, Kamesha, and Lakia tripped simultaneously and were picked to bones by vultures.

The Boogieman threw the sickle through Ricky's leg, and he screamed, grabbing Lawanda and Evelyn. They tried to get loose, but he had them in twin headlocks. The Boogieman punched holes through them, then looked down at Ricky.

"You feel lucky, punk?" the Boogieman said and ripped the sickle from his knee to his shoulder.

"To the house!" Kevin said and everyone followed.

They pulled on the door, but it wouldn't budge.

"Hurry, he's coming," Deon said.

Kevin and Rodney went in first and he followed Jamie with Toni coming last.

Deon and Jamie rubbed heads, and a spark flew off, setting Toni on fire. She writhed, screaming until she'd burnt to a crisp.

The Boogieman ran in and tripped over Toni's smoking corpse just as they ran upstairs. Deon tripped and fell down the stairs. The Boogieman picked Deon up, took him to the kitchen, and put him through a giant cheese grater, turning him into chop suey.

The Boogieman returned to his killing spree. Kevin and Rodney ran into a room and shut Jamie out. Jamie begged them to let him in as he went insane and began dancing like Michael Jackson, moonwalking right into the Boogieman.

The Boogieman beat on the door as Rodney and Kevin barricaded it. The banging stopped.

The door burst open, broken furniture flying across the room. "Which one of you wants to go first?"

"You don't have to ask me twice," Rodney said and shoved Kevin into the Boogieman.

The Boogieman turned Kevin around, grabbed him by the band of his underwear, and pulled them over his head. Kevin snapped into the air, through the roof, and landed on a pole.

"I hate a traitor," the Boogieman said. And then Rodney was dead.

I'm glad I was absent that day.

Hoo boy. Okay, so that was the last story *for obvious reasons but these are the last poems for the same reasons. They are really really bad. I wrote them all for my girlfriend in high school (and subsequent wife). I should have deleted, erased, and burned every copy in existence. These are all embarrassingly awful.*

Close My Eyes

When I lay at night,
And I just can't sleep,
I close my eyes,
And reminisce on our love so deep,

I go through the wonder whys,
Of what went wrong,
I close my eyes,
And swear I hear our song,

I know as time goes by,

The ache can't last long,
I close my eyes,
As a tear streaks my face,

I wonder why my heart defies,
The love my mind says is no place,
It's been forever,
Since I've lain in this bed,

Listening to this argument,
Between my heart and my head,
I don't understand,
These things I feel,

I gave my heart in my hand,
Now it's torn apart piecemeal,
The ache will end,
Only with time's will,

But in the midst of my heart's mend,
I know I love you still,
But through all my cries,
And emotions I can't disguise,

I just lay down at night,
And I close my eyes.

No More Tears

There are no more tears,
All that could have been shed have been,
Life must go on,
Broken hearts must mend,

Spirits must heal,
And tears, much like the rain, must end.
Like an empty well,
Once full with water,

Overflowing with life,
And then suddenly black,
Black with dull heartache,
Black with empty anger and revulsion,

...Black with loneliness.
From the fire in the night,
To the smoldering flame in the early mourn,
And inevitability, life will begin anew,

Where there was a heart that would never love again,
There is hope for new effervescence,
Where there was struggle to survive,
There is complacency to live on,

To make it through the night,
And the night after, and the night after......
Until there are no more tears.

Untitled #1

To be enraptured in your fiery passions is what I've waited for all my
life,
I can stand to be without you no longer,
All I want is for you to love me like I love you,
Can't you see it in my eyes?

Can't you feel it in your soul?
I wanted you then,
And I still want you now,
Forever,

Be mine forever,
You can't imagine the heartache of seeing you,
And not having you to call my own,
Something I can hold on to,

Curled up in front of the fire in the fireplace,
Making promises to the world,

Gerald Dean Rice

And only keeping the ones we say to each other,
The 'I love you' you say doesn't mean half as much as the one I see
in your eyes,

I hope you can see it in my eyes someday,
Someday soon,
Because I can't stand to see you and not have you to call my own.

Untitled #2

How could I ever say goodbye to you?
I tried my hardest,
But always knew deep down,
I was at your beck and call,

Still in love,
By my side,
It's always been what I wanted,
Us forever,

Trying to stay away was nothing but agony,
My faces, you could always see through,
But how would I, how could I tell you?
My heart and soul always had to be half of what it should,

But I was always there,
Waiting…waiting,
For you?
Through all the pain,

The patience,
The anger,
The separatedness,
Yes,

I was still there,
Waiting…waiting,
For you.

Untitled #3

What waits for me at the end of time?
A fate unjust or a destiny I've always longed for?
Could it be my envisionment of beauty,
My angel wrapped in flesh?

Does she love me or does she condemn me?
To a damnation of loneliness where there is nothing,
Nothing but the full sound of emptiness,
Emptiness of my heart.

As hollow and dark as the bed of the earth itself,
I never wished for an angel,
Never thought one would descend from the heavens,
Solely to love,

Mine alone,
A predestined ending never to come,
I never thought you could love me,
How full my empty moments have become.

How such sweet torture,
Tearing my soul apart and I can't say no,
The pain, sorrow, guilt, and unendurable, patience,
But enduring it all the same will all be worth it,

At the final moment at the end of time,
When you finally love me,
Making everything have worth,
The world is born anew in my eyes,

The wind sings an untrained song,
The sun radiates warmth and shines bright,
In a sky that is blue once again.
I see through the light you shine in my soul,

With eyes opened by your hands,
Hands that hold me and tell me those unutterable words…

Those words at the end of time.

Thank You

For all the love you've given me,
For holding me on lonely nights,
For every day you've made me sad,
For every day you've made me happy,

Thank you…
Because you love me,
Because you let me love you,
Because you let me in your life,

Thank you…
For being my friend,
For just being there,
Thank you…

Because you've given me all the love I need,
Thank you…for love